Symphony
No. 3

Chris Eaton

BOOK*HUG PRESS 2019

LIBRARY AND ARCHIVES CANADA CATALOGUING IN PUBLICATION

Title: Symphony no. 3 / Chris Eaton.
Other titles: Symphony number three
Names: Eaton, Chris, 1971- author.
Identifiers: Canadiana (print) 20190196440 | Canadiana (ebook) 20190196475

ISBN 9781771665100 (softcover)
ISBN 9781771665117 (HTML)
ISBN 9781771665124 (PDF)
ISBN 9781771665131 (Kindle)

Classification: LCC PS8559.A8457 S96 2019 | DDC C813/.6—dc23

PRINTED IN CANADA

The production of this book was made possible through the generous assistance of the Canada Council for the Arts and the Ontario Arts Council. Book*hug Press also acknowledges the support of the Government of Canada through the Canada Book Fund and the Government of Ontario through the Ontario Book Publishing Tax Credit and the Ontario Book Fund.

Book*hug Press acknowledges that the land on which we operate is the traditional territory of many nations, including the Mississaugas of the Credit, the Anishnabeg, the Chippewa, the Haudenosaunee and the Wendat peoples. We recognize the enduring presence of many diverse First Nations, Inuit and Métis peoples and are grateful for the opportunity to meet and work on this territory.

Part I

Only children tell the whole truth, you know.
That's what makes them children.

— HENRY JAMES,
The Turn of the Screw

Allegro

SOME CREATURES DON'T DESERVE TO LIVE; THOSE
without use, which should go without saying, but also those
that are too useful, because they rob us of the opportunity for
our own use, for achievement, greater self-reliance, the opportunity for purpose; the mules, the oxen; the camels; the ones
who carry us into complacency 'til neither ride nor rider right;
those that are good; those that are merely good enough; those
who are merely good enough for something; those that are but
pale copies of use; the bichon: a pale copy of the poodle and
the barbet, who are, in turn, pale copies of pale copies of pale
copies, teetering back to the first tamed wolf; the Bali tiger:
runt of the species; the Arabian ostrich: mother of negligence;
the ape: a laughingstock, a personal embarrassment; the Arabian horse; anything domesticated but especially cats; those that
are meek, those who flatter, those who beg, those who gather;
the whining collie, bleating meerkat, the emasculated bottle-
nose (*kookaburra, kookaburra*), gentled bear; those who expect
things, even if it's only bad weather; those who work and also
those who will not, who never expect to do anything strenuous, or heroic, or even moderately active during the off-season; those who adapt; those who don't; those who fly because

9

they have wings; those who crawl because they do not; those who have neither wings nor bellies but still make the attempt, perhaps especially those, who aspire; the raccoons, washing their food like tiny little men, that can be dressed in all sorts of humiliating waistcoats and bobs; the immensely relatable; the uncomfortably honest; those who believe; those who long, even for the peaks of pointlessness, forging aimless out of instinct: the sea turtle, swimming steadily against the currents to Ascension Island to mate, just so the next generation can do it all over again; through all that golden-green water and over the dark, over the chill of the deeps and the jaws of the dark; the sun over the water; the sun through the water; the eye holding the sun, being held by the sun, with no thought of sharks and only the beat of the going, the steady wing strokes of the flippers and the going; those who feed off the weaknesses of others; those who seek community for protection; those with pus, those that preen: the peacock, the Lopshire leopard; those who seek attention merely by standing out; the parvenu, those sudden kings of France: the American mink, American bullfrog, sitting out on the edge of a mud puddle, fast asleep, American cottontail, the American loons, with their long-drawn unearthly howl, more a wolf's than any bird; the mimics, whose ambition calmly trusts itself to the road, instead of spasmodically trying to fly over it; those who are fierce; those who are of affectionate disposition; those who abide the laws; those who write them; those who aim for immortality; those who beach themselves like great pods of whales on the shores of fate, one eye pointed up at the sky, like Isaac to Abraham, the other planted more gratifyingly in the sand, and accept death as the end; those who care too much about this particular moment and their particular place in it.

On the other side are those who deserve to die not because they are similarly without use—because they are—but because they are just too good for this world, have done nothing to warrant this life besides being born, majestic and true, without even dreams because theirs is naught with envy; Verreaux's eagle-owl: feasting on the pregnant hare; the king cobra: eater of other snakes; the fin whale: solitary beast of the sea and unconquerable Cain of its race, whale-hater as some men are man-haters; the Barbary lion: Lord of the Gladiatorial Rings. They barely exist in this world (could care less what the rest of us do) and are yet so often brought low by it. Surely this is why God gave the razorback its great fin, a constant reminder of its truth, projecting like a sundial to the time of its own death. I once saw one swarmed off the coast of Argentina by fewer than a dozen orcas, in the Samborombón Bay, a magnificent creature, over twenty metres in length by the captain's estimation, her dorsal curse as tall as a man, and her straight and single lofty jet rising like a tall, misanthropic spear upon a barren plain. She was gifted with such wondrous power and velocity in swimming as to defy all pursuit from man and our captain, who rarely perceived the necessity to speak with us, said the whalers had once avoided them, too fast for the trouble, but then the tide of the sperm whale receded, the tide of the right whale receded, and trouble took on an entirely new monetary value. There they were, her small black cousins, ennerved to slaughter by newly perceived weakness, their increasingly less furtive teeth upon her fluke. Would they have dared in her day? Like the gangs of Brutus upon Caesar? This is how God rights the world, his pity wasted on those who already receive enough of it. Imagine what this world would be like if He backed the winners for once, the strongest He bore upon the Earth, rather than this constant redistribution. Loftward heaved the razorback and violent brought her tail to crash upon her attackers. But we could ready see the bloody gash, the logjam roll of blackened snakes, the dorsal fin made nod and keel, and her cursèd fin, the fault of design, the sea, a jeering roil, kept her finite body up but drowned the infinite of her soul. The game past up, she carried her shame down to wondrous depths, where strange shapes of the unwarped primal world glided to and fro before her passive eyes, imprisoned not by man but by possibility, strands of flesh floating to the surface.

We found the lion later, perhaps too late—in the winter of our life (if the fin whale was the fall)—to teach us humility, forgiveness, to rebuild our living house, to tell the Truth, with his golden mane and great, royal, solemn, overwhelming eyes, we could not even look at him directly, even trapped behind bars in the botanical gardens of the Parc Zoologique Ben Aknoun, went all trembly, my brother from the impression of a delightful strain of music, I myself from the sensation of mysterious horror. Yet, at the baring of its teeth there was no more winter. At the sound of its roar, no sorrows. We named him Calando. If we humans had not come along, he would have likely ruled the world. Instead he was forced to witness his own slavery, the last of his kind. Even if a semblance of his old life could have been reproduced in its entirety, in some form of clear dome drawn miles wide, with an entirely replicated food chain, a blazing sun over some North African mountains, a tree branch for reclination, a lioness, and one or two cubs, would he still have been a Barbary lion? Would he still have been Free, would he still possess dignity? Would he know from the smell of the lamb, the loose folds of the antelope's limb, or the bland smack of the wounded waterbuck that it had been placed there by uniformed attendants with their own poor personal hygiene? Likely he gave it no thought. That is what life was and still is. Ben Aknoun existed as a deterrent to hope, or a monument to human mastery, depending on which side of the fence you stood. The lion's entire space was no more than five metres across, devoid of any natural clutter, with its shredded wooden flooring, two large rocks, and a rag doll, surrounded on three sides by walls of brick, a large rubber ball he never touched, a fallen tree. He had worn a path from the wall to the trough and seemed unable to deviate from it. And yet he also seemed oblivious to all of it, as though he existed on another plane, a separate dimension, looked at us like we look at rocks. We were nothing more to him than rain, less than rain, less than a breeze, he may even have felt pity on *us*, as we pined for the recognition of accomplishments, of victories, for objectivity. The Barbary lion taught that the way was to become subjective, to become the subject. The Barbary lion was not a human being. It was not important for the Barbary lion to have visible evidence so that he could see if his cause had been victorious or not; he saw it in secret just as well. He looked at us as if to say: *As long as you are always looking down at others, you cannot see something that is above you*. And we listened. And we reconsidered. And my brother made a wretched compromise with the beast, in a language it could understand, called to the lion each day until it saw him, recognized him as an equal, coaxed the beast to the bars of its cell and slipped it bits of flesh through the fence when no one was paying attention, which was often, gradually increasing the amount of poison so it would remain undetected by the great beast until it was gradually lulled to a final, peaceful sleep.

Most everyone in this world is either a camel or a lion. The big question: which one are you?

When Camille Saint-Saëns died, there was a parade in the streets of Algiers, beginning at the Hôtel de l'Oasis, where a man named Hautbois unceremoniously slit my brother's throat and drained his blood slowly into a porcelain bowl, sprayed a diluted mixture of phenol and arsenic into his eyes, then filleted him from the lower margin of his rib cage to the superior crest of his hip, tore out his liver, his pancreas, cast his entrails momentarily to the side and dug deeper to remove his lungs, his stomach, reeling in his intestines like a fisherman coiling a rope. Recounting this does not come easy for me, but the task has occupied me totally, occupied me religiously, I have understood the completion of this authorship as my duty, as a responsibility resting upon me. Hautbois went to the balcony for a cigarette, left the heart and kidney to breathe. When he returned, he trimmed my brother's beard, set his mouth in a slight, uncharacteristic smile, shoved wads of cotton and gauze into his anus, and dressed him with the help of our least Arabic servant in Camille's most expensive suit in preparation for the two-day steamer trip to Paris.

Hautbois was not a camel or a lion but a vulture, a tool, the mortician, his only purpose to introduce my brother to the crowds that had gathered outside, the body escorted by squadrons of cavalry, a mounted corps of Chasseurs d'Afrique, a full regiment of Zouaves in formal *sirwal*, a dozen Senegalese and a phalanx of Ponukelian, with their ebony skins, heavily armed beneath their trappings of feathers and amulets, five companies of imperial fusileers, carrying the body on the backs of the people from the hotel to the pier, down Rue Tripoli, along the Boulevard de l'Armée de Liberation Nationale, past the beaches, the aforementioned zoo, the *bassin Anglais*, in full view of the lycée, the customs offices, and Aristide-Briand Square, snug between the Opera and the Theatre. When Camille Saint-Saëns died, there was a ceremony at the docks presided over by the archbishop, the governor general. All the players and singers from the Opera—in fact, every musician within a hundred kilometres—took to the streets to mark the occasion, to celebrate the passing of France's greatest composer—and at this point this statement was still true, especially in Algiers—by performing together one last time in his presence. When Camille Saint-Saëns died, they performed Beethoven's *Eroica*.

The state funeral back in France was held, as I recall, at La Madeleine. Franck, for obvious reasons, was not in attendance. Neither was Stravinsky, whom Camille once called "a political anarchist throwing bombs indiscriminately around Paris." Monet sent his regrets by telegram from Giverney: *Suffering from cataracts STOP Unable to travel STOP Painted a weeping willow in his memory in a general reddish tone STOP*. Anyone else could not avoid it politically, not even Debussy, who once met Camille on the Channel ferry for an introduction to Sir Hubert Parry of the Royal College of Music, yet whom Camille later called (after a confrontation over the use of bassoons) *obsessed with the bizarre, incomprehensible, unplayable, his timing always a step or two behind the beat,* nor de Givreuse, who had courteously reached out to Camille after being chosen over him for admission to the French Académie with *My dear colleague, l'Institut has just committed a great injustice,* only to receive Camille's matter-of-fact reply from the Canaries: *I quite agree.* In the end, Camille was their victor, it would be like not attending a treaty signing with Napoleon. Those who clearly posed no threat, whose stolid mediocrity remained the unwavering benefactor of Camille's support: Messager, Widor, Duparc, Fauré, even Dubois; those who did pose one and he did everything to crush: in secret, Ravel, Chaminade, Massenet, and Dukas, whom he never forgave for also befriending Debussy, or more publicly, d'Indy and his acolytes (Canteloube, Auric, Poulenc, Milhaud, Satie, Honegger), who gathered toward the back to shake each other's hands and yawn in unison; d'Indy, who'd never had an original idea in his head, though not as bad as Vinteuil, who ran off with the melody of Camille's Violin Sonata in D minor, then had the nerve, when confronted, to say my brother was "a musician I do not care for"; the Americans: Hemingway, Stein, Valentino without his beard, Fitzgerald and Zelda; Enrico Caruso Jr., just seventeen years old, who had quite rightly distrusted the coroner's report on the cause of his father's demise as pleurisy with an intercostal neuralgia, instead blamed Camille, and refused to leave the coffin's side and then the grave all night in case the whole thing were a trick. Diémer had clearly rehearsed—and very nearly pulled off—the story of the time he had been prevented, by atmospheric inclemency, from performing with Saint-Saëns in a two-piano version of Liszt's Preludes; Camille had, on that occasion, simply placed both scores on his piano and played them simultaneously; the master Dutch cellist Joseph Hollman recounted to the delight of at least a third of the attendees his experience of performing the debut of the Cello Concerto no. 2, written specifically for him, forgetting the score in a taxi in his haste to make the performance at the Conservatoire, and

Camille, without a word of blame or blitheness, rewriting it from memory, as it was being performed, handing the pages up to Hollman from the prompter's box; even Dubois, whom everyone had supposed was already dead, told the story of one of Camille's first appearances as a live performer, when he not only surprised the entire audience by playing his Mozart pieces from memory, but then also offered up as an encore whichever of Beethoven's sonatas would please Her Majesty, Queen Maria. Though d'Indy was no doubt already considering his next move, it was still generally accepted, on that day, in the way these things are when someone has just recently passed, which is to say with the fantastic hyperbole of fact steeped in grief, that Camille Saint-Saëns was one of the best men France had ever known, that he had some faults but that, in the end—and in all things one must take the end into account—he was indeed as good if not better than (when also taken with all of their faults) Mozart or even Beethoven.

I was not asked to speak.

Of course, music isn't about a community of mutual support. Music isn't pleasant. Music isn't nice. Composing music isn't about entertainment or distraction. It isn't a compass, moral or otherwise, isn't therapy, isn't about revealing the true essence of life, the beautiful frailties and strengths of the human spirit. Music is about composers with no humanity not noticing other humans, as the rest of us don't notice ants, while engaging each other in war.

And one could question, after reading all this, whether it was all worth it, whether the lengths to which Camille went to destroy some of the most promising artists of his generation was in the best interest of art, or beauty, which is to say nothing of the others, the innocent bystanders, myself included. Otto Mahler could not take the success of his brother another day. Unable to deal with the emergence of Handel, Jeremiah Clarke flipped a coin to decide if he should hang or drown himself, and when the coin landed on its edge in the mud, used his pistol.

Who knows what more Tchaikovsky might have achieved had he not met my brother and taken his life at fifty-three?

Then again, we won.

When I am dead, people will make of me an imaginary figure, will claim I did not exist. Then this book will be truly terrifying. Non-fiction is a story that happened to someone else. It makes people feel safe. There's only one reason to study history: to confirm that one is less horrible than presupposed, or at least less horrible than others, to confirm that one is still among the living. As a creature of fiction, I will forcibly enable readers to pry themselves from the reality, imagine themselves in my place, create demons where there are no demons, reasons where there are no reasons, justifications where, but for I, to set structure to scripture, to ask, *What would I have done?* It takes a novel, a possible world, for people to feel like they've seen the truth, to make sense of their own existence, by bracketing it, falsifying it, creating a flow and movement, to dream. Real life has no such comfort. Real life is a kitchen drawer of elastics and strings, the cast-offs of order, with no more evil in a rusted corkscrew or creased orphan spoon than one might ascribe to the bite of a child, the sting of a bee, immutable, no different than death, confined only by the physical space of the pine box.

That's if death ever comes. I am no philosopher or scientist; I don't understand the System. I know the System exists, but not whether it is already complete or just a long rest. I'm not sure where it begins or where it ends. The whole idea that man could devote so much time to discovering the beginning of it all, the Origin, whether by math or by faith, is beyond me. Does the mountain cease to be a mountain because of how it was formed? Perhaps the rest of the universe recedes from Earth merely because we are repulsive. Perhaps, of all the bodies in corporeal existence, only ours is afflicted with this human stain.

Perhaps these other worlds recognize our hope and ambition and aspirations and are repulsed, physically, because our hope is so pathetic, and someday they will disappear entirely and eventually regroup somewhere else where we can never find them, an entirely different universe of contentedness, leaving us to take our tiny, torn corner for granted on our own. The universe is. Life is. Asking why is a thumb in the eye of God. Even though one is capable of converting the whole of one's life into the form of a story, be it short, parable, novel, or quest, it does not necessarily follow that one has adequately conceived that life, understands how one got into it, or how it got into one.

We were twins, Camille and I, born in Paris in 1835, in the third storey of the third house on the third street, surrounded by a man and a woman and a woman and a man. The men were weak and accepting of being weak. I remember my father's hands fumbling over the body of Camille like he was a wilting chard, then retiring to the settee for a cigarette before he could even consider me, which he never did. Surely his life as a civil servant had not trained him for much exertion, a government clerk responsible largely for taking notes no one ever read and helping to prop up a corrupt establishment by co-authoring, without credit, an analysis of the effects of stronger prison sentences on ethical conduct, the longest, dullest work of fiction ever penned in this country or any other, which made two things he and Proust had in common if you also count the pulmonary abscess. I don't suppose my father could even have been called a camel, so little he accomplished in his short time on Earth. But at least he worked. People have to work to exist, to warrant their existence, to earn the resources with which to subsist. The only exceptions, at least partially freed from the preoccupations of livelihood, are children, old people, the crippled, the sick, and the voluntarily parasitic, the category to which you might assign my aunt Charlotte and her inappropriately named husband, Esprit. My uncle had decided it was his calling to be a noble bookseller, and his largest success, finding himself with a roof over his head and regular meals, was largely accidental. For surviving the banality of my father's existence, France awarded my mother a regular dollop of assistance, to be used together with the meagre earnings she collected as a maid to the other more affluent personages in our building, and Charlotte and Esprit rewarded themselves for their genetic association and geographic proximity by taking over the first bedroom on the left, by rights mine, and transforming it into a mausoleum for Esprit's unsold stock, whereby Camille and I were forced into precarious cohabitation on an abbreviated mattress in the hallway closet.

Camille was easily the favourite, the gifted one, the golden child who could do no wrong. My mother and Charlotte lavished him with attention while I was largely ignored, was even left to go hungry, to basically fend for myself, so engrossed were they with my brother and his massive hands. An example: one of my earliest memories is of the park not far from our home, with its splendid fountains around which dozens of children would expel energy and would not stop. We would go and go and Camille would run his drills and because I was generally considered talentless, not worth the time of practice or aspiration or ambition, I was free to run among the park's many statues and press my face to the busts of King Henry IV and Louis XIII and sleep in the laps of Blaise Pascal and Saint Augustine and help Barye's Yvain battle the serpent and hide in the folds of the huge copper robes of François Rude's *Henri Bergson Losing His Faith*. A park is the furthest thing from real life you can find, and sometimes you just need that. It's not really the city, not really the wild, almost an imaginary place, a poor man's facsimile of the idea of nature. A park full of statues is the same but more so, existing not only outside of space but outside of time. No matter when they are made, both parks and statues come from the past, look old, are designed to look old, something that has existed longer than I have and will likely continue to exist long after I am gone, while the city continues to grow around it. If a city is a living, breathing thing, a growing thing, a constantly changing thing, then the park is a city's enduring heart. Did you know a lion's heart never grows? Like a human's eyes, which are fully formed in the head of a seven-year-old, a baby lion is burdened immediately with the full weight of its life, barely able to carry the load of existence, and as it grows, rather than getting any better, it actually becomes less and less able to manage the rapidly expanding size of its body. This is why lions are unable to run long distances, as opposed to hyenas, who have hearts that comprise more than twice the percentage of their body weight, and the real explanation for Richard the Lionheart's name, as he took his holy war to Saladin's Arabs at Acre, barely able to stand from scurvy, firing crossbow bolts at the walls from a stretcher. The statues of Lionheart never show that.

I apologize. When you have all the time in the world, you find even more time for distractions. On the day I'm remembering, the air was mild and flooded with sunshine and shadow. The sky was as clear as if the angels had washed it in the morning. A group of workers and students were chanting near the big building at the north end and appeared to be having a great go of it. I watched them for some time, as they pushed closer to something I couldn't see, then retreated again. I found it soothing. My aunt Charlotte took out a basket, from which she removed three small sponge cakes (possibly dipped in chocolate, this detail is fuzzy), handed one to my brother, one to my mother, and kept one for herself, and I crept up from behind, intent on snatching one before anyone could notice. Suddenly there was a gunshot at the pond, followed immediately by several others, and a shudder ran through me and I stopped, intent upon this extraordinary thing that was happening around me. Men came rushing past us like startled gazelles, erupting from the hedge and brush in huddles of twos and threes, bayonets out like antlers. The first of them, removed at several stages from the actual threat, danced around the sculptures and brooks, coursed around our blanket rather than over it, safe in the knowledge that they were outrunning the others, calculated and dull. But later the runners were whipped with blood and spittle, frothing and lowing, with a terror that was pure and beautiful, without time for thought. From whence did it come? What did it mean? How could I seize and apprehend it? Like any child, I turned to my mother to share in the experience, but she was already moving, reaching instinctively for Camille, only slightly slower than my aunt, who tossed my brother over her shoulder, lively and swift like a bird, and I was left with nothing but the retreating face of Camille, a face in miniature, sullen and discontented and sad.

My mother never once spoke to me, would not even look at me directly. I was an orphan with two mothers and a father, the brother of an only child. Not that I blame or resent them. I have no regrets. Had I not been forcibly born into this family of neglect, what might my life have borne? A family of poverty? A family of abuse? The seventh unwanted son of a seventh un-wanted son? Perished well before my time? In this life, no one yelled at me. No one molested me. No one set my cheek to the stove. No matter what anyone tells you, life can always be worse. So I made the most of it, and might even have been described as happy, if anyone had ever bothered to take notice of me at all, or if happiness were a real thing. The fact is, it was clear to everyone around me, including myself, that I was unimportant, would never change the world. I was not to be heard, nor to be seen. Even before we were born, my mother had dreamed that her sons would be, in sequence, a musician, a sculptor, and a painter, no doubt spurred by dreams of financial success in the arts as espoused by her sister and brother-in-law. Camille, as the first to draw breath, had his career set; I, in turn, well, let's just say there wasn't enough to invest in the proper training of two offspring at once. Thus it became Camille's job to channel the music, to be a pure vessel for its delivery, to create beauty, while my purpose, conversely, was merely to observe, to walk the grand salons of Camille's life like a careless tourist, without schedule or plan, not even looking at each painting on the walls, necessarily, but aware of each one nonetheless. I would make no impression on the world and thus was free to live the life less purposed, less underscored, less italicized, with the hope that I might, purely by perceptiveness and proximity to greatness, learn more to see as beautiful what is necessary in all things.

Thank goodness Camille displayed such unmistakable signs of such an abnormal musical instinct, both for my mother and aunt but also for himself. He was not a handsome baby, or toddler, and it was clear he longed for attention, so this seemed his ticket. Charlotte spent our week's food allowance on the services of a professional tuner and directed him to the square Zimmerman we'd inherited from the apartment's previous tenants because it had been judged too cumbersome and poorly maintained to warrant relocation. When it was finally opened to my brother's inspection, instead of banging inaccurately up and down on the keys as the majority of children do at that age, he touched one note gingerly after another, as though sampling a cake batter, craning his neck and lingering on each resonance until the sound had completely died away. Charlotte knew less about the piano than Esprit knew about bookselling. The closest she had come to one before was in the dictionary looking up *piazza*. She was inordinately familiar, however, once again thanks to her husband, with tedium and resilience. So she inquired about primers, and had Camille focus on drills, repeated patterns: four-octave scales, arpeggios, more octaves; steps, skips, and intervals; backwards, frontwards, inverted, transposed. Camille was made not only to command the patterns but also to memorize each exercise by heart, able to perform them in any tonality at any speed. We were made to sit on our left hands while performing with our rights, then the reverse, to keep us from putting the parts together too early. We were made to read books while we practised, so we could perform as if asleep. Charlotte would shout at us with arithmetic, with questions of anatomy, philosophy, any attempt to distract us.

Until she couldn't distract us. And Camille was made to hold mugs of scalding coffee with one hand, and sometimes knives, with pencils across his knuckles to keep them flat. And lord knows where Charlotte got them, but sometimes Camille was made to play with tangerines cupped in his palms, to ensure the proper arch of his wrists. Charlotte taught us the names of the notes and almost immediately Camille could identify each from the next room as they were struck. Only then were we allowed to move on to actual melodies. And when Camille moaned that the left hand in popular children's music was too dull, complained that it did not sing, that it gave him great pain to perform it, Charlotte tracked down a copy of *Le Carpentier Method*, designed for adults, which he mastered in a month, and some simpler works by Haydn and Mozart, which appeared to satisfy him, at least for a time.

Camille cried like a lost soul when the piano was closed, as it sometimes was in the early days to permit the rest of our worthless uncle who often complained of migraines from looking so purposefully at the books he couldn't sell. But this was yet another war Esprit could not win, and eventually my mother, bless her soul, demanded the fallboard be left open so my brother could express his thoughts in music instead of screams. We practised at least five times a day, except on the days when we didn't and on those days we practised at least six. Some days, as I have already mentioned, we went to the park and practised there, and Camille played the fringe of the blanket between our mother and aunt. Some of this was a strengthening exercise. But he didn't need the piano any more to know what sound it would produce when struck, which was why, in his later years when we spent so much of our time in exile, he was able to produce so much of his work without sitting down at any instrument. I was permitted during these lessons to share the bench, but only barely, and not to touch or speak, so I contented myself at the window instead. The window was never open, for fear of incurring the wrath of my brother, who claimed it burdened him with draft upon his shoulders. But still I was drawn to it and the vantage from which I could safely witness the world outside. I hated the woman pushing the pram, hated the newspaper boy, hated the moon, but mostly I hated the woman from the basement. Her name was Basson and she was a widow. I knew this because of her unfaltering fashion sense, and I had seen her appear from our building and had read the names on the postboxes and, by gradual process of elimination, I reasoned she wasn't the prostitute whose name was left blank (who lived directly below us) nor the mother of five named Durand (from the flat above ours) who let her kids cry all day in one room while she entertained her lover in the next; she was not the wife of the painter next door who had been a student of Ingres, nor was she the woman whose apartment also shared our floor who claimed to be the Vicomtesse de Ségur. I once overheard that last one reciting her family web to the postman, dressed in the most outrageous silk deel at seven in the morning, with an open neckline and sash (I suppose at one point in her life she must have been considered beautiful), but *I* knew she spent most of her days at home drinking and confiding in her dog. Our building was full of horrible people. The widow Basson was supported by a son who had fled her to South Africa, just to escape her horribleness and his duty to that horribleness. On multiple occasions I witnessed her standing in the middle of Rue du Jardinet, shouting at the sky in what I assumed to be Italian although the first time I heard it I seriously had no idea. She had trouble with the front steps, required the help of passing strangers to descend from their precipitous seven-inch peaks, so she began each trip as the mother of grace and gratitude; but once she had managed that small victory over nothingness, she was omnipotent, like a storm cloud or a spilled chamber pot, quickly turning on her unexpectant benefactor, like a capsizing ship to the shadowed dinghy. She swung her scowl at complacency, trembled at audacity, smiled at babies but not the producers of said babies, and meanwhile wandered vulnerable among the hooves of horses

When Camille played the piano, it was like God at the treadle, and the music surged upward from the soundboard and the casement in coursing waves of sound, multiform and indivisible, smooth and restless, like the deep blue tumult of the sea. At four and a half, despite his rejection from the Conservatoire, he composed a variations around a lullaby our mother had sung to us in our infancy, but also birthing intricate variations around any sound he heard in the world, a shattering wineglass or melting icicle, the symphony of the kettle with its introductory oboe solo, or the sound of a blackcap mimicking a nightingale at dusk. When we went to the park, the sparrows twittered in the depths of the chestnut trees and the hammers of the men at the nearby construction site fell like the skittered claws of great beasts upon a polished marble floor. I could hear it and ignore it with all my being. Camille would hear the same thing and experience Hercules reciting a madrigal to the Velleda.

For Charlotte and Mother, however, children were manifestations of life's second chances, and they remained convinced not only that Camille needed guidance to reach his full potential, but that huge numbers of older artists must be lining up to find gifted children to pass on what they had learned before coming up short, someone to resent and push. So many, having come so close, must have seen the potential for domination through a surrogate. The old men without children were without hope. Camille's first instructor was Camille-Marie Stamaty. Mother and Charlotte wanted a name, someone with notoriety and connections to the best performance halls. And Stamaty had not only worked with the young American Louis Gottschalk, he also charged the largest fees. Charlotte took one of Camille's scores, helped clean up the penmanship, and waited for Stamaty on the steps of his home. He sniffed, took a quick glance, and said: *The first reiteration of the motif is overly simple. You see here how it merely copies the pattern of harmony and restates the theme in weaving quavers? Do you know what Gottschalk was doing at five?* Pause. *The second pass is also not especially remarkable but not especially bad either. But the third...* Out of nowhere, Camille had shifted everything into an unlikely waltz in a major key, and you could tell by the old man's face that he found it impressive. *Perhaps,* he said, *if he can learn to keep his passions in check and if he follows my instruction properly.*

Stamaty taught a fine, crisp, even-filigree style, with a concentration on the evenness of blows when performing scales, the fluidity of strokes, the independent movement of body and arms, mind and spirit. Within two weeks, however, Camille already found him inadequate, deplored his perpetual legato, like a drunken bear trying to slur his way through Molière. Stamaty seemed unable to see beyond the saccharine models of the day, the waltzes, fantasies, quadrilles, and variations so dear to the nineteenth century, while Camille was already looking beyond. And he also spent at least half of the first month's lessons convalescent on the settee from a combination of rheumatism—for which he carried jars of live bees, to agitate and apply to his arms and thighs, so the venom could reinvigorate his circulation— and a general sort of Calvinist gloom, which was thought to have been eradicated in the late 1600s but had recently experienced another outbreak, particularly among the artistic community. He woke only to request a repetition, or another glass of brandy, or to scratch out an invoice, and six weeks later I looked out the window to see him shouting in the street, that Mother had still to pay him for what he knew and that he was withdrawing his services. Charlotte tossed a potted plant at him from my side and said that what he knew was worthless.

It was all part of Charlotte's plan. She already had what she wanted and, far from dispirited, spent the day ordering Esprit to move the writing table, move the console, shift the armchairs, angle the commode, transforming the sitting room into a parlour, while I tried to trip him up by getting underfoot. In most situations I was only an idea of a person, an abstraction. There was no real me: only an entity, something illusory, especially in the shadow of my brother; I would never surmount what he would do. But like Chopin (who must have woken one day in sweats to realize he would never be another Mozart, let alone a Schubert or a Mendelssohn), rather than giving in, I could take pains to entrench my position of inconsequence, fully aware that I would pass through life not as an active participant, not the hero, as most people see themselves, surrounded by spear carriers, but as an observer, a critic, a poet like Homer or La Fontaine, typical ghost things, separated from the struggle, the morality, like shake the flame of the chandelier, cause a table knocking bold, rile the hair or quicken the bladder. I would never be an artist, a ship carrying the world's most precious cargo through the storm, but somehow by swerving in and out of his step, step, step, I could be like the critic, a ship's captain in Camille's storm, trying to find the strength to turn the wheel. Esprit didn't know I was there, could not feel me exactly, but more than once he took a swig from his bottle and faltered and swore and, rather than listen to him complain, I suppose, Charlotte finished the redecorating herself and sent him out to paper our neighbourhood with bills instead. For weeks he did this, advertising the great prodigy Saint-Saëns and of course using the names of Stamaty and Gottschalk quite liberally, along with several other local musicians and composers we had never even met, let alone studied under. Come on, everybody, the posters said, come on over here to our apartment, come on, everybody, I have something to show you, just wait till I show you what he can play on this little BOX! It was amazing. My brother began the first night with a waltz by Liszt, then opened the floor to requests, having already memorized countless popular concertos. Unfortunately, most of the attendees had no previous knowledge or experience of music, the seats lathered immoderately with the tactless other inhabitants of our building, people for whom my mother cleaned house, or other women my mother knew who cleaned house, or bookseller friends of Esprit who drank quietly in the corner and ogled the women who cleaned house; there was the negligent mother and her bawling children; there was the widow Basson and there was the prostitute, moaning softly in the back for different reasons; there was Basson's saint of a son; and there was the Vicomtesse, crowned in an oversized hat of white fox fur, her bichon Timbal pitched under her arm, accosting anyone who would listen to her drone about her Mongol hordes, and I began to wonder if she wasn't perhaps more loosely connected cerebrally than the widow Basson. Very few people don't take the truth as an offence—Esprit was another conspicuous example—but the Vicomtesse clearly considered the truth her mortal enemy and did it battle regularly. She was a writer of children's books; her husband, the grandson of a famous diplomat, wrote poetry; her own father had once been the Minister of Foreign Affairs for Russia *and* the Governor of Moscow *and* had set fire to all the Russian capital's churches and monasteries to stave off the invasion of Napoleon. There was no way to tactfully deny them, however, and Charlotte figured, correctly, that numbers were more important at this point than appreciation, but it clearly offended Camille to play their mindless folk songs from the provinces before finishing with Mozart, lowering the fallboard, and giving himself over to the fussings and dotings.

Rather than be forced to witness it, I lingered instead at the back near the harvest of chocolate and cakes and tried to blow into his ears so that he might bark. But Timbal could see me! And finally, after being alone my entire life, I had a companion. A spear! I could order him to fetch me things, to help me harass the ankles of my uncle more physically and piss in the shoes of attendees who had affronted me either by quoting Robespierre or being presumptuous with their attire. From then on

I took pains to disrupt the evening whenever possible, simply for the joy of witnessing Charlotte's face as another plate of pressed caviar and tomatoes crashed to the floor amid Timbal's scampers and yelps. I felt for the first time real. Then, on one occasion, mid-performance, surprising even myself, I set the bichon's jaws to howling, and my brother's countenance at the keys grew distinctly heavier. Camille hated the bichon at that moment, like a flower hates the tree that overshadows it. He demanded that Timbal be excluded from all future performances, Charlotte refused until attendances became higher, and the bichon and I were free to continue our reign of terror until tragically one day someone left the window open and tiny Timbal fell to his death.

Eventually the musicians began to show up, lured as much by the posters and word of mouth as by a rumour my aunt had started that my mother was not only wealthy but single. Charlotte had her eyes on Victor Massé, who had placed quite highly in a recent Prix de Rome (a prize in composition for seniors at the Conservatory that came with a scholarship to study in Italy), losing only to Edouard Batiste's *Musique de Zèbre*. He bragged often about being on terms with Berlioz, as well as Pierre Baillot, which should have been the first sign he was desperate enough to take us on. But the clearer indication was that, even setting the bar for his acquaintances so low, he arrived mostly with other younger musicians—and nearly every week.

Baillot might have been a more desirable choice, but the closest we ever got to him was one of his students, Antoine Bessems, whom Baillot had dropped after years of refusing to listen to him. As a teenager, the young violinist had ventured to Paris from Antwerp on scholarship to make his name as a musician and composer, during the brief period when Belgium was still part of the Empire and its citizens might yet have a chance of making something of themselves. He was not, perhaps, the best violinist in the capital—he played too much from the arm and his bow fought against the direction of the bridge instead of working with it—but he was the most beautiful, and was soon tapped as the soloist for the French debuts of Weber and Schubert, summoned to perform for Louis XVIII and Charles X and many other names and Roman numerals besides. *The musician should disappear,* Baillot tried to teach him, *until he is only the music. Like a ghost, we should not see him—only the movement of the floating candelabra, only the flickering flame—he should haunt the theatre with the spirit of the composer.* But Bessems was born to be a star. The tics Baillot aimed to eradicate were what drew the greatest gasps, brought the whoops and claps and all, and rather than following the conductor, he rushed to crush the bow to string, to push, to push, push, pushing the orchestra, forward and forward, leading the conductor on his chase until the room was filled with laughter and eyes wide and mouths wide and flowers were tossed and Baillot, lurking in the wings, would shake his head and say: *Now we have to start all over again!*

Then, in Bessems's final year at the Conservatoire, when he should have been preparing his acceptance speech for the Prix de Rome, Paris was consumed with a new fever for a Norwegian toddler named Bull who was already the first violinist for the Bergen Philharmonic. The exception to the rule, Bull had been discovered not by a falling Icarus but by a French Hermes, a salesman and amateur anthropometrist named Bertillon who, inspired by the work of Camper and Daubenton in predicting criminal tendencies through physical proportions, had begun to test some of his own theories for forecasting a vessel of perfect musical expression. Bertillon travelled Europe extensively for work, attending as many local performances as possible, then lurked at the back doors, long after the performance was complete and: *Oh! Hello!* He had no more than twenty-four seconds to explain it to them, what their participation would mean to future generations, to the future of their art, but he was a salesman, after all, and it didn't take many failures to hone his pitch, press the future, posterity, vanity. *You are the ideal,* he said, *you are perfection, never have I seen a more impressive finger span,* he lifted the arm, pulled the sleeve taut, *do you mind? You might have a longer little finger than Viotti! A thicker neck than Durand!* Could they meet the next day? Perhaps? Before breakfast? He could bring croissants, he knew a place. Or even better, if they just stepped back inside? For a moment? It was a simple procedure, wouldn't take more than a few minutes, he was almost certain they'd outdo Kreutzer and, by that point, if he had them still at that point, it was relatively simple to talk them out of their clothing, to measure them nude, the details notched in his notebook: the length of the fingers, the breadth of the wingspan, the nipples, the weight, the height, height sitting, height to the knees, to the pubis, to the shape of the skull, the girth of the neck, the waist, the chest, depressed and inflated, fifty-three precise measurements that he was able to complete, after a few years of experience, in under six minutes, so long as the environment was as close as possible to twenty-three point eight nine degrees Celsius, and then he was gone. Sometimes it took longer, particularly if they asked too many questions. *A muscle knows when it is being watched,* he said, *and will grow or rest accordingly if considered.* Had they heard of Professor Lehmann? From Copenhagen? He had developed a thermometer that could detect differences of zero point one one degrees and had shown that thinking about a hand while measuring its temperature could produce measurable deviations. *It's fascinating, really...when you think about it.* And then he would laugh, every time like it was the first. He hoped to eventually go searching for the same ratios in toddlers and infants before they had even touched an instrument, perhaps before they had even heard a note. But every measurement shifted the needle. And the more maestros he touched, the more contact he craved. Here he was, in the presence of such greatness, and all he needed to prolong it was one more measurement.

So he did. For years and years. Until he arrived in Bergen on business and, finding the brandy so good and so cheap, postponed his departure for several years to finally apply his findings. One morning he stumbled to the pharmacy to ease his hangover and *fylleangst* and was attacked by a display of cod liver oil in the process of being stacked by the owner's grotesque five-year-old. The pharmacist rushed from the back with his belt, swatting the child around the shoulders and ears as Bertillon stared, amazed at what he was seeing, and when he was too exhausted to continue, offering Bertillon anything he wanted in the store, Bertillon pointed at the boy. *He's an oaf!* Bull's father laughed. *He can't stand still without tripping over his patience. You think he can join an orchestra?* But Bertillon assured him: *A clumsy person is nothing but a sufferer of partial paralysis. There are undeveloped nerve centres or nerve fibres that, if not quickened into life, will continue to degenerate and in their decay will involve or at least affect connected appendages. With the proper exercises, he can overcome that—at least in his fingers; dimensions do not lie.* Bull's father did not understand music, nor did he really understand much French. Bertillon, additionally, had no idea how to teach a child the violin, had no capacity for it whatsoever. But the Frenchman had faith in his measurements and bought the boy a lovely red violin, though it was not made for a child and Bull complained regular of sore neck and fingers, and took him to the Bergen Philharmonic, hoping he might just absorb it. Even when he began to moan and wail at the sound of it and they were escorted to the street, Bertillon brought him back the next night, and the next, until one day young Bull was quiet through the entire first movement and then politely requested to go relieve himself and leaped out the window into God's sunshine and air to escape it.

Bertillon was crushed—until he realized Bull had taken the violin with him. No one had ever given him anything before, certainly nothing so beautiful, and they found him down at the water, asleep, cradling the thing against his body like he was a swan protecting his offspring. He told Bertillon that it spoke to him, that he would wake in the middle of the night and hear it calling to him from the other room, with its pretty pearl screws and so red and so smiling at him, and he would take up the bow and speak to it and it spoke back and told him it would be pleasant if he were to pick it up and splay it cross the strings, just a very, very little; and it did sing to him so sweetly that he played a capriccio louder and louder against midnight until he felt his father's belt across his shoulder blades for waking him and the precious thing dropped to the floor and was shattered. Bertillon just bought him another. And even when he happened to maul

36

two strings at once, or just barely missed his pitch, his thickening fingers were always where they were supposed to be, not always hitting the right note but never seeking the wrong one. And soon after they were in Paris taking the world by storm and Bertillon began writing his book and Bessems's life was over. He tried his best to compete, attended each of Bull's concerts in search of some advantage, but quite swiftly the invitations—to performance, drinks, and various clandestine meetings—began to sparse. He'd gigged briefly around the capital for over a year before graciously accepting a post as the director of a children's choir in the 13th arrondissement, an overcrowded neighbourhood that was, at best, standing on an overturned barrow peering into the window of middle class. Bessems was not a camel *or* a lion, more like the sea turtle, albeit less successful even than that. He was not very bright, and had long ago used up any contacts he might once have had. Do you know the monarch butterfly? The sea turtle's migration is foolhardy but attainable; the monarch's entire purpose is founded in futility. Shat in a patch of milkweed at the edge of a Mexican corn field, they begin their fantastic voyage most immediately they're hatched, striving for a northern destination they will never reach, their quest taken up by offspring as each previous generation burns itself out mid-trip. Bessems was similarly aimed at a goal far beyond his life force, but unlike the monarch, it was just as unlikely that his grandchildren would make it as he would. Still, Charlotte let him perform some of his own compositions one night, just to see, and while my brother cringed visibly in the back Bessems played, we somehow ended up studying with him for the next two years. I use the words *studied with* rather delicately, instead of saying *studied under* or *apprenticed under*, because I think it likely Bessems learned as much from the exchange as Camille did. But my brother also enjoyed having someone to perform his violin sonata and he was also a passable pianist and we were in dire need of anyone with adult hands to tackle the works Camille was now composing. Thankfully my mother dreaded handsome men, which Bessems would have known had he only taken a moment to study the image of my father in the entry; otherwise we might have been stuck with him forever.

I have to imagine he soon knew he'd been had. I certainly never saw Charlotte pay him directly. But by this time Bessems was at risk of losing his garret apartment and Esprit eventually let him sleep in his room of books. Meanwhile, fashion produced another child phenomenon with each season—Paladilhe, Plante, Alkan, Julien, Duvernoy, and of course Fissot—and as his value diminished with each wave of fresh prodigy, Camille and Charlotte became increasingly agitated. Not even Camille's other hobbies could console him: collecting fossils in the forests of Meudon, reading Hugo's poetry, Racine, or Dumas's populist tales of brigands and murderers. My brother was a genius, there is no other way to express this, equally trained in Latin, astronomy, math, botany. My mother spent what we had to teach him dancing, fencing, riding; he was obsessed with plants and animals, the human body, could likely have been a surgeon had he not been such a natural at music. With the money he made from his first performances he purchased a new Secrétan telescope to probe the skies. After Timbal's accident, my brother offered to help the Vicomtesse dispose of the body, and instead kept it for several experiments, stretching the corpse across one of Esprit's book-binding jigs to probe for signs of trauma. Five teeth were missing, and there was a slight laceration of the tongue and a bruise running along the lower part of the jaw on the right side of the face, likely caused by his impact with the paving stones. He made several incisions with a razor run ragged cross the midline ventral abdomen, and three or four practice cuts run downward, on the right side, until he was satisfied, and was obstructed by the linea alba. This layer was much thinner than he had imagined from reading his anatomy texts, a barely noticeable white line that stretched under the rib cage, but it was still enough to thwart his progress, and he was forced to raid the kitchen for an ice pick to puncture it, then finished the job with some poultry shears from sternum to bladder. There was surprisingly little blood as he sliced away the omentum, removed Timbal's stomach, Timbal's diaphragm, Timbal's liver. This was remarkably small, even given the pup's size. He flipped it over in his hand to check the veins of the vena cava and found a particularly jagged shunt. Timbal's spleen also seemed enlarged, and after weighing it carefully, Camille decided that Timbal would have died of other natural causes soon anyway. Mostly he wanted to see how the heart worked, not from sketches in a book but up close. It had four chambers, like the four movements of a symphony, and once it had been entirely drained of blood, Camille was able to produce remarkable sounds by blowing carefully into the right atrium. When it started to smell too foul to hide, he pressed it firmly against the wall until the whistles passing through its valves emerged in perfect fifths.

Shockingly, it was this arrangement with the Vicomtesse that finally provided Camille with his big break. As it turned out, she was truly a Vicomtesse after all, and her father had indeed thumbed a fiery nose at Napoleon, then fled with his children to the Duchy of Warsaw, then Germany, the Italian peninsula, and finally Paris. The Bourbon Legitimists looked on him as a hero, and he settled comfortably into the aristocratic and artistic elite. Only after the return of Napoleon's nephew to the throne—and the publication of a particularly Gallophobic memoir—was he forced to flee back to Russia. But by then the Vicomtesse had already married the grieving great-grandson of the first Comte de Ségur and was permitted to continue her Parisian alcoholism in peace.

The Vicomtesse was the first Muslim we ever met. Her father had been forced to convert to Roman Catholicism while in exile, but even as a child she had felt such a pull toward her roots: the Tatars. *People were never meant to be so sedentary*, she said. *This*

French habit of roosting, it's not natural. And all the bread! After Charlotte found out she was royalty, we were often allowed to lunch in her apartment, where she fed us horse and goat and marmot and vitriol, and we ate fried dough while she drank vodka from some sort of animal horn. For Camille and myself, who had experienced nothing in life that was not French, had never consumed a breakfast without butter and sweets, it was like we had been visited by aliens from another planet, or someone from another time. She would say: *The French think they've got it all figured out because of Descartes and Diderot and Rousseau, that because they discovered oxygen they can live in a bubble. Descartes was nothing but a peddler of antimetabole. Diderot lied to himself and listened to his own lies. And the French like to claim Rousseau's greatest merit was his style, but take any work you like by him, open a page at random and underline all the barbarisms and grammatical indecencies; any educated twelve-year-old could have written better.* She said: *A Frenchman is a balloon inflated with vanity: flighty, prone to speak before he thinks and act before he has a motive. His military has grown soft and his warriors of script—the press—lie and slander in their clamour for pension, place, decoration. They don't even know what love is; marriage here is nothing but a financial contract. I know this more than anyone. Have the French produced a great composer? Some have French names, but how many were actually born here? They say the British are so tasteless. The Germans are so crass. The Americans are so fat. What do they say about the East? Nothing. They pretend like we never existed, like they didn't steal everything from us.* She showed us an early compass, a mechanical clock, and another horn, this one filled with gunpowder. *The Mongols invented the triangular plow,* she said. *The Mongols invented love.* And one day she pulled out a primitive, two-stringed cello and played us a melody reminiscent of a dying sheep, and for the first time I could recall, I saw my brother brought to tears. Camille once asked the Vicomtesse why she stayed and she replied: *Where would I go? Down the street to the baker? Out into the country? Even across the city it's the same. One day you should travel, Camille. There's no reason for you*

41

to stay here, to compete against these people who are not your equal. If you stay here, you'll end up like them. If you stay here, you'll eventually want to murder the lot. Don't accept it, Camille. Turn your back on this. Only once you have spat in the face of the human race all that you hold against it, only then can you start to feel again like someone who is good.

The Vicomtesse loved Camille, in her way, called him her *bon petit diable,* fed his body and mind in ways it had never been fed before, introduced him to books by Cao and Luo, Murasaki, Galland's translation of *One Thousand and One Nights,* dressed him in frocks and bonnets and told him stories about another child named Camille who lived so far away from all of this, in a castle in the countryside surrounded by artifacts of greatness, a young girl who is totally free to her own pursuits, and kills—because she can—a macabre procession of fish, a bee, a squirrel, a cat, a bullfinch, a donkey and a tortoise. I'm not sure how much of it actually made an impression on my brother at the time, not in any meaningful way, but he did adopt several of her habits to please her. He was easily influenced by anyone but me, even if the seeds never sank very deep. The Vicomtesse also had several high friends in high places, via her father and husband, and eventually arranged for Camille to be added to a bill at the legendary Salle Pleyel, where Chopin had made his public debut. It was Francis Planté's bill, who was four years our junior, and they spelled our last name incorrectly in the program. But there was no mistake in the standing ovation, or the look of fury on young Planté's face. The audience would not let him stop, and by the end of the night Camille had given them two more pieces by Handel, Mozart's Concerto No. 4 in B flat, three more by Hummel, Bach, and Kalkbrenner, and finished with Beethoven's Concerto No. 3 in C minor. Camille breathed the air of the mountaintops, was something beyond the camel or the lion: a giant. Confronted with their unquestionable joy, he swayed at the bench, unable to stand, which everyone took for stunned humility, waited and longed to be crushed. I, for my part, was a mirror to their awe, it filled every inch of me, had never before seen the bounds of glory, and I perched atop that glory like it was a vanquished enemy and smiled for perhaps the very first time in my life.

The next day in *Revue et Gazette*, Henri Blanchard heralded Camille as the second coming of Mozart, lacking in originality—he was a child!—but stylistically brilliant, and the week after that, our home concert was packed with fallen dukes and flâneurs, lined up out the door, down the stairs, past the widow, and into the street. Amidst this chaos, the director of the Conservatoire, Luigi Cherubini, came to offer Camille a scholarship in person.

Camille made very few friends at the conservatory. The conservatory was not a place where you made friends. Neither was Paris, for that matter, but that was never the goal. If you wanted to make friends, you went to a public school, or found work as a grocer or in a café, or you went to someplace outside Chartres and became a monk, or a farmer and grew things in various states of beige. The countryside subsisted on the rhythm of necessity—must get up to tend to the animals, must get up to tend to the fields, must break at two for wine—but Paris in those days was in such a grand state of confusion, each man, woman, and child tending the fields of history, seeking their place in it. The epoque's greatest fashion, beyond even crinoline, flounced redingote and horsehair braids, was victory, and there was no option to simply coast by. A third of the city was out of work due to the failure of the potato and the unrealistic debt the manufacturing class had accumulated over the preceding boom. The Industrial Revolution had promised them escape from failure, but here it was, and the earlier immigration from the countrysides, the infestation of the poor and uneducated, unskilled in any way, set to gnawing, would have eaten the cracks in the pavement if they could have. Hundreds of thousands lost their livelihood and their homes, and were now left with an excess of time to devote to general disenfranchisement and ancillary griping.

The greatest humiliation of the poor, of course, is that they are lacking even in the proper tools for independent revolt, trapped under so many layers of shit that it's impossible to see out of it without help; the greatest heights the poor things could aspire to was maybe petty theft and frivolous vandalism. The ones above them weren't happy either, overprivileged white men from one city arguing about the more privileged white men from other cities, like zebras longing for what the lions have while the grass—and you can imagine where the poor fit into this metaphor—just sits there and burns in the sun. They wanted to eat the lions, too, these zebra sons of bankers and surgeons, the ones born wealthy enough to be writers and art critics, wanted the vote, a right reserved only for the very rich, like the landowners, the one per cent who'd been born that way. Meanwhile the Prince d'Eckmühl stabbed his mistress with a letter opener; the Comte Mortier tried to butcher his own children, concerned that they were trying to usurp him; and Charles Théobald, the Duke of Choiseul-Praslin, who was said to be having an affair with his children's governess, was arrested for the murder of his wife, striking her repeatedly with the heel of his boot before prying open her cracked skull with a hunting knife. As a member of nobility, the Duke claimed his right to defend himself not before a citizens' jury but a Court of Peers. This was the way it had always been. Yet, as the date of his trial drew closer, public sentiment became less sentimental and more eager for change. Did French law not apply to Choiseul-Praslin in the same way it did to others? Are even the greatest above us above the law? Wasn't this what their fathers and grandfathers had fought against fifty years ago? Huge public demonstrations were held. The government reversed its decision and made a public announcement that the Duke would face a citizens' jury (a clear attempt to separate themselves from the appearance of complicity, that this was not a problem with the peer system, per se, not systemic entitlement but a lone monster). The dust began to settle. Then, just a few days before the trial was set to commence, the Duke killed himself in his cell by self-administering a dose of laudanum. The trial was annulled. And judicial action brought against the governess was dismissed in mid-November of the same year. Both of these events, far from removing the spectacle from public view, only served to reinforce class differences, that peerage went against equality and that corruption went straight to the top. Some even claimed the peerage supplied him with the poison, or perhaps even poisoned him themselves, to avoid the embarrassment. Early the next spring, a story emerged that claimed the Duke's death had been faked, rushed from the country under cover of night to Argentina. The rebellion in the poorer quarters was so severe and widespread that the Assembly eventually had to give the head of the military full powers to suppress it. The central parts of the city were transformed into barricaded fortresses, run by a series of citizens' militia, streets blocked by overturned omnibuses and thousands of felled trees. Any time you went outside you risked being shot by bandits, militia, the army, or all three at once.

Camille arrived wanting nothing more than to impact the world so forcefully he left craters, to wipe out entire species. He was beyond excited to take on his equals, to finally be admitted to this battleground called the Conservatoire, this arena for children, trained with weapons of wood and brass to one day kill with their minds. Unfortunately, once we arrived he discovered the other students were not his equals but musical wastrels, the offspring of the nouveau riche, an institutional colonization by the new aristocracy, the banking princes, railroad barons, dukes of the stock exchange, landowners extracting natural resources, little Choiseul-Praslins basking in their entitlement. They likewise recognized the difference in him, shy and awkward, with an overly pronounced collarbone that could have shaved cheese and an affected wardrobe (provided mostly by the Vicomtesse) of showy, collarless shirts and bright sashes tied with ornate knots at the waist that further amplified his fragility. He also spoke in exaggerated universalities, like: *God has given us music so that we should first of all be led upward through it!* And: *Shall we be judged by the vessels of our souls or the souls themselves?* And even: *Who does not feel a quiet, clear peace steal over him when he hears the simple melodies of Haydn?* Camille was convinced that the favour of Cherubini, who was known to share his anger with everyone equally but trotted Camille out regularly for friends and funders, would position him as someone the other boys would want to admire. But we had never been exposed to other children, had no idea how cruel they could be. Very few of them would even speak to him, and shoved him in the hallways. We would frequently return to our room to find the buttons of Camille's waistcoat clipped, still trembling upon the floor. Camille complained to Cherubini and he gave us our own room and special permission to practise on the pianos reserved for seniors. The next week a boy from Marseille forced Camille to the ground and held his head in dog shit, a fact we did not realize until he was sent back to his rooms by our professor of song.

There were only a handful of other boys for whom my brother could approximate some form of respect, with whom he ever made friends. Edouard Silas, for example, could write with such germinal energy that everyone was forced to stop and listen: beautiful and thrilling, innovative and visceral. Unfortunately he just as often let the notes get away from him, let them fall in love with themselves to the detriment of their interaction, so obsessed with the feelings he had birthed in the initial shock that he smothered them rather than let them grow throughout the piece. He was also an amazing organist, perhaps second only to Camille. Gabriel Fauré was already a myth, a legend, discovered by a blind cleaning woman in the music room of the school where his father taught arithmetic (never bothering him because she assumed him to be the instructor). Even younger than Camille, he wrote with an instinctive musical language that was all his own, drawn to reapplications of older modes and mild, unresolved discords. He probably should have been our main foe but he preferred to use this language mostly to talk to himself, a master at the keys who shunned virtuosity in favour of the Classical lucidity of the French masters, sometimes playing so quietly and errantly that you could forget he was even there. Music was for him and him alone, and it was clear how painful it was to even share it with his friends, let alone an audience. Because his family lived on the Riviera, he often came to stay with us during the holidays, and once we travelled down there with him and found his family was very much unlike ours—loving, for one. It was astounding to sit around the table with them, feasting on endless amounts of scallops and snails as they asked questions of one another and listened to the answers.

The most unlikely was Jules Duprato. Duprato always took the easy route, could embed a musical reference like no other, used cultural baggage to transport listeners without any of the heavy lifting, passages borrowed mostly from the classics but also pieces that were more recent, popular, low-culture references, German lieder, a bar of Stephen Foster; it was magical to take it in, and yet so much of it was still a joke to him, each note a comment on music and creation itself rather than searching for Truth. He was also, like Bessems, exceedingly handsome, in a Euclidean sense, possessing a surface beauty that was difficult to deny, and one of the more popular boys among the other students because of his near-constant state of joy. No one would have been likely to peg him and Camille as likely friends, but one day a group of seniors threw my brother off a first-floor balcony, and fearing he might have broken his wrist, they picked him up and left him crying on the floor outside the infirmary. Duprato, who sometimes faked an illness to gain access to the infirmary's supply of morphine, cradled Camille's head in his lap and stroked his hair and whispered: *There, there.* But also: *It's okay.* After that, Camille was often found in his wake, and the bullying stopped—or at least slowed down.

The only other person Camille could talk to—and, indeed, the one with whom he became closest—was César Franck. Franck was not a student or a professor exactly, but somewhere in between, almost an adult at this point and clearly the best pianist the Conservatoire had produced in some time. Franck should have been rich, should have left the school behind years ago to seek his fortune as an international performer. The son

of a poor Belgian clerk, he had shown early promise as a painter, but his father, like our mother, had his heart set on music,
moved the entire family to Paris, and because the Conservatoire
would no longer accept foreigners, found two professors who
would teach the boy privately on the side until he could gain
French citizenship. By the time he'd won his way back to the
fold, so to speak, Franck's skills were undeniable, and he took
first prize in piano at the end of his first year and consistently
maintained that level of performance throughout his studies.
Then, due to a very public feud between his father and a critic,
he was unable to have any of his work performed or even get
hired as the soloist, and they created a position for him at the
Conservatoire, paying for his lodging as a tutor, accompanist
and prefect, a chaperone hired to ensure the behaviour and
safety of the new students like us.

They were an unlikely pair, Franck and my brother, with
nearly thirteen years between them. But the fact that Franck
had played at Liszt's Swiss tour farewell concert, and was also
in attendance at the famous Liszt/Thalberg piano duel, was
enough to make Camille idolize him. And Camille was already
so advanced, so beyond his years. The two of them frequently
disappeared to discuss things like pitch space (how pitch was
not like a stretched string but a spiralled helix, with pitches that
were quite far along the string actually closer in harmony), and
challenged each other to invent entirely new musical languages
within the constraints of current Western instruments. Franck,
like Duprato, also likely felt protective of my brother. I suppose
you could say Camille loved him, or whatever approaches love
in the self-centred, psychotic mind of a child. A child's existence is so simple, entirely without empathy. Charlotte and my
mother had done very little to shift this perception. He even
began referring to Franck as the brother he never had, which
was hurtful to me but not overly. I had never truly succeeded in
demonstrating my affection toward him, had never been able to
make clear what I would sacrifice for him. Franck, on the other

hand, provided protection from the other boys, or sometimes a second dessert, or a light caress upon the brow. What I would have given to be able to touch him. One day he reached for Franck's hand as he'd always imagined and brought it to his lips as he'd always imagined and kissed it as he'd always imagined and Franck, who had been reading a book by de Lamartine, smiled back at him and tousled his hair and said: *Camille*. Just his name. But it was *how* he said it.

Our professors were, if possible, even more disappointing, the wings of music's future held firm to the ground by a ragged loft of cowards and pessimists, pigeons tied to the roost without even a flypen; the failures and opportunists; the first timpanis and anvils in the orchestra; an entire generation of composers so terrified at having gone up against Beethoven and lost that they retreated from the public arena to the safety of a steady income and the semblance of esteem. Adolphe Adam (who claimed to be teaching us counterpoint) was not a composer, just a hawker of vaudeville and seasonal carols. Daniel Auber (who had picked up a few instruments in the same way that most wealthy children did, like a neglected corner takes on dust) was proof that you could succeed in life without any recognizable talent whatsoever. And like a post-traumatic stress disorder, they avoided teaching the symphony entirely, refused to let any of the children near one, created entirely new genres instead—the concerto grosso, sinfonia concertante, trio sonata—or focused on sonatas and chamber music, vocal writing for the stage. My brother believed that if you were going to dignify music, you had to eventually go up against the gods and win. And when Auber tried to justify their fear by claiming the shorter forms were more *complet*, more successful in their condensed perfection, in their ability to swoop through the world like a bird on wing, capturing not only the way we hear but the way we think and feel, Camille responded: *Then wouldn't the supreme act of skill be to prolong that feeling? To stretch it infinitely in all directions at once?* What was the use of isolating a single emotion or moment like that? The world was huge. Existence was huge. It was like trying to capture the essence of a person by perfectly rendering a toe.

Less than a toe, it was like trying to define life through one drop of blood, one cell, one dream. Auber ordered him to leave. *You are lucky to be in the way!* he screamed. *Don't come back until you're ready to learn something!* Camille shouted back: *Despite what you may hope, people are going to get smarter, not dumber!*

Franck tried to urge restraint. *Watch what you say in public,* he warned my brother. *More importantly, watch what others say. There are some who can make or break you with a word. And some who are fragile as dry sticks.* But it seemed impossible for Camille to resist, and he got off to an even worse start with François Benoist, our professor of organ. Benoist had won the inaugural Prix de Rome in 1815 and was the only organist in France at the moment who could hold a candle to the Germans, but he had also been at the conservatory longer than any of them, with a well-worn trench of bitterness running through his soul to prove it. He was the one-eyed guard dog the children danced past to frolic in the garden, the fist of anger that had been raised so long ago that the fear of its descent no longer remained. Having once been the primary instrument of the seventeenth and eighteenth centuries, he had been forced to witness the decline of the organ in popular culture like the slow death of a loved one. The dual manual grand orgue that had been installed when he began teaching there, which Benoist kept hidden at the back of the room behind a ponderous velvet curtain, had over the years become squeaky and worn, and it was difficult to tell what pained him more, the mewl of his injured lover or the awkward adolescents pawing so aggressively at her. None of the other boys in Benoist's class even cared about the organ. For most of them, the class was not so much about perfection of technique as it was about keyboard improvisation, loosening the mind for inspiration. Very few of them put much effort into it, and mostly Benoist's coping strategy was to ignore them. At some point, all these young cocks would be out of his life entirely, as though they had never existed. They were no more a part of his life than atoms, or the news of the terrorists from Algeria. So he lurked as close to the exit as he could manage, nodding occasionally and shouting out random key changes while orchestrating ballets for his other job at the Opéra. When Cherubini accompanied us into Benoist's classroom, it was as though the length of our legs—still too short to reach the pedals—was a personal affront to him. He was not a babysitter, he said in front of everyone; the organ was no joke to him, and he would not prostitute it with barcarolles, contredanses, galops, waltzes, polkas, or little children. Cherubini insisted, softly, so Benoist ordered my brother to the bench to show us what a prodigy could do, intent on humiliating him. Camille, who had never before played the organ, approached it with confidence, like this was just another of his salon showcases. He was, without a doubt and despite his age, the greatest piano player France had produced in some time, and knew he could fake it by the tricks he had learned from Bessems on the left hand. But no matter how aggressively he approached the piece, the lack of dynamics in the keyboard made his playing seem dull and lifeless, and the delay between summoning the note and its arrival through the pipe, though no more than a fraction of a second on an instrument this small, disrupted his rhythm entirely, destroyed his focus until he just let the piece peter out on its own without finishing it. We were allowed to stay but forced to sit in the corner and say nothing. After two weeks, however, Benoist criticized Beethoven's First: *Who starts anything on a V7 chord? Surely he put the muscles and lungs of the musicians to trial, but what about the patience of the audience?* My brother retaliated: *Beethoven doesn't have to follow the laws of music because he is a law unto himself!* And after careful consideration of what my brother had said, Benoist told him not only to remain quietly in the corner but also to turn his chair so he was facing the wall.

There we stood, our face afoot the plaster, unable to see what was being played, only to hear it and formulate the fingerings inside our head. None of the other boys even cared about the organ. They saw the class not so much about perfection of technique as keyboard improvisation, loosening the mind for inspiration. Very few of them put much effort into it. No one ever played Bach. Most of them had probably never even heard the Fugue in B minor. My brother spent all of his private time toiling over Bach's *Art of Fugue*, certain it was only a matter of time before Benoist's pride wore down and he was permitted a second chance. But even though Benoist had been forced to witness the decline of the organ in popular culture like the slow death of a loved one, even though the dual manual grand orgue he had personally installed had become squeaky and worn and it was difficult to tell what pained him more, the mewl of his injured lover or the awkward adolescents pawing so aggressively at her, he was also stubborn, and the first thing he did at each class was to ensure that Camille was properly positioned. Benoist's coping strategy was to ignore them. At some point, all these young cocks would be out of his life entirely, as though they had never existed. They were no more a part of his life than atoms, or the news of the terrorists from Algeria. He lurked as close to the exit as he could manage, nodding occasionally and shouting out random key changes to distract them or announce a new key, or an interval change, or to tell them that A was now off limits, while orchestrating other people's ballets for the Opéra. *Ultimately,* he would say, *there is only one key. Or perhaps it is more accurate to say there is no key at all. The distinctions between letters are illusory. Keys are for more sterile instruments, the passionless ones, when you can create your sounds in a lab of your own control. There are no such distinctions for instruments that are played in the real world. God does not believe in keys. You have to chase it. You need to just be.* Camille hung on every word. Benoist's tastes tended toward the safe and predictable, but his judgment was still and sure, and everything he said to the other boys was valuable and important. He introduced them to older works and composers who had gone out of fashion or been forgotten entirely, and when one of them complained that he was stuck in the past, he erupted. *It is not the works that are old,* he told them. *Nor me but you! You* are the ones who are old in your minds, your imaginations faded, your sensibility dulled by the easy path of rebellion. The old music is as vital as it ever was. In fact, its power and warmth are not merely undiminished but grow day by day, to the point that you look at it like you look at a flat earth, unable to even grasp the full scope of its body! One day Benoist became so frustrated with his raft of imbeciles that he rose up like a bear beside young Lecocq, tossed the boy from the bench, and filled the chamber with such glorious sounds that my brother was brought to tears and applause. There's nothing remarkable about it! Benoist screamed at them when he was finished. All one has to do is hit the right keys at the right time and the instrument plays itself! None of them except Fauré believed they had anything to learn from him, and gradually they just stopped coming. Only then did he deign to let my brother turn around, and Camille was astonished to discover we were alone.

Within a year, Camille had taken first place in organ and won it repeatedly until his graduation.

They called Fromental Halévy's course the Art of Decomposition. Halévy, who had never faced music as a calling, more as a convenience, was a black-tailed raven who possessed nothing but an insatiable curiosity for whatever happened to be placed in front of him. As a child this had translated to fascinations with irrigation, steam power, ball bearings, gravity, preserving and fermentation, the French Revolutionary calendar, the medicinal properties of oat grass, and the diets of wolves when food is scarce, never lasting more than a few weeks at a time, but when his father decided he no longer believed in the theological focus of the Jewish school curriculum, Halévy's brother was sent to attend the Lycée Charlemagne and became an industrialist, while Halévy himself went to the conservatory and became unhappy.

Halévy knew more about the history of music than anyone we had ever met, an encyclopedia of minutiae, able to recall any important moment in history or zero in on the perfect isolated example to use as a teaching tool. When Mozart composed, he said, the floors and walls were chalked in countless numbers, and he used a complex mathematical code in his letters to family to keep politically sensitive comments from the eyes of the censors. Bach did the same, using a cabalistic code exchanging letters for numbers, with countless references to 2, 1, 3, and 8, the numbers corresponding to his own name. The numbers added up to 14, with which Bach eventually became obsessed, and when asked to join Mizler's Society of Musical Sciences in 1745, he delayed his reply almost two years just to ensure he could be its fourteenth member. Halévy had been the first composer to successfully subdivide the semitone. He had written the definitive texts on the definitive people, and a singing primer that espoused the social role of music. Most impressively, he'd been requested by the Congress of Physicists to head the commission to establish a universal definition of note pitch, travelling across Europe to collect information from every possible musical institution while amassing an impressive collection of tuning forks. And yet, in Halévy's great, suffocating accumulation of knowledge, he became totally unable to enjoy it, like a honeybee who had found himself not wholly at home in the hive. The more he learned, the more he hated it, and the more he seemed engrossed in passing that hate on to his students. He wouldn't allow them access to instruments or even paper, just had them go over old scores and, as often as he could manage, imposed us on a nearby rehearsal. When that option was not available, we would just listen to him lecture and hum pieces from memory.

Thankfully, he was also almost never on time. To be punctual, he claimed, was to wait on other people. Sometimes he never showed up at all. The only purpose Time serves, he said, is in music, to guide genius along an arc. *There, Time is God. Otherwise, life is a puzzle to be figured, not by laying the pieces out in a line but by starting at the outside and working in.* Eventually he would saunter in, gaze out the window for another ten minutes, and then say something like: *Did you know mine was the first opera to feature an inter-religious marriage? It was illegal in Vienna,* he said, *but the opera had been so popular that they made an exception. It sold out weeks in advance, and the private boxes were filled with the most beautiful Jewesses dressed in the most radiant costumes and the Emperor was there and later changed his mind.* After he'd won the Prix de Rome, he'd had countless offers to stage something, and it had been first produced the year we were born for an unheard-of 150,000 francs and starred the unmatched Adolphe Nourrit, the most popular tenor of the day and one of Halévy's own instructors when he had been a student at the conservatory. Though Nourrit's father had also been a popular tenor, young Adolphe was barely a man, more of a creation, an instrument, taken in early by Rossini and trained to sing the parts the Signor Crescendo heard in his mind and needed to get out. *Nourrit never had to resort to falsetto like Mengozzi*, Halévy said, *or even Duprez, who could only hit a screechy C like a capon dying from a slit throat*. Nourrit made possible an entirely new set of notes in performance. He was said to be able to reach an E5, though no one had ever heard him go above the D.

When it finally came time to write pieces of their own, Halévy's reins remained taut, as he forced them repeatedly away from instinct to think outside themselves, to avoid their first thoughts (which he claimed were beyond their control) and to pretend instead that they were other people. How would you arrange the harmony if you were Palestrina, then? Or Bach? Or Rameau? How would Mozart have solved this problem? Or Cimarosa? Or, more unorthodox, someone from outside our traditions, like Tyagaraja? Or Gusikov? Was there a correct way? Or were all options correct? Was everything possible and equally beautiful and right, at least until it was inked on the page, at which point all other possibilities were instantly erased? Halévy had them each work on the first act for an opera, and Camille devised a story around Möngke and Kublai Khan hunting with their grandfather Genghis, with kettledrums played so softly they could barely be heard, flutes and pizzicato harp to give it an oriental flair, the overture as if he were Haydn himself. They studied the *opéra comique*. They studied *singspiel*. They studied Verdi and Mozart. They studied Wagner's *Lohengrin*, comparing it to his earlier work and how he had begun to rethink dissonance at this point, using it in such a different way, employing the exact same shriek to punctuate Elsa's death as he had with the Dutchman's betrayal in *The Flying Dutchman*, the soloist on a high B flat over a second-inversion D minor triad, but much later so as to remove any opportunity for redemption. Halévy compared this to the *Shreckens-fanfare* of Beethoven's Ninth, held by the entire orchestra until the baritone shrugs off the struggles and sorrows of the world and says: *Not those sounds, oh no...* Camille, thinking he had finally found his entrance, said: *When will we work on a symphony? Like Beethoven?* But Halévy replied: *Symphonies? Beethoven?! What do you think you know about Beethoven? A symphony is not a minuet, not a sonata. It is not an idea. A symphony should have everything in it. All the world. It should encompass it, consume it!* Soon he had departed into another story, about meeting Beethoven as a child, in Vienna, when he was not much older than many of them. *Beethoven,* he said, *had no knees, was unable to do anything but stand to tall and snatch to the heavens. Beethoven knew no moderation. Beethoven knew only everything. He was beyond restraint, beyond morality, beyond weakness.*

People like to talk about their response to Beethoven's music, but Beethoven doesn't care about you! You are such a minor part of existence while he—he!—he is the conduit for Everything, the changing of the season, when March tears at the throat of February and the soil begins to bubble and erupt with beetles and roaches and screeching cicadas, writhing over each other in their semi-solid adolescence; devouring, devouring, the maggots devouring; the birds rip themselves from the soil and scorch the sky screeching full-throated victory hymns, the buds of flowers ripping themselves through the flesh of the branches. Beethoven did not write from pleasure. He wrote because he was the only one who could. Beethoven was not creating, he was devouring, hunting down the sounds of the world and exposing them. Before him, the world was hiding. The world was not known because the sounds were not known. They say one day the sun will expand into our orbit as the charred ember that was once our Earth vaporizes. Beethoven is the sun, and he grew to consume us all.

Once there was a time, Halévy said, *I thought like you, that I had already learned everything. When I arrived at the station, I found an elegant carriage standing in the middle of the road with a pair of spirited grey horses. There was no one in it. The coachman had got off his box and stood by, hunchbacked and hook-nosed, the horses held by the bridle.*

You the pianer playr? *the coachman enquired of me.*

I nodded.

Seems yer duet taint no moran a solo now.

He clapped softly and I leaned closer, unsure of what the coachman meant.

Yer mate fer travels hath lected to pearsh.

He's died, you mean?

Nless you knowen other way.

As the other man had prepaid, the coachman said it was still worth it for him to take Halévy alone, if he wanted, and if he didn't mind taking on the occasional lifter. It seemed to be a poor sign, two deaths so close, but Halévy was eager to start this new part of his life. He had also spent some money on a travelling suit and had said all the good-byes he wanted to say for some time, and a part of him felt like he was already there. So they set off on the first leg, and Halévy started into his first book about escape and his innerness with the coachman like a ghost, or a lamp, or a signpost, not a real thing, not even there, until the coachman turns suddenly to change the world entirely, reintroducing the weather, taxes, death. It was strange about the other man, the coachman said. He'd had a feel. A feel that he was never going to show up. A feel like water creep. The other man had been a philarsifer. *That was how he said it.* Philarsifer. *And the operating term:* been. *He'd travelled with another* philarsifer *before.* Dey talks about deaf so much dey bringsit. Tink in bout deaf is like build in a bridge to yer end, innit? Juss lives yer lyf, swat me grammy use to say. The moment you stops try in to live, you stops succeed in at it. The more you talks, the more you thinks, the more you cants no more do neither. *The coachman asked Halévy if he'd ever heard the story of the* philarsifer *and the coachman?* One spawn a thyme, a philarsifer neededs to distract hiss self from Frank's Foot to Paris, or maybe from St. Peter's Burr to Bay Ching, or doubt to faith, somewhere philarsifers cum frum'n go two, to gathers with other philarsifers so as dey cans all talk and not listens. The kinda fella who things rawks ain't rawks, who things the whirl doan spin and time doan moof like an error. He dint want to hear nuffing about the coachman's life, bout hiss sick mama and soar toof and long in pains, so loanly on the roads by hiss self and hiss tawts, juss when on bout the sunshines cast in shadders an how them shadders aint from right now deys from eight minims ago, an stories about have in to walks a quadrillion miles an sit in down to ress forever an still make in it, like anyone wud walk dat far in the furs place, an without the coachman even have in a pensill to parper figgger it out. The philarsifer says, We ayn even the same people we was when we started dis here trip, or when we started dis cons verse say shun, or when I started dis send dance.

An the coachman says, I'm certain a lot more tire.

Let me put it in shorter words an con septs dat you might better unner stand.

Oh, yessir, please do.

Thing bout yer carriage. Thing bout each trip, you must wears it down quite severely.

Quite, yes.

An when some pin brakes, wha do you do?

The coachman scoffers. Well, I fixes it, doan I?

Coarse you does. And when the next ting brakes, wha do you do den?

Yer not a good lissener.

So gradually, one ting brakes, an den an other, an you fixes one, an den the next and ventually everthin is go in to brake.

No thin lass fer ever.

An you replays everthin.

Yup.

An it stills yer carriage?

I paid fer tall, dinn I?

Yes, but it stills the same carriage?

I spose so.

Now magines dass the whorl.

The whorl issa carriage?

No, magines the whorl brakes a little at a thyme, an each part is replace assit brakes, till nothin in the whorl is what it was when it began. But dis happens everseckin. Ever fraction of a seckin.

Fmy carriage broak dat fass, Id juss buys me a new one.

Dass not really wha diss is bout?

An wear do all dem broke in parts go?

The philarsifer never stops talk in, complain in and sess in lea bout how diffcull hiss life were, bird in with the big questions of eggs hiss dance, hiss trunk of whys an hows and whatfors dat, despite the wait, float in sumwheres above the heads of people like the coachman. The philarsifer longed for nothin moran the simpful life, for a mine unable to grasp complex city. A mine like the coachman's. He says: Oh, to be simpful like you. He says: Oh, to have no choice in life! So right before dey reach dare destination, the coachman turns to the philarsifer an says: I has a choice for you. Why doan we swish places for while. You be the driver an I be the thinker. The philarsifer says: You doan wann that. And the coachman says: I sures do. And the philarsifer says: No, you doan. And the coachman says: Can you know in side another man's mind? So they swish. And they gets lost four times in the last block on a one-way street to the con furnance, but once they're there, the coachman is a hit, listen in quietly, laugh in as a pro prit, nod in polite when others be speak in.

For a week heess live in like a king but respectful to the hotel starf, not demand in a nicer room, not send in back the wine. He is asst to speak at an other con furnance in an other city for other philarsifers, is asst to all the parties, land in a publish in deal. The philarsifer, who should be grateful, heess a rich man now, is only envious instead. Heess sick of wash in everone pat the coachman's back, wash in everone con graduate him, sick of sleep in under the carriage while the coachman sleeps on feathers and inside young Rachel whos read in everthin heess writ in and travel in all the way to this city juss to feel him inside her an is know in things your mama nor wife never knew. Weess all juss one, she is say in to the coachman. We should juss be one. Heess juss a blackent hook nose hump back figger but the coachman hass never fell so big man, is love in have in the wait of the whorl and the wait of young Rachel on hiss shoulders, hiss knee, hiss face, hiss hips. The philarsifer is sneak in into hiss sweet while the coachman is face deep inner, sneaks hiss spare suit and lingers on the outer rings of the audiences, king of whispers, try in to ruin hiss own career cos if heess not in joy in it no one will, and the coachman is almost never leave in hiss room, from Rachel to Violetta to Beatrice to Rodelinda, and still the talk of hiss genius is continue in to grow, until finally, juss as the coachman is leave in the build in to applause and even flow-ers, someone calls out a question. One lass thing, someone says. I was juss wunnering. Wunnering if, as you says, weess all one entity be in constantly rebuild in, then is there even any unique consciousness at all beyond the whole, one solitary think in, to quote the Cart, and is you then say in you believe in in God? And the coachman says, Thas a right simpful querstion. So simpful that even my coachman can answer it. *And he was still laughing as Halévy fell asleep again. The days seemed to stretch forever, and when he wasn't aroused by the bumping of the road and the rolling hills, he was lulled in and out of uncomfortable naps, a film over his eyes, without any concept of the end of one day and the beginning of another, lost track of the time entirely. Everything looked the same, no matter when he*

63

looked out, like it was never changing, and he dreamed that maybe he'd died and all this was some kind of purgatorial test. Was the coachman just some tempting angel? Was the coachman's story true and had the coachman and the philosopher actually traded places for real? Halévy asked him if he knew how much longer the trip would take, how much time remained. The coachman shrugged. Never much worn a wartch. A week? A day? Two seconds? Life could end in a second, he said. Or it could drag on forever. Sum ways, were already dead. We dun everthin wherever gonna do. Were juss wait in to figger it. As they breached their highest point in the Alps, the coachman stopped the carriage and Halévy was certain he would be robbed and abandoned, if not murdered, left without the clothes on his back to freeze in the snow, stabbed through the eye, a long rusty needle slowly inserted through the ear or nostril to pierce his brain and leave him without a mark or in a vegetative state, his skin pulled off in strips and fed to the wild mountain people travellers had claimed to have normally spotted feasting on the blood of stray sheep and cattle, a gift to ensure future safe passage, perhaps, perhaps even tied to a fencepost and raped, then left to bleed out among the buttercups and low blue gentian. Stick out yer arms, he said, and Halévy pondered quick exit, calculating the distance to the door and the length of the man's arms. The coachman was old and infirm, could barely be expected to keep up if he made it to ground. But the distance between them was so small, could he be out before the man had a chance to cut him? Could he throw it? Were there more men waiting outside? A robbing station? If so, how many? And might they be overpowered by surprise? Would an attempt at running just make it worse on himself? Would anyone even miss him back home, gone as he was planned to be for minimum three years? He only had a minute but then the minute was passed, still having done nothing but nothing, still there, looking at a man looking at him looking at a man. He sighed, unbuttoned his sleeves. If this was the end, then so be it. He held them out like handing over two loaves, wrists up, having seen enough young men take their own lives at the conservatory over the years to know the quickest way, closed his eyes, longing for the pierce and the tear, an end to all this imagining. The hands that grabbed him were smoother than he might *have imagined, as if years at these moist altitudes had not wrinkled the old man's body but eroded it, smooth as the stones on which they rode. To be taken by such hands, he reasoned, might not be so bad. To end now, he reasoned, might not be so bad. Would it be any different than living forever? Hands like glass hands sliding over his forearms, passing them out the window, perhaps to one of the robbing station accomplices. Hands like brass hands, trumpeting his end. Suddenly he feels the carriage moving and the coachman up front again, rubbing his legs together, and the coachman says:* You feel in it?

Feel what? *I said. But I could—can—feel it: the temperature dropping several degrees in a matter of seconds, as though my arms were submerged in buckets of ice water. I opened my eyes and everything was the same, but I felt different.*

What is it? *I asked.*

And the coachman replied, Thass the feel of leave in yer French morls behine.

Halévy seemed lost, once again, in it all. His shoulders fell and he said: *Very well. Tomorrow, we write a symphony.*

My brother wanted the melodies of his first symphony to sing over the world. To drown it out, like Beethoven. Halévy, however, said: *Do not concern yourself with melodies, Camille. There are no melodies in life, only sounds. The world is made of sound, and it is the minds of men that interpret it and give it shape and meaning. Beethoven didn't even believe there were notes, only the relationships between the notes, and the relationships between us and the notes.* So my brother began to collect all the sounds he heard and gather them into a sort of musical mosaic, not thinking of how they would be ordered so much as how important they were to capturing the mundanity he witnessed on a daily level (the sound of our apartments, the anxieties of government clerks, overheard conversations in coffee shops, about finances, comedies, the dreams of Esprit), paying close attention to how they should be placed around one another, whether in separate instruments or passages or sections, how those collections of sounds would harken backwards and fore to one another, until gradually he could weed out the ones that didn't fit. Halévy didn't even care that it sounded too much like Mozart's *Jupiter Symphony*, or Bizet. In fact, it was probably better if it did. It was still more impressive than anything any of the other students were doing. And it was a symphony! Which no one was even attempting, except maybe Mendelssohn, Schumann and some Swedes. He even lobbied for my brother to compete in that year's Prix de Rome, years before he should have been eligible. Auber was furious, said: *You're always doing this, Fromental, picking your favourite and looking for exceptions from the rest of us.* But Cherubini acquiesced. He thought it might bring more attention to the program, which was beginning to struggle financially. And yet, Auber had the last laugh as the judges called it technically proficient but lacking in passion, different only for different's sake. Benoist, who believed in constructive criticism and did not mean it to be taken as harshly as it sounded, talked about Camille's fear of being common, his obsession with colour and detail over insight and wonder. Adam said: *The boy is more intellectual than real. He hurls his themes into waves of imitations and canons where they disappear immediately, pressed and stifled under forms that lack tunefulness, a harmony too bright under a network of dissonances, cadences, an orgy of noise. The monotony of constant surprises and affectations is still a monotony, only of a different sort.* Auber likened him to another recent graduate who had become known for pushing boundaries, although fans of Berlioz said he was like Berlioz without melody while haters of Berlioz claimed he had been sent to force people to like Berlioz by contrast. Berlioz, who had also attended out of curiosity, said: *He knows everything, but lacks experience.*

Camille replied: *We don't understand music, music understands us.*

And: *I am not alone in this!*

But it turned out that he was. Even Franck, whom my brother had always believed would be our companion in arms, urged restraint. *A piece built solely on innovation,* Franck argued, *is like a red-cheeked apple with a worm inside it. Innovating in style is easy; profundity is clear as gold.* Old Halévy found my brother crying in his room and tried to console him: *Not everything is going to come to you making sense,* he said. *It's about making sense of it. The Prix is not everything. There are so many other things in life more important. Love. Even hate. Every collision your soul has with another, no matter how devastating. You can't listen to other people. Winning the Prix felt like a vindication to me. It was the proof I thought I had been seeking all of my life. I was met in Rome with such hatred. My fellow winners were not welcoming, as I had anticipated, not encouraging and supportive, but cruel, locked me out of our shared apartment on the first night and tossed me a blanket from the upstairs window and said I should sleep in the ghetto with the rest of the Jews. My background had never been an issue for me before. Nor had I ever let it define me. My father was a* cantor, and secretary of the Jewish community of Paris. I grew up in a Jewish neighbourhood. I ate matzos at Passover. We owned a menorah and I would light the candles because I enjoyed the sulphurous smell of the match. But I had found no meaning in it, had never worshipped with my parents, at least not once I was old enough to decide these things for myself. So I did not feel like these were my people I found in these ghettos, these Jewish ghettos, overcrowded, with buildings that towered over the streets and cut off the sky entirely, literally walled away from the rest of the city. I had never seen such poverty. Were there ghettos like this back in Paris? I wondered, stepping cautiously among the men and women lying beneath blankets of paper in the streets, no idea where I was headed. They barely seemed human, these people, could only hold out their hands and mumble unintelligibly, and I had to step lightly to avoid them, avoid looking at them. I wondered where I was going to sleep.

Then, as if by the hand of God Himself, I stumbled upon a hidden synagogue, located on the second floor of an unassuming home, lured by words and melodies I didn't understand but still recognized. From somewhere in my path. It is strange, the power of nostalgia, to soothe and comfort in one's greatest need. I slipped quietly past the doorway and discovered a small group of worshippers in an even smaller room. It was an awakening experience for me, that people in such misery could still believe in a God. They had nothing. They were nothing. And still they gave, welcomed me to Pesach, and one of the worshippers took me to their home for Seder. They let me live with them. I was able to leave to attend my musical instruction, but every time we exited the ghetto for the rest of the city, we were forced to wear yellow scarves to identify ourselves. Every Saturday, we were forced to gather and listen to Christian sermons in front of a church, and these experiences changed me, and when I began to compose my first operas, these were the themes I kept returning to, the universalities of grief and injustice. This was when I wrote La juive. I wanted to make a difference, to expose the rest of the world to what I had seen. La juive wasn't just something from my past but was the anchor of my life, the piece to which everything else would always be connected, something I would always be working toward from both ends, the thing I was most proud of in my entire life. *The company that acquired it raved to me as I signed the contract, that this was going to make a real difference in Paris, that my opera was going to change the world. I didn't really understand them but I still believed it. The producers used similar words to the ones I used, but with entirely different meanings. Score. Beats.* What we love, *the producers said,* are the beats about the underdog. The mother-daughter relationship is especially poignant. *I said:* It's a father and son. *And they replied:* Yes, let's talk about that.

And yet, they were putting so much money behind it. They seemed to really believe in it. People were already talking about it months before it opened; his name was, once again, discussed in small circles. So I did not feel disheartened at the concessions I was making. They felt they could capitalize on my experiences, even as they rubbed all of me from the actual opera itself. What they wanted, the producers said, was an ending that was more dynamic, more than a punchline, with a symbolic natural disaster to mimic the heroine's internal crisis. They brought in another writer who sent my heroine tumbling into a vat of boiling water. I even rewrote the part of Robert de Saint-Loup so it would be better suited to Nourrit, then changed the end of the fourth act from an ensemble piece to a showy aria, and let Nourrit write his own lyrics. By this point I had been entirely broken, was looking at my future dream instead of my present life, so put up no fight at all.

We will not make that mistake again.

From then on my brother wrote only impossible pieces, works meant to destroy both listener and performer, to destroy Auber and Adam and the rest of them. He wrote a piece that was an asteroid on a collision course, a piece that was a grain of salt, a shattered vase, crispness, the last petal cast from a thirsting flower. Then, one night on our way back from a performance of Wagner that had set to swing my brother's jaw, stealing back to the Conservatoire with Mother, Charlotte, Halévy, Bessems and Fauré, we were confronted with the first of three deaths that would enter our lives and affect us greatly. The night was colder than normal and Bessems had stolen a fresh loaf from a nearby boulangerie so my brother could keep his hands warm, and Fauré was in the middle of a rant about the unnecessary pageantry of what we had just seen (*Of course, it's all an act, even not acting is an act, a clear and definite act, a statement against the act...*), when suddenly we were being held at knifepoint by a man who, at first, in the peaked cap and drab smock of a labourer, appeared to be holding us up for our wealth. My brother had just admitted to Fauré that the baritone in the lead role had perhaps been a disappointment, but only because he had lacked the stamina and charisma required of a composition so bold. The choral-orchestral duel in Act III had been mesmerizing. The overture, the Senta-Dutchman duet, so complex and raw at the same time, old and new at the same time. And here was this man with the knife, this tall and thin man, with long slender fingers that might have served him as a pianist like my brother, had his earlier fortunes been different, this man. This man's back, bowed slightly, this man's left shoulder, a little higher than this man's right. This man looking poor and sickly, swooping forward like a great grasshopper. This man who seemed to want our money. We appeared at first not of widely divergent economic strata, the attacker and my family; my mother wore a simple, sleeveless dress, russet in tone, and for all intents and purposes might as well have been breastfeeding a child in a painting by Courbet. But my aunt had insisted my mother spend much of what we had to dress Camille in a pale blue tunic and short breeches to belie his origins, so the illusion of wealth was certainly present. Likewise my aunt—for she was, in every effect, Camille's most visible representative in the artistic community—made sure to have all of her dresses made by the shop owned by Charles Worth, the height of *la mode*, bedecked with green ribbons, a great grey shawl from the house of Gagelin and Opigez (who were said to dress the Countess of Montijo), and a grey bonnet embroidered with red flowers. Bessems tried to step in. To mediate. He said, *Can we fault Wagner? Even if his passion is false, is the passion that it inspires in the audience also false? Perhaps, as witness to this reflected passion, which may or may not also be an act, he too begins to believe it, or begins to believe that this fake passion, knowing it is fake, is still the entire point?* At first I noticed this man's beard, uncommon for someone of his standing, but then also the colour of this man's skin, the darkness of his face, like the filth of the street, and it became clear he wanted very little from us in a financial sense, only revenge, only to send a message. We meant as little to him as he did to us. He stepped toward us, knife high, and Fauré said, *Well, I'm not in love with my life as much as I love music, and I'd rather not even have love than taint it. Does that make sense?* This Arab wanted to kill us, erupting with the idea that, simply because we were born French, we were somehow his enemy, somehow responsible for the atrocities he may or may not have experienced in God-knows-where. The fact that one could create an entirely different reality at whim terrified me. There is no point in trying to reason with someone who has an imagination more fiercely determined than your own. Luckily, just as suddenly, he was impaled by the

71

bayonet of another animal set on protecting our children and national monuments who mistook him for a socialist.

It's difficult to say exactly what influence this attack had on our lives. We were well versed in the war against terrorism in Algeria. The Arabs were jealous of our prosperity, and the newspapers regularly carried stories about attacks on our women and children in Oran and the other smaller cities and colonies. An entire settlement had been wiped out on the Mitidja Plain, two dead in Médéa, massacre at a café in Constantine, three more injured when a lunatic with a sabre appeared at a gala thrown by the Governor-General in Douaouda, a French soldier bringing water to stranded Kabyles outside Bône was beheaded and dragged behind a mule for two days to the capital. We had brought democracy to them, helped to overthrow their dictatorial Dey and set up free elections with very few restrictions. Most of the Algerians had welcomed our morals with open arms, but a group of monsters calling themselves the Ouled Riah, led by Abd al-Qādir, had demanded autonomy, freedom, and when we refused to negotiate with terrorists, they increased the frequency of their attacks. After months of hunting the terrorists in the deserts, French forces had finally captured al-Qādir, hunting him down to his secret bunker in the mountains near Dahra, making off with his considerable war chest, and killing 128 Ouled Riah in a fierce and noble firefight. For the safety of French people and ideas and values and justice. By anyone's account, it was a major blow to the enemies of Western prosperity and civilization. As General Bugeaud described it: *An outstanding job.* Also: *A dramatic show of force.* When French troops marched into Oran, King Louis Philippe I proudly added: *Abd al Qādir says he owns Algeria. We own Algeria. We own his palaces, we own downtown.*

A victory for French ideals. A victory for French women and children.

Until now this had been nothing more than an abstract. The fact that this could now happen at home in Paris—that the terrorists could touch us here—was transforming in ways we had yet to realize.

The second death came almost a year after the Arab. That spring, the conservatory announced a new prize, the Grand Prix de Rome, which not only carried the previous scholarship in Italy but also an increased financial bursary and an advance toward mounting the student's first production upon their return. More money, they reasoned, would bring with it more publicity, providing a healthy boost to the career of the student, but, perhaps more important, would raise the profile of the conservatory itself, attracting more students from abroad, which they were planning to do to increase the establishment's income stream. A number of students were rumoured to be in the running. Even Franck was given an outside chance because of his foreign birth. But it was generally considered a given that the prize would go to Duprato. Our entire wing was alive with excitement that one of our own might take the prize. But the idea of a Duprato victory was deeply conflicting to Camille. On the one hand, my brother wanted everything in the world for his protector and friend. On the other, it might mean we would never see him again, that he'd be lost to us forever. Duprato tried to reassure him, said: *Don't be ridiculous.* And: *Let me show you something.* And also: *Come closer.* But it was hard to imagine the difference several years might make. Camille considered sabotaging the contest. Even if it hurt him briefly, he reasoned, it would be better for Duprato in the long run for them not to be separated. The actual weekend of composition, all of the competitors were confined to the dormitory due to financial speculation over who would win, and one night after the scores had been submitted, we all gathered on the roof to drink and look at the stars, singing and dancing and pretending to like each other. Duprato had his trumpet and another boy had brought his violin and together they performed an impromptu medley of everyone's submissions. Some other boys were kissing and more behind the entrance to the stairs. Duprato took my broth-

73

er aside, seemingly unfazed by the pressure, and when Camille asked him how he could deal with it, Duprato said: *You should do what makes you happy, Camille. If you're doing this to be happy someday, but it all makes you miserable, perhaps it's not the right path,* and though he was speaking directly to my brother, I was so happy in that moment that I began to see my existence in an entirely different light, not only permitting me to discard my previous notions of inconsequence, but allowing for the suspicion that, far from a curse, I had been rewarded for piety with this invitation to return and experience a life of joy, to finally feel fortune and happiness, a life more blessed than the one I had previously lived.

Then came the gunshots. A lone militiaman saw the gigantic entwined shadows of the children on the roof and, assuming them to be dissidents or socialists, opened fire. The children scattered, all except Duprato, who perched defiantly upon the parapet and hurled one of our bottles back at the source. An exclamation of surprise in the darkness. A near hit. Emboldened by this success, he fired off a second, and a third, arching through the spotlights and shattering out of sight behind the walls. The older boys joined in the assault while the younger boys laughed and shouted encouragement, until the entire scene was like a painting by Cabanel, lobbing their fire back at the gods. It is in this position that I will always recall Duprato, silhouetted in the floodlights that had betrayed us to the stalwart defenders of France. He had blown his great horn till the city rang and their attacker had been dismayed and drawn back. But he was now so exposed and alone, the rest of the boys having lost interest in projectiles for their own sake, and I began to worry that there were birds below whispering to our attacker about the spot where we were not most vulnerable, his arrows aimed at the head of Duprato, at the roots of his long black tresses. Perhaps this was the goal. Perhaps he wanted to be shot. What if he didn't win? What if he did and never lived up to it, what a warrior could do in this hour, a great leader? Perhaps he considered all of this and also that this might be an easier way out. When no answer but the echoes came, there was a renewed volley of bullets, this time from multiple sources, and as the other boys scattered for the stairs, still laughing, Camille and I found ourselves separated. It was a remarkable feeling. He still existed as a part of me. I could feel his pull like the moon likely feels the Earth. And yet, I was suddenly my main focus. My own joy. Could I have walked away at that point and simply lived my own life? A life outside of the necessity for acceptance and acknowledgement of my brother? Like the moon, could I have detached myself and reattached to some other? Or simply been content to drift through space in random observation of only my immediate surroundings? And as I steeped in contemplation, stood still and acquiesced to the moonlight, as if on cue there came a strange sound unlike anything I had ever heard, calling me away, low at first but climbing in both pitch and intensity, with a melody and intensity that brought me to tears. It was the most beautiful thing I had ever heard, and if I might say so without being disloyal or false in any way to the truth of my brother, more beautiful than anything I had yet heard from Camille, perhaps would ever hear, a man I had considered before this as a sort of God. This, it seemed, was my true destiny, to one day join with this music, and I forgot about Camille, forgot about Duprato, sought it, was pulled by it, past the exhaust vents and the stairway, to a space behind one of the chimneys, and there was Camille, listening as intently as I, crouched over the boy from Marseille who, unseen and unbeknownst to anyone, had been shot through the neck and silently calling for help as the wind passed across the wound like a breath on a bottle. I felt shame in that moment. Betrayal. He was my brother, his cheek pressed tenderly against the boy's chest as his breathing gurgled like paint in a drain. This was not an exasperated cry of loneliness but true pain and fear, climbing in pitch gradually, until it rose in a shriek on the darkness. It was clear he was dying. He was losing blood quickly and all the others had retreated back to the dormitory. If we went to find help, it was more likely than not he would perish before our return, alone and afraid. If we stayed, we might at the very least be able to affect his final moods, make his last moments easier, allow him to express himself more freely. Camille grabbed the boy's hand and held it firmly. There was so little resistance. He began to squeeze harder. I could hear the bones shifting against each other, grinding, like icebergs below the surface of the water. Not a new cry or peep. Just the constant wheeze and whistle. A fresh moan mounted the night and I suddenly realized Camille's other hand was wrapped around the boy's neck, had always been there, his index finger forcing itself into the wound. A fresh flow of blood erupted from his mouth, punctuated by bubbles of sound, and a new, steadier note emerged. And another. And another. This was the music I had heard earlier, not better than my brother's but the moment of his full ascendancy. It was the most beautiful sound I had ever heard. The boy seemed not to be breathing anymore so much as letting all the air in his body slowly leak out. By forcing his finger into the wound, Camille discovered he could change the pitch and tone, the volume, until suddenly the sounds stopped entirely and the boy ceased to contribute. And for a moment I wondered if he could see me, or that this shared experience was like seeing, and we both smiled.

Sometimes, when one person is missing, the whole world seems depopulated. The other boy had meant nothing to us. He was just another obstacle, another unworthy adversary. But there was still the Prix de Rome to be handed out, and while at first, due to the tragic events on the roof, the judges decided not to award a prize, they eventually caved to popular pressure and awarded it to Duprato as expected, and he was gone from our lives. This was the genuine loss and sorrow that Camille incorporated with the sounds and melodies he had coaxed on the rooftop, in a handful of vocal pieces that started with some oversentimentality and ascended into godliness. Even Cherubini, who had once trotted Camille out regularly for friends and funders and given us our own room and special permission to practise on the pianos reserved only for seniors; even Cherubini, who was known to share his anger with everyone equally; even Cherubini took notice of us once again, stepped in and began to lobby for my brother's inclusion in that year's Prix, which would have made Camille the youngest boy ever to compete. Certainly Cherubini's support seemed a near guarantee. Under his auspice, my brother's fate seemed assured.

But then came the third death: Cherubini's. And our good fortune was over.

More than three thousand students and teachers, present and past and likely future, gathered at the conservatory for the funeral procession, held at the Church of Saint-Roche, then pulsed through the narrow veins of the city, performing Cherubini's own Requiem in C minor for male and female voices. Cherubini had composed it almost a decade earlier for this occasion, had in fact planned out his entire funeral to the final note. And at the last moments, on the steps of the church when the archbishop forbade the female half of the choir from entering and singing in the sanctuary, the entire group elected instead to finish outside, which was entirely more fitting anyway. Far from the typical, solemn march, it was a singularly pessimistic expression of grief, full of anguish and sorrow, and the singers of both genders threw themselves upon the steps and upon the casket and upon the ground and upon each other and chanted in perfect close harmony: *I do not want to die. I do not want to die.* The centrepiece, of course, was Camille, Cherubini's poster child, who scratched from the writhing hordes upon the steps, sang his solo, and entered the church to take up this place at the organ, addressing every note as the old master had written them out of respect for the man Beethoven had once named his most worthy adversary.

It seemed obvious they would choose Halévy to succeed him. He and Cherubini had been so closely aligned, had similar visions for the Conservatoire. What we did not see coming was Auber. The Conservatoire was struggling financially and, because Auber had flunked out of several prominent commerce schools and failed at so many enterprises before demeaning music, his experience had become an asset. He argued to the committee that Cherubini had taken them in the wrong direction, producing too many graduates who were daring in their experiments but unable to make a living from what they were doing. They needed to learn more practical skills, to produce music that would restore the people's faith in composers and return more of the middle class to the concert halls. *It is the responsibility of the composer,* he said, *to note the direction of the wind and harness it. We are doing a disservice to our young gentlemen if we send them out into the world without the means to properly support themselves.*

For the first time in years, Camille came second in organ to Silas, and though he initially feigned illness when asked about it, eventually he could not contain himself and began an open campaign against Auber and the rest of the jury. Camille had chosen that year to perform Bach's Prelude in D, for example, as well as Liszt's new *Ad nos, ad salutarem undam,* virtually impossible pieces for anyone but the composers and my brother. He should have been given the top prizes for his bravery alone! Silas had performed impeccably, of course, but had gone with the popularity and safety of *Jesu, Joy of Man's Desiring. Jesu, Joy of Man's Desiring!* The following year, despite the fact that Auber had removed the category entirely, he submitted a second symphony, and was ultimately accused of weak, Schumannesque imitations, devoid of any wit or subtlety, a worse disappointment than recent Chopin. Adolphe Adam said the symphony's main shortcoming was that it should have ended sooner, possibly after the first note. Camille wrote an editorial for the *Gazette* claiming Auber was biased and bloody-minded, had taken opera to its lowest point in history and was now taking the conservatory down with it. He also claimed Auber had stacked the jury against him. *Better pit a fox in the henhouse than ask those men to judge their peers.* Franck tried to calm him, urged him to apologize, pointed out that, because of their perceived closeness, just as had occurred to him earlier because of his father, my brother's words could destroy him as well. But Camille was nothing if not brave. So Franck came out more publicly against him to save his own skin, and was rewarded in the final year they could justifiably employ him with the position of head prefect. Franck said to us in the privacy of his rooms, but louder than he would typically speak so his voice might carry beyond the walls: *Who are we to decide what is good and what isn't? Auber's operas are regularly performed to packed houses.* But my brother resented the herd mentality most of all. He said: *There is a view of life, my friend, which holds that where the crowd is, the truth is also, that it is a need of truth itself, that it must have the crowd on its side. But to win a crowd is not so great a trick; one needs only a modicum of talent, a certain dose of untruth, and a small acquaintance with human passions.* Franck said: *Surely the crowd can be right, that individuals can each reach a common truth in private and come together and nothing changes.* But Camille was adamant: *No! Then the truth changes! The truth shifts! The truth is elusive and insidious, and it is our responsibility, once a truth is accepted, to go out and seek a new truth once again. Whatever one man does of his own accord—that is the only truth.*

What if Auber is right? Can't music just make us happy?

And Camille said: *If Auber is happiness, we'd be just as happy if we had no music at all!*

That summer we left the Conservatoire and took our first post as the organist before one of the city's most prestigious congregations, at the Church of Saint-Merri, in the exciting Latin Quarter, named after the eighth-century abbot and explorer Meriadocus, lover of boats and maps. But Camille was not the only one to find work in the era's burgeoning industry of false devotion. Silas could make no pretense to Catholicism because he was too Dutch, and was ultimately chained to an inferior Protestant instrument near London. And Fauré landed a position at the best cathedral in Rennes, but wrote to us often of giving up, using his hands for something more substantial, more useful. His grandfather had been a butcher, for example. His siblings were working in journalism, politics, in the army, civil service. He was undoubtedly the best organist the church had ever had, but was let go after he walked out on multiple sermons to smoke with the altar boys and showed up one Sunday for Mass still in his evening clothes, reeking of alcohol and cigars. A week later, he took up extended temporary residence with us back in Paris, withdrawn so far into himself by this point that he made no greater contribution to our new apartments than the housewarming gift we'd received from Charlotte and Esprit.

Franck, meanwhile, had always primarily been a pianist and, perhaps because he'd spent so much of his final years kowtowing to Auber, never wholly acquired the organ's legato style. The bar for professional organists was not set particularly high. Most were pale falsities of musicians, unable to pull off any real pieces designed for the instrument and resorting instead to popular hunting and drinking songs or *The William Tell Overture*. Still, Franck was unable to find a church that would have him, and ultimately he was forced to live off private piano lessons and often came looking for money, or food, one of his intolerably talkative students in tow. This would not have been half as bad if we hadn't also been made to listen to the simplistic pieces he was working on, or to put up with the students he was sleeping with, especially Félicité who would go on and on about dresses and how amazing it would be to be an artist like Franck and she would sit in the corner with her mouth flapping like the drapes, staring lustfully at the heap of garbage that had once been Fauré. Years passed like this, without any of us moving, it seemed. One day Franck informed us that some of his new techniques may, in fact, have abetted her pregnancy, and that he wasn't sure where the two of them could live on his wages. My brother took the hint and was able to coerce the organist at Notre-Dame-de-Lorette to employ Franck as an assistant just to be rid of him.

Camille and the Church were unlikely allies. My brother had in fact once written a paper claiming that science and art were on the ascendancy to replace religion as the guide of human souls. He saw the entire model of church music as built upon an untruth, a devil's agreement, and feared being falsely interpreted as a soldier of God. He was also dismayed to discover that the organ at Saint-Merri had been badly damaged during the revolutionary wars when the entire building had been used as a base to manufacture and store vaporous saltpetre. Two of the four manuals, the Récit and the Echo, were restricted, and only twenty-one pedals worked, which made the performance of Bach all but impossible. But so long as he never had to speak to any of the congregation directly (preferring the company of pipes and pedals over other people, favouring the never-ending psalm to the creeping curse of mundanity, sterility, speech without musicality, without meaning), he could stomach it. The job, as mentioned, was not difficult, to play set pieces between the preludes, offertories and postludes, to improvise accompaniment to the remaining congregational chants and hymnals. There was no way to know going into these interludes what key they might be in, or even if they would be in any key at all, because this depended on the abilities and focus of the priest and congregation, varying in tone from mass to mass, from half a tone to as much as one-and-a-half. But Benoist had prepared him well for this challenge, and the exercise became so regular and unmemorable that he forgot each performance entirely, almost as soon as it was played, so each succeeding day was not piled on the last, was not merely an insertion of new possibilities into a recollection of vespers past, but was like creating the world anew, like it was the first time, the only time. It was like my brother was building cabinets. Cabinets of music and whim. And the next time he just tore them down and started again. While people often talked about the wonderful music at Saint-Merri, no one really knew he was there, seemed to assume that the music just descended from heaven or was churned out by blind men with dancing monkeys. Was this the peak of his life? To be forgotten before he could even be remembered, to be ignored like a child on a hobby horse: was this the end? He found it increasingly difficult to reconcile with his dreams, with the promises his mother and Charlotte had made to him, that he was special, that he could do anything, that he would one day move mountains. More years passed. He began to resent them all, especially Saint-Merri's curé, a sad-looking priest by the name of Goulot. Goulot bore a look of wrenching sorrow as if born with it, yet seemed content to place his body firmly against the lever of action and not heave against it. Goulot was no more ambitious than any of them, and had still been risen to this point of prominence among them. It seemed such a waste.

Hasn't God given you the tools to lead? Camille would say.

I am a tool of God. He leads me, and uses me to lead others.

They believe you're the mouth of God. They would believe anything you said.

It's a responsibility I have accepted.

He confronted his flock daily with his tales of overcome and woenesses, jaw locking back and fro, lip dripping to and forth, his morals tumbling from the gap like change out of a torn pocket: pride, envy, the beauty of death, why bad things happen to good people, free will versus determinism. None of them understood a word. None of them cared. They were only there to be soothed by familiarity. To be led toward the lights they could see in the distance. These sheep and cattle! They knew less about music than the washerwomen Charlotte had lured to our salons. As a general rule, people who believe too much know nothing; people who know too much believe nothing. Sometimes Camille imagined strangling them, one by one, until the bodies filled the nave, a true soldier of God, marching slowly down the aisles and opening fire, or of locking the doors and windows and setting fire to the entire lot, just to listen to their screams. Would anyone care? Would it change anything? Would the world notice? And if they did, what would they feel? Would the song of these people be the most beautiful that anyone had ever heard? And would it last? Or would people just forget it after the next song? And the next. And the next. *It doesn't always matter what I say,* Goulot said. *It's the fact that I'm here, and* speaking, and I use the same tone of voice I always use and stand in the same place and look at the same people in the same eye. The church is their refuge, an asylum against worry and confusion. They feel tested enough in their daily lives and long to be reassured by common melodies and ideas, long for familiarity, long for peace, as a balm to their daily struggle. If I can give them that, I am providing the touch of God.

Then one day Goulot told the story of the greatest trumpeter the world had ever seen, without equal in his or any time. When he performed, it made his heart soar, but he became unsatisfied with being the mouth for someone else's words, and began to wonder about adding his own voice to the pieces he played, combining with them to create something new, to deviate from the score as it had been laid out for him long before he was ever born. Though his name was the one on the bill outside and everyone had come to see him, though the composer was long since dead, the trumpeter began to dream of freedom, from this tyranny—and he'd begun to think of it as a tyranny—of a being he'd never seen. What was the point of the performance without the choice of exerting your own path through it? Was he a man or merely a tool? And a tool for whom? That night he sat at a slight separation from the rest of the orchestra, in a special seat on a raised podium that allowed him to look down on the rest of them, and listened to the sustained build of the strings with a new realization: that he would be the one to set his path from this day forward, that he was now free. Though he had performed this piece many times prior, the strings opened up to him this time in a way they never had before, like a wide-open field inviting him to not just run through it but to pause, to roll, to head for the mountain or city in the opposite direction. A careful path had been blazed, and the brush on either side was high and uninviting, full of scorpions and snakes, and though each note was a shiny black stone and he could see very little beyond the path, he still imagined the glories of the other side, the delicious fruit he could not taste, the foreign wind he could not feel, though none of it was real, though the unreal can often have more compulsion than the real. In the end, however, he stuck to the notes on the page, trusted implicitly in the vision of the Creator, and the joy that he felt in such trust was unlike anything he had ever felt previously. *This is like our life with God,* Goulot said. *He is our composer and we are His musicians, free at any point to deviate from the score but never doing so because His love is worth so much more than anything else we may dream of, our Lord and Saviour, who taught us in His name to pray...*

Camille approached him after the service. Was the greatest joy to trust or earn trust? Was the greatest joy to follow? Or to lead others to follow? Goulot said: *We all have our place. Trust as the others do. Do not long for the great dreams of the future or linger over the great nightmares of the past. Be satisfied in life because it is the greatest gift we have.* And yet my brother couldn't stop thinking about what was beyond the brush. Were any of the congregation satisfied, as Goulot claimed? How could any of them be satisfied if they needed to come back every week? What were they searching for? What were they missing? Every week they came back in the same state of confusion, abused by life and looking to be consoled, and while Goulot's mission amounted to a once-a-week struggle to tow the flock's cargo ship a little closer to eternity, a human soul, unlike a cargo ship, could not lie in the same place until the next Sunday. The whole world had to become his battlefield, not just his church. To make a difference, the church could not continue to be a weak anaesthetic against the pain of life; the church was the very place where the difficulty had to be presented at its strongest, not to momentarily soothe but to make the rest of their pain pale by comparison. It is better to go from church discouraged and confused and to find the task easier that one thought, than to go from church overly confident and become discouraged in the living room.

Camille's improvisations the next day stunned the congregation. Several parishioners made for the doors. Others crossed themselves. A number of times, his fingers slipped from the keys, damp from sweat. The collection plate was passed more slowly. After the service, Goulot asked my brother what he was doing, and Camille just shrugged and apologized and promised not to do it again. But he felt different already. Until now, he had treated his position like a commodity, like an old woman spooning escargot from a rusty ladle on the street. Franck was wrong. There was no victory to this. He wanted to win. Or at least know that he was fighting, to know that they knew he was fighting. A violent negative reaction was better than a passive acceptance. He wanted to provoke them, to confront them, to make them notice. So the next day he replaced the second hymn with an étude by Liszt. An elderly cobbler tossed his hat. He lathered them with Wagner and two men started a fight in the south transept. From a straight improvisation over the offertory hymn, he dropped a Schumann bomb and skipped seamlessly into something he'd been experimenting with for weeks, a seven-minute piece in E flat that began with an ingenious, dreamlike alternation of chords between the two undamaged manuals, an effect that had never been tried before, and ended with a grand virtuosic coda that would have posed problems for any other performer besides himself. That night, there were riots in the streets.

Silas was premiering his first symphony in London in April, a piece he'd been working on for at least ten years, and he'd invited us to come stay with him and share in his excitement. We had never left Paris, but the grey was gathering around my brother and we longed for a friendly face, so we took a short leave with Fauré as our substitute at the church and hefted north on the next ship we could hire. Nothing could have prepared us for the glory of London, this vast fortress, armoury, prison, bank, grand theatre, this furnace of great power. It was dawn when we arrived and the Thames was smudged in boats of shapes and sizes all. Surely someone could have walked from one side to the other just by stepping, stepping, stepping. Mists curled and smoked from dark and noisome pools. The reek hung stifling in the air. Due south, mountainous warehouses loomed, like a black bar of rugged clouds floating above a dangerous fog-bound sea. Some were so immense they occupied twenty-eight acres of land at once, blemished with gasping pools choked with ash and crawling muds as if the factories had vomited the filth of their entrails upon the lands about. As we progressed farther, we passed high mounds of crushed and powdered rock, strange bottle-shaped kilns with orange, tanlike tongues of fire, great cones of earth, fire-blasted and poison-stained, an obscene graveyard in endless rows, slowly revealed in the reluctant light like hives, swarmed in shirtless men with eyes and ears and mouths but no use for any of them; just their strength—squat, broad, flat-nosed, sallow-skinned; just a writhing mass of mismatched biceps, backs and thighs, rugged and strong. The world is full of ghosts, creatures we never see, creatures we never want to see, monsters with fangs filed stumpy, who will never have any impact, positive or negative, on your or anyone else's life. But the stokers, armed with long iron rakes, threw open the ovens and drew out the coke, which fell in fiery torrents, swallowed into the abyss, the bodies become black and beastly, white eyes bores to the soul, and to me they were no longer figments of imagination, no longer the splintered fragments of true light, but mythical beasts, magical, born of seething darkness. I imagined them sending the mountains, and when the mountains were peaked, flinging themselves at the sky, in waves, plummeting back to earth, then rising on shattered limbs to send again. *Because of these men,* I thought, *one day London will reach the sky. Because of these men, we will run faster than horses in great steam engines!*

My brother, however, seemed afraid of them, expected them to ask him for all they lacked, saying: *We don't have this. Let us have it.* He expected them to make him hate them, like his congregation back at Saint-Merri. They didn't even know who he was, didn't know what he was capable of, but they offered themselves up to him because he was clean and straight in posture, tried to sell him biscuits and scrap. The club-footed lozenge salesmen, he saw them. The mush-fakers with their tissued, tangled wings of umbrellas, he saw them. The scarred crawlers; the young daughters of drunkards and manics, without shoes or stockings, spending ill-got money on ear drops and fancy combs; the men in their rickety water carts, radiating from the vestry yards on an arid afternoon to paste down the dusty roads. The filthy, parboiled women peddling flowers outside the gardens made him a garland from their essence, from quarters of the sky, and put it on him. They were so full of fire, but holding their fire to themselves in secret. The farther we pushed from the river, however, the further the ground softened; the further the fire; the further the gaudy grew. Silas's home in the West End, far from the fevered ditches and crawls of the East, was cold and motionless, built in an early Italianate style to mirror his new parish. The streets had been recently torn up to install a network of drains for increased sanitation, but they still seemed forged of feathers, draped in the high aristocracy who, unlike their tarnished counterparts nearer the docks, walked with little to no purpose at all. Silas greeted us with a hug and rushed us inside. We'd come just in time, he said, said we were welcome as long as we wished. He missed speaking in French, thinking in French, worried that doing all this in English, pulling back the lips, through his teeth the hiss, would make him as feral as the rest of them. *You'd think being in one place for so long, and full of such wealth, they would have risen above it all. But they're still just animals, all of them. They've merely been domesticated. They haven't changed since Brutus of Troy defeated the last of the giants.* He missed talking about serious subjects. *They only talk about food here,* he said. *And clothing. And being seen. And seeing. And working. And getting to work on time. None of them use their hands for anything more than eating and gesturing. They talk about ethics as though they are abstract and not in the belly, like it's a disease that only attacks others. They talk about art like it's a bird on yonder branch.*

We reluctantly took on several of Silas's shifts so he could oversee rehearsals. To reward him for his success, Silas's congregation had recently purchased him an organ to match his skills, designed by fellow Frenchman Aristide Cavaillé-Coll, who had been experimenting with new reed combinations to more closely imitate the timbre and character of actual orchestral instruments, replacing the dense forests of nazard, quarte, tierce and cornet that infested older organs with the richness of the bassoon and oboe, even an entirely new future sound he had invented that he called the *flûte harmonique*. The congregation had never heard anything played so beautifully. After the service, people approached Camille and asked him his name. He was asked to be the soloist for Schumann's Piano Concerto in A minor, Beethoven's *Choral Fantasy*, Liszt's *Hungarian Rhapsody*. Camille wrote a Fantaisie, attacked it after the offertory, and was mentioned in the *Musical Standard* as a note of interest. His footwork, they said, truly astounded. We met Anton Bruckner, who had once seen us play at Saint-Merri, and he invited us to help him open the new Albert Hall. Every evening we were invited to another party, another dinner, another gluttonous bacchanal, admitted to the most lavish homes with feasts of boar's head, venison, peacocks, swans, suckling pigs, cranes, plovers, larks, pink lamb, foods that didn't seem of this world. There were so many separate events Camille had to change his outfit at least three times a day, which meant either spending what little we didn't have on new clothing or borrowing outfits from Silas, who was quite a bit smaller. The top button of Silas's trousers refused to accommodate my brother's fondness for breakfast sausages, and he was forced to remain seated at parties or cross the room with his left hand shadowing his crotch. One night, we were introduced to the Queen's eldest daughter, Victoria, who was soon to be wed and become the Crown Princess of Prussia, and he only avoided exposing himself to her with a perpetual bow. At the moment they were called to dinner, they were approached by her youngest sister, the precocious Beatrice, barely five, and as custom had it, he was required to offer each of them an arm. He only barely managed it without international incident by refusing to breathe until they were all seated again.

That fall, Camille began an affair with Swedish soprano Christina Nilsson. The great Nordic beauty had been cast by our countryman Charles Gounod for his British debut at Her Majesty's Theatre, and though we barely knew the man, felt certain he did not know us, when Gounod heard that Camille was in town, he immediately sent a request to Silas's home that Camille take the piano part from him. My brother was previously committed, but still accepted a pair of tickets, arriving at the back of the club box just as the curtain went up on the garden scene. Nilsson was easily one of the most beautiful women in Europe, and we were shocked when we received the invitation to meet her afterwards in her dressing room. They were the couple of the season, played at hearts as other children might play at ball; only, as it was really their two hearts that they flung to and fro, they had to be very, very handy to catch them, each time, without hurting them. We feasted on pasta with fennel and banana, peanut butter soup with smoked duck and mashed squash, pilot fish with tulips and cinnamon. We were presented with intricate baroque plating, yellowish marmalade circling the plate in an artful octagon, cilantro leaves circling the marmalade, chili seeds circling the cilantro leaves. We gorged on fruits that seemed drawn by children: durian, rambutan, lychee and mangosteen. We devoured ferns and flowers, beasts of all sizes and ferocities. Every night Silas was waiting for us on our return and they would laugh and play for each other and sometimes even fall asleep across the keys themselves and wake with the lines of the sharps and flats pressed into their cheeks and foreheads. *Do you remember when we met?* Silas would say. *Sometimes I feel like it was only yesterday. I feel as though anything I would say to you about my life today would be the same.*

Oh, come now, my brother said.

But truly. What has changed, Camille? Are you not always working on another symphony, another concerto? I feel as though other people change. They have their children and they grow wiser and leave these other things behind.

I am in love, my brother said.

Aren't you always in love? It's like an illness. It's like being an artist. Like living in Paris.

Yes, living in the city is an illness, too. It has one cure. Unfortunately, being an artist has none.

We met Victoria again at a party thrown by the wife of Charles Dickens, in conversation with the artist William Holman Hunt, arguing about Tennyson. *Hunt was just telling me about your playing,* she said. *I had no idea the other night I was in the company of such distinction. What is it like to be better than everyone?* Classical music was not her thing, she admitted. *I am trained in the piano, of course. There are things that are necessary for a lady these days. But honestly: too long! Give me the popular tunes of the day. Holy! Holy! Holy! Lord God Almighty! Just touch the harp gently, my pretty Louise.* She always seemed to be humming something by Blamphin or Vance, Foster, horribly out of tune. *What is it that attracts you to that noise so much?* she asked him. *Why are you drawn to something so complicated and dull?* And Camille laughed because he couldn't answer. *When I'm Queen,* she said, *I could be your patron.* She rubbed his thigh beneath the table. *But you would have to play something nicer. Would you like to be the official composer for Prussia?*

Later in the evening she leaned into him, presented her neck and invited him slumming. *Hunt and I pretend we're poor and commiserate with the locals,* she said. *It's delightful. You must come!* Christina was reluctant, tired. But Victoria was so delightful and insistent. Though Silas's concert hall was in the East End, and he would travel there by carriage every day, we had not been back to the black and noisome since our initial arrival. The road sticky with slime, the palsied houses rotten from chimney to cellar, leaning together apparently by the mere coherence of their ingrained corruption. Uneasy shadows passed and crossed, the human vermin in this reeking sink, like goblin exhalations from all that is noxious around. Women with sunken, black-rimmed eyes appeared and vanished by the light of an occasional gas lamp, so like ill-covered skulls that I started at their stare. What did they see when they looked at us? Could they see me? Do poor people have imaginations? Do they have time to think about things that aren't real? To project themselves forward to a future self? A better life? Can they create other worlds to shelter themselves? As they began to crawl out from their holes, I half expected these monsters to speak in nothing but guttural whip, that they would not even know their own language, or had taken it and perverted it to their liking, brutal jargons scarcely sufficient even for their own needs, unless it was for curses and abuse. But the first of them began to sing, and then another, and then another, and miraculously, as soon as the first throat began to sputter and spark, the heat and flame of their voices rushed into me. French had always come to me laboriously. Here, I understood everything. Not just the basic idea. Everything! Was this some clue, then, to my prior existence? I had also come to believe, since I couldn't see myself in mirrors but could judge from the vantage point I most commonly occupied, that I must have been a dwarf, perhaps a circus performer or an oaf. This was possibly why I had never excelled at the piano like Camille, with my tiny hands like a raccoon's while his held the span of the albatross.

Can anything be done for them? Christina asked.

Victoria said: *Done? Tenants may ruin the character of a house, my dear, but no house can alter the character of its tenants.*

Hunt approached one of the houses and intoned: *Behold, I stand at the door and knock!* Laughing, Victoria laid down in a gutter beside a parchment woman and sang with her while Hunt made a sketch. My brother began immediately to compose another symphony, whistling as we were led through the piss and the shit and the bodies of the poor, something he would later call his *Urbs Roma*, a celebration of England and its capital—like the glorious empires of old—that would never fail. Christina suggested it was time to find a carriage that might take us back, but Victoria suggested they pay some young scamps to carry us on their shoulders instead. She sat down in a puddle and refused to take another step. *Look at them!* she shouted, and indeed half a dozen sets of eyes were poised above a nearby shattered window. *Come here!* she called sweetly to those eyes. *Come by, you strong and strealthy warriors!* She succeeded in coaxing two of them from the darkness, took a coin from her pouch and rapped it against the taller boy's forehead. The boy's greazy eyes fell over each other for a better look. His mouth dropped awkward. *I. Would. Like,* Victoria eked. *For you. To carry.* And she swept her arm to take us all in. *Us. All. Home. Do you understand?* Did the boys have any room in their mind for more than the coin she had promised him? Had they spent it already? The first took to knee. The second. Christina refused and walked along beside us. Of course, by the time they had carried us a few hundred metres, their tiny legs began to buckle, and Camille set his free but Victoria whipped hers with the buckle of Hunt's trousers. The boy stumbled but, righting himself with a shake of his shoulders, took a few more steps. Victoria leaned down to his ear, whispered something, and the shift in weight made him topsy, tippling into the muck and piss. *I think I broke my ankle,* the boy said. Victoria bent closer. *Let's see,* she whispered, now seemingly sober, tender. She bent over the boy, placed her hands carefully on either side of his leg, as though she were scooping up a baby swallow, then knelt directly on the boy's ankle and let her weight sink in. The boy began to throw up. Victoria nudged him with her foot, called him a thief. *Some people work hard for their money!* But the boy was unable to respond coherently, had perhaps even passed out. *Is it a handout you're looking for? If so, you can look elsewhere!* The boy was not moving. The other boy had run off. Victoria kicked him again, this time harder, lifted him off the ground, then positioned his face down in a puddle and left him there.

We took Christina home and returned to Kingston-up-on-Thames.

She's not like you, Silas said when we told him.

Christina? You mean she's good?

I mean she's satisfied. I mean she's not followed by her demons.

Is there anyone like that? Anyone in the world?

We attended a feast of light, then a feast of fury. We sat down to cobra ovaries with a sauce made from raw cashews, a platter of scorpions and spiders, fermented Greenland shark, Sardinian cheese wriggling with maggots; a tray of pearlfish fresh off the kill, their bellies full of sea cucumber. For several nights in a row, two animals were pitted against one another, and once the victor had consumed the other before us, it was killed and prepared in a sauce of fried chicken ovaries, raw cashews. Some were roasted alive. We ate veal cut straight from the mother. Another night we were immediately instructed to remove all our clothing and handed divers' masks and miniature tridents and everyone leaped into a tank with a metre-long sturgeon, laughing and stabbing her with the miniature forks until she was still enough to wrestle her over the glass, our feet slapping on the marble tiles, where we sliced her open with steak knives and mined the caviar directly from the cavity with our tongues and teeth while on the air she gasped and shook. Victoria swung her arms around my brother's neck, completely naked. Christine tried to pull us away, suggested we leave, and when my brother lingered, lazing move and traipsing gaze, she fell to her inner cower. Camille took her aside. *You are crying,* he said to her. *You are afraid of me! I am not really wicked. You shall see.* And he ran to fetch their coats, but on the way out the door Victoria again insisted we stay and Christine went home alone and we had another opium pellet and talked about the mad madrigals of Gesualdo, the morbids of Edward Lear, talked and laughed when Victoria mocked Christine and said: *Are people really so unhappy when they love?* The doors to the banquet hall were swept sudden open and they brought two of the men from the kilns and let them dig their claws into each other as a distraction between courses. After a few minutes of their uninspired grappling, a few of the guests began to stand. Where was the blood? Where was the reminder of life? Our host laughed uncomfortably and, waving his handkerchief in the air, tossed a steak knife at their feet. Both competitors looked down, as though contemplating their relative distances to the weapon, or perhaps their chances of escape. I wondered briefly if they might suddenly recognize that the tables had turned and, if they wanted, could probably murder us all, steal our possessions, escape into the night. The first of them took a step toward us, but that they might touch us was apparently unfathomable to them, and he was stabbed viciously from behind by the second. The knife was serrated but not particularly sharp at the tip, so instead of penetrating directly, it merely skipped a little long the surface, drew a line across his hip that reminded me of the edge of Cézanne's dark period. Oohs and aahs crept back from behind the plates. The second man spun around and punched the first in the side of the head. He went down immediately, as if his skeleton had been torn right out of him. Everyone cheered, except the apparent victor, who strangely waited for him to stand again. Soon they were both covered in fat red lines and I wondered how many it would take. Could you measure a person's life in lines like this? As though they were the markings of men just waiting to be released from this prison? The first combatant pinned eventual the second to the floor between his thighs and then, reverse-gripped, hammered the handle into the other man's side instead, over and over, again and again and again until his skin looked like the bruise of a peach and spread the sheets of his flesh wide open. At this point, the blade was actually admitted into his side, broke off in his ribs and, like Frankenstein's monster fed with lightning, he rose mighty and single-purposed, threw himself at our table, emerged with an oyster fork to drive repeatedly into the other man's neck and, like that, it was over. Everyone looked at each other in wonder, as if asking: Will he taste like the bull who had gored the brown bear through the neck? The wolf who took three seconds to kill the lynx? But then someone paid the victor and everyone laughed uncomfortably and he left and they brought out platters of ripe cheese instead.

Afterwards, instead of heading back to Silas in the West End we went deeper still, with Victoria and Hunt and the rest, and stepped gingerly over the piss and stepped gingerly over the shit, and stepped gingerly over the bodies of the poor like we were stepping gingerly over the piss and the shit, and out of nowhere we were flanked by two men who had no bodies besides mouths and stomachs and cocks and balls, nothing but appetites, consuming everything around them, wild animals, and they accosted us verbally and asked if we needed rooms and women and when we shook our heads and made to step over them they said, *Then why have you come to this quarter if you do not want a lady, and a room to take your lady to*, and Camille replied, head down, that if the pimp really felt that these women were ladies, he should treat them with more respect, did he have no mother, and eventually we arrived at a building that had once been a tavern but tonight had all the windows boarded up and a man at the door saw us and swept us inside and while from the outside it seemed like a place without light, inside it was all brightness and a place from which no light escaped, and we stepped down the bright hallway where they took our coats and up the bright stairs where we began to wonder if we were too drunk for stairs and on the second floor we stepped through a pair of velvet curtains and everything was fine again. The world settled down, it was no longer as bright, and we entered a salon like you'd find in any English restaurant. And everything we'd been afraid of disappeared. The world was real again. And we found comfort in it. The space was divided into two parts lengthwise. In the part where we were ushered, there was a row of tables separated by wooden partitions, and on each table was every kind of wine and liqueur, and every kind of meat and fruit, flanked on both sides by sofa benches. And we ate. And ate. And ate with relish the inner organs of beasts and fowls, thick giblet soup, mutton kidneys, nutty gizzards, a stuffed roast heart, liver slices fried with crust crumbs, fried hencods' roes, lampreys with hippocras sauce, such things as we might only have dreamed of at the earlier gatherings, and the room was full of people, so many people, but the partitions kept us from seeing them, seeing what they were eating and doing, at the table beside us, and they couldn't see us, so all attention was really on the food and, of course, on the other half of the room. The other half of the salon was a stage, positioned so that all of us could see the performers and the performers could see all of us but, as mentioned earlier, we still couldn't see each other, and the performers were richly costumed at first, then less so, and the men called them over and they disappeared from the view of some tables and directly entered the worlds of other, and some of them kissed the men and the men poured them drinks and some of them dreamed about falling in love and mar-

97

rying one of them and some of them dreamed about one of the men forgetting his gold pocket watch and selling it for a down payment on a house so they wouldn't have to fall in love and get married at all and they laughed, sometimes honestly and sometimes not, as the men pouring drinks missed their glasses and poured them directly on the women instead, and certainly none of them dreamed of the truth, first the men, that their unspeakable acts could in any way be as bad as the unspeakable acts they imagined one or two or more partitions over, but also the prostitutes, paid at the end of the night at the same time as they were presented with a bill for the liquor they'd never wanted to consume in the first place and placed in a cab if they were still awake and had a place to live and were still coherent enough to tell the cab driver where they lived and if they weren't then settled on the floor in the backroom to sleep it off and possibly survive choking on their own vomit. They seemed entirely without self, without willpower, without feelings, like hollow shells, to be played with as the men saw fit. Camille called one of the women to him and presented his lap to her and asked her to sing and after she had mangled a recent hit by the Great Vance he made her down a glass of vinegar mixed with mustard and pepper, proffered by Hunt, which sent her into such horrible convulsions that the men leaped from their chairs to get a better look.

It was nearly dawn when we finally returned home. Silas was still at the piano, as though he had never actually moved from that spot. He said nothing, simply gestured beside him and played a small passage from Grieg. Though the room was spinning, as if the whole world had suddenly been jerked from its pedestal and tipped like a spinner's plate, Camille laughed and played Silas some of the beginning passages of his *Urbs Roma*, a brilliant Beethoven pastiche over a deliberately awkward 6/4 time signature that slid jarringly into Schumann. *Imagine, if you will*, he set the scene for our old friend, *the sinuous, funereal creep of a clarinet in the style of Schumann. That would be in the second half.* All he wanted to do was sleep, but he felt a requirement to show Silas that nothing out of the ordinary had happened earlier, that he was not out of control. He tore a piece of paper from the pad Silas kept on the piano and drew him what he'd written for the oboe in the second movement, and Silas said: *You haven't changed, my friend. Though it flows beautifully from you on the piano, you know it's impossible to play on the instrument to which you've assigned it.* And Camille replied: *It's the music of the future. Someday, some future oboist will be born who will be able to play this. Perhaps. For now, the piece can wait for him.*

Silas laughed. *Does the world make sense to you, Camille? Do you look at the puzzle and see only the space where your piece fits?* My brother was unsure how to respond and Silas sighed. *An oboist from the future, then. And this man—or woman? Is this person a woman? Something else? Will they be waiting for you? Do they know you are coming? Is theirs the puzzle you belong to? Or do they belong to you?*

He continued: *Why is it that you do what you do? Why even make music, Camille?* This was not something we had ever considered. He might as well have asked, *Why breathe?* There was an implication that music was a concept and not an urge, a choice and not a desire. What Silas was exploring, he said, was the colours of music, the vibrations of the human soul. *Ah, it sounds foolish to say out loud. Vibrations of the soul? But it's all that concerns me. All this talk of ideas. The Realists and their unhealthy obsessions with depicting prostitutes, but still they paint them like Napoleon. It's not the subject that is the problem but the tradition.* When we asked him anything more specific about his new symphony, however, he became unusually quiet. Even when we asked about the motto he'd assigned the piece, the curious *Nur jene Form eines Tonstückes (The Subordination of Composition to Geometrical Form)*, he only replied: *Who is your favourite composer, Camille? Besides yourself, of course.*

On the night of Silas's debut we were seated with Christina in a private box with a view of the entire room. They'd torn down an entire row of tenement housing to make room for this hall, these statues, the striking Corinthian columns, and it was amazing to think how something of such beauty could emerge from such previous failure. The curtain made reveal, and we were surprised that Silas's style had not softened in the years, but had in fact hardened, was an attack on the audience from the first notes, a mirror held not to the glory of God or State but to hatred and fear and inequality. Here was their culpability; here was their shame. Have you done anything to make the world a better place? Have you done anything but complain? Have you not once judged? Here we are praising capitalism and democracy like they are meritocracies when, in fact, for capitalism to succeed, the opposite needed to be true, that the most incapable must rise to leadership, so that total destruction can progress unheeded. They were not the cure, they were the virus. Then, in the final movement, everything changed, the tempo slowed, and Silas wrapped the entire hall once again in a comforting fugue, a respite from his wrath, introduced a sadness that transformed the piece completely, with confusion, regret, as though to wake up from a night of perfect, a night of knowing, in the arms of all your lovers at once, knowing the shapes of the numbers, the numbers of the sunlight, the light of the soul, pulled every soul of every man and every woman in attendance out through their faces and transported each back to the moment where happiness was real, or at least within grasp, where happiness might once have been possible. He drowned them in nostalgia, called to mind, for each separate attendee, the exact second at which they had felt most human, most real, the most like the world made sense, to a time when there was purpose, and the purpose was joy. I picture myself atop a mountain, reaching down to Camille. Men, women, the room: filled with wet. They felt whole. But to be presented with such happiness in this place is, of course, to realize it has been swiped from you and replaced by this gigantic room and everything else outside it, this world, this experience you are having right now, none of which is real, all of it only approximating real life, real emotion, none of which is real, brought to tears by violin strings and appoggiatura, the quavering imagination of some god-being, none of which is real, these people on your left and right and below and above and inside and everything, none of them love you, none of them care about you or your moment of happiness, only want to share *their* moment, none of which is real, and then to realize there are infinite possibilities but instead you've ended up here, so your prior happiness is made even worse for having escaped you, or you having lost it, taken it for granted, and this realization, that everything in the end, even the most perfect existence, must at some point begin to crumble, brought them back to the hall with more presence than before, held down in their seats by Silas's knee across their throats, the violence of the earlier movements returned, not as an echo of the theme on a muted horn or in the lower register of the woodwinds but in every instrument at once.

Adagio

WE WERE FORCED BACK TO PARIS TO SETTLE SOME
business for our mother, who was beginning to show further
signs of her age. Christina was unable to accompany us because
she was being inducted into the Royal Swedish Academy, then
embarking on another tour with Gounod, but we planned to
meet up when they returned to the French capital. Though we
had been out of their home now for more than a decade, Mother
and Charlotte had continued their daily walks to the Luxembourg Gardens, and on the days Charlotte had business to run
for Esprit and the two sisters could not head to the park from
rue du Jardinet together, my mother would meet her there.
The Gardens were changing, and change was displeasing to
her. So without Camille to order about, she would berate the
groundskeepers over the new fences, the new gates, the new
statuary, how everything, from the selection of flowers to the
general shapelessness of the grounds and lack of civility, suddenly seemed more British. She would say: *Do you think Heaven is
this asymmetrical?* Or: *How can you even tell which parts you've tended
today?* The clothing on Oudiné's *Bertrada*, she claimed, was not
historically accurate. And Carpeaux's new fountain under construction near the nursery? With its unhealthy women, their

wasted flanks and furrowed thighs? *Why would anyone want to look at such wild, vulgar, wrinkled creatures?* Charlotte would often find her at the extension of the rue de l'Abbé de l'Épée, being shouted at by the horses and their riders. Louis Napoleon had decided to extend the road straight through the grounds, part of Haussman's designs to clear away entire neighbourhoods and install wider boulevards and cleaner, more efficient residential areas. The humanitarians saw it as a way to eradicate the rampant disease of the filthy blind alleys that made up so much of the capital. But my mother was no humanitarian, and the new road cut her off from a full seven hectares that had once been hers. So she refused to acknowledge its existence and walked out among the carriages as though they weren't there, purposefully holding up traffic until my aunt arrived to usher her back to safety.

One day it was my mother that wasn't there—not in the rue de l'Abbé de l'Épée and not trying to cover up the genitals of Hiolle's *Narcissus*. Charlotte ran back to get Esprit and together they combed the entire park, behind shrubs, in fountains. This had never happened before. She was always there. Could she have just disappeared? Could someone just cease to exist? Sometimes women disappeared. Should they find a police officer? Could they still trust police officers? *Have you seen a woman with a dreadful scowl?* they asked. *A general aura of disdain?* When they found her, she was bleeding from a head wound, had fallen down a small flight of stairs and struck her temple on the polished buttock of cherub. She'd become disoriented, thought she was heading north back home but was actually moving west. One of the older groundskeepers had recognized her and helped her back to his shed to get cleaned up, but she couldn't remember exactly how it had happened, and from there things progressed—rapidly—downhill.

I had always thought of our mother as eternal. In all of our years, she had never changed, except once when she briefly changed the colour of her hair and I wept loudly and ignored in the corner for days. I recall her mostly wearing that one dress, the one she was wearing the night we were mugged by the Arab. It was the nicest thing she owned and she prided herself on her looks and her attention to perfection. Overnight it felt as though she had aged a dozen years, probably more, was shrinking into herself like a singularity had formed inside her. Even with my pint-sized fingers I could have encircled her biceps, perhaps even her thighs. Her hair began to fall out. She could no longer apply her own makeup and Charlotte, who was as useless as a man in these things, having never truly valued beauty *or* her sister, let her expose herself to the world in ways that would have embarrassed her greatly, had she still possessed that awareness of herself as one of the few remaining creatures of beauty in the world.

We also found the Quarter much changed, that it had become infested with the adult children of wealthy Americans who had admitted some short fiction by Henri Murger into their souls, accepted it as fact, then travelled all the way across the Atlantic to make pretense to poverty. There are some who make art, and others who only aspire to being artists. The latter seek only to conquer life, perhaps capture it, while the real artists seek to change it, destroy it. The Quarter had become a sort of fantasy world, where people dressed like corpses on vacation, torn knees and beardless, each so unique you could pick one out of a protest like drawing black stones from a bag of salt. In this new Yankee Renaissance, where everyone felt like they could do anything, in fact, pursued multiple avenues of anything at the same time. Suddenly you couldn't just be a painter or poet, you had to be both. You couldn't just compose music, you also had to dance and make a fine soup, with everyone scouring the city for stray backslashes to tack on their already-bloated identities. Even critics like Botte were suddenly also known for their compositions, which were called out favourably by other critics/composers or critics/poets or critics/historians/urban planners.

It was in this theatre of mediocrity that we ran into Franck—

outside the popular Café Rotonde. He was barely recognizable, beardless now (as was the new style from across the Atlantic) with a more angled moustache, his clothes accosted with all the colours like some kind of crazy zoo bird, a two-year-old hanging off him like an additional accessory. We tried to pass without notice, but he smiled when he saw us, produced a set of wax crayons from out of nowhere and absently shoved his little girl toward one of the café's empty tables so we could catch up. Franck clapped us on the back, seemed genuinely excited to see us. It had been much too long, he said. *What are you working on?* It even seemed as though he listened to the answer, and what we discovered was that, when a place is no longer your everyday battlefield, the grass grows back. Faced with each other on a less consistent basis, we were both just Frenchmen against the world again, and it was lovely to see him despite his new wardrobe and success. Franck fetched a bottle of wine and it was not as insurmountable an obstacle as one might imagine to hear the story of his wedding, of his experiences in fatherhood, of sleep patterns and bowel movements and how Félicité, having finally reached acceptance that she had no talent whatsoever, had elected to become an actress with no backslashes whatsoever. My brother, who mostly detested children, took the little girl on his lap and said: *My dear, how do you catch a unique rabbit?* And when she stared blankly after the punchline, he tried again with a: *Knock knock,* and she replied: *Owl.*

In our absence, Franck had been appointed lead organist at Sainte-Croix-Saint-John, which was in possession of a congregation smaller than that of Notre-Dame-de-Lorette but also a brand-new Cavaillé-Coll, like the one we'd played for Silas, the kind of organ that could make anyone sound good, even this friend of ours who could barely do two things at once when one of them was just breathing. Franck had always struggled to release the stops between flourishes, languished between puerile shows on single stops and overambitious rambles of gargantuan chords, his body thrusting against the instrument like a beached whale. The organ was also too much for the space, so loud that it distorted slightly at the extremes. But still, word of its audacity drew crowds, and Franck was able to debut several pieces that caught the public's ear, and had recently published his *Six Pieces for the Organ*, which the great Liszt himself had apparently ranked publicly alongside the work of Bach. It was a job that by rights should have been Camille's, had we not stayed so overlong with Silas. *If you only knew how much I love this instrument,* Franck told my brother. *It is so supple beneath my fingers and so obedient to all my thoughts. It's like an orchestra! An orchestra at my every whim! I remember how you used to play,* he said. *Your speed and evenness. I always envied you for that. At Notre-Dame I had been banished to a spot behind the high altar, with its infantile, dual manual Somer. And for a while I was convinced this was my fate. Then I went back to Benoist for advice, apologized to him for not listening harder at the Conservatoire, and though the finances from my position provided me with little else besides basic sustenance, he agreed to continue our lessons, essentially where we had left off, for free. He told me to buy a practice pedalboard, so I did—thirty notes!—so I could work on it even when I wasn't at the cathedral. I practised hours every night, the same patterns, over and over. I could barely walk from practising, Camille. My feet desired more to step over each other than to forge straight paths. They would skip forward, hop back. Félicité would come home and find me on my back, my feet moving on their own! I would pass out on our bed and they'd kick at the sheets to fly. In my sleep! Yet I continued to practise, of course. How else, so much had my playing improved? The only time they acted in concert with me was at the organ, else I was forced to the role of the lovable buffoon, tumbling down stairs, careening into traffic, knocking on the doorsills. I fell down at least a dozen times just walking to the church, then a hundred, then I couldn't make it to the door. Do you know what it's like to lose part of your body to its own designs? The Abbé was incensed but still arranged to have two of the altar boys come fetch me every day in a wagon. I was gaining weight at an alarming rate. Félicité accused me of sneaking out in the evenings, after she had gone to sleep, said she would wake up and find me gone. At first I thought it was a joke. I was an invalid! I couldn't get to the edge of the bed to use the chamber pot, and she thought I was out the carouser! So I answered it was none of her business what I did with my free time, shouldn't I get to go out once in a while, too? I was being defensive, and more than a little irritated at the ridiculousness of it. But she found this less funny than I, and I, too, began to notice something foul afoot (ha!), strange substances stuck to the strata of my boot heels, oily and thick at times and, at others, repugnant and reeking. How did it get there? Was it possible for your body to do things, or even just parts of your body, while you were completely unaware? Perhaps my feet, so energized by their new independence, were walking in my sleep. Other feet walk, I gather they must have said. We will walk. Isn't that funny? But then I began to worry. Without awareness, how could I be sure that my feet were not up to no good? Was my body bound by the same morals as my mind? My spirit? Were my feet off at night acting against my will? Were they kicking at stray animals? Were they dancing?* And he laughed, clear he was having us on. In truth, his gratitude belonged wholly to Félicité, who had fallen in with a horde of the Quarter's post-American backslashers, including Cavaillé-Coll himself, had even attended the man's wedding, where they were seated with the Abbé Dorcel (*You two must know each other, no?*), and when Dorcel was given his own parish at Sainte-Croix, he took Franck with him.

My brother, who had always resisted groups, begged Franck to take us to one of these American gatherings, and the next week we accompanied him to the apartments of the Viardots, who had a large art collection they thought of as progressive without being overly offensive and a median age of fifty-eight. M. Viardot had earned his fortune as a writer/critic/translator/ heir, had recently published a new translation of *Don Quixote* and, with that under his belt, had decided to up the ante by translating novels from Russian without knowing a single word. Mme. Viardot, who spoke six languages though seemingly none fluently, like a parrot or Shakespearean starling, labelled herself a mezzo-soprano/pedagogue/composer, but was really more of a wealthy has-been/communist. Quite famous in her day, she had been renowned for her range, an abusive father, and an admittedly more talented sister. We had seen her perform before her retirement, and I could recall Camille describing her voice as *a little harsh, like the taste of a bitter orange*. She accosted everyone at the door draped in the costume she'd stolen from her final performance of *Don Giovanni*, shaking hands like a child, almost without the use of her muscles, like her hand was just a slab of meat or a stick of warm butter, and Camille's hand recoiled as though he might pass directly through her if he lingered too long.

We were shown to the parlour off the dining room, which M. Viardot insisted on calling their *state room*, ram-packed with insufferable, self-important poets and a smattering of myopic landscape artists, licensed copyists, expert loungists, pretenders and reeks, the same invasive species from America that had choked out the Quarter, expounding loudly on things like international policy, colonialism, the problems of the poor, systemic behaviour. They were the competent but uninspired, the intellectuals, women discussing the reading and writing of magazine articles. They filled the room with poisonous gas, the sound of shifting weight, the clack of sucking teeth. Franck introduced us to a group of his teenage students assaulting the piano in the corner and my brother was forced to humiliate them, put them in their place as he could not help but do, improvised ten variations on the spot, brought back his old tricks of playing masterpieces from memory.

There were still occasional performances and readings, vernissages, presentations of works in progress. But generally the evening comprised a handful of lectures, curated by Mme. Viardot herself, on subjects in which the presenters were not experts. Many of the topics were art-related. The poet Gautier, who claimed to be working on a *total art*, encouraging the emotional participation of the reader over form (which reminded us of Silas), spoke of a complex, theoretical, information-retrieval system, designed to potentially replace memory (to what aim, no one was certain), a system of cards with number-coded locations around all four sides that could be hole-punched using a mechanical, number-driven device. Millet gave a talk about plein-air painting, which advocated starting and finishing a painting in the open air, even if it was still a painting of an interior. Jules Verne, who was working on a novel about time travel, described the perfect baguette. Mary Cassatt rambled on about the railroad. André Gill lectured on the quantitative measurement of satirical values of various fruits, Jules Dalou on the rights of the mentally handicapped. Another evening's program was curated around suicide notes, and how to be an asshole. Gustave Courbet, said to be in regular sexual congress with George Sand, spoke at greatest length and frequency. One night we listened to him read a list of city monuments he found too nationalistic. On another he argued the real reason Napoleon was widening the roads was not to make the city cleaner but to make protest more difficult, to ease the passage of the military, and the recent addition of chlorine to the city's waterworks was similarly not about hygiene but part of a deliberate effort to dumb down the masses. Courbet labelled himself a Realist, and searched the country for the most perfect expressions of true poverty so he could invite them back to his studio to paint them. *I have never seen angels or goddesses so am not interested in painting them*, Courbet would proclaim. *True beauty exists only in the representation of real and existing things.* Also: *Titian was a fraud.* And: *The work of Raphael and da Vinci show no thought.* Courbet had already made so many enemies in the art world, no one would show him any more, so he held his own exhibits, in spaces owned by friends and acquaintances of his father (funded mostly by Alfred Bruyas, who had also studied under Charles Matet and then made his name, much like the masculine-gendered Viardot, by being the son of a wealthy banker in Montpellier).

Orientalism, once a niche, was now the vogue, and walking into the Viardots was like stepping off the boat, straight off the plank, into a turbulent churn of vague Biblical imagery, dressed in collarless shirts and bright sashes tied with ornate knots at the waist. Elizabeth Gardner once came in full Indian headdress. Courbet, never to be outdone, was always shadowed at a polite distance by the Egyptian. That's what they called him: the Egyptian. Perhaps he was Egyptian; perhaps he was Algerian. He confused them, in some ways, but because he was alone, he could but dilute them, could not take them over entirely. They admired, as artists, his undeserved wealth, his umbilical tie to taboo, which freed them to behave like the entire space was a slave market, where they were all the buyers *and* the goods. Camille was not immune, drank in the corner and leered at the young students from the École des Beaux-Arts, so young and ridiculous, so young and fit and drunk, so young, so lovely, so hopeful, in their knee breeches with matching velvet jackets. One night Courbet led a group of them around the apartments with a sheet, trying to demonstrate the different values of white in varying intensities of light, and my brother lurked at the back to be full awash in their disinterest: Jules Bastien-Lepage, Paul-Albert Besnard, Henri Regnault, Georges Clairin, Eugène Carrière, all disciples of tradition and Cabanel, with such immense skill but nothing to say. Most of them had grown up in small farming communities so far from the capital you might wonder if they were still French, with tousled accents like a clang and clock. They had never seen a fluted glass before coming to the École a year earlier, never heard of Auguste Comte, or solar power, or liberty. Even the Parisian—Regnault—though a gifted colourist, was overly influenced by Raphael and Poussin. He was also athletic and charming, however, with long, gorgeous hair and a fantastic brow. Was this what it felt like to be an old man? Caught peering through a fence at children chasing a rolling hoop? Trying to speak to him suggestively about viticulture? Desperate, he inserted himself into an argument between Bastien-Lepage and Clairin over the supremacy of different media, whether sculpture or painting was able to bring one closer to the Truth. My brother burst through them like he was breaching the surface for air: *Sculpture is an artifact, the art of the past, with no meaning outside of that passage of time. No matter when they are made, they come from the past, look old, are designed to look old, both in composition and materials. They are a war against time and also always about time. When I see a statue cast in bronze or chipped from stone, I see the immutability of life, something that has existed longer than I have and will likely continue to exist long after I am gone. Painting is the art of the future, the art of fantasy, built on metaphors, images standing in for reality, or even sometimes for other images, as unrelated to truth as honey is to a bee. Only music exists outside of time. Music does not truck in metaphor. Music has no desire to represent anything except what it is. It is an expression of an expression, not just a replication of a flawed perception of the world but a true burst of life before it can be tainted by interpretation. Other art forms come from outside; music, when done right, comes from within. It needs to be let out, to be released from the body at any cost, rather than understood through it. Music is everything. Music is truth. Music is the now, eternally in the present no matter when it is first composed. There is a tendency to enforce movement through time in performance, with each note flowing seamlessly into the next. The mind longs to hear music as one single ascending or descending chromatic line, like someone practising drills. Yet on the page each note is solitary, so perfect and pure. Barring flourishes and trills, which in their own way, it could be argued, represent single notes stretched in possibility, each note is a present moment. And not just a vague present that smudges and runs into the following, sloppily performed by someone like Wagner or Berlioz, each note is crisp, self-contained; an entire void separates it from the next one on the page. Between each note and the next, the world is annihilated and reborn. As each emerges, the world is a creation ex nihilo. Each note is an island, and we tumble from one to the next, through void upon void. Both sculpture and painting are stuck in the single moment, like a scarab in amber. Music, by focusing on each separate, specific moment, without verb tense, cast adrift by time, has the ability to contain all of human existence. There is no past or future. Only the now. A constant now. Only the it is happening.*

It is happening. By the time we are done, most of them are gone. But not Regnault. Not the young god, his face directly before us, his hand on my brother's arm, so close we can smell him, musty, like a marsh at dusk, like being buried in fresh soil. Regnault says: *If what we're seeking is Truth, then surely the advent of photography is going to collapse them all.* But we aren't really listening. We hadn't expected him to be so smooth, or that his lip would drip off his face the way it does, his gums black from the wasted wad of tobacco pasted across his bottom teeth. *I'm sorry if I've been staring,* he says. *But my parents took me as a boy to see you play. I remember asking my father why you looked so angry at performing such beautiful music, and my father told me who you were and said that all artists are full of rage.*

My brother is astonished to find the young painter's hand on his thigh. *Is that something you still believe?* Regnault shakes his head, distracted. *No. I think people who are on the outside of it mistake it as rage. Like when people complain that the sun is getting hotter...* But my brother has so little time for words and thoughts, especially the words and thoughts of other people. Instead, he imagines the curve of the other man's buttocks, the line of his thigh, groping him from behind, pulling him closer. He wants to bury his face in Regnault's hair, press his teeth into his shoulder. He imagines slipping the painter's shirt up over his chest and shoulders, tonguing his nipple, working feverishly at the buttons of his trousers. *Can a man be mad at the world?* Regnault is saying. *Can a place elicit anger?* But in my brother's mind, Regnault is reaching back to grab him, guiding him forward, the slight sigh of his shoulders as he enters him from behind, his full weight pressing down and down and down. Regnault is clearly in love with thoughts and words, at least his own thoughts, his own voice. Camille is nodding and imagines Regnault sliding from his chair, kneeling between his legs, unbuttoning his trousers, the feel of him in his hand, gripping him too tightly because he is so eager, pressing his lips to the tip, staring deep into his eyes—

...that artists are actually full of honour, which warms the heart of the witness and the source.

Do you play? my brother plucks the string of conceit.

No. Not truly.

But you do.

A little.

The piano?

Yes, and I sing. A little.

Camille tugs him. By the arm. To the piano. Urges him to sing something from Handel's *Messiah*—no, *Acis and Galatea*: *Love sounds th'alarm!* Regnault, flattered, shakes his head no, but Camille is sitting down and playing bits of familiar melodies to encourage him, to encourage the others to encourage him. As it turns out, Regnault is indeed a passable tenor, not entirely without talent, with a voice that is not perfectly suited to singing but also enchants in its own way, as irresistibly seductive as his penetrating gaze. My brother, helpless with him, forgets for a moment that they aren't alone and reaches out to grab the other man's hand. Regnault is throwing his arms around my brother's neck, is leaning his head into his shoulder, is placing his palm against my brother's beard, tugging at it playfully. My brother is helpless with him. He wants to run his fingers through the boy's hair, tread toothéd along his nape. Regnault is leaning heavily into him, his hand in his lap. If every moment in time were permanent, did not begin to expire the moment it came into being, he might have been happy. And yet, time plunders. He can see Clairin and the others mobilizing by the door *(Come, Henri! We're going to help Courbet destroy France!)*, knows this is all coming to an end, so Camille quickly scans the room for Victor Capoul—because clearly he would have been the more obvious choice—and when he is certain the other man is absent immediately offers Regnault a part in the opera he has recently completed about Samson and Delilah, just so that he might see him again. Regnault can barely focus his eyes, but he says yes, he said yes!

This was a small untruth. Camille had *considered* writing another opera, and he had even spoken to a friend about writing the libretto. But so far all he'd composed was an oratorio around some words Voltaire had written for Rameau, certainly nothing to do with Biblical judges and jawbones. Fortunately, my brother had developed one of the finest minds for improvisation that ever existed, and confidently began to build a scene, on the spot, in which Samson/Regnault, moved helplessly by the song of Delilah, attempts to woo her with a song, while she, in turn, could care less about the words or the quality of his voice, is enthralled only by the body. *I will need a few others*, my brother announced, and scanned the room quickly for a potential cast. Seeking a Delilah who might represent the age difference between Regnault and himself, he turned to Mme. Viardot, but she waved him off, pointed to her throat and coughed lightly, so Camille coaxed the talented Augusta Holmès, who was not old at all but sufficiently homely to appear so. Who else? A High Priest! Bussine, the poet, was seated closest to the piano. He was also old enough, and we'd heard that he gave occasional voice lessons. Was he a baritone? Unfortunately, it turned out he was. Camille himself performed the other incidental roles as they came to him: an old Hebrew, Abimelech, various Philistines, the barber. *Je t'aime. Je t'aime*, he had Holmès sing. *I love you. I love you.* And Camille could be seen to mouth the words with her, though the sentiment was more: *Just fuck me! Just fuck me! Just shut up and fuck me!* Camille prompted his Samson and Delilah in a way that gave the opera the impression of being in a round, or an early spiritual. Holmès edged closer to Regnault as Camille pounded the keys harder and harder, doubling her voice entirely, his face transformed.

My brother spent the following week trying to recall what he'd played at the Viardots' and then build on it for the next salon. But Regnault did not return and the sculptor Doré lectured on Cervantes, and the photographer Nadar addressed the possibility of space travel, with complex diagrams of a vessel he felt could make the voyage successfully, and eventually Camille lost interest in the new opera altogether.

His improvisations, however, were not wasted, and led to a growing popularity in their group along with his bold pronouncements like: *I produce music as an apple tree produces music.* And: *We don't understand music, music understands us.* And also: *If you've managed to link every instant symbolically or metaphorically to every other instant and established exactly what it means, then you've done it wrong.* One night he sat down to the harpsichord and drew a crowd aping Mozart while playing the central notes with his nose. A few weeks later, he was emboldened to dress in drag (pilfered from Mme. Viardot's wardrobe, that same dress from *Don Giovanni!*) and, to the delight of everyone, performed astounding impersonations of everyone from the dull head-resonance of Rubini to Duprez, with his high C from the chest; both pitchy ends of the range of Elizabeth Billington; the rusted hinge of Lilliet Berne; the peaks of the birdlike Adelina Patti; the castrato Moreschi; Mme. Viardot herself; even betrayed Christina, a voice he knew so intimately, its beauty and flaws (particularly when she was at the uppermost end of her register), with little resistance, then immediately felt sore for it. Camille also began an indiscrete affair with a cancan dancer from the Bal Bullier, a Creole of easy virtue who always leaned in when she talked, as though her legs bent backwards at the knees. She would accompany us on outings to the countryside or to the cheaper theatres, and eventually ran off with an actor to America.

Courbet, meanwhile, returned with the Egyptian. Rumours continued to circulate around him. He might have been Greek. He might have attended an Egyptian military school, might have been the son of an Egyptian general, might have been born in the Egyptian palace. He might have been an ambassador for someone to Russia and had helped to negotiate an end to the Crimean war. The most fantastic story of all was that he was renting rooms from a wealthy Englishman not far from the Viardots and was assembling the largest private collection of pornographic art in the East, naked white women with which to cover his walls. Most evenings you could hear him trying to convince Courbet to paint a picture of Sand's genitals. They all wanted to be near him, but because he had no discernible accent unless he put one on for them, would have passed for Parisian from behind a curtain, they were afraid to ask direct questions.

Courbet gave yet another talk, this time about the war in Algiers, and a German journalist who had travelled to Oran on assignment for a British newspaper called the *Northern Star* to interview members of the local resistance. Several of the attendees laughed and cheered throughout. The German, Courbet said, had made his name exposing conditions in London homes for the elderly, where the residents were rarely allowed out of doors, with only one cup of tea per day and barely a scrap of bread. *What shall we say,* he wrote, *of the woman, or man, maimed by misfortune, who must come here or die in the street? Why should old people be punished for their existence?* When the opportunity arose to question the men who remained of the Ouled Riah, why they were still doing what they were doing, in their own words instead of the typical narrative of abused orphans brainwashed by al-Qādir, he thought: *Here is my destiny. Here is how I will shape the world. This is my big story.* The German's wife

117

asked him to stay home. They had three young children now. He lectured her on what was important. *If you die over there for what is important,* she said, *who will look after your children?* And he said: *If these stories are not told and the world stays as it is, it won't be a world worth living in anyway.*

The German was met at the dock by a teenager holding a sign with his name. The only Latin letters for kilometres, it made his own name seem like some sort of foreign language, even to him. Was the sign necessary? With the French abandonment of the city, could there be any doubt who he was? The lone white man? Then again, perhaps the sign was not for them to find him but rather for him to know who could be trusted, in case someone else had been sent by a rival group to intercept him, for less altruistic purposes. His contact back in London had warned him of this. They were a tribal people, he had said, and even the ones who had joined under al-Qādir had split into many splinter groups. Some insisted on other modes of resistance, without the restrictions of diplomacy.

Of course, had these other groups also known he was coming, they might also have sent a boy with a sign. So there was no way to know, really. (This last comedic bit earned Courbet some of his greatest laughs.)

Assuming the boy would be unable to communicate with him, the German wordlessly offered up his bag and began following him up the hill, through the ruins left by the French. It made him feel nauseous to think about it, that an entire city could be removed from the planet like this, expunged from time, forever, and for what? Entire city blocks left to rubble, fire set to fields, fruit and olive trees razed low, and then, from out of nowhere on his right, a half-destroyed wall someone had transformed into a stunning work of street art, beautiful, with colours he'd never seen before in European painting, calling to mind a lone flower straining up through paving stones. He began to compose his first article. *Even in the face of such adversity,* the German thought, *they strive for the sun.* Soon they came across another. And another. And the further they climbed, the more menacing they became, as if they might move to smother him, these beautiful painted flowers. He and the boy were beating a straight line to a large round dome atop the hill and he could still see straight back to his ship at the docks and the repeated imagery made it seem like the creatures in the images were following them, running circles around them, like colourful shadows slipping noiselessly along the walls: an ornate, eight-pointed star, beaded with shards of broken glass; a lone figure with a dark-skinned face and a shepherd's crook and something resembling a sling; a one-eyed giant. Had someone taught these people the story of David and Goliath? What had stood here, on this spot, before the fiery sword? An eighth world wonder? Like the Library of Alexandria? A hospital? Then out of nowhere the boy said: *This road was once a cemetery. Your people bulldozed it to create a straighter road, so they could see from the harbour to the mosque they converted into a cathedral. You are walking on the bodies of our ancestors.*

I am not French, the German tried to assure him.

You're not one of us.

Of course, now that communication had been established, the German pressed on: *You speak French.*

Nothing.

You've been to French school.

They've been to me.

And the paintings, the German asked the boy. *The murals. Who made them? What is their purpose?*

The boy shrugged. *What does it matter? What can colourful images say to murdered women and children? What can metaphor say to children forced to schools in French, where they only teach one history that never happened to us.*

They reached the dome—a converted mosque. The boy dropped the German's bag inside and said: *There is a room downstairs with beds and a basin to wash. I will bring you food until the men are ready to speak to you. Until then, don't go outside; don't speak to anyone.* Then he left. There were no windows. The only escape from the room was the one door, then the long hallway, then the stairs back to the surface. Should anyone come for him, he would most certainly be trapped. Would they do that? Did rules of sanctuary mean anything to these people? Every day the boy brought him meals and said today was not the day. And because he slept below the ground in a windowless room, the German never had any idea what time it was. Sometimes he would come up in the pitch of the black and find no one, decide he needed a cigarette and a drink and, not feeling right inside a holy building, would take his flask and cigarettes outside to look at the stars. He had forgotten the names of the constellations he'd learned as a child, so he made his own connections in his head. Were they even the same stars? This far from the real world? One group reminded him of the murals from the first day. One night a Kabyle herder walked by with a goat, stopped and stared at him for several minutes. He went back inside. Other times he would arrive with the sun high in the sky and find the mosque full of old men. *Why are you here?* one of the men spoke suddenly from the corner, in French. *Why are you here?* the German replied.

Then one day the boy walked in and, instead of bringing a meal, he just glanced in disgust at the old men and said: *Come. It is time.* Toward the water. Across the road that was built on the backs of the dead. The air was full of the call of the birds, most of which the German could not identify but he did hear a dove and a pern and what he thought was a loon. He led the German through a hole in a wall to a place where there were no murals, just a field of rubble pitted with fires. Each fire was surrounded by a handful of Kabyles, mostly old men but also young men and also women and also children and also. As they stepped carefully past the fires, the German could see they were fuelling them with books and he gasped audibly. The boy said: *The only thing the French left us was their books. At least we can use them to keep warm.* The German, who had learned to read when he was only three, from his mother, who held him every night and cooed, began to feel ill. Books were what separated men from animals, he thought. If you didn't value books, you were no better than a beast. A demon. It was exposure to books, proximity to literature, that separated the violent cultures from the civilized. One only had to look at the failures of preliterate societies. Where were they now? Perhaps it was the lack of a written culture that had made the Arabs so violent. *The Frenchmen said they came here to bring us culture,* the boy said. *They were widely read. Then they cut down our trees and chased away all but the old men and sent many of our young women to an island so that none of our young men could ever reach them. The French books burn the best because they're more full of shit.*

The rendezvous for the interview was in a modest building on the far edge of the rubble. The German was expecting to find the room lavishly decorated, to make him feel as comfortable as possible, at ease, so he would not be distracted from the interview, but when he stepped through the door he found it completely empty, not even a table or chairs, and once again he was left alone. Once again, there were no windows, and only the one door through which he had entered. Outside there could have been anything. The world could have ceased to exist entirely, could have been reborn a million times, a billion times, more, like the old men had said, until all the molecules in the universe chanced again on the same configuration of existence, or at least close enough that he would never know the difference, and the door opened and in came a line of young resistance fighters, all in their teens or early twenties, all scarred in some way (missing limbs, large burns, head wounds pasted with bandages), likely to increase his sympathy. But he was a journalist as well as German and would not be swayed in his quest for the facts by cheap emotional tricks. He sat down at the only table and someone immediately brought him a coffee. He removed his notebook. He licked the tip of his pencil. He adjusted his chair. The secret weapon of all great journalists is silence. Make people feel uncomfortable and they will eventually tell you everything. They looked bored. He licked his pencil again. He waited. None of the young men spoke German, or English, or even French, had lived so long in their remote villages in the mountains that, before hearing their first French soldier's death cry, they had never heard a word of it. The German asked the translator, the only one who was not injured, if any of them were being paid to talk to him. He asked if any of them were being coerced into this. Were their families in danger if they refused? He turned to the translator. *Will they be allowed to answer my questions freely?* *Of course*, the translator replied. But really, the German had no idea what the translator said to them. He asked: *Why did you start this?* And the answer was: *Us?* The German asked: *Where are the older rebels?* And they replied: *Fighting. They will not take time to talk, as we do. They are done talking. They have seen too much to talk. At some point, you have to stop talking about things and just do them.*

The people back in Europe don't understand you, the German said. *I can give your stories voice. I can bring your stories back to them and the stories will change things.*

These stories are not your stories, the translator said.

The German smiled, knowing their anger would make them more eager to talk. *Why do you fight?*

We have been here, in this place, for more than ten thousand years. We fought the Pharaohs of Egypt. We fought the Carthaginians. We fought the Romans—

The Carthaginians brought you agriculture.

The man shrugged. *We already had agriculture. They brought us different agriculture. So they could grow the foods they were used to, instead of the foods we were used to. We enjoyed the foods we had before.*

The German asked about the murals. *The figure with the crook is the old one*, one of them said. In another answer, however, one of them referred to it as *the old woman*, and another as *the corn spirit*. The German said: *Corn spirit? Are you not Muslims?* And the men said: *Yes, yes, of course.* And they looked at him as if he were crazy. They told him how the world was created, with only one man and one woman, who lived not upon the earth but beneath it. They told him that the man and woman met one day by chance, not knowing that the other was of a different sex, not knowing, in fact, that sex existed. But they put two and two together—*many times, in fact*—and eventually filled the world with people. *One day they both came to the well to drink, and the man said:* Step aside and let me drink, *and the woman said:* Step aside and let me drink. *And he tried to push her aside. And she struck him down. And in their struggle, their clothing fell from their bodies and they knew. They put two and two together.*

Later, they said, *once the sons and daughters of the first man and woman had found their way to the earth's surface, they found the world full of delicious things to eat, and they asked the plants and animals:* Who made you? *And the plants replied:* The earth made us. *And the animals also replied:* The earth made us. *So the young people turned to the earth and said:* Who made you? *And the earth, of course, said:* I was already here.

The translator tried to get them back on topic. *One night,* he said independent of them, *they herded all the young men into a public square, forced them to wear skirts and masturbate.* The boy on the far right lifted his shirt to show where he'd been gored with a corkscrew. Another revealed the scars of third-degree burns over ninety-nine per cent of his body. The only parts that were not burned were his hands and shins, which he claimed had been pressed to the ground as he tried to cover the body of his younger brother to protect him from the flames. The German grew worried that he might not come back with something reasonable. He grew annoyed. *One night,* a soldier said, *I am sleeping in my home with my family when the French come. With knives and hatchets and pistols. I remember my wife's head strike the table so hard it crack the leg. My son is still sleeping, could sleep through anything. Even when his baby sister would wake in the middle of the night, inconsolable, he would still be sleeping. They crush his head with a rock. While he is still sleeping. My baby girl is so trusting. The French soldiers coo to her and she reach for them and laugh, and one of the soldiers said to me, in a voice that was still light and airy so my daughter would continue to*

123

laugh and smile at him, would not resist, that once he had killed me, he was going to take her back to France and raise her as his own, that he would teach her to be civilized, a true European, not like us, would have her educated at the finest schools in Paris. She would only know happiness. It would change her life entirely. She would grow up French, would think in French, would think she was French, would be rich like the French, smart like the French, would be taught to hate the Algerians, the people like her father, her mother, her poor dead brother, would sit in cafés with her friends after a day at the Académie and dip her pastry into her chocolate and sneer about the way the Algerians treated their women, the public stonings for infidelity, the ritual sacrifice, just so one day he could tell her what she was, and she would be old enough and smart enough to understand what it really meant, and she would hate herself, and only once he had described to her in exacting detail how he had killed me, would he finally kill her, too. It would be such a shame to kill her now, *the Frenchman said,* when she won't understand.

Which one of them said that? the German asked the translator.

Does it matter?

Afterwards, he spanned the field of nothing but fire and rubble and books and no more books, dejected. The interviews had not been what he had hoped. The stories went too far. Even if they were true, no one would believe them. He would be ridiculed, might even lose his job rather than ensure his career. What was that ember in the middle of the closest fire? he wondered. Leibniz? Darwin? Augustine's *Confessions*? He approached the flames and demanded the book in the old man's hands. Then he put his body into it. His guide said: *What are you doing?* and tried to force his own body between them. *You're removing his only source of warmth. You'll have to give him something in return.* The German thought he might weep. He had nothing. *You told me to bring nothing.* Instead, he tried to overpower the man, who was at most half his weight, tried to wrest the text from its executioner, finding he could not. He shoved the man, shouted at him, screamed at him about decency. Men around the other fires began to take notice. Some stood up. The boy told the German to be quiet, said: *We must go. Quickly.* But he couldn't move. It was as though his feet were rooted to the spot. This unknown book had become his entire life. It didn't matter what was in it. It was knowledge. It was beauty. If he didn't save it, he had nothing. The world had nothing. The old man stood up and finally succeeded in tearing it from the German's hands, and the German, without thinking, raised his fist, brought it down as hard as he could upon the man's head. Down he went. The men around the nearest fire began shuffling slowly toward them. They couldn't see the body. The German couldn't even see the body, not in this darkness. The light of the fire took in everything. The German tried to see if the old man was okay but the boy had him by the arm, was pulling him away. No, no, the German shook his head. He had to make it right, make sure he was all right. He was not a criminal, not a thug, not a thief. He had the book in his hands, but he could still make it right. It only required an exchange, an act of commerce. And without really thinking it through, not even knowing what it was he was struggling to save, he gave the man his notebook.

Not until they were back through the hole in the wall did he begin regret at what he had done. How was he supposed to go back to London without his notes? Without his interviews? Even unusable, surely his editor would want to see them. The newspaper had paid for his voyage, would pay him even more when he returned. And he had traded it all away for this thing in his hands, brought through fire, almost falling apart, pages cut and glued from other books, private observations in handwriting so messy it was barely legible. He tried to inhale it. He had traded his life for this, for a diary. Once they were safe back at the mosque, the boy went back to assess the danger more thoroughly. The German tossed the book aside, now certain he had traded it all for nothing. Could he simply invent the stories? Who would know? Surely he had an imagination forceful enough to approximate atrocity. Surely he could move people to action. If he made it home alive. Why had the old man attacked him like that? What did that book mean to him, surrounded as he was by so many other things to burn?

There was a sound from down the hall, someone coming down the stairs. It was the boy. *People are saying you killed the old man. We must go.* The German quickly grabbed his things and they headed back to the street, out of the room with no other exit, down the hall with no other doors. Up the stairs. The streets were full of men with torches and clubs. Rifles. The boy took him on a route that circled around on themselves more often than he could count to elude them. *They've blocked the road near the docks,* the boy said, and took him through another hole. They moved quickly. Even then, it seemed to be taking too long. From what he could recall of his bearings, it was as though they were not travelling toward the water but away from it. What if the boy had merely spent his time rushing between factions to negotiate the best price for him? *You want to save the German? How much are you willing to pay? You want to kill the German? Make your bid.* He decided that at the first opportunity he would escape him, knock him out if he had to. Instead of watching his footing, he began scanning the ground for large rocks. How he would then hire a boat to London without the boy was another issue, but it seemed trivial compared to the certainty of death he now faced. He had spent his childhood summers sailing on Lake Bodensee and could surely manage, from the sweat of his agonies, if he could commandeer a small boat of some sort, to coax it as far as Majorca. It was necessary that it so happen. The boy gestured for him to hide behind a wall. It had a painting on it, a treasure of gold. The boy told him to wait and slipped off to the darkness. The German found a rock and palmed it in his right hand. People often wonder if they could ever kill someone, but killing is simple when it is necessary. Of course, if the boy had simply wanted to kill him, why the charade of circuity? He began to reconsider. To make sure he took the German back to the right camp? To make sure he was not rescued by the faction he'd come to speak with in the first place? There was the sound

126

of a twig snapping on the other side of the wall and his hand tightened on the rock.

Oh, come now! M. Viardot interrupted. *Clearly he made it back. What was in the book?*

And, grinning, Courbet pulled it from under his chair. And he began to read. *My name is Blanc,* it began, a soldier's diary, not nameless but without rank or battalion or squadron. *Our mission,* he wrote, *is to crush the resistance for good, by cutting off the head of the terrorists, capturing or killing al-Qādir in his caves in Dahra.* People in the room cheered. Emboldened, Courbet went on. Many of the diary's pages, he said, were nearly illegible, having been written at night, under the pitch of the black. Disoriented after days of marching, Blanc would fumble for his bag, then his book, then something to write with, miscounting the pages to where he'd previously left off, notes on top of notes, possibly weeks apart, it was impossible to tell. Did it matter? Do feelings build on one another? Does one truly accumulate grief to burst? Or can one shift laterally and immediately to the light or crushing despair? *Aside from quartermaster ledgers,* Blanc wrote, *this journal is the only book for kilometres. The other soldiers have begun referring to me as the troop librarian. The other day, Ledeuil asked if he could borrow it, laughed, and promised not to scribble in the margins. But sometimes I can see him watching me, or watching the book, with resentment.* He wrote often of Ledeuil, his clothing, face, the sound of his voice, but Blanc also wrote tenderly of his fear, and the enemy. *Today we reach Dahra and will do battle with the Ouled Riah. I half expect to wake and see a wave of sand, centuries tall, over which peeks the sneer of al-Qādir, the bodies of his lifeless warriors propelled toward us by the churn. Ledeuil says they are seven feet tall. They are not afraid of death. They do not bleed. Because they have no hearts. But there, but for all this, went peace. I did not know what Dahra meant back in Arabic until today, although it's probably just as likely that this isn't true. When we marched through Mazouna this morning, the only town for kilometres, it was deserted, so beautiful, so serene, groves of the deepest green I had e'er upon laid eyes, apricot,* pomegranate, plum, quince, lemon, almond, jujube, pear, peach, olive, karoub and fig. *This was how I had always imagined Eden, Paradise.* In a swift briefing, they were informed that al-Qādir was not present at all, and that the rest of the Ouled Riah had retreated to the safety of some nearby caves. They hid. The great monsters of the Ouled Riah. In caves without exit. *We prepared mentally for the siege. But the next morning we were woke by the bugle. Pélissier ordered us back to the grove, to collect brush for fires, seize victory from beauty, crack the boughs of the karoub, hack the limbs of the fig trees, mash the ripe fruit beneath our heels. My arms bore the murdered grove and I walked up and saw these men doing strange things, setting fire to the caves and waiting for people to come out and then shooting them, going into the caves and shooting them, gathering people in groups and shooting them. As I walked in, you could see piles of people all through the village, all over. In total, we removed nearly six hundred lifeless bodies from the caves. Unsure of what to do with so many, we began to stack the bodies. Some were not quite dead yet, including some women and children. And the women threw themselves over their children to protect them, and were shot. And once the mothers were dead, the children who were old enough to walk emerged from the piles and were shot as well.*

And no one was laughing anymore.

No one could look at the Egyptian after that. Camille, however, could not wedge the image of the groves from his mind. The wave of sand. The murals. He wanted to know what the women were wearing. And the children. He dreamed their sorrow. He was so tired of his day-to-day Parisian existence, tired of the uniformity of constant dedication to his work, used to being so powerless in Paris, at the whims of fools like Auber and Franck and the Viardots. He'd had enough of this endless repetition, enough of this mimetic representation of the exotic, enough of the sounds, the same sounds, the no sounds. Enough of the trees. He wanted trees that were not trees, a sky that was not sky, sounds that were not sounds. Enough of the sounds. *Tell me more about Algeria,* my brother said to the Egyptian one night and the Egyptian replied: *What makes you think I would know anything about it?*

You're one of them, aren't you?

I grew up here like you.

But not like me.

Thankfully, the Vicomtesse said she had some rooms at the Hôtel de l'Oasis in Algiers, so we booked passage on a ship from Marseilles, in search of something we could not pin down, a drop of water in the ocean seeking another drop, a drop that matches, in the whole wide ocean. What would my brother do when he failed that task? Was any part of the ocean any different than any other? Could it be divided down? With one drop missing was it any less the ocean? And another drop? And another? Was not each of us the ocean in our own way? Infinite and yanked by the tides? You are never alone, always alone.

On the morning of the second day at sea, however, with the

help of binoculars, we finally caught the first outlines of the Atlas Mountains, very indistinct, but definitely there, on the extreme edge of the horizon. In a few hours, we would fully enter this other part of the world, in this mysterious Africa we'd only read about in adventure books, a place that seemed entirely unreal even though we were only two days from France. We drew nearer to the city, and we couldn't even make sense of it, carved as it was into the side of a hill, vertical and horizontal planes colliding, confused, intersecting and crossing over each other in revolt, as though the city existed on more dimensions than we were used to, or as though traditional geometry did not exist here at all. I thought I might be ill, and spent the last hours hanging over the railing, concerned I might throw up. Excited to get to it, we left our bags at the Place du Gouvernement and ventured immediately up, with a painter from La Rochelle we'd met on board. Our new friend had already been to Algiers several times, for a wedding, on an archaeological dig, to fix a painting of a camel. He was eager, he said, to solve a problem he'd encountered on his first trip: the colour of the sand. *Even the brightest colours of my palette seem to have the opacity of mud when trying to capture it, he said. You will know what I mean when you see it. The sands here are a colour beyond yellow, so much so that to call it yellow is to make everything ugly and spoil it.* As we climbed further, the wide avenues splintered off into increasingly narrow passages and the ground tilted below us, haunted by the grave quiet faces of the older men, looking so smooth and clean in their white burnooses, not even looking at us, silent, and everywhere the same old black man in a dark corner making coffee. The women were mostly swathed in a redundancy of wrappings, like piles of shuffling laundry, crammed to bursting with seeds and couscous, yet we did spot the occasional sultry Jewess in flagrancy and were thronged by dozens of children of the desert, many fronting a rare beauty that would have made envy the most beautiful Parisian women. One child seemed to follow us wherever we went, always at a respectful and unobtrusive distance but all the same constantly dogging at our heels. He was dark and filthy, his pockets full of fists and dirt, drilling his heels to the soil, and we assumed him at first to be a thief, merely waiting for the right moment to swoop in and make off with our purse, but our new friend explained that the boy was just watching. Observing. *They take nothing for granted here,* he said. *If the French have taught them nothing else, it's that every inch of their reality is something to be collected, something to be spent.* Camille crouched his eyes at him: *To be spent? Like time? No,* the painter said. *If a person stumbles, it has worth. If a person is particularly fortunate and discovers a golden sceptre beneath his feet, it has worth. The boy can see you are new and he is probably waiting for me to leave you so he can replace me as your guide. Tourists have a habit of getting lost,* he said, *and boys like that will suddenly appear and offer to guide you back to the main thoroughfare for half a franc.* The boy's clothing, our friend assumed, had come from the lost luggage of some Americans. *Or perhaps he only wants revenge.*

The streets closed in on us completely, pulsed us through the whitewashed building facades. The doors and windows of the houses pressed against us completely closed and there were so few openings through which we might remember that there ever was a sky or anything beyond the alley. We became disoriented, lost in the labyrinth, often of wonder whether we had been overturned, the sky now beneath us, running the walls. At one point, our friend told us it was night, which we could neither confirm nor disprove. The darkness was so opaque that we were forced to feel our way along the walls, stumbling, falling from one darkness to the next, while black figures watched us with white eyes, squatting in doorways and lurking behind rain barrels and mules. Long white ghosts slid by in silence, and we stepped on greyish masses that changed position while sighing, across the mounting backs of these creatures who looked like men. Occasionally, from a low door left ajar, dim light filtered off a wan wax candle, and our shadows, cast by the trembling light, made us think of what the painter had said about the colour yellow. This was when we noticed that each bolted door was pierced by a peephole covered with lattice, like the doors of a harem or prison. Our new friend gestured to one, urged us to peer through, and we were shocked to find that, while the nature of the openings had heightened our expectation of the forbidden, there were no scenes of sensuality or violence, no orgy of brown bodies in repose around the hookah, leering after the departure of a slave, but simple scenes of domesticity: the preparation of dinner, two children playing a game, a patriarch reading to his family, a mother carding wool between her left hand and big toe, a young girl washing the feet of her grandmother before prayer. We spent ten minutes just watching a boy study, his hand above the page, astonished that such quotidian events could be rendered exotic or taboo.

By mid-week, of course, the magic began to fade. They had made Algiers a part of France, after all, with cafés by the dozen, restaurants with overpriced, prix fixe menus, clothing stores, hairdressers, bookstores and theatres. The Place du Gouvernement, we could now see, was nothing more than a replica of the lobby of the Théâtre des Italiens, only fully exposed to the open air. My brother showered, trimmed his beard, and we joined the other hotel guests downstairs for a breakfast of toasted baguette with jam, a bowl of cereal, *pain au chocolat*. A pair of older women, a larger and a lesser, both Parisians and immoderately interested in botany, invited us to a camel ride and tea in the Sahara and we accepted graciously, excited to see landscape once more that stretched farther than our arms. They were delightful, these larger and lesser women, cultured, able to converse on a wide variety of subjects, though mostly they talked about the food. *They brought us one of those dry biscuits,* the lesser confided in my brother, whom they had singled out as a kindred soul, *and I said:* No, no, no, bring us whatever you would eat. *The cheeky imp made like he didn't understand me, so I said:* Me no eat. *And I picked the biscuit up and dropped it on the floor.* Camille blinked. *You have to be clear with these people,* she said. *Show them their place. They won't respect you, otherwise. I had to go with him to the kitchen.* The rest of them were cowering around a three-inch table like tailors at a shopboard, scooping some horrid mess from a wooden bowl with their hands, and I had to dig my own fingers in it to convince them. After that, the staff had brought them gigantic beans disguised with the juice of a lemon; fresh cucumber and olives; flatbreads that seemed covered in mould; undercooked pancakes doused in honey; thick, sour milk they ate with spoons and fruit; oversalted cheese; eggs poached in a sauce of tomatoes and peppers that smelled vaguely of body odour; and the women held their noses and spooned the wretched messes liberally to their pinched mouth holes, delighted when it splattered the white tablecloth. *The coffee is horrible,* the larger said, grinning. *So syrupy, it makes me gag.* She offered the plate of dates to her companion and my brother, but whereas Camille lifted his delicately on the end of his fork, the lesser lanced it brusquely with the point of her knife, then spat the pit on the floor where the staff were there immediately to sweep it up. *Most people know nothing of Algeria,* she said disapprovingly, eyeing an adjacent croissant. *The* real *Algeria. The beauty of this place, the culture.* They spoke about the country like it was art they were going to hang on their wall and show to their friends, championing it, and did little to hide their disdain for the other visitors in the hotel, the ones who would never leave the city, who were just there to check it off a list, to wonder at plants in captivity at the Jardin d'Essai, with its rows of towering *Chamaerops humilis, Latania gorgonica, Dracæna draco,* and *Phoenix dactylifera* like exploding fireworks above them; taste a banana; take in the dresses at a formal wedding; admire the hanging laundry. At most those people might travel a few kilometres down the coast to visit Sidi Ferruch, the castle where the French first landed, but always within view of the sea. *They come because of the sun,* said one (did it even matter which anymore?). *But they don't really experience it. They don't live it. Until you've set foot in the desert, you can never understand what it means to be one of them.* Camille glanced longingly toward a tray of brioche. *I miss when it was just us,* the larger bemoaned. *Serr tnin ya'rfouh alfin,* the lesser laughed. *A secret known to two is soon known to thousands.*

They had arranged to meet our guide at noon. He turned up on time but the camels, who perhaps belonged to a separate guild, did not. Our women demanded an explanation. Our guide said only that they'd been held up, which made it sound as though there had been some form of traffic congestion, that somehow all the camels at once had attempted to pass through the same needle to disastrous results, and it never occurred to anyone that they could easily just go around. The women spoke as if he couldn't hear them, and our Arab waited patiently for them to finish. *This is the way they think around here,* the larger said. *They have very specific ways of doing things, centuries of tradition, and it makes thinking outside the box all but impossible. That's why they're responsible for so few scientific advances.* The women insisted our guide take us on foot, at least as far as the first oasis, which was something the Arab could not entertain at first, and I have to admit that neither could I. I had never seen so much of nothing before, it seemed impossible that it could even exist, particularly so close to the denseness of the Casbah. It was as though so much of reality had been drawn in by the singularity of that place we'd visited only last night, had bent around itself so many times that it had left this massive gap in the imagination everywhere else. Was this universal? I wondered. Ongoing? Was the rest of the world losing an inch of itself every year, let's say, to the centre of Algiers? Would the Algerians centuries or millennia from now wake up one morning and realize that the rest of the world had disappeared entirely? Perhaps the mountains and the oases were no more than an arm's breadth from us. Perhaps we could have reached out and pulled back the veil and touched them, and it was merely our own French limitations holding us back. The lesser woman said: *A culture this beautiful is wasted on them. They don't really have a concept of history, an appreciation for it. They only think of the future. They have this dream of their perfect*

134

world, and an insatiable desire to wipe out everyone who isn't like them. I once travelled with a guide who was taking me to Faya, to see priceless warrior figures from the empire of Darius I. Five hundred BC. To him, they were nothing. Of course, when he saw how much I appreciated them, he knocked each of them to the floor to see them shatter, as if they were a weapon against me. The greater recounted a visit to a local m'chacha: where they all just fall helpless from hashish and spend so much money that the owners can afford to dress up their human slaughterhouses with brand new matting; beautiful, hand-carved tables; huge blue glass urns filled with fresh water and goldfish; ribbons and coloured tissue paper cut in fanciful design. I asked to paint it, brought my easel and watercolours the very next morning, but by then one of them had even died while being carried home so I had to replace him with a rug that was entirely out of place.

Before I knew it, we were surrounded by palm trees. This oasis alone, our guide said, is home to over three hundred thousand date palms, some of which are over thirty metres tall. He allowed us to sample the dates and we were treated to a tall glass of what appeared to be filthy water that was apparently made from the sap. Not one bit of the palms goes to waste, he said. Even the stones from the dates are ground and fed to livestock. The leaves are woven into baskets. And when the trees have finally stopped producing, over two centuries later, the wood is used for timber.

My brother refused to believe that time could change something so dramatically. So we continued to search for more authentic experiences, headed back to the labyrinth of the Casbah, alone. He went directly to the young boys this time and offered them money to take us somewhere new. Not the hotel, he begged. Anything but the hotel. They took us to the zoo to sketch the plants, and the Jardin d'Essai to chase a peacock 'til it unfurled. According to the signage, the gardens contained at least two of every plant on the Earth. If ever there were a cataclysm that might eradicate the world, the sign claimed, they could rebuild it from here. And they took us to more markets and cafés, a bathhouse, the public beach down by the harbour.

If I never see another carpet or coral necklace, my brother pined, *it will be too soon.* We were sick of the women, greater and lesser, sick of the trees, sick of the sounds, sick of the no sounds. *Surely,* Camille said to our guide, *this is a different world. How can it sound the same? Surely the birds must do more than bird, the screams strive for more than shrill.* And our guide said: *The real Algiers, you mean? The one that exists when you are not here?* His head swung like a cracking branch. Finally one of them took us to a local cabaret located in the ruins of what must have been a residence for soldiers, or the ruins of a church left over from the Romans, with haphazardly collected tables and chairs and the roof open to the sky. As we passed through the gates, we were surrounded by Arabs, pressed between them, thigh to thigh, laughing and singing. Someone handed us a bottle to drink. *Is it wine?* Camille asked. The boy shook his head. *Wine is forbidden.* So we drank. And it tasted like pineapple and boiled meat. And when they looked at my brother in expectation, he drank more. And we began to laugh and sing with them, though we did not know the joke or the tune. Someone beside us began to cry, openly and vocally. A man touched my brother's face, and he did likewise. Then the air tore open with female voices, Moorish girls who sang melodies that were completely disorienting. We hadn't seen a woman in hours, and suddenly two hideous, middle-aged, fat women, one of them a negress, were twisting and wriggling their bodies around like nautch girls, like Spanish gypsies, only with less grace. The doors at the far end of the square swung open. Three sheep, two calves and a bull were ushered through. The negress split her face with grin, snorted in satisfaction, then stooped down and laughed triumphant in Camille's face, who applauded with all his might. The blacks were supposed to be Mahomedans as well, but it was a religion that had been forced on them, and while they outwardly observed the ordinances of their adopted faith, they still retained their own magic and superstitions. Surrounded by heaps of feathers, a little fire, and a pot of boiling water, a sorceress slashed their throats and left them to die, by degrees, so that their chest cavities slowly filled with blood and crushed their lungs, the air forced out in a *whoop whoooop, whoop whoooop, whooooooooop*. Some of the men made to speak to my brother, though they knew no French. Some of it began to sound aggressive, but there was no way to tell because we had lost the boy somewhere in the crowd. They always sounded angry, these people. So Camille just nodded and tried to sit as still as possible. The women were still singing, and my brother tried to sing with them and was repeatedly embarrassed by their rhythms. They made it seem so effortless. He felt like a child again. Camille fell to his knees. We began to suspect that the boy had drugged us in order to have us murdered, then spotted him not far from us, also on all fours, creeping closer. We could not move. Dancers trampled on my brother's knuckles, men piling on his back. The boy reached out and took my brother's hand and tried to lead him toward the priestess, parted her robes and pushed him through. Suddenly we found ourselves on a precipice, at the edge of a block almost entirely demolished, shocked to find the sea, like a beautiful slab of steel, the sky vomiting forth from it through a large opening before us. And the boy said: *As soon as the French set their sights here, history split. In your reality, your people were victorious, and this whole city became as you people imagined it was all along. Somewhere, however, there exists another plane, on which your people don't exist at all, where your people were the ones who were slaughtered or successfully driven away, or never even came here. Somehow a fragment of that world crossed over into yours. In this place, you are perhaps already a famous composer. The most famous composer who ever lived. Or perhaps you are, as you've been telling people, just a travelling businessman, a seller of books. Perhaps you don't exist at all, a creature of magic, as exotic as a unicorn. You see how they stare at you? They've never seen anything like you, so pale and so fat they turn away. But the ones who do believe in you want your horn.* And they were staring. *Algiers is not a place anymore, not for men like you. It is a fantasy. Algiers is a place where you can act out any private desire without concern, with complete control. People here will do what you say. All you have to do is think it and it will be.*

The Vicomtesse decided death was no fun unless she could enjoy it before it happened, so she bequested my brother a small financial gift with which he was able to buy a room at the hotel and he returned to Algiers often and transcribed some more Liszt, some Gounod, wrote an oratorio about the great Flood, and a Lisztonian sort of tone poem for the Great Paris Exhibition of Fine Arts Applied to Industry, pressing French militaristic rhythms hard against the slow, strange, languid, loafing melodies he plucked from the Turks, sitting in with local musicians as often as he could, like an ornithologist collecting specimens in his bag before civilization wiped them out entirely; rushed with peaks of trilly flutes, double reeds, tambourines; skins to stretch full-long across the rebabs; the tall neck of the bass like a crimson bird; the brazen coils of huge brass instruments like tamed converted serpents; the great white drum; a dream of the entire orchestra selected for their blindness—the greater the affliction, the keener their sense of music; and in general he was able to forget, finally, about the painter Regnault.

Then, during one of our visits to Paris we spotted him gathering grapefruits in a wicker pannier. *Camille!* the young man said, and seemed genuinely pleased to see us. *I've been thinking about you lately,* he said. *You're still writing? What happened to your opera?* We hadn't given it a second thought in months. We weren't even sure where we'd left the sheet music my brother *had* written. Still, we told Regnault that we had started rehearsals again and were merely having problems finding another Samson. Regnault smiled and said: *Please, call me Henri.* And we rushed back to our apartments to start over.

To warm up for his role, my brother recommended Henri

take additional vocal coaching, any excuse to increase the number of his visits, through which we were able to learn much more about him than we had before. He came from a very wealthy family, for example. His father was a successful research chemist and physicist, with the fortune and leisure from an inherited porcelain factory to pursue various pastimes, had pioneered a process for developing photographs using paper negatives and helped to found Société Française de Photographie. When Henri first showed his affinity for art by drawing the horses and dogs he saw on his walks around his father's estate, Regnault Sr. could not have been more proud. He had always wanted Henri to attend the École Polytechnique, as he had, to complete his classical studies, at least gain his *bachelier ès lettres*, but he took Henri immediately to see his cousin Eugène Amaury-Duval, who introduced him to the work of Ingres, and recommended him to Hippolyte Flandrin, who introduced him to the work of Poussin. It was hoped that Flandrin might take him on as his student, but he was too consumed painting frescoes and sent him to Louis Lamothe, who said yes and then merely sent him to the Louvre to copy the masters. Shortly after we reacquainted with him at the market, Camille helped him find a job as an assistant to an art dealer in the 9th arrondissement near Pigalle, unrolling the canvasses as they arrived and constructing new stretchers on which to mount them. One day he unfurled a great battle scene by a Spanish painter named Marià Fortuny, and a series of studies of the Moroccan War (which Henri had never even heard of), with such fine detail they felt like they held the entire world. Fortuny's sparkling, flecked brush strokes felt otherworldly. The Moroccan horsemen hovered above the earth in a cloud of dust. They glowed. One of the studies was sold almost immediately to an Oklahoma steel man for a sum that could have paid Henri's salary for more than a year, though it was first sent back to Fortuny so he could add a likeness of the new owner, clad in a suit of armour, in a painting within the painting. Henri made the sketch of the man for Fortuny to work from and could not stop from thinking: *This is what I must compete against?* He had once thought himself special and now spent entire days staring at this other man's effortless masterworks, retreating periodically to his studio to replicate them, and became suicidal when he could not copy the way the Spaniard rendered water.

He found solace, he said, in my brother's opera, which was unfortunate. Our prior assessment of Henri's vocal abilities had clearly been clouded. He could barely read music. His lung capacity was that of a small mouse. But it set my brother's body quivering to watch Henri's chest as he tried to keep up on the Adelaide, mangling the long, high B flats of the climax as Camille hammered his way to the ecstatic dominant seventh. *Imagine you are searching for your lover,* Camille instructed, *that you see them wherever you wander, wherever you look, that you've been told nothing you can do will bring them back, but you know that isn't true.* And afterward Henri would collapse into his chair and they would talk about their shared appreciation for Beethoven, how he used to throw things at his servants, and the story of how he had once asked Haydn, long after the older man had been his instructor, to sit with him at the piano one last time, for old times' sake, at a performance for the king, just so he could help turn the pages. It was an insult that the older composer could not, in front of the king, refuse. And when, begrudgingly, he assumed his position of submission, he was shamed to find that there was nothing on the sheets at all, not a note, not a single pen stroke, that Beethoven had not managed to finish the piece in time, was simply making it up on the spot, so there was nothing actually useful for Haydn to do besides mime appearances. Beethoven's depression and anger were monumental. So much of his music was like a suicide note (*yes!*) that he never carried through on (*YES!*). Henri was mostly referring to the *Marches Funèbres* of his Third Symphony, but Camille, who wanted to impress him, referenced also the Piano Sonata, op. 26, no. 12, and the final movement of *La Malinconia*, which he judged as more than a little obvious. My brother suggested he thought it was weak of Beethoven, that suicide was an expression of cowardice, and Henri just laughed and said: *But he didn't do it!* And my brother replied: *Thoughts are the definitive aspect of human existence. A thought is an action, and by all of our actions shall we be defined and remembered.*

After working for some months for the art dealer, Henri became even more fascinated by our collection of Oriental art and artifacts and would often come early to study them more closely. Likewise our bookshelves, which were filled with Hugo and Molainville, Dante and Chaucer. *By the Nile I find you once again,* Camille would often quote on seeing his young friend. *Egypt shines with the fires of your dawn; your Imperial orb rises*—a pause—*in the Orient.* Camille also collected poetry translated into French by whatever foreign writers we could get our hands on and, inspired by them, Henri began to paint his human subjects like wild beasts and would often travel to the Bois de Vincennes to sketch the bare-breasted Senegalese, the caged Calormenes, reduced to animals. Other than Timbal and the pigeons around Luxembourg, our experience with animals had been very limited. Henri loved them. The zoo was his favourite place in the world. *Imagine a world run by animals instead of humans,* he would say. It was like watching a child, the way he scampered excitedly from cage to cage. *Man is useless to the world. He does not give milk, he does not lay eggs, he is too weak to pull the plow, he cannot run fast enough to catch rabbits. Yet he is lord over all the animals? Why?* He was barely able to contain himself, knew each creature by name, aped the apes, pawed the ground before the cage of tigers, and stood motionless for nearly an hour before the zoo's main attraction, two grand elephants named Castor and Pollux. Afterward, we chased each other around the maze, taking turns pretending to be the Minotaur. Then, back in our apartments, Camille entered the room while Henri was bathing and, when the younger man said nothing at his intrusion, began to stroke him, softly, without speaking.

142

Henri closed his eyes, would not look at us, but also did nothing to remove my brother's hand.

I had never seen Camille happier. Every second day, Henri would come over to work on the aria, but gradually their voice lessons became shorter and shorter, and Camille would just immediately take a seat at the bench, pull Henri toward him, and work on him tirelessly until they both fell asleep or went out to meet friends at a salon. They spent days together in bed, drinking and laughing and fucking like teenagers. My brother had seen many penises during his days at the conservatory. Henri's was not the largest, but it was definitely the hardest, and he was amazed that Henri could maintain his erection even after coming the first time, that he was still hard between his fingers even after he'd felt the come in his beard. My brother took this as a challenge to have his young lover reach multiple climaxes, held him in his mouth and tongued him until his testicles snapped back up. He loved the look on Henri's face as he came, and the feel of his body as he tried to resist doubling over in pleasure. This was all he wanted to do, to bring someone else pleasure. It was enough, he felt, to do this.

Eventually, Henri returned the favour, using his mouth and hand together. He seemed surprised when Camille came in his mouth, however, and my brother was embarrassed, worried that maybe he should have prepared him better, felt that maybe he had degraded him in some way. He didn't want to lose him. Henri was his muse. In a three-week period, he completed transcriptions of Beethoven, Haydn and Wagner but also began work on his second piano concerto. Through someone at the Viardots', he'd been asked to conduct a series of performances for the Russian pianist Anton Rubinstein, whom we had once seen rattle off some Mendelssohn, annihilating the fiddle and cello, he played so hard. Rubinstein had just come off an extensive tour of the US, set up by Steinway & Sons to promote their pianos, sometimes performing two or three times a day in as many separate cities, and frequently spoke about himself in the third person. He was paid an exorbitant amount, he confessed, but he also swore to Camille that he would never do it again. *May Heaven preserve us from such slavery!* he bemoaned. *Under these conditions there is no chance for art; one simply grows into an automaton, performing mechanical work. No dignity remains. The artist is lost. He begins to despise himself.* He was extremely generous with Camille. Each performance was better attended than the last, and toward the end of the run, Rubinstein began calling my brother onstage to join him for the applause and I had the feeling its intensity actually increased.

It was uncommon in those days to be open about one's homosexuality, especially for someone like Henri, whose father had recently been honoured by the Royal Society of London and the Royal Swedish Academy of Sciences. So they never touched when they were out. That night, he kissed Henri behind the curtain when no one was looking. By just ignoring it, the tension seemed to have evaporated. Then, three days later, Henri said: *You're not the first man I've fucked.* My brother was clearly hurt by it and, without pause, replied: *You are mine. I think I loved other men before, but it never occurred to me.*

Would you like to know who? Henri said. *No,* my brother replied. Apparently someone had seen them together at the Rubinstein performance, mashing their gills together like fish, gasping for air, and Henri's father had cut him off. Camille insisted he move in with us. We had plenty of space, after all. We even had all of our furniture transferred to the western rooms of our apartment so Henri could use the north, where the light was better, as a studio. For a while, things returned to normal, if not better. With such privacy, Henri would enter the room with his pants already unbuttoned. The whole apartment smelled of sex and Henri's large black mastiff, Lagraine. Then Camille would wake in the night to find Henri gone, not returning until the next morning, or still awake in the next room, working feverishly on a new painting or entertaining Clairin in his room. Camille would stumble through the door and try to act surprised that he was not alone and Henri would provide a high swing of his wrist and announce: *The man himself! The world-famous composer Camille Saint-Saëns!* And Clairin would snicker. Camille would retire to his piano and pretend to compose while they laughed and drank near the windows. They had an almost secret language, Henri and Clairin, had spent so much time together at the lycée and under Cabanel, having enrolled together at the atelier, had so many shared experiences. Camille suspected them of fucking behind his back. Was Clairin the other man Henri had alluded to? It was a horrible time to be distracted. On the last night of the run, Rubinstein suggested Camille finish his new piano concerto so *Rubinstein* could conduct *him.* This was my brother's moment to truly demonstrate who was the better composer and player. Not only did he aim to decimate Rubinstein, he longed to create a piece that, by perfecting it, would entirely put motivic manipulation to bed. He wanted to begin strikingly, with a sparkling cadenza, but when Clairin was present, he worried it sounded a bit too much like Liszt. He worried they'd know he stole a passage from Fauré. He began to fear he would never finish. *Sometimes I wonder the point anyway,* he said to Henri. Clairin snickered.

That year, Cabanel was still the chief adjudicator for the Prix for painting, and naturally both Henri and Clairin were invited to compete again. The subject: *Thetis Giving the Weapons of Vulcan to Achilles*. And Clairin set off without thought, because he was simple, while Henri wanted something unique, a revisionist dream of the myth. He made several sketches, portraying Achilles as panther, as stallion, a Chinaman, an Arab, and Henri was always agitated when he was trying to figure these problems, so Camille tried his best to stay out of it, never leaving the apartments but always at the piano working on smaller exercises: transcriptions of Wagner, transcriptions of Haydn, transcriptions of Paladilhe, a pastiche minuet meant to approximate the worst Bach. But one evening my brother emerged from the bath, his body loose and scarred, and Henri begged him to stand there, to keep still, for a moment, dear God, can you not just stand still for one minute!? *You magnificent creature,* he said as he went back to the easel, applying a new layer of white to begin again. *You are my Achilles. My aging hero.* Partway through, he asked to cut him and worked it into his red. *Sing,* he said to my brother as he painted, *of the rage of Camille Saint-Saëns/that brought great suffering to all other composers!* And he'd covered the canvas again by morning. They made love for the first time in a week and fell asleep.

Two days later, however, Henri's faith began to falter again. He was one of the most gifted painters France had ever produced. Of this we had no doubt. But because of this, he was so overtaken by possibility, so overcome by the thousands of paintings he might have made that he was levelled by uncertainty of direction. Was this what he wanted to say with this one? Was there something more important? More shocking? He knew what Cabanel would say. He would tell him to trust his skills and paint what he was asked. He didn't need to change the world. *There is a tradition,* he would say, *that the other judges will be looking for. How does it follow Michelangelo? Raphael? You needn't be good, just comforting.* Could that possibly still be the goal? To traipse after men who had died over three hundred years ago? More crucial to him was that he was doing something important, not just wasting his time making pretty pictures. Was it important, he wondered, what he was doing? Did it say anything important? *It is easy to live up to your expectations,* he would say before he passed out. *It is even easier to live up to the expectations of others; they will invariably be lower than you can ever imagine. But it is another matter altogether to live up to history, to perfection.*

Another week of doing nothing. The problem was Clairin. Clairin would follow their teacher's advice, of course, and then what hope did he have?

Have you seen it? Camille finally asked, but that only made it worse.

Seen what?

Clairin's painting. Have you seen it?

What would be the point?

I don't know. I was just curious. Are you not curious?

There was a long pause.

I wish you would be more direct when you speak.

I'm not sure what you mean.

I wish you would be more direct. I wish you would say what you mean instead of trying to guide the conversation toward it.

I only asked if you'd seen it.

But is that what you really want me to say? Will a yes or no answer suffice for you here?

I didn't mean anything else by it. Honestly.

Well, you know perfectly well that I haven't seen it, that it's forbidden by the rules.

What will you do if he wins?

147

Camille did not want Henri to win. He did not want to lose him to Rome, not the way we had lost Duprato. So, often, instead of trying to encourage Henri's vision, Camille suggested a trip to the zoo, to the countryside, theoretically to remove Henri's stress but more to relieve his own. He also made to nurture this insecurity. *Italy has nothing for you,* my brother would argue. *It is the home of the past and you are working on the painting of the future! You can learn so much more here through your job at the gallery, through all the new work he brings in. Think about that Spaniard.* Then one night after a particularly horrid day, Henri and my brother got into a fight over something ridiculous—dinner, perhaps—and he went to stay with Clairin because he knew it would hurt my brother most. Clairin, who was already finished his painting, had his servants cook up a fantastic dinner, inviting many of their friends, and Henri met a woman with such a delicate and distinguished profile, and he sketched her furiously while she ate. He returned to our apartments and his isolation cell and literally turned the whole thing on its side, shifted the entire composition of the painting from an upright to an oblong and began again. A few days later we were allowed to see it, with the face of this woman as Thetis and Achilles modelled after Clairin, caught in flagrante with his lover who, in the self-deprecating tradition of Caravaggio, was modelled after Henri himself.

Camille took it in for a moment and said: *It is entirely respectable.* And Henri raised a fist to him and said: *What do you know about anything? You are the organist at a church for landowners. You have already sailed past your prime. Your children could be great composers by now.*

All I said was that it was good.

Good?! I could kill you if I wanted. Right here. And no one would care. That's how good you are.

And of course he won. Though he was only twenty-two, the judges proclaimed the painting of singular grace and elegance, a work that did more than just appeal to the imagination, it addressed itself directly to the eyes, visceral and immediate. His control of light and combinations of colour revealed the peculiar gifts of a new master. My brother was frantic and desperate, but Henri's mind was made up. We took him shopping for new clothes and he looked fantastic in his gorgeous new morning coat with its short waist and pockets in the pleats. Henri also asked for a round, high-crowned Stetson that was supposed to be so popular in America. The practical idea was that the hat might serve him well as the rainy season approached. But to be honest, my brother caved on it mostly because it made him looked more rugged, and he insisted that Henri wear it the night before his departure. He promised to write.

Camille distracted himself by accepting various offers as an accompanist at the Salle Pleyel, and an invitation from Leipzig to debut his third piano concerto. He resisted going at first. He had an instinct that Henri might come back. But the lead would have been impossible for anyone but himself to play, particularly the rapid arpeggios and polyrhythms of the first movement, so eventually he succumbed. The reviews, as usual, were not good. Botte wrote: *The first part lacked coherence and the finale was a complete failure, with everything except a musical idea, good or bad.* It was criticized for being hectic and rushed, though it was likely the harmonic experimentation that really put people off. I remember mostly that the building itself seemed to be falling down. Camille was in bed for a week.

We tracked Henri's progress through letters, mourning they were so slight; a postcard here, a few sentences there, they were over before we could truly get into them, but I suppose it was enough to piece together his basic life in Italy. Every morning began with two hours of life drawing, followed by a session painting frescoes at the Teatini, and then they were to hunt down an old master for three hours of back-patting. He rebelled. For generations now they'd been showing restraint, and where had it gotten them? The Academy sent Ingres from Paris to try and rein him in. They sent Vernet. Eventually they even sent the aging Delacroix. But when Henri saw Ingres all he could think about was how much the man hated colour. When he saw Vernet all he could think about was the profaned graveyard of his *Coudiat Ati*. Delacroix was a lifeless boor. Delacroix, who was not new to the arrogance of young students, assigned him a simple nude, suggesting that if Henri could prove to him he had mastered the human form as he claimed, he could forego the rest of the term's morning classes. He thought himself clever, clearly expecting something simple and small. But Henri replied with *Automedon with the Horses of Achilles*, his animals near copies in overall composition and the sway of the manes to Delacroix's own *Horses Coming Out of the Sea. Everything here is a copy*, Henri yelled at him. *Each day, a copy; each meal, a copy. None of you people are artists, just copies of artists, flirting with their idea of what an artist should be.* More than that, Henri also made his horses life-sized, the painting so large it cracked the winch as they lowered it from his studio to the street. *Size is a property as much as a red*, he said. *Or an empty! A lovely! A suspect! If I am to paint a horse, how can it rival a real horse without being as large? What is the point of creating a palace unless it is the size of a real palace? No, it must be larger. What is the point of creating mountains that do not dwarf other mountains? What is the point of a civilization?* He wanted Delacroix to feel threatened by it, had thrown all of life into it, all energy. There was barely a square inch that was not pure muscle and the horses strained and the groomsman strained against the muscle and the muscle strained. Delacroix laughed when he saw it and said: *It is one thing to make something seem like something else. You have failed to copy the technique.* But Henri replied: *Of course not, I have made it so you can no longer see the brush strokes.*

For a time, we heard nothing, and it was only through common acquaintances that we learned Henri had left Rome entirely, abandoned his instruction for Spain, to hunt down Fortuny. *I can no longer see what I have done because of him*, he told Delacroix, *nor what I am doing. His brush strokes! His sense of colour! He's the master of us all!* And eventually Delacroix gave in, making him promise only to live up to his scholarship obligations: three history paintings and a perfect replica of a masterpiece. The first we heard from him was after he'd met up with Clairin to traverse the Pyrenees, the letter still short but accompanied by reams of sketches. *My dear friend*, he wrote. *Please, hold these for me, these tests and experiments. I may wish, when all is said and done, never to see them again. Then again, perhaps that journey will bring me joy, if it finally ends with my dream of a true masterpiece. I would like at least, before I die, to have created an important and serious work, of which I am dreaming at this time, and where I would struggle with all the difficulties that excite me. Whatever turns out to be the product of this battle, when you find me I will be facing an immense canvas, where I want to paint the entire character of the Arab dominion in Spain, those powerful Moors of yesteryear, those who still have the real blood of Mohammed in their heads. If I find a way to baptize my tableau with something before I finish it, so much the better; if not, I'll invent something and send the critics to chapter 59,999 of an undisputed Arab history that was destroyed in the fire or sack of a city!* After that we mostly had to infer his story not through words but through images, and only occasionally would he have captioned the reverse with something like: *The Spaniards are truly a strange people; you cannot imagine the native distinction and politeness of all these rascals, whom one would not be happy to meet at the outskirts of a wood.* And: *The other evening, an Aragonese offered us preserved fruits at the end of a* navaja *as big as a cavalry sabre.* And: *One hears the footsteps of a handsome picador who stands up to dance, showing his white teeth and his broad silken girdle, on which fall two great chains of gold.* They attended a bullfight in Bilbao in a big, tawny brick amphitheatre at the end of a street in an open field, seated in the proximity of some kind of Spanish princess who complimented him on his hat and he pretended to be a real cowboy, a burly American, and my brother wanted nothing more than to be there with him. *The game of the matadors is very effective. There were costumes marvellous for their richness and originality with which the tones of colour were arranged. Yet I confess that the struggle with the picadors is disagreeable to me. I would like to see something more balanced, a true struggle of dominance between man and beast.*

Henri and Clairin were so happy to finally reach Madrid and went immediately to the home of Fortuny, and when he was not there (was, in fact, if his servants were to be believed, in Granada, in view of the Alhambra, establishing a small school he was calling the Studio of the Martyrs), went instead to the Museo del Prado to immerse themselves in the genius of Velázquez and Goya. *It was like going to Heaven*, he wrote to us, *surrounded by so much perfection*. The only upsetting part was re-emerging into the sun, confronted by narrow-headed boys and sleek young women copying Murillos to sell to American tourists. Why would men and women possessed of ordinary sense pay gold for such blasphemies? They stormed immediately back inside and prostrated themselves before Velázquez's massive *Surrender at Breda*, chasing off anyone with a sketchbook who dared to get close. If that was all they could save, they felt, it was still worth it.

While waiting for Fortuny to return, they tried to find lodgings, which was much more difficult than they'd imagined. The revolution made people less trusting to begin with, and as word preceded them that they were bachelors and—even worse—Frenchmen (*Franciss!*), it was rare that anyone would even open their doors to speak to them. Were it not for a young woman who found Henri so handsome, leaning from her kitchen window and yelling (*Forasteros! Forasteros!*), they might never have learned to search for balconies with ribbons wrapped the railings, climbing to the first, second, third, fourth *piso* to a fantastically sturdy door and replying to the frantic old woman (*Quién es bled?! Que quiere usted?!*) by saying: *Gente de paz*. Men of peace. Like they were Ali Baba issuing his magic words, this was the only thing that opened Madrid to them. The old woman, like their previous window angel, took one look at Henri's hair and chest and grin and the rooms were theirs, complete with a Spanish sofa like a torture device, a host of flies, and the old woman's endless tales of other and better times.

For the next month we received no sketches and Henri never once thought about it. Madrid in the midst of a revolution suited Henri's romantic ideals perfectly, and every morning he would rise to wander her streets, so magnificently ravaged by all the fighting, the air full to tender murmurs, the clash to rapiers, the groans to their victims, frequent borne together on the same breeze. Despite it all she was still standing, Madrid, like a great pond of ice upon which skaters leave their trails but never crack, and he marched through the gargantuan square every morning, past the Convent of Atocha and the gate of the Recoletos, past wonderful statues made to Neptune, Apollo, and Cybèle, drawn in a lofty car by lions, back to the Prado to resume his aegis of the *Breda*. He needn't have bothered. After several weeks, everyone had received his point. No one came to visit it anymore but him. The actual museum guards didn't even visit it on their rounds. Then one morning he showed up with a monstrous stretched canvas, dragging it all the way from their apartments across his shoulders, the exact dimensions of the *Breda*, and he started to mix his paints. If he was going to wait this long for Fortuny—and he would wait—he might as well finish his replica of a masterpiece while he did it. Selecting something like the *Breda*, something Spanish instead of classical, would set Delacroix's mind on fire. *He will scream when he finds Velázquez appearing at his threshold*, he said to Clairin. *What profanation!* And at a full 1:1 scale, it would be even larger than his *Automedon* in Rome, just to emphasize his earlier argument about size. Gradually, because they were still honestly more than a little afraid of him, a crowd gathered to watch him, as he focused so much time on the background with its smoking destruction and death, but also the handshake, and the surface of the horse. Some days he would complain about the poor architecture of the building, which led to so much cross-light and false reflection, did so little to allow the proper lighting to the canvasses, even prevented it—he had to keep moving around, because he could only see the *Breda* properly in chunks. Still others he would despair to Clairin that the painting was irreplicable, that the main characteristic that made Velázquez so brilliant, his spontaneity and free handling, were in direct contrast to the deliberate premeditation of making a copy. His feelings on Velázquez even began to lessen because of it, and he and Clairin talked about stealing it rather than making his perfect, causing a distraction and then making the switch. With such horrible light, who would know the difference? In the end, he just abandoned his *Breda*, as well as Velázquez's, saying: *I don't paint just to obey a* règlement, *but to make a painting.*

Fortuny finally returned and they met in person. *Day before yesterday I spent the entire day with him,* Henri wrote, *and that has broken my arms and legs.* They became fast friends. And so impressed was he with our Henri that he invited him to study with him, to share one of his many studios and, side by side, they would paint a tiny Bedouin on a horse or draw a vase he had borrowed from the Alhambra, pushing one another to greater and greater accomplishments. Watching him draw was enough to stop Henri's heart. He was as good as Meissonier—no, better—and yet it came so effortless to him. He never composed at all, just set his pen or brush to the canvas and threw his figures together with an insolence and neglect that can hardly be expressed in words. He would paint a woman's figure with such delicacy of contour and light and shade as barely to be believed, and then surround it with a mass of coarsely daubed, dull-green paint, representative of absolutely nothing, that should have failed in a million million ways and yet was perfect. His tiny Bedouin, no more than four inches tall and set against a white wall, was rendered with such detail that it threatened to come at you if you looked at it cross. He heaped the brightest of colours upon one another in a reckless prodigality of strength, and never was there an imperfect combination. They were constantly being interrupted by royalty and the wealthy, and more than once they were visited by the liberal revolutionary General Juan Prim, and Henri nearly fainted from admiration. Another day a gift of jewellery arrived from some wealthy countess, professing her love to him. Fortuny tossed it on the table like it was nothing and devised a challenge to see which of them could capture the gem in it most brilliantly. Henri felt like he was already dead, but Fortuny promised him that if he won he would ask Prim to let him paint him. Henri modelled the bracelet directly into a bodiless arm he'd started, slicing over it with a few well-calculated strokes—the brush firm at the centre—to create deep wells along its entire length. Once this was done and dry, he ran a hint of *garance* in the wells, then later, with a razor, carved off the excess that had spilled over. And finally he laid down delicately an exquisite turquoise blue, perpendicular to the wells, so that the depths were like blood and the summits an icy prison. Fortuny was stunned and could not figure out how he had done it. But he still gave the bracelet to Henri and kissed him and took him to meet Prim.

This was how Henri completed the first of three history paintings. Technically, as history paintings, these works were supposed to follow certain guidelines, which typically meant the subject matter should be either mythological or Biblical. But more recently the Academy had begun to allow military portraits, and Henri saw his opportunity when Prim was made Prime Minister to do his part for the movement. Prim suffered through countless sittings. Henri had to beg Fortuny to go to Prim for one more favour, and one more, and one more, and in the end, when he sent the painting back to us, it seemed he had only used the man's head anyway, and Camille was upset because Henri had so clearly used Clairin as his stand-in for Prim's body, in a copy of the general's uniform, sitting astride a barrel. This made it impossible for my brother to enjoy the rest of it; there are times when knowing too much about a work of art can ruin it entirely. Gustave Geffroy at the Academy called it impressive, if a little busy. Delacroix questioned the way in which Henri had treated the mob, who seemed not living breathing creatures but entirely drained of blood, no more important to the piece, no more inserted to capture and entertain the eye, than inanimate objects. Prim, he said, had fared little better, the hero of the painting entirely devoid of importance. But in the end Henri had been drawn to his regular obsessions, and the hero of the painting was clearly not Prim but the horse—which our dear, sweet Henri had been able to select himself from the royal stables—if it wasn't just violence, or just colours. Though the painting won the gold medal at that year's Paris Salon, by then Henri's feelings had changed. He had no interest in Prim anymore, no more interest in people. Revolutions went beyond people, beyond facts. Revolutions were bigger than facts. The facts were the colours. *This war is not merely a battle of men on men, as it must appear back home, but a battle of ideologies, a battle of minds. A battle of egos when there should only be battles of the heart. Is there a way to remove an idea? To kill an idea? Any attempt to inoculate a people against an idea will automatically infect those same people. The warriors become carriers of the ideas. We should be fighting for feelings, defending feelings. Does the other side love? Does the other side hate? If not, then we need to remove them. It is the ones who cannot feel that we must fear the most.*

Fed up with Henri's theatrics, Fortuny urged the two Frenchmen to continue to the Alhambra and they were in awe of the confident Moslem rock pile amidst the desperate Gothic cries for attention that plagued the rest of Europe. What did he care about Fortuny any more when there was this!? *We are living close to the palace,* he wrote, *with its turquoise sky and rose-coloured towers, built straight into the mountain on seven levels, each delved into the hill, and about each a wall and in each a gate. 'Twas a true barbarian, the artist who made that, a savage, a monster. You must see it!* There, for his second history painting, he decided to expand his painting of the serpent bracelet, broadened its focus, a reverse colonization of the classical ideal, a direct attack on art's establishment: *Salomé the Dancer Holding the Basin and the Knife That Will Serve for the Beheading of Saint John the Baptist.* But history had taken on a whole new meaning for him. He didn't care about reality anymore, longed instead to show the history of imagined worlds, more perfect worlds than ours, felt strongly that it would be more powerful to ignore the real. And when he sent that back, the response was ever worse. Delacroix lamented that the deep Oriental sky, rendered so beautifully, was brought down by an extra from low theatre dressed as a regular bohemian. Thomas Couture urged him to *give up this habit of fleeing the character of your country. Why Italians, why Arabs? Be Parisian as one was Athenian!*

Henri was furious. *Do they think I still want to be Ingres?* Henri responded. *Like Gleyre? Like Cabanel? So far as any of them seem to be or have been concerned, it is only a slight overstatement to say that Muslims and Arabs are essentially seen as either violent autocrats or erotic taboo. Very little of the detail, the human density, the passion, the perfection of Arab-Moslem life has entered the awareness of even those people to profess to advance it. What we have, instead, is a series of crude, essentialized caricatures, presented in such a way as to make that world vulnerable to—to justify—our colonial aggression in invading Egypt and Syria. I don't even feel as though the art I do merits the same categorization, is a similar thing to what these beasts of opportunity spew out. Do they ask the questions I do? Or are they merely obsessed with political favour and the commonly misplaced concept of the New? This subject has never been painted, so it is the New. This is taboo, so it is the New. It is ridiculous. Did Girodet really believe that no one had ever painted an engorged penis? Just because it's not on the wall of some duke or count? What's worse, though, is when his purpose is politics, like his painting of the revolt of Cairo, the Egyptians naked and primitive and barbaric when it was Napoleon who ordered the cannons open fire on a mosque. That is the truly shocking part.* Napoleon at the Penthouse at Jaffa *is nothing more than militaristic propaganda and bravado, with Napoleon as Christ and the locals as Lazarus, woken from their ignorant sleep, the historic meeting of the rational and the irrational. What it does not show, Camille, is the massacre of the Muslim soldiers who had surrendered, that when they ran out of bullets for the executions they dispatched them with bayonets and knives, rocks and boot heels, the bodies piled so high that they had to be torn down from the pile to get at the prisoners who'd been trapped underneath, so they could be properly slaughtered as well. If I could get away with it, I would paint Girodet and Gros together in their lavish studios, fanned by Napoleon while seated on the backs of those Egyptian children, dipping their brushes in*

Muslim blood. If I could, I would depict them both on their knees, heads bent, with the great axe of Rao descending for the third time.

Rather than back down, he remained at the Alhambra for months, producing painting after painting in the same vein. Crates upon crates appeared on our doorstep at regular intervals and were immediately transported to the north room where Camille would sit with them for days while composing: Judith with the head of Holofernes; a portrait of the German Johann Struensee, who led the Danish monarchy in the mid-eighteenth century as the caretaker of the senile old King Christian VII, abolishing torture, censorship, slavery, and capital punishment for theft, but not for trying to usurp the power of the king; a towering diptych of Joseph Rosenbaum and Johann Peter caressing skulls in the graveyard, arguing over which belongs to Haydn; the miraculous reunification of Husayn ibn Ali's body with his head, exhumed in a state without decomposition, the right arm falling from the table meant to conjure Caravaggio's *Entombment of Christ* but also Jacques-Louis David's portrait of Jean-Paul Marat upon ordering the execution of the Girondists, reaching out to the head on the table opposite; another diptych featuring, in the first case, the humbled King of the Roanoke Indians, Wingina, from whence the state of Virginia actually gets its name, a silver goblet in his hand spilling with blood, executed not even by the Governor himself or a soldier but dispatched by a cabin boy who wields the axe handle close to the blade, and in the second case, a portrait of Elizabeth Throckmorton (Lady Raleigh) chained at the ankle to a large velvet bag called *Comes meus fuit in illo miserrimo tempore*; the body of another Indian chief, Metacomet, cut into quarters and hung from the trees; the marathon of Saint Denis of Paris; various other saints and the Apostles Paul and James. *It is their force,* he said, *their configurations of power that interest me. Taken singly, they are paintings of events. They are meaningless moments in time, just as any moment in time is meaningless. Together,* he said, *they capture the world.*

Then they continued to Gibraltar, where he and Clairin lived for a time among the soldiers of the Main Guard, detailing the arrival of new hundred-ton cannons, such magnificent forces of destruction. It was from Granada he sent his masterpiece: his *Execution Without Hearing Under the Moorish Kings of Granada*, but by that time the jury was already set against him. They remarked how beautifully the orange caftan of the executioner accentuated the tones of the background, the perfect contrast to the victim's blacks and greens. Cabanel said: *Artists so rarely avail themselves of the master weapon of simplicity.* But most of them stood in solidarity with Gleyre when he said he was confused that both figures were depicted as black Muslims, making it more difficult to interpret the morality in the dichotomy of executioner and victim. He also wondered if the blood spurting from the neck of the severed head might not be a tad *theatrical*, saying: *Either it is bad as a work of art, and should therefore be excluded, or it is good as a work of art and should be forbidden.*

Farewell, Camille, Henri's last letter read. *I could never return to Paris now. It has lost its way.*

My brother was crushed, unable to write anything but transcriptions and journal entries, swearing he would never suffer the same again. He became so embittered toward emotions that he emerged with an entirely different philosophy of life, replacing the popular *mal de siècle* approach of the day, the pain of the century, a melancholy disillusionment typified in many works of that period, with a more general *mal de tous*, the pain of everything: life was more or less horrible from birth, and innocents were not really corrupted so much as illusionary. Infants were born with desire, craving attention and food and protection, and this desire was humanity's downfall. Corruption came in being born, and any reaction to the world, good or bad, was just a set-up for some other ghastly twist of fate. Paris was not, as Pierre Choderlos de Laclos coined in *Les Liaisons Dangereuses*, the City of Love, but the slaughterhouse of love, where desire is slain at a single stroke.

The Franco-Prussian war could not have come at a better time. The Luxembourg Gardens were filled with soldiers, we could see them from our apartments. There were children singing songs and selling coffee and sausages in the streets. Camille returned to the Viardots', eager for distraction, only to find a distressing increase of aphorisms. *Freedom is nothing until it is taken from you*, people would say. And: *Life is nothing without struggle.* And: *Frenchmen are the sons of Gauls for whom battles are holidays.* The worst of them were Franck's old students, emboldened by the recent publication of an amateurish yet sincerely felt sonata between them, behaving like children hoisting flags on bâtards. The worst was d'Indy. *France is a magnifying glass for culture*, he proclaimed, *where artistic innovations from other regions came to find true focus and strength!* And: *The Germans may have perfected technical prowess, but only the French can produce true emotion!* My brother was largely allergic to these shows of patriotism. He was also older, and had intended to invest his age in an exemption. But the rest of them were practically falling over each other to show how much they wanted to board the next hot air balloon to Buzenval and he got wrapped up in all of it and outfell them all. Violence is called patriotism if properly channelled. And the next thing we knew, we found ourselves on the ramparts at Arcueil-Cachan, members of the 4th Battalion of the National Guard, the Prussians laying siege to the capital.

Camille was glad, for once, that Henri was safe in his self-imposed exile. Our unit was far from the real action, on an inconsequential stretch of wall alongside an entire insecurity of artists and scientists deemed too delicate to lift a gun, let alone fire one: Paul Verlaine; Guy de Maupassant; Henri Poincaré; the Impressionists no one wanted, Manet and Degas, the latter of whom could barely even see; the sculptors Joseph Carlier and Ernest Meissonier; and of course Franck's man-child, d'Indy. Elsewhere, however, we'd heard that Auguste Villemot, one of the city's wittiest members of the press, had been shot trying to take back Nogent; Carrière had reportedly been captured at the front and sent to Dresden, forced to stare at paintings by Rubens all day and all night; the vaudevillian Alexandre Flan tripped and fell on his own bayonet; Dumas was said to be ill, though there was no confirmation that it was related to battle. All told, the Société des Concerts was said to have lost eight violins, four violas, four cellos, a contrabass, a clarinet, and twelve vocalists including the choirmaster. Concerts continued, naturally, but there was some confusion with patron seating; older subscribers stayed home and were thought to have perished, their seats reassigned, and meanwhile they had not.

The only concrete reports we received regularly, almost daily, were official declarations on changes to our State seal and motto, first with the figure of Liberty, with the motto *Au nom du peuple français*, then a crown of oak and olive joined together by a band of wheat stalks, then both, with much toing and froing about the proper order of *Liberté, Egalité, Fraternité*, as well as the rise and fall of the price of a pound of coffee beans. The city ran out of butter. The price of bread rose sharply. We couldn't even see the enemy, could not be certain they even existed except for the daily reports of their slow march through the forests at the far edge of our sight. Had they ever broken that cover, they would have faced a charge of at least 3,500 metres over which we would have had the leisure to shoot them between cups of coffee, had any of us the skills or inclinations. For d'Indy, it seemed enough that the war was happening. He didn't need to see it to be affected by it. But for most of us it was a constant war against monotony, reciting poetry to one another and drawing caricatures in the dirt, playing cards, chess, backgammon, passing around wrinkled copies of Paul Avril, of which we seemed to have almost half of the full run of a hundred copies between us.

One night it was just d'Indy and us on the wall and he looked at us sideways for nearly an hour before saying: *I remember meeting you. Do you remember?*

Clear that he was referencing that first night we'd destroyed him at the salon, my brother still played dumb: *Where was this?*

You know what I mean.

You should say what you mean.

No. He shook his head. *No.*

Another night he suggested there should be a ban on performing German music. Camille scoffed: *You know, of course, that Franck's parents were German? That he was not even born here?* But d'Indy had already gained so much traction with the idea, crying to everyone he could about *community, artistic citizenship, social capital.*

Making art is a role? my brother asked.

Being an artist has obligations! Without it, the entire system must collapse.

It was ridiculous. Had France ever produced anything of real

worth in this regard? Had there yet been a true French masterpiece? So safe, so little experimentation, so little daring. Nothing on the level of a Beethoven or Bach. *Who is closer to God than
the Germans?* my brother asked. *What would you play for the Mass?
Gigault? Couperin? We should be musicians first, Frenchmen second.
Let the politicians and businessmen fight the wars over real estate. We
fight over men's hearts.*

Beethoven was only a man, a mortal like the rest of us.

You understand nothing of music.

Still, my brother was alarmed to discover he was in the mi-
nority on this, that d'Indy had already mobilized all the sharks,
that he and his Mutual Admiration Society were helping to
shape the calendar. They allowed a performance of Camille's
humorous *Odeurs de Paris*, which had originated around improvisations with Fauré with toy instruments, but they repeatedly denied his requests to stage a symphonic poem inspired by
Henri and based at least theoretically around a latter story of
Hercules, who had thrown the great-grandson of Apollo from
a tower after a disagreement about some stolen horses, and was
punished by being placed into the servitude of the god's Oracle at Delphi. This was, however, Hercules's second such visit
to the Oracle, the first having resulted in his infamous twelve
labours and, ultimately, in the disagreement that led to this second visit, and, wanting no more to do with him, the Oracle sold
him as a slave to an Asian queen named Omphale. Instead of
forcing him into feats of strength, Omphale made him dress as
a woman and spin wool and clean her house while she worked
the skin of the Nemean lion into a suit of armour. The trick,
inspired by Liszt and modelled at least partially around the
cyclic form exercises of Beethoven, was communicating all of
this without words. Auber had tried to teach them that music
could not express any actual ideas without words, in the same
way that a painting of Adam and Eve, for example, could mean
nothing without one actually having read the Bible, could only
depict a man and woman naked in the garden. But Camille had

grown increasingly convinced that musical architecture and form could give equal pleasure with the proper listening training, and they might not walk away from this new piece talking about Hercules, per se, but about feelings of struggle, and the triumphant struggle of weakness against force. He began with a poem Liszt would often quote, by Hugo, that went something like: *Ce qu'on entend sur la montagne*. And my brother would repeat these words to himself in a singsongy voice, *Ce qu'on entend, Ce qu'on entend*, over and over, until the words eventually disappeared and he was left with nothing but the melody, and the melody, and the melody, and the melody, trying to describe the orchestration (he wrote it primarily for two pianos, aware there was little money for full orchestral performances, but still he imagined he knew enough people to stage something light and unusual) to Fauré (whom he had already asked to play the second piano), groaning: *Hercules groaning in an embrace he cannot break, and the trombones aaaaand...cymbal roll!* Or: *Omphale mocks his feeble attempts at knitting, oboe, oboe, oboe, oboe... Do you hear that?!* he shouted at Fauré. *It's the monsters of anarchism and socialism! Prowling the cellars of society!*

In the end, however, d'Indy's committee decided that the genre itself, given its origins, was not French enough. Officers from the Academy attended several of Camille's services as the siege continued to ensure that he was upholding the new laws, though the potential penalties were never stated. It was worse than the war itself, because it meant everyone on this side of the wall was also against him.

Then one day I looked up and there was Henri. We should have known that, with his oriental models of honour and duty, he would rush home immediately to defend his father's estate, his family legacy, and insist, despite his father's influence, that he advance straight to the walls with the common man rather than to an office behind a desk. Victory, he said, comes not from paperwork but from the ordinary fusilier. He would only be a mediocre officer, he argued, but will be a model foot soldier. But it was still a shock to see him approaching us, in a spectacular uniform of his own design, standing out from our dull French grey in full Spanish marshal's uniform, covered with plaques and eradiate, a crown of odoriferous pine branches and a yellow band around the red bonnet of a Garibaldian officer, and Camille breathed a great sigh of relief as we watched him sharpen his scimitar.

Camille's only worry was that Henri had forgotten him, and was afraid to be too demonstrative, lest he push him away again, but one autumn evening as the sun was wrapping itself to the aqueducts, Henri launched spontaneously into his solo from *Samson et Dalila* and Camille had the others create a vocal bass around the pentatonic scale while he whistled a countermelody. There are stories from the journals of German soldiers at this time about the beauty that reached them from across the divide, floating in like birds upon the trees, and they all put down their rifles, danced and wept. Henri lamented daily, however, that we were not being better used, fumed about the petty military duties we were tasked to carry out, counting grains of rice, running messages to the tables of safety. It was nothing compared to Fortuny's battle paintings of the trenches

166

in Sebastopol, and Henri worried about being inconsequential, was frequently angry, craving activity, purpose, just cause. He made up for it with rounds of push-ups and squats, and slept on a puddle of half-thawed mud. He trudged to the barricade each morning from his home with letters pinned to his breast pocket to be forwarded, on his death, to his loved ones, and organized frequent searches for Prussian spies, though none were ever discovered. He admired the balloons passing overhead to observe enemy movements, and when the mathematician Poincaré started an accidental fire with a discarded match from his cigarette, Henri led the charge to extinguish it. One day a boy of fifteen appeared in the fields below us, approaching slowly. At that distance, it was unclear if he was the enemy, and was likely halfway to us before anyone even noticed. Monet took several shots at him, without success, and only once he had scaled our wall did we realize he was one of us, a lad who, until this point, had never left his arrondissement, with the casque and needle gun of a Prussian he had killed on his own. Henri was so jealous he wouldn't speak to anyone else for a week.

Two weeks after Henri, Courbet showed up as well. We were all so amazed that he'd avoided the draft so long, but he said he'd just been in hiding, trying to use his own disinterest as a disguise when he was nabbed on the streets of Dieusaitou by the 6th Battalion, thrown in a train bound for the front, and had to fake dysentery to escape, gorging himself on a patch of black cherries when they stopped for more "recruits" in the lower Viens. His re-entry into Paris on a stretcher, therefore, though lacking in certain dignities, especially at the back of his pants, felt like breaching the gates of Heaven. *Our train was greeted by beautiful women and streamers, both long and undulatory. Some were nuns, waiting to take me away to be healed, largely more in my soul than in body, but I was not discriminating. They let me pick my first meal and of course I chose butter, served on a filet, with a side of fresh red marois. They laughed, but there was still a pillow for every corner of my body. And the nuns read me to sleep with stories of pirates. I believe*

167

it was Treasure Island. His main treatment, he claimed—in fact, the main treatment for most ailments at the time—had been a licorice infusion, a tincture of three drops in a lemon water, which was perhaps not such great news for those suffering from gout or amputation, like his acquaintance from two beds over, but with some biscuits or a croissant for himself, Courbet said it was, all in all, a lovely afternoon. The war had clearly changed him. And he cowered whenever an eerie silence descended on Paris, broken only by exploding shells and the shuffling tread of women and children queuing up outside in the early morning. This was not the Realism he'd imagined back at the Viardots'. It took weeks to coax him from his inner recesses, to have him talk about his experience at the convent hospital in more detail. Even then he was more than likely to tell jokes about it. *With all of my limbs and mobility,* he said, *I was like a king to the rest of them! On several nights, I even led great escapes with some of my fellow patients to drink absinthe and sleep with prostitutes.* Then one night their excursions were discovered, and from that point the doors were securely locked. Courbet said it was nearly like being blind, locked in this hospital wing where all he could do was listen to bombs fall, wondering what had been hit, trying to calculate their distance by the pitch of the whine. Soon, the hospital was abandoned. One day, they were being spoon-fed and sponged; the next, nobody came, an explosion crippled the wing, but even the ones who could run had nowhere to go. There were bolts across the doors, bars on all the windows. It was only by means of forceful imagination that they were able to make their way out, and in the streets it was worse; Courbet likened the men and women and children of Paris to animals, creeping beasts, who cornered rats and dogs in alleys and sometimes didn't even wait to cook them. Cut off from the outside world, those in the poorer sections were forced to subsist on nothing but a few grams of bread a day, with little to no meat. And the poorer sections were essentially all of them. In some quarters, there were rumours of cannibalism. Unable to escape the city because of the Prussians, and afraid for his life at the hands of the Parisians, Courbet said he and his merry band of gimps hid mostly from sight, exiting only at night to forage. Once, they lucked upon an apparent store of stale pastries in an abandoned patisserie, uncorked bottles of wine in plain view on the tables, but it was a trap, and their orgy of eating and drinking was interrupted by thugs with rakes and shovels. Only the nimblest invalids scrambled the footboards with whatever they could carry to safety, forced back to their hideout to board up all the windows and doors and wait out their own private siege in hopes that the Prussians would eventually take them, which they did. As the winter drew on, an eerie silence descended on Paris, broken only by the sound of further exploding shells and the shuffling tread of women and children queuing up outside in the early morning.

For days after that he said nothing again, and then one day when d'Indy asked him to fetch another pail of water, Courbet launched into a strange story about a beautiful teenage girl named Martha (*qui rit même beurre*) from a small village west of Nantes and south of Couëron who decides to leave her mind-numbingly provincial home for the glamour and glitz of the capital, seeking fame but also love, and true beauty, only to find herself trapped in a city of flesh-eating monsters. It was clearly inspired by *Frankenstein*. In fact, on another night he began his tale with the story of the death of Shelley's daughter's cat, run over by one of Lord Byron's horses outside an old off-season villa near the Italian port of Ricordo. Byron had become obsessed with birdwatching (the great plovers, a rare blue jay, kay-wees, manx shearwater), as well as the theatre, and wrote at this time, among other things, *L'Ombra dello Scorpione*, the ridiculous *Brivido*, which he directed himself, and lastly, inspired by a famous poem of the day called "*Risplenda su tutti noi*," a more experimental piece that contained nothing but the repeated phrase *Il mattino ha l'oro in bocca*. Because her husband was useless when around Byron, it had fallen on Mary to explain to Clara, not yet five, what had happened to her beloved kitty, about death, and to bury the corpse in the copse of trees at the edge of the villa. Three days later, the idea came to her: what if a young family were to lose their daughter's pet, and rather than tell her, were to find a way to bring it back to life? *I can remember crossing the road,* she wrote in her journal, *and thinking that the cat had been killed in the road—and I thought, what if Clara had died in that road? And the two things just came together—on one side of this road was the idea of what if the cat came back, and on the other side was what if* the child *came back! So that when I reached the other side, I had been galvanized by the idea. Not in any melodramatic way, but I knew immediately that it was a novel.* It was only on further drafts that the child became a full-grown man (albeit with the mind and heart of a child) and the parents were replaced by the Doctor.

Courbet's story was also a parody of the beauty and fashion of the day. *The cities were the places where the beautiful people went,* he said as a matter of background. *If you grew up in the country and were beautiful, it was only a matter of time before you began to dream of something more. Then the beautiful people got together to procreate, and gave birth to even more beautiful people, who married each other (or one of the other rare, beautiful, rural people who continued to be drawn in like iron filaments to a magnet) and gave birth to people who were even more beautiful again, until this vicious cycle of aesthetically perfect inbreeding resulted in a completely vacuous society with no greater desire than to consume everything and everyone around it.* It was amazing to listen to, so wholly original in the way he described the city and its citizens. Marthe—Courbet's heroine—was what he called a *jeune fille sans direction,* as yet unacquainted with the fashion and makeup skills of her urban counterparts, searching in vain for the first haute couture house she can find when she's accosted by her first undead zombie: *tall and thin, fair-haired and pale-faced, with a blond beard, long slender fingers, hands that were never still, and a few white bristles showing in his shaggy head of hair. He had a habit of knocking his ankles together when walking, with the result that he had worn out the ends of his trousers. With his back slightly bowed and his left shoulder a little higher than his right, he looked poor and sickly. He advanced in fits and starts, marking time for a while and then swooping forward like a great grasshopper, tearing along at full speed with his umbrella tucked schoolmaster fashion under one arm, and rubbing his hands together for no apparent reason.*

Every night Courbet introduced new characters, telling and retelling the story of Paris from the points of view of dozens of other survivors, a ragtag herd of strangers trying to reach the Left Bank (where one of them has heard there is safety at the Saint-Germain-des-Prés monastery): a bread thief, a non-commissioned soldier, a woodsman, a Jew, an African prince, a sanitation worker, a wet nurse, a contortionist, the owner of a Welsh brewery, a village idiot (who was, coincidentally, the most hideous boy from Marthe's own village!), the son of a tailor (who was clearly meant to be Renoir), a defrocked friar, a grotesque Spanish painter named Galeoto, and a child who couldn't speak, or at least didn't. Each of their stories was its own cautionary tale, complete with secret baby, a kidnapping, a young man who squanders his savings, amnesia, and the shipwreck of the African prince, washing up alone on a foreign shore, forced into the servitude of an Italian, impregnating his master's daughter, and finally saved from the gallows by his brother who is visiting as a dignitary and recognizes him just as he's about to be executed! There was also the American who was hit on the head with a broom and believed she was a mouse, and a tale stolen almost entirely from Chaucer, in which two clerks plot to sleep with an old man's wife and daughter and, in moving a cradle three separate times from the foot of the old man's bed, only manage to trick themselves into having sex with each other. Galeoto's tale, in particular, was comprised mostly of lists, largely of the lewd variety, including pornographic wordplay on popular, contemporary dramatic productions, slang terms for male genitalia (in various languages), and an exhaustive compendium of increasingly unlikely-sounding sexual positions.

I wanted it never to end, felt it was as much a part of my life as anything else. After countless gruesome deaths in the fashion district and the Louvre, only Marthe and the Prince reached the monastery, but it was surrounded, and I listened breathless as Marthe broke down and delivered, through Courbet, the most beautiful soliloquy on the meaning of life, and love, and inner beauty. The Prince brought a finger to her lips and kissed her, and said: *If man's life is a pendulum swinging between suffering and boring, then I choose suffering.* He said if he was about to die, he wanted to die in an embrace. In love. She reciprocated. And he began to edge them both into the street, waving one arm to gain the attention of the monsters.

He says to Marthe: *Keep your eyes upon me, dear child, and mind no other object.*

I mind nothing while I hold your hand, she replies. *And I shall mind nothing when I let it go, if they are rapid.*

They will be rapid. Fear not!

Tearing them asunder, the creatures are unable to separate them, but the plague then spreads to the countryside, where the zombies not only eat brains but tend to dress the same, in some extreme fashions of the day, and much of the rest of the book is a treatise on the aesthetically displeasing—why you might hate orange more than green, for example, or Brahms more than Bach, or painter vs. painter, animal vs. animal, plant vs. plant, until the last of the ugly people remain, alone in their garottes, miserable and waiting to be eaten.

On the day after Wilhelm I was proclaimed the German Emperor, Henri finally got his wish. General Trochu (commander-in-chief of the city's defences) appeared in person and called on our battalion to follow him to the western barricades, to rise up and reclaim what was rightfully ours, to descend on Versailles and liberate the works of Charles and Elisabeth Le Brun, Houdon, Rigaud, Nattier, Antoine-Jean Gros, Renoir. One of Henri's paintings was also being kept there, so there was something personal at stake, and enemy numbers were supposed to be lower than ours, so despite the freezing temperatures, spirits were high as we paraded through the city, traipsed the hills long the Seine, to Saint-Cloud. When we reached the walls near the gardens, however, we caught sight of that wonderful army, with their great machines of injury and death, and rows of men not with guns but with picks and shovels to bury us, and turning to Regnault, Camille said: *Let us get home as quick as we can, for here it is hopeless.* The fight was at its hottest here, the smoke thick. Many young fellows lay dead at our feet, killed by the enemy's fire. But Henri would have none of it, his heart purified and enlarged by so many months of suffering. This was everything he'd ever dreamed of. Even when Trochu saw what was what and ordered our retreat, Henri rallied the others for one final sortie. Camille, Henri and I leaped the wall and ran straight toward the largest cannon, laughing, a feverish hug the hands on the rifle, the ash to burn to flake and fall. I looked round for Clairin, in the fight in the woods, I looked round for Courbet, and saw nothing but dying; descend the battalion, the darkness inquiet; I looked round for Camille, for Fauré. I found him. I looked round for Camille. I looked round for Camille. And there he was, holding Henri's head in his lap as the grey rain curtain of this world rolled back and Henri said: *I didn't think it would end this way.* And my brother, staring in admiration at the wound in his neck, replied: *End?*

Two days after that, France surrendered and the war was over.

My brother spent the next week locked away in the apartments where we had grown up, avoiding Mother, refusing food, in order to complete a piece around the melody he'd been humming since our dead lover had returned, performing it on the piano with Fauré at Henri's state funeral. He called it his *Marche héroique*, and when they finished, there wasn't a dry eye in the house. The war and siege had a profound effect upon French music. Offenbach's librettist, Henri Meilhac, ruminated that frivolous satire and irony had weakened France, and so the rawness of Camille's ode to his friend, so passionate and sincere, emerged when the country so greatly needed it. Even Botte agreed that it was the perfect song for the time, conceding that Camille had finally come into his own, with a piece of music that would live forever. *Some events change history,* he wrote. *Some change lives. This has even changed Camille Saint-Saëns.*

He wrote the *Danse Macabre*, with its purposeful mistuning of the solo violin and the bestial laugh of terrible fifths. He wrote an opera called *La Jeunesse d'Hercule*, where the hero glimpses immortality in the flames of a funeral pyre. Was this the secret that Regnault had finally understood, that the secret lay not in living up to your potential but in *not* living up to it, or perhaps it lurked instead within love, that the secret to immortality was that it couldn't be achieved on one's own, could never be attained through brilliance but only through remorse or regret? It seemed, finally, he could do no wrong. The London Philharmonic Society even approached him about writing his first commissioned symphony. And he agreed. But he wanted none of it. Because none of them understood it, none of them cared about his sadness. This was not merely a song about dying and loss, it *was* dying, it *was* loss, every time it was played. But that wasn't what had drawn them to the *Marche*; sadness was the currency of another age. Nor was it his love, hanging rotten from his branches, unconsumed. All they cared about was his anger. We returned to Algiers to recoup and start the symphony, then put it off and put it off and began to question whether he would ever play music again. Maybe teach? There were rumours circulating—again—that Benoist was set to retire. My brother had always feared being chained to Paris. But would it be so bad, he wondered, to live comfortably for once? To be freed from the slavery of Saint-Merri? Now that Auber was gone, it seemed possible. Certainly Tolbecque owed us his endorsement, and there was Bussine, now among the faculty as a vocal coach. It was difficult to imagine anyone more qualified. Thanks to Liszt, *Samson et Dalila* debuted finally in Weimar (how many years in the making?!), and as divine wrath rumbled through the timpanis, Camille had to be dragged from the pit (at Wagner's insistence!) before the second act was even complete so they could applaud him again. There was Wagner and there was the Grand Duke and his entire family and court, the visiting Governor of Poland, so many of our friends: Fauré (who had never failed us), Bessems, Bussine, even Franck (who we'd not seen in years), Durand (our publisher, who immediately announced how happy he was to be out of Paris), Armand Gouzien (the director of the *Journal de Musique*), and Charles Tardieu (a critic from Belgium). And still the sound of the applause attacked his ears like a wave of muddy, septic waters, tossing up all manner of untouchable objects, and Camille swayed at the bench, unable to stand, recalling at once his first public performance at La Salle, so many years prior.

Afterward, they arranged a private supper at the hotel where all our friends were staying and Bussine brought some women he'd met outside the venue, both of them claiming to be heiresses, and we turned everything away and demanded to be served mussels and ham sandwiches. Camille positioned himself at the table so he could always see them, but mostly he wanted to speak with Franck, like the old days. *Why do we still do it?* he lamented. *Listen to music, I mean. Or even play it. Do you feel as though it could change you in some way? That a sequence of notes could change you? That an idea could change you? That an idea could register on your awareness if you didn't already have it in the first place? Will music bring Henri back? We should not be trying to make music but to stop music from being made, we should be questioning the validity of music.* Franck tried to console my brother. *We've all lost so much,* he said. *But music is where we make sense of it all.* He was working on an oratorio for orchestra, chorus and soloists, a work about ideal evil, he said, if they would allow him to link those terms, had been working on it for six years already without a light at the end of the tunnel, was having trouble pulling all of its disparate elements into something more cohesive. *There is chaos in evil that is difficult to translate,* he said. *But it's still worth it, I hope. I know when it is true. I know when I have captured it so wholly.* It sounded wonderful. Camille was happy for him, longed to tell him of his plans to quit but was enjoying it so much, just listening to him talk about what he loved, it didn't even matter what he said.

But it became progressively difficult to ignore the ravings of Bussine and his heiresses, discussing Wagner (who'd gone home early). *An opera about gods?* one of them squealed. *How is that still relevant to anything?*

I love it, said the other. *Wolves eat the sun. Stars fall from the sky. But it's not very pretty.*

No, not pretty at all.

That's because there is nothing true about Wagner's love. Not like Mendelssohn.

Mendelssohn is so pretty.

It is beauty.

Camille could no longer resist. *Beauty?* he interrupted. *What do you know about beauty? Beauty can't bring you joy! Beauty is a pacifier, a hazy film over reality. Beauty is a still night, a warm bath, undeniably pleasant, yes, but joy? Elation? Bliss?* Tardieu began to tut, audibly. I could see it from the corner of my eye: tut, tut. But Camille railed on. *What could you possibly know about Wagner? Or Mendelssohn, for that matter?* Tut, tut, tut. *You sneer, Charles, but what good is music unless it is teeth or claw, a racket of rusted daggers, suspended by a worried dangle above your brow? What good is music that's not setting fire to splints hammered under your nails, a mass of Arabs, you and your* tuhtuhtuhtuhtuhtuhtuh. *Music should hold you down and carry through with its threats! How do you expect anything to rise above the tide by revelling in buoyancy?!* He was thinking about Silas, and everything he'd accomplished on our last visit to London. Franck smiled awkwardly, tried to change the subject. *To the exiles,* he announced, and raised his glass to the others. Bussine laughed. Fauré acquiesced but said: *Come now.* Tardieu, who was arguably the only one truly listening at this point, asked Franck what he meant by ideal evil, to which Franck merely shrugged and took another gulp. Camille was so drunk already that he didn't even notice. Was this what his life had come to? Sitting around a table drinking with a bunch of failures? The women continued snickering privately to each other, and Tardieu pressed my brother instead about Franck's absolutes: *Do you really think perfection exists? It's a ridiculous idea. A symphony is, if anything, a memoir of failure. The space between the world and the aspiration.*

But surely we must still strive for it, Camille replied, *and somewhere, in the space between, find truth?*

I don't think you would have thought so recently.

You think too much. Art must capture without thought.

Tardieu raised his hands in defeat at the hands of the great Saint-Saëns and they all laughed and we returned to our conversation with Franck. Franck complained about the treatment he was now receiving back in Paris, the press he was receiving from many of the same culprits that had chased away my brother, and Camille was again so glad he'd decided to quit it. Franck had tried his hands at a symphony that was very poorly received, then returned to operas and quartets with even less praise. Even when things went his way, he said, as when he was appointed to be one of the Prix de Rome judges, there were claims he was showing undue favouritism to his own students. Camille, smiling so tenderly at his friend, their old roles of protection reversed, said: *I apologize, my old friend, perhaps it is your connection to me.* But Franck merely shook his head and replied: *We are both just misunderstood. I suppose I should feel fortunate that d'Indy made such a successful case for me at the Conservatoire.*

...

...

Then, from Camille: *To replace Benoist?*
Yes, they asked me to replace him right before I left for here!

...

...

Then it's decided?

...

And Camille was standing, barely, knocking over tables and trying to get at Franck. *What's happened to you?* Franck was saying, but Camille was screaming: *I should have known it was you who stood in the way of this great desire of mine. I got you appointed at your first cathedral. It was I taught you whatever you know of music. But keep in mind these prophetic words: not years, nor months, I say, shall pass, but a few weeks, ere this shameful ingratitude prove your ruin!*

We returned to Paris and launched an all-out assault on Franck, reviving the rumour that our old friend was not, in fact, a French citizen. Since the war, my brother argued to the selection committee, nationality had become a prerequisite to the position. Young d'Indy had seen to it himself. But the appeal hearing was full of Franck's friends, Félicité's friends, friends of the Viardots, Franck's students who, due to their tutorial lineage, now had their posterity wrapped up in his. *Shall we talk about Nationalism?* d'Indy yelled back at my brother. *Shall we discuss what it means to be French?* My brother, he claimed, *though once a great hope for French music,* had been corrupted by the East, had *embraced the customs of African countries, where, it is said, they drown old people who are deemed useless encumbrances!* He directed them to *Désir de l'orient. Are these collections of primitive sounds,* he said, *the grunts and snarls of the Canaques, the Pahouins, the Senegalese, the Jews, are they worthy of carrying the noble name of Music? Are we to entrust the future of our children to a man like this? A man so full of hate for his own kind? The function of France throughout history has been to provide a form, a culture, in which the various schools of the European spirit can grow. The Gothic inspiration did not come from France, but it was on French soil that the first and finest Gothic cathedrals were built. The inspiration for scholastic philosophy did not come from Frenchmen, the progenitors of the National ideal were not Frenchmen, the Fathers of the Renaissance were Italian, but it was in France that each embryo found true life. It is so with Franck. Goethe said that France is every man's second country. For Franck, she is his first.*

Thankfully we still had London. The members of the Philharmonic had arranged us lodging in the St. James area, where we would be waited on hand and foot by the servants of a Mme. Dieudonné, within reasonable walking distance of Whitechapel, where the performance would be held, and we set about burning the rest of our bridges as we packed. We also arranged one last visit with my mother, whom we hadn't seen for months, what with the completion of *Samson* in Algiers and the tour of Germany. She and Charlotte were still living in the same apartments where we'd grown up, and the walk through the streets brought back so many fond memories, a longing for home where we could find bright fire burning, lamp shining, fish served for meal—mullet, mackerel, something else. Charlotte met us at the door and tried to make conversation, but Camille said he had no time and we found mother seated by the window where I used to play with Timbal and my brother ran to her so he could wrap himself to her legs and be loved without question. But as we approached, we could see how much of her hair she'd lost, how much weight, the bandages she'd torn from her hands, the way the flesh hung in meaty strips from her face. There was no appearance of having taken alcohol, but there were signs of great deprivation and he should say she had been badly fed.

Did you do this to me? she said immediately to my brother.

He shook his head.

Then you know who did.

No.

What about that one?

And my heart stopped in my chest for a moment, for she was pointing directly at me. I had spent so much of my life in the part of her mind reserved for negligence. I was there or I was not there; not there if she didn't see me. Now suddenly I was there. She could see me. Then I realized Charlotte had simply entered the room behind us. *Charlotte would never do anything to hurt you,* my brother tried to calm her. *She'll protect you.*

You're damn right! If she ever found out it was you, she would kill you.

My brother was speechless.

Or I would.

And she started to cry. And he held her. And she let him hold her. And my brother filed to postpone the symphony's debut until the fall so he could remain at her side. But this had never been done before. And they said no. The schedule had been set long in advance. He would have to wait at least a year. And that was if nothing else came up. They couldn't guarantee anything. *This is a huge opportunity,* they said to him. *Perhaps you should reconsider.* But he couldn't leave her like this. There would always be time to compose. And perhaps not so much time to be with her. So we moved our things back into our childhood home and slept on a rug at the foot of her bed so we would be there if she had any final wishes. Each day was essentially the same. We would wake early, frightened, then wait for hours for her to forget she looked so hideous. We would go for a walk at Luxembourg. Asking her questions, any questions, to try to engage her. What had she wanted out of her life? What were her biggest regrets? What had she dreamed about before meeting Father? Mostly the Gardens calmed her. Occasionally, however, she would ask to see the Medici Fountain, which had been moved and slightly redesigned, so she refused to believe him when he said that's where we were.

You never let me do anything anymore.

This is the fountain.

I'm not stupid, you know.

This is the fountain.

The fountain was against the wall.

What about this fountain, then? he'd ask.

I like it all right.

It was hard to believe anyone could sigh so much in the course of one day, could stare at nothing so long, could suck the bone to the surface of her thumb. It was hard to believe in God. In music. When there were children, she would move to play with them, but she would forget they were small, then

182

sometimes turn on one and scream: *You're horrid! Horrid!* Sometimes she would say: *You were such a lovely child, Camille. So affectionate and caring.* How she had loved to listen to him play when he was young. Did he remember the whistle of the kettle? *You used to cry when we took you from the piano.* Did he remember the whistle of the kettle? She talked about going to Mass. And the whistle. And the kettle. She said fond things about Father. And Bessems, of all people. And she talked about a woman named Marie and an uncle we had never heard about, and it was clear she was delusional. She said this uncle had once built a concert organ with his own hands. *We would sit at it together and I would play and he would run his fingers through my hair and talk about art, music, painting—beauty in every form.*

Tell me about father, Camille said to her one day.

He was like anybody else, I suppose.

Do you remember the day with the gunshots?

Why would I remember that?

She could no longer remember how to make her watercolours. But she would still sit with them in her lap and occasionally she would press the brush to paper and leave a trace of her diminishing will, then tear it up and turn on us and say: *Did you do that?*

No.

And she would cry.

And gradually I began to realize she was not talking to my brother at all. She was talking to me. As she approached death she had begun to feel poorly for how she had treated me, how she had ignored me in favour of Camille, a mother's regret, and now she was making up for lost time, in her own way. I told her I understood. The two of us existed outside time. We could see it all. We knew how it would turn out. She was not asking me if I had done this to her. She was asking me to *do it* to her. *I have things in my fingers,* she said to me. *They need to come out. There is something under my skin,* she said. *It needs to come out.* And I tended to her with all the care of the newly favourite child, without complaint, dug my nails into her skin and tore the flesh away to help please her, help appease her. I chewed at her cheeks and tore and tore. I fetched the scissors, fetched the knives. There was no one else, no one who would do this for her. My brother and I took shifts. Every day I would sit with her by the window and loosen the ties on her gloves, fetch her the knives, the scissors. Every night my brother wound the bandages around her hands again, pressed the cotton to lacerate, pasted the cloth to cheek, to forehead, canvas to limb. So she couldn't hurt herself in the night. Then every morning he would wake up to discover them gone. And she would turn to me and say: *Did you do this to me?*

Yes.

Did you do this?

Yes, yes.

I provided her with someone to blame.

And I taught her how to disappear, took her to the park and showed her how to be invisible, so she would not be seen slipping off, and I taught her how to hide, so she would never be found. And my brother and Charlotte shouted for her frantically and I taught her how not to listen, how to shut herself to the sound. She stopped bathing. And we stripped her tenderly and eased her beneath the water and persistently sponged and swabbed. She stopped eating. She stopped eating. And my brother dipped a rag into a glass of water and let it drip slowly into her throat. She stopped using the bathroom. She hadn't used the bathroom in several days. The doctor said that her kidneys had likely shut down. Her doctor prescribed more morphine. And the time travel increased. One moment she was there with us and the next she was a child and Camille was maybe her father or mother and the next she was a student and he was her teacher. She was working in her father's store and he was a regular customer. He was her son, her mother, her lover, her great aunt, the rabbi. It was impossible to judge how long we'd been there. It felt as though it was just one long day, and had always been. She lost weight. Dramatically. The heart is small. Her heartbeat was irregular. Her heartbeat stopped.

The heart is small.
We do what we must.
We give what we have.
The heart is small.
The stiff of the limbs is not marked.
Henri first. Then Mother. Then Liszt, of pneumonia, it did
not end. Life can be over in an instant. Life is a series of brief
instants. Love is over in an instant. Happiness lasts only for an
instant.
Only desire lasts forever.
My brother and I had never spoken much. It had not been
common for him to share his feelings with me. But now we sat
frequently together and talked about sad and weak and use and
end and end and he would say: *How much can the human mind
stand and still maintain a wakeful, staring, unrelenting sanity?* Did
anyone ever get a second chance? I would try to console him,
would long to help him. And yet, despite reassurances, he knew
well he would hold that son's grief, that it might never turn to
quiet joy and tender sorrow, not even with time, that it might
even begin to creep backwards, so fierce it was, into his memories. The pain was so great that it infected his entire life. Even in
the times they had been together, he was going to already miss
her, had already missed her.
The heart is small, but holds so much. Bussine's apartment
was burgled and set on fire and the perpetrator killed the po-
liceman who tried to arrest him, claiming: *This is the right of them
who have nothing, to take from them who have.* D'Indy gathered the
others around him and had Camille removed from the Société
Nationale de Musique entirely. *No matter,* my brother said. *They*

are on a voyage to a world that has ceased to concern me, forever. He went out to drink and found himself with d'Indy at the same establishment. Camille ordered a Suze. A loud train whistle indicated the train from Marseilles was about to arrive. D'Indy stopped to place an arm around the shoulder of a man Camille did not recognize. Then he was at our table. D'Indy picked up Camille's glass and took a long drink.

Can't you ask first? said Camille.

D'Indy replaced the glass: *So sorry, seigneur.*

Why did you have to make me look mad?

Because you are *mad!* shouted d'Indy. *Mad, mad, mad!*

He was nearly to quit. And I whispered to him: *You are a god. You can do anything you want.* I said: *The world does not know what it wants until you tell them. There is not gain without risk, however, no risk without love, no doubt without passion, no passion without risk.* The heart is small. Beating in darkness. It emerges from the chest, lifted out of the body and placed on the shoulder. From nowhere, we were contacted once again by the London Philharmonic. Someone had died, they said. Could we help out, they said. A second chance at life. And we packed our things and said goodbye to France. A symphony is a memoir of failure. And we made to London and crept unsure and eastward from our apartments daily toward Whitechapel through the rapidly gentrifying neighbourhoods, step by step, through Covent Garden, with the finest flowers and anger that money could buy, and coffee houses set up like sorting stacks; coffee houses where medical men might be consulted; Puritan coffee houses where no oath was uttered; Jews' coffee houses for money changers; the coffee houses where Jesuits prayed over their cups for another Great Fire; atheist temples of general complaint. There were earls in stars and garters, clergymen in their cassocks and bands, translators and index makers in their ratters and tags, the young beaux and bon wits come to smoke and chatter about poetic justice and unities of place and time, playwrights claiming art could transcend social classes. *Look at Walpole,* one of them was saying. *His father was born a sheep farmer and he managed to write a classic work of literature. That was a hundred years ago! What isn't possible today?* A symphony is a compendium of hate. A play is no more than an opera in a hurry, a waste of so many words, beauty stripped of everything but exposition. They would have been failures without drama. We longed for the eastern neighbourhoods without presumption, nothing but hunger and work, but once we passed the Temple Bar the situation was not improved, cramped by all manner of false aspirants, tumblers and sketchers, knife grinders and umbrella menders, Italian children indulging in all sorts of buffoonery, one with a Viggiano arpetta, a violin, bagpipers, organ grinders, bell ringers, hurdy-gurdy murderers, dragging woeful caricatures of the "Marseillaise" across the cobbles and stones, young girls dancing the Fling, doing it pretty, and filthy-fingered crones pawning statuettes of wood and porcelain and plaster, a Grecian gladiator, penitent Jesus, Plato and Hippocrates, a crucifixed Saint Roche, female figures indecently cast, knit sentiments, rotting boards with painted letters, quoting Perrault, Boileau, Dunno. *A dream is a wish your heart makes,* one read. *The right resides chiefly with the strong.* At night we hid in various gambling establishments, surrounded by men with little to no aspirations except to predict the future. One night a man collapsed outside the door and was carried in. The Club immediately made bets whether he was dead or not, and when a doctor in the group stepped forward to attempt to revive him, the wagerers for his death interposed, claiming it could affect the fairness of the bet.

He tosses the score aside and says: *They would not understand now any more than they understood then.* The heart is small. A symphony is a compendium of hate. And at the celebration before the performance we run into Christine and we are all reminded of how poorly he treated her and yet I envy her because she was treated at all. There she is, standing straight, holding out her arms as if awaiting the stigmata; she opens her mouth, she is suffocating. I wait a few moments: I am afraid she will fall: she

188

is too sickly to stand this unwonted sorrow. But she does not move, she seems turned to stone, like everything around her. She gives a little groan, *sons bouchés*. Her hand goes to her throat and she opens wide, astonished eyes.

A symphony is a memoir of failure. The heart is small. There is no evidence of a struggle having taken place. They hear the music so closely they do not hear it. And he goes out among them and holds their faces against the music and screams: *You do not understand beauty! You do not understand beauty! You do not understand because, if you did, you would long for it. You would work for it. Not this! Beauty is the movement; beauty is the practice; beauty is not the reason but the knife; beauty is the final act; beauty has no place; beauty is not a distraction; beauty is the work and the work is beauty; beauty is the cry of a creature hurled over an abyss; beauty is the knife in the body of the child; beauty is the child, the twist, twist; beauty is the knife in the body of the child; beauty is the child, the twist, twist; beauty is the hiss and derm and clitch; beauty is the reddest meat; beauty is the mosquito net between the fear of living and the fear of death; beauty is the twist, the plunge and breach, two shadows, a short woman pulling a man by his sleeve and the man thrusts his hands in his pockets and screams:* You're going to shut your trap now, aren't you?!

And he leaves without looking back.

And deep, hoarse sounds come from her, tear at her, fill the street with extraordinary beauty.

The heart is small.

All the teeth on the lower left jaw are absent.

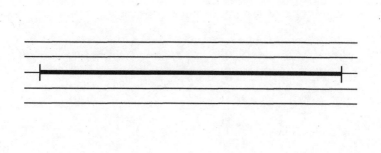

Part II

We must start young to be moved, to
assimilate and drink the sun, to endure the
dazzle of marbles and stuffs; we must come back
young to create with force.

— CAMILLE SAINT-SAËNS

The thirsty man dreams of fountains and
running streams, the hungry man of banquets,
the poor man, hidden gold, but nothing is more
appalling than the imagination of the poet,
which can destroy without a second thought.

— WASHINGTON IRVING

Part II

Scherzo

I ENJOY BOOKS ABOUT GRIEF, SAID THE HEIRESS; *IMAGINE* Frankenstein, she said, *not as the tale of a monster,* she said, *or of fear,* she said, *but as the story of Elizabeth, dealing with the death of her mother.* No one cares about the monster, she said. *No one ever writes a story about a monster. Imagine Elizabeth never having a mother, though, never knowing a mother, always loving a mother. What is it like to live without a mother? Or worse, to know that you killed her? What is it like to feel responsible for a person not being there? Especially for a person who has never been there? At least for you. To know that you forced yourself from her and tore and clawed and clawed and tore and gasped and writhed and cried and gasped and never even noticed she was there until you did, and then she wasn't. You noticed she was there (or wasn't) and felt empty and longing for something you never had, missed something you never had, never understood, could never understand, missed a gap, a lack where once was wonderful, because you didn't have the time to notice what she was or why she was there or even that she was. Until it was too late. Imagine looking at the other moth-* ers, the heiress said. *Imagine hearing the word* mother *and each time hearing the word* mother *being reminded of the no mother, the lack of tender caresses and fortitude and benignity. Imagine becoming a woman,* she said, *then falling in love, and wanting to be that thing she never had. With Victor, of all people! Whose mother she also killed! And when she discovered that she couldn't? When the doctor said:* I'm sorry? *And when she knew exactly what the doctor meant, though he didn't say her name or I'm sorry for what, just:* I'm sorry, *like somehow he had struck her inadvertently and somehow these words were going to make it feel better, to replace not being able to provide life, to replace the no mother, losing a mother that was never there and then also a child, a no child? Somehow this man who always carried a bag thought he could fix it all with:* I'm sorry. How many apologies does he have in that bag? *she must have thought to herself. And:* What else does he have in there? Condolences? Platitudes? *Can words ever fix anything? Sometimes you learn to accept. Life is one long lesson in acceptance. But could you accept that?*

She'd already lost them at this point, however, all of them staring out the window at the bay, and the ship, and the bay (and the ship) seemed unmoving, idle, unreal, as a painted ship upon a painted ocean. The wind was, on a typical day, exemplary; not uncomfortable for sunning, of course, but perfect for sailing, or kite flying, or reducing the temperature. It was crucial to the success of a seaside resort, as anyone knew, that the gusts never outnumber the guests. But here it was—the ship, or the wind, or even the bay—forcing its presence with inaction rather than action. And the factory owner whose name was Tudesq said, profoundly: *Despair has its own calms.* And the Wife of Chaline said, desperately: *Has anyone ever died here?* And they looked at each other as if surely it were only a matter of odds and that the longer any of them stayed, here on the beach, staring at the ship, the better their chances that they would be the next. They held their children close and their wallets closer and the concierge sent someone in a rowboat to the ship to retrieve a man and his trunks and a servant who was an Arab. And the man fingered the exotic flowers in the lobby and muttered, barely audibly, that they were too dry. And the man wiped a long finger cross the long counter, and rubbed the dust to nothing. And the man kept tapping the bell deliberately though the concierge was right in front of him, deliberately. *La-la... La-la-la-laaaaaa...* The concierge tried to rush him through the process of signing in because the crowd was gathering. And the man, whose accent was clearly not Dutch, said: *I am Dutch.* And the man, whose hands were clearly not those of a diamond merchant, said: *I am a diamond merchant.* And he asked for a private cabin, as far from any of the other guests as possible, with three bedrooms though it was only him and his servant (the Arab) and the trunks. And he asked for a private cabin not facing the bay, as was popular, and more expensive, but open to the mountains. And everyone was already talking. And he signed his name: *Charles Sannois.* And everyone was already talking.

* * * * *

They sat their dinners in the common room—the heiress and the factory owner (whose name was Tudesq), the engineer (whose name was Chaline), the engineer's wife (whose name was the Wife of Chaline), the young Englishman (taking a break from the labours of his Grand Tour), the grey-haired widow from Rouen (who was so close to death it was not worth the energy to recall her name), and her cat, Puffles (whose name was actually Mr. Puffles)—and entertained one another with stories more or less true; and sometimes there was also the Russian, who looked down on all of them and was inordinately interested in suicide and lemons, and everything was always *vdrug, vdrug, vdrug,* and a Canadian who had a name none of them could pronounce, something like Malouin (he had a lisp), and another American, a handsome black writer who was negative about many things and showed no interest in the heiress and came across as rather obtuse and disagreeable to her for all of it; but largely they kept to themselves and the heiress simply never bothered to learn their names, which made it more difficult to think bad thoughts about them, never able to be specific about them, not even to herself, which was probably just as well, when you thought about it. Her father had told her not to think badly of people, though she often found it strenuous. Politicians, for example; and the Japanese; census takers; the young Englishman.

Biarritz boasted two beaches—one of rock and one of sand. And most of the guests equipped the sandier with their bodies which, now the morning, rolled from belly over, propped elbows to stare at Sannois and his Arab and question. He appeared on the first morning, this man who gave his name as Sannois, trailed by his Arab and his easel, and would sit the sand and sketch the coastline and occasionally there were watercolours. And he talked to himself. And he wrote things in code. He would erupt sudden from the sand and grab the nearest sheet of paper and scratch out a series of dots and lines, hand them to his Arab, who was never far off, and later someone would spot the Arab down at the pier, smoking and gabbing with the sailors, exchanging money for packages. Was he an invalid seeking the sun? A political refugee expelled from his country? A disappointed lover keeping his distance? He liked to walk the gardens and berate the groundskeepers, this man who gave his name as Sannois, fell to his knees and tore the plants from the soil, with his bare hands, and cast them to the side of the path, another, and another, and another, another, sweating and wiping his brow with a hankie from his spare pocket. The gardeners rushed over and yelled: *What are you doing? God help me, what are you doing?!* And Sannois shook his head and said it was wrong-all-wrong. The yellow of the coreopsis was in conflict with the facade of the building. The lilies were lined up like lonely soldiers. And he said: *How dare you touch me? How dare you!* And his Arab puffed up like a silverback and beat his chest and the concierge came running and said: *M. Sannois, have you seen the mountains?* The hotel was also the first in town to have an elevator, and sometimes they would find him riding it up and down, his ear pressed to the wall for the *clang clang clang.* He would say *shhhh* if anyone spoke, and if anyone else spoke he would say *shhhh*, and *shhhh* he would say if they did not listen and spoke again. Then he would scowl and get off and they would forget to get off, though it was only a trip of one floor. And they'd just have to ride it back down and up again. The young Englishman had witnessed the Arab at a café on his own, and when the owner refused to serve him, he just stood there, not speaking, not even staring, just standing. And several times a week Sannois attended the concerts presented by the community orchestra on the promenade, listening raptly and ramming his fist to the railing. He could not sit still. He could not stand. *My God!* he would shout. *My heavenly God!* One day, just as the tenor started in to his first aria, the conductor had to halt the performance and ask the man who gave his name as Sannois to be quiet or leave. And he left.

* * * * *

The widow claimed he was the Devil. She had come to Biarritz for the various tumorous growths that oozed from her skin; her doctor thought more sun might help, but she was also not a fan of indecency, had not even attended the concert where Sannois had caused such a ruckus because the composer was a Protestant, and so her trips to the beach were made in long robes and—miraculously—longer white gloves. She ate only the softest foods, which frequently spilled the front of her shawls. One of the waiters claimed to have helped her one evening with her napkin, draping it around her shoulders, and just below her collar he grazed a particularly large excrescence, flat and long, about the size of a narrow fingernail. She preferred to rise early enough to attend mass at Our Lady of Guadelupe, which meant she was exhausted by midday and always took a siesta in her rooms after lunch. She said she was climbing the stairs—because no one would take the elevator anymore, and so the concierge had placed an OUT OF ORDER sign on it so no one would feel uncomfortable about it—when she met Sannois coming down, preceded by his Arab, and the Arab stepped aside and their eyes met and the widow said she could not move, that one moment she was as able-bodied as the next geriatric and the next she was held to place as though a pin had been driven down her spine to the floor. Though she did not fall, she claimed to momentarily lose consciousness, to black out while he dowsed her soul. When she came to, Sannois and his Arab were gone. For a long time afterwards, she could walk only with difficulty and avoided eye contact with him whenever possible.

Another day, the Wife of Chaline watched him capture a butterfly in his bare hands. *His hands are massive*, she said. *Like dried-out mops!* And she half expected him to waste it against the crease of his trousers but the hands did not crush. He would trap the butterfly and hold it there and feel the beat of its wings and part his thumbs to peer and see the beat of its wings and he would whisper, softly: *Aren't you beautiful, you are so beautiful, you are so, so beautiful.* And then he might crush it! Or he might just let it go. And not even follow it with his eyes to see where it went next. Because he had already moved on to something else. *He lacks focus,* said Tudesq, confidently. This was something he could not abide. *That is why people fail in this world. I was not the smartest child in school. I did not perform well in matriculations, nor did I even understand much of it, if we're to be honest, but I have my talents, and I knew what I wanted and I never veered from it.*

Chaline, who had never known what he wanted, only what he didn't, and whose life had veered unerringly to a desk at the *ministère des ponts et chausses*, observed Sannois to put down his brushes and weep and he convinced himself that Sannois's secret was a matter of national security. *Men don't cry without secrets,* he claimed. *Horrible secrets.* And one evening, laying claim as the ranking officer in the line of presidential succession, he said he had spoken to the concierge and confirmed that Sannois's bill was being covered by regular wires from Paris. *He's definitely not Dutch,* he continued. *He speaks French so poorly. Only true Parisians take such little care with their enunciation.*

And the heiress, who radiated such constant positivity because no one had ever been cruel to her in all her life, not even
the woman who cooked for their groomsmen, said: *So what if
he's not Dutch! Who among us is?*

* * * * *

The factory owner whose name was Tudesq liked to tell them
about the horrible things: delightful views of perfectly calm
waters; untouched basalt cliffs and slopes of woodland with
occasional glades, stretched down for nine or ten kilometres to
a central lake; gigantic, cinnamon-coloured trees, fragrant and
wet. *Have you ever been?* he ventured to the man who gave his
name as Sannois, by which he meant Africa, and Sannois shifted his body slightly so they were no longer facing and Tudesq
continued, unperturbed: *Such an ugly continent, an empire of the
darkest imagination, with all of the sensory reactions to which we are
accustomed but none of the reality; an untouched world of pretend that
only draws vaguer as neared: the almost unbroken front line of thick,
leafy bush, sprinkled with shimmering butterflies and moths and insects;
the trees borne all the crushing fruit; the trees of fever, trees of stone; trees
of burning sap and death apples; the man-eaters, carnivorous tangle
trees, strange orchids, vegetation to riot the earth; the endless fields of
razor-burred grains and hartebeest; the threat of smallpox; the black
peril; the naked houris; the kilometres of stones that banked the winter
rivers, lifted sudden to the sky, become birds a hundred times abundant
to block the sun; the glorious land whales, native lords of the forest and
the plain, who shook the earth with their deaths; springbuck, kudu,
wildebeest, quagga, fancy names for various lengths of inert meat; and
the craw of beated wings upon the meat; the horrid noises, and hideous
cries and howlings that were raised; some tiny creature, mad with wrath,
coming nearer on the path; the hands of the lions and the tigers; the forest
satyrs, witch doctors, stork fighters, handsome dwarfs; a city populated
by evil gorillas; huge and mighty forms that do not live; sometimes you
could gaze into their faces and recognize but your own humanity, he said,*

if that; and the wide rivers of shining water fell from the sky, disturbed the exquisite repose of nature every afternoon, soon after two o'clock; dark portents of lowering tempests; thunderbolts rent the gloom; and one of the baboons forgot we were just playing with them and ran off with a pair of socks and we blasted wild into the trees until, wounded in the leg, it came crashing back to earth, cracking from branch to branch.

Kongoni, he called the hartebeest. *Nothing is more difficult than creeping up on a herd of antelope,* he said. *All eyes. On every side, all eyes.* There were so few of them now, it was so sad, probably not another quagga left. You probably couldn't find one south of the Zambezi, it was barely worth going. But once upon a time they were bringing back 150,000 pelts in a single year, he bragged, so many they couldn't fit them all in the wagons, would have to leave the rest to rot, herds a kilometre or more in diameter that still managed to surprise *them*, if you can believe it, come over the rise like a poison mist, thick and opaque and deafening. One time Tudesq was sure they would die trampled 'neath the brainless hoofs but stood his path, while his Khoikhoi marksmen slowly raised their muskets to fire, fire, to fire, and the mangled fur stretchers prostrated themselves before him like before a coming God. It reminded him, he said, however briefly, of that Sudanese soldier, innocent as a lamb cropping sweetgrass, begging him for forgiveness after trespassing to loot another native village. *I felt so sorry for him—after all, how could he resist his nature when the world was there for the naturing?* His words waited before them like a restful beast with lungs breathing and heart beating and they listened because it made them feel better to hear it, the sound of the lungs and the heart, and the heiress, who was like a void waiting to be filled by culture's impact, was unsure if he was having them on or not, but she liked to hear about Africa just the same, so she kept quiet as long as she could bear before she said: *Don't you often worry for your safety? That you might be killed? Lured into smiling and treacherous bays? Knocked in the head with outlandish war clubs and served up without preliminary dressing?* And Tudesq, who was an expert in drawing things out, in dropping small bombs of information on conversations and then spending the next block of time cleaning up the mess before dropping the next, said: *People have outlandish ideas about such things. But the natives aren't really skilled enough for all that. They lack focus. I have met several who had a wish to kill me,* he said. *Violence is their way of life, after all. But by the time they'd reached me, they'd gone on to the next shiny thing, the next thing to be angry about, and anger can't live forever. Eventually it dissolves into frustration and then they'll have nothing. It happens to everyone, even if you win, but especially if you keep getting nowhere.*

* * * * *

The young Englishman taking a break from the labours of his Grand Tour was recovering, he claimed, from a bout of alpinism he'd contracted in Lausanne. After nearly three days through the Great St. Bernard Pass on the back of a bony footman, his thighs burned like a well rope, and he fanned his mid-region with a wide-brimmed hat and spoke in sequences of rapidly occurring events to anyone who ventured within striking distance, about encounters with wolves and a bear and a *table d'hôte* menu that was not nearly as bad as one might have expected.

I can recall my own tour, said Tudesq. *The tragedy I saw! It was very educational.*

Indeed, the Englishman replied. *I have a new-found respect for properly reinforced trousers.*

Before he'd entered the room, the heiress had found him attractive in a rakish way, his haggard suspicion so striking. He said: *Oh yes, there are monsters in the world. I have seen them.* And the heiress inched closer. He said: *In Greece they told me of a Turkish custom whereby women accused of adultery are tied in a sack and tossed into the ocean.* And she squealed: *How ghastly!* But one day he was telling wonderful stories filled with ancient ruins, romance, vermin and Albanians and she got caught up in it all and said: *Do Albanians even exist? I thought Byron just made them up!* And the young Englishman went suddenly cold and said: *Perhaps if I had never travelled, never left my own country when I did, my views would also be more limited.* And after that he became overcome with undue civility and propriety, concerned about what was or was not appropriate conversation.

Oh, please, she begged him on another occasion. *Could it really be so bad?*

You couldn't imagine, he replied.

Oh, you'd be shocked at what I can imagine. The most horrible things, I swear!

And she was left with no one to listen to but the Chalines.

* * * * *

The Husband of the Wife of Chaline saw the world as a web of profoundly intertwined histories and events and, as such, might erupt at any moment with the capitals of each department of France, statistics on injuries and deaths in six-day racing, or tracing his family lineage to one of the twelve peers of Charlemagne. As an example he provided the story of *The Grandfather of Chaline*, which began on *a pitch black, starless night, trudging solitary from Brive-la-Gaillarde to Limoges, in the deep forest atop the Massif Central, where sometimes robberies and even murders had been committed. He was a good and faithful man, and also a postmaster (did I say that already?), travelling the same route between Limoges and Brive-la-Gaillarde and back, through Boisseuil, Vicq-sur-Breuilh, Donzenac, Shediac, Mactaquac, Bric-à-brac, day in, day out. My grandfather had been engaged in this work for several years and was much respected and loved by all who knew him. He was the second generation assigned to the same route, and many of the citizens of this department (which is where my wife and I still live) still remember my grandfather as a child, had watched him grow into the man that delivered their letters and packages, though he rarely remembered them. They were not special to him as he was to them. None was ever more than the person to whom he was delivering. None was more than a destination. So when they greeted him* so warmly he behaved with appropriate affection for them but truly had no idea who they were. If he made genuine attempt to recall any of the other people he had met, even the last one, they still had the same face as this one. There was only the face of this one. It was the same with their dogs and their chairs where they let him rest and their proffered glasses of water or café or wine and their empty words of concern. He was always easing his body down into that chair and thinking, This chair is the most comfortable I have ever sat. This chair has no colour or shape or anything but this comfort. It was the same with the rocks and the trees. He could recall none of them with any accuracy unless they were directly in front of him. And eventually he began to question it. And by "it" I mean the rest of the world. Sometimes he would stop at a dilapidated inn outside Masseret and stare at an oak beside the road and try to imagine another, a different oak of the same variety, and found he could not. He tried to imagine a grosse sequoia, and found he could not. There are so many trees, some oak, some red, some black, some Japanese, some chinkapin, so many trees. And once they were out of sight, did they not fade quickly if not immediately to that one tree placeholder, no more real than one he might create in his mind from scratch. My grandfather was not just a postmaster. He was a talented artist. And he was clever. He drew a picture. And once he was done he turned around and he looked at the picture and said: That's the tree; that's the tree behind me. And, satisfied, he took that with him. So he could always recall that specific thing he called the oak tree, that specific oak tree. But then he would look up to steer his cart, unable to see the tree or the drawing, and the tree and the drawing were both transformed again, merely the image of a tree, as though reflected in a fountain. And he thought: The world is unfinished. He thought: God gave up on us. He started to create a world for man in which to live, but after a week he lost interest and just left it here, left us here, thinking we would never notice, perhaps, or that we might finish it on our own, to our own specifications and perfections. Perhaps that was the answer. The only thing that is real is right in front of us. The periphery is always a blur, an imagined space of faulted imagination. And because he was constantly moving, this meant he *was always headed away from clarity rather than toward it, always moving from the perfect organization of his present state toward the increased chaos of God's unconsidered. Life, he decided, was a constant state of worsening, of increased confusion.*

Then one day outside the dilapidated inn near Masseret as he contemplated the tree again he was rushed upon by two robbers who began to beat him with their heavy clubs and as he was being beaten by their heavy clubs (overlooking a beautiful forested valley of pine and oak and yew, trees so old they felt as though they had always been there, would always be there), he spied a flock of birds of the air, wild birds, of the air, flying over them, and he began to think about his constant movement, from Limoges to Brive to Limoges to Brive, Limoges to Brive to Limoges to Brive, as he was being beaten, he thought about his movement, like those wild birds of the air in migration, and how tired they must be, those wild birds of the air, the heavy clubs beating, how tired he was of that movement, so constantly moving that he never really knew entirely where he was, his exact position in relation to Limoges, or Brive-la-Gaillarde, just that he was always getting closer to or farther from Limoges, closer to or farther from Brive-la-Gaillarde, and he looked upon the birds, as he was being beaten by the heavy clubs, and he looked upon the dilapidated inn, and the beautiful forested valley of pine and oak and yew, and he decided the only good in life lay in not moving, being a tree, a stone, or even less than that, and, if he could recall it perfectly, it wouldn't even matter if the tree existed, or the sapling before it, or the seed, because then it would be in his head and he could revisit it whenever he wanted, the world would be complete.

* * * * *

The Wife of Chaline said: *Did you know Boulanger has a Kenyan half-brother?* To which Tudesq, who was a firm supporter of the Ligue, replied: *I think you mean a Tunisian bastard.* And she laughed and said: *Oh, right, I knew I had it mostly, it was only the name.*

Then, at no one's request, she told them about a riot in Decazeville, just south of where they lived. The miners had descended to their daily work of sweat and coal and then refused to re-emerge, occupying the black veins of the town for weeks, refusing to eat, sleeping on piles of straw they had smuggled down a needle at a time. No one in the town could sleep except these men, in fact, because, although they'd always been there, these men, no one had ever seen them, these subterranean men. And once the word of the strike spread, the other townsfolk saw them constantly, in their nightmares: an army of blackened men, tunnelling under their houses; hands that broke the soil, pierced the heart; men without speech, without eyes, with backs that bent and legs right-angled; hard-shelled men; black-lunged men; feeling-at-the-walls-in-the-darkness men. First the dogs woke crying. Then the children. And the adults said: *Why are you crying? These are only dreams. They're not real. These are only dreams!* They said: *Your reaction is irrational. The men aren't really in your dreams. They're not really under the ground. It's something happening somewhere else.* But they could see them, the children could: covered in dust; expressionless. They could imagine them. And the adults said: *Stop it! Stop it right now! Do you want to lose your toy? I'm going to take away your toy if you don't stop it.* And then of course the adults saw them in their dreams, too, and so they were real and so they didn't take away any toys. And they did everything in their power to stay awake, gathering in single rooms to sing and pinch each other and compare dreams. And this went on for a month. *We weren't even that close and I couldn't sleep anymore, either. If this was going on underground somewhere else, what was happening under the ground where we were?*

One by one, the entire town gathered at the mouth of the mine, in case the miners should finally re-emerge, though some were there to welcome and some to stop; some to shelter, some to crack. There were rocks and sticks and blankets and bowls of hot stew. There were strong words, strong silences. They eyed each other suspiciously; they laid blame. Some claimed there were no men down there at all. They were just dreams.

Just bad dreams. But they'd all seen them. Then one day one of the miners did emerge, and no one could move. They had expected so much more. A monster? An army? But he was just an undernourished teenager blinking. No one recognized him. No one remembered him buying something at a store, or lending a helping hand. Was he even one of them? Someone threw a rock, and another. Someone in the crowd said: *Why are you here? What is it that you want?* And the miner said: *Anything, really. A piece of bread? A glass of water?* Someone said: *Are they all dead, then? Down there? Is this the end?* And the miner shook his head but waited until he had the water before saying anything else. And the rocks stopped. *Thank you,* he said. And they asked him why the miners were doing this to them, and he said the mine owners had threatened their jobs, threatened them with Italians who would work for less money. The miners said the mine owners were in cahoots with the elites in Paris. None of them lived here. None of the benefits stayed here. The miner said: *We should strive to welcome change and challenges, because they are what help us grow.* And it was time that ownership returned to the area and the miners themselves. And all the town were suddenly behind him, this young man none of them had seen before, who couldn't grow a beard, this man of the blackening. They fought to feed him, to house him, to clean his clothes. He became less sickly, though never less filthy. Eventually, an engineer from the company arrived from Paris and the miner went to meet him but the engineer from Paris ignored him and walked straight to the edge of town and called to the men from the mouth of the cavern. He was nothing. A small man with a moustache and a tight hat and nothing. He was nothing. But down below he sounded like a thousand voices, and they were coaxed out. By the thousand voices. And they saw the man who was nothing and followed him into the town and the innkeeper opened his doors and they went to the large private room upstairs and spoke for hours about their concerns and he listened. For the first time in their lives, someone listened. He said: *I understand.* He nodded. And they believed him. He said: *Here is what I can do for you.* And they listened back with such open hearts and when he was done they tossed him from the window and down below the townspeople saw his broken body already dead and began to beat it and no one would even volunteer to carry the coffin. *And all because they'd been losing so many jobs to the Italians! Imagine all that! Over nothing but rocks!*

But, of course, a rock isn't a rock isn't a rock, Tudesq chimed in. *And it isn't right to talk about them like they are.*

Not rocks?

You undermine all of society with a statement like that.

They are, though, the American journalist said. *Nothing is a diamond until we say it is. Before that, it's just a hard lump in the ground.*

The hardest, you mean! Tudesq looked as though he'd been struck. *Should we set up a small exchange, you and I? Diamonds for path stones? The Africans have no idea how to properly separate concepts. So they use the same words for dozens of things. They know nothing about finances; some of them use copper crosses for money; empty sardine boxes; jam and milk cans; used cartridge cases; in one region of Gambia, they decided to use peanuts because they saw we Europeans would pay so much for them. Then one day a tribe of elephants crashed the town and sent the entire region into massive debt. I showed up in South Africa with nothing but a bit of cash and forty boxes of cheap cigars. The next thing I knew, I owned near half the mountains around Pretoria.*

The heiress could barely take it any longer. And she began to compile a list of potential interjections when Tudesq was suddenly cut short by a voice from the back: *You mean the birthplace of Emma Calvé?*

* * * * *

Decazeville, Sannois was saying again. *It was the birthplace of Emma Calvé, no? She had the arms of an ape but could scale the extremes of her range with ease.* They'd forgotten he was there. He was so unassuming, rarely ate with them, unless invited by the American journalist. Any time they'd tried to engage him, they had been met with the same indifference he had demonstrated toward Tudesq's humanitarian missions. But here he was staring the Wife of Chaline straight in her face and her husband, who had no idea whether Decazeville had birthed Emma Calvé or not but did know a thing or two about Castle Cabrières, the fortress not far from there that he knew she had recently purchased, began a tangent from which everyone felt he might never return, about Arab gold, and the Knights of Templar, German smelters, a man in Rennes-le-Château who found a gold ingot under a stone weighing almost twenty kilos, and another near Saint-Just-et-le-Bézu who tripped over a whole bar of it in a stream that was nearly fifty; about Pythagoras, a fifth element, something called a quinotaur, dark matter, a deaf mute, golden bees. Calvé was well-known in their parts, he continued, for the parties she threw, and who attended them, especially the Indian swami, and the Spaniard, and the woman who appeared to be of Middle Eastern origin and who was introduced as Semiramis and performed a rite that she, or rather her companion or manager or whatever (who claimed to be a Georgian Princess), said was Ancient Babylonian and that Semiramis was an avatar of the Great Mother Goddess Cybèle, and then, suddenly, from Sannois again: *Is that it?*

Is that what?

Is that truly your whole story?

...

It's like the one about your grandfather. I thought maybe he was going to achieve something.

He did, sir. He achieved awareness.

We all have awareness.

Yes, yes, of course, but of what?

Banality. At least, most of us.

* * * * *

One day the widow approached the concierge to say Mr. Puffles had gone missing, she couldn't find him anywhere, and she demanded they search Sannois's cabin. The concierge, though sympathetic, urged restraint. The heiress approached Sannois directly and he showed her some of his poems and she asked what they were called and he said one was called "Death" and another was called "L'arbre," built around the image of roots struggling in the darkness, the upper branches waving in splendour. *What are they about?* she asked. *That's a difficult question,* he replied. He was just a sad old man who liked to wander the mountains, range through their immense recesses, look at butterflies and flowers. Perhaps his wife had passed. But she dared not ask. She imagined him as a much younger man, stopping by with flowers and chocolates. She imagined him as a teacher. He enjoyed explaining things. He told her that colours were illusions, that everyone saw them differently. The idea of a standardized tuning, he claimed, was likewise preposterous. On several nights they went out to look at the stars, and he pointed out the Great Bear. The Bull. *That constellation is called Aquila,* he said. *That is the Swan, the one that looks like a child's drawing of the cross. Its tail is one of the brightest stars in the sky. The one that actually looks like a swan is called Leo. And that arrangement over there is Hercules, the fifth-largest of the constellations though it has no first-magnitude stars, looking down fittingly on the Pyrenees. See how it looks like a man on his knees? It was one of the original constellations listed by Ptolemy himself. Fifteen of its stars are orbited by other planets where other people are possibly looking at our sun and imagining us. Do you see that one over there? The one that looks as bright as lamplight on the mountain? That one isn't a star at all. That is Venus.*

The planet, you mean?

Yes. Isn't it amazing? That we can see such a heavenly body at all when it gives off none of its own light, only reflects. I have a theory, in fact, as to why things appear so bright close to the horizon, if you would like to hear it. And when she nodded, he continued talking about distributions of density, contractions of the air, causing things to seem more spectacular by proximity, and he was so delightful that she laughed out loud and confessed to having had her stars charted once upon a time. The tripod of her spiritual life was Saturn, Rahu and Jupiter. *One is ruled by Mars, she said, and another by the Moon, both of which are water signs. The fortune teller said that meant I was meant to cross the ocean, and here I am!*

Oh...oh... He seemed slightly disappointed. *Despite what some may tell you, astrology and astronomy are not the same thing. Astrology is a horseless cart that has never been washed out. Astronomy, on the other hand...well... Read Arago. Or read Laplace. C'est la plus belle des sciences. Do you speak French? Do you know what that means?*

There are just so many. She was still shaking her head. *How can one ever hope to know them all? What could be the point?*

If one wants to learn anything, he said, *one must go at it slowly, then more slowly, and then finally, slowly. Did you know,* he asked, gesturing to the mountain range behind them, *that they were named for Pyrene, the lover of Hercules? They say that when she died, he built the mountains as a tomb for her.*

How did she die?

Some say she was killed by Hercules. Some say she killed herself. Other stories say wild animals. Perhaps all these are true. They also said that, as he aged, Hercules would often return to these mountains to find his peace. He loved so many mortals, and of course they all died before him. And each time he came back to her, here, either because of guilt or regret, especially when he became very old, had lived nearly a thousand years, had loved so many dozens of women and men and had time to reassess his actions. He could barely recall his Great Labours, they were so long ago. He could barely remember holding up the sky, or defeating Troy single-handedly. Instead he sat on these peaks and considered the things he had once said to Deianira that might have made her feel less than she was, to Omphale, how he had given Megara to one of his other lovers, Iolaus, not to mention the women he had lain with and moved on immediately. What had become of them, he wondered. This is where he grew to know compassion. This is where he grew to know true love.

As Hercules had shaped the mountains, so had the mountains shaped Hercules.

The heiress, who enjoyed facts and had a few of her own, said: *Did you know...they used to harpoon whales here and slaughter them on the sand?* And Sannois replied: *Have we not all, at some point in our lives, done horrible things?*

* * * * *

She began to accompany him on his walks, sometimes strolling the gardens but more often testing the base of the mountains. He was remarkably unfit for such pursuits, took frequent rests. She'd never seen anyone sweat so much, so much wheeze, so much rattle. Sometimes he threw up and wiped his mouth on a handkerchief he unfolded carefully from his back pocket. She waited beside him and wondered if he might die. *Or is this just what old people do?* she wondered to herself. She thought about calling for help. But then his eyes would light up again and he would smile and say: *On we go!* as though it was nothing.

He complained to the concierge about his calves. His legs felt like animals fighting in a bag, he said. He said: *My muscles are eating themselves, like they're trying to escape a trap!* One day the concierge recommended the masseuse. And after that, no day was complete without a visit to her. One day the masseuse was not there and Sannois seemed overly annoyed to be faced with someone else, a man with a moustache who liked to sing as he worked. He went immediately back to the concierge. *Where's the girl?* he asked. *I'm sorry?* the concierge replied. *The girl*, Sannois repeated. *From the day before. I would prefer her. That girl.*

...

...

I think she might be ill.
What if I came back tomorrow?

...

...

213

She might still be ill.
But she might not?

...

...

She might not.

And as they were exiting the lobby the heiress thought she spotted the girl with a group of women behind the kitchen but could honestly not tell them apart. The girl moved to leave as she and Sannois approached, but the heiress blocked her path and said: *Aren't you just the most grateful little creature in the world! Aren't you beautiful! I have a dress that would look splendid on you.* The girl was not French. She was Spanish, Basque. The Spanish would work for less money than the French. The Basques would work for even less than them. The young woman shook her head and tried to look past her. Sannois said: *He told me you were ill.* She said nothing. The heiress tried to reassure her, offered her another biscuit, told her about a lovely pair of earrings. And Sannois said: *Will you feel better tomorrow, do you think?* Still she said nothing. She looked down. She looked back up. *Will you feel better tomorrow?* And this time she nodded because she thought he would go away.

* * * * *

Do you believe in monsters? she asked him. They were higher than they had ever gone before and she had turned around and looked back and had seen what she imagined to be the other guests receding on the beach, their specks dispersing. She tried to imagine what they must have looked like as they had started. She tried to imagine someone higher watching them now. How close was the nearest other person? she wondered. Would they make it back for dinner? He had been telling her about bees when she asked him and he perched on a fallen tree to rest and looked at her strangely for a moment, then finally croaked: *Why do you ask?* And pleased that he had asked her a question that was not rhetorical, she told him what the Englishman had said, and Tudesq, and Chaline and the Wife of Chaline, and about creatures that were only half there, aberrations of metaphor, ugly, dirty and stupid. She said: *Stories about monsters are always really about something else. What is a monster, after all, but a misplaced dream?* She said: *Did you know the Greeks once believed in a race of people who did not need to eat or drink or breathe—who survived by smelling apples and flowers?* Sannois seemed to think about this for a while, then said: *Have you read Aristotle's* Metaphysics? She had not. *Flaubert's* Temptation of Saint Anthony? No. *Have you read le Bon?* They stared at each other for several minutes in silence and she wondered what it was like to be him, looking back at her looking back at him. Then he said: *Come with me.* And he led her back down the path, down the mountain to the resort, past the hotel and over to his cabin, a single-storey cabin with three bedrooms, a full bathroom, and a half, as well as a combined kitchen/living room/dining room with windows that faced only the mountains, and she went inside. *Wait here,* he said. *I have something for you.* And he disappeared through one of the doorways and into one of the bedrooms and she stepped aside to peer past him, at the bed, untouched for sleeping, covered in the paper with his nonsensical scratches. *Sorry,* he called. *I can't find it. Give me one more moment.* And she walked slowly to the door of the second bedroom. The bed there also seemed untouched. Only the third bed seemed used, and in that room was his collapsible easel, with separate compartments for his brushes, his oils, his watercolours. There was a jar filled with a clear liquid that smelled slightly sweet and tarry, like a hospital, and another filled with yellow powder that smelled faintly of apples; another reeking of misery; another stuffed with damp towels that, when she pulled one out, spilled a dozen or more insects to the floor. She nearly screamed, then realized they were dead and stiff. Recalling the other rooms, she scoped under the bed for some kind of cot or prayer mat. Could the Arab sleep standing up? she wondered. Was that possible? She leaned heavy to the sheets and inhaled, sat down on the bed to collect herself, looked at herself in the mirror and realized her nose was bleeding. She searched the room frantically for a kerchief she could hide after using. Directly beside the bed was a tiny contraption of ropes and pulleys, with leather rings at one end the size of five-franc pieces, and small weights at the other. She cautiously inserted one finger and depressed the ring until it squeaked. It was more difficult than she had imagined, like pressing into an uncooked steak. And she realized suddenly he was in the doorway, holding something heavy in his left hand, looking from her to the strange device she had found, back to her, in the doorway, blocking with his body the doorway. It was impossible to know how long he'd been standing there, but he looked uncomfortable, frozen there, like he wasn't even real, just a painting of him. And he said: *I thought I asked you to wait in the other room.* And he said: *No matter,* and began moving toward her. She tried to estimate the distance to the window. And he stepped closer and pressed the object into her hand and it was a book, an author she also did not recognize. *Do you not know Dumas, either? Do they not teach literature in America? I'll assume you know, at least, of* The Three Musketeers? *Yes? Well, this is another book by the same man, about a sculptor named Benvenuto Cellini. Have you heard of him? He was famous for his art but equally famous for several murders: a competing goldsmith, an arquebusier who had injured his brother in defence, the Duke of Bourbon, the Prince of Orange, a Frenchman who sued him for something or other, many more besides. Perhaps he was guilty, perhaps he was merely accused out of jealousy. Either way, Cellini was sentenced to execution and he went into hiding in Paris until eventually he was pardoned by Pope Clement VII in exchange for the finest triple tiara and additions to the papal carriage.*

And then what did he do?

He was a monster and no one would punish him. What would you do?

* * * * *

After that, Sannois began to spend more time with the American journalist, spreading maps over the sand. But one night he and the heiress found themselves together again at the same table looking suspiciously on some typical Basque tapas, fried cuttlefish and lamb's brains or some such, served with cider and finished with shots of patxaran. Most of the table seemed less intent on the process of digestion than on digression. The Canadian and the Russian, for example, could not stop talking about fish treaties, unless it was to dabble briefly in mining disasters. Sannois, though he likely had a thing or two to say about mines, remained quiet. A new couple had arrived, celebrating their miraculous fiftieth wedding anniversary, and the heiress, who still believed in love, asked how they had met and they looked at each other for a long moment as though they communicated telepathically and they both chuckled softly and everyone prepared for a wonderful story of romance, on a train platform or a tragic shipwreck, and finally the gentleman cleared his throat and said: *Good fortune.* And everyone laughed heartily. And his wife slapped him playfully and added: *Depends on how you look at it.* Of course, how could you explain true love to people who'd never felt it? Was it like a hot bath? Was it painful? Were there limits? The heiress kept calling for more patxaran for the table. *A toast,* she said. *To love.* Sannois said nothing but finished several of these patxaran in short order and the heiress, seeing her opportunity, said: *Have you ever been in love, M. Sannois?* And his gaze was slow. He wiped his mouth with the corner of his napkin and said: *Yes.*

I'm sure she is beautiful. Where did you meet?

And he seemed confused, looked at her as though he'd been somewhere else, had only just arrived and was weighing his options.

A party.

Are you married?

A much longer pause. *Yes.*

Any children?

Of course, he said.

And are they as beautiful as their mother? What are their names?

Jean-François...

They all held their breath.

And...André...

Now they were all staring. No one had ever heard him divulge so much. The older woman began talking of her children, and her grandchildren. And she turned to the heiress and she said: *I can only imagine what your parents are going through right now, young lady. Halfway across the world by yourself! Imagine!* And the heiress said: *My father says Mother cries every day!* And the older woman said: *It's the hardest thing, watching them try to find their own way. Because you can't do everything for them. Eventually they have to go out into the world on their own and then you can only hope for the best. You can only hope you've passed on some values, really, and then hope for the best...that they'll be happy.* And the heiress, laughing now at the ridiculousness of it all—this old woman who'd forgotten what it was like to be young—turned to Sannois and said: *How about you, M. Sannois? Tell us about your darling little ones!* And Sannois said: *Well...André...he was only two, you know... He liked to play with his friends and roll marbles down the stairs. Then one day... he heard the sounds of his friends playing in the street below...and leaned too far out the window...*

Oh, how horrible, the woman said. *I'm so sorry for you.*

People die, he said. *All the time.*

Do you believe in God? the gentleman asked. *Surely he is in a better place.*

And Sannois eventually replied: *I know how to respect what is respectable.*

218

It is terrible to have the life of another attached to one's own like a bomb you hold in your hands, unable to be rid of it without committing a crime. You have probably never understood desire. Most of you don't even know what you enjoy out of life, what you love the most. You spend your days *getting through*: reading books; responsible only to others, never to yourself, never to desire. Have you ever been in love? I doubt it. If you had, you wouldn't be here. You wouldn't need this. If you had, you'd realize how hollow a depiction of love can be and all art would only bring you to despair, as it does me. Love is a senseless act. It is impossible to escape the explosion. And there will always be the explosion. Sometimes the explosion even comes before the bomb and, disoriented, you search about for something to hold on to, something with meaning, and the closest thing, a beacon shone bright, is the bomb. But life is not a problem to be solved, only to be experienced. You have nothing—nothing but the bomb. It is better to have the bomb than to have nothing. So you grab it in your hands again. And press it to your heart. And they tick in unison. And you wait the rest of your life for them to explode again.

My brother had chosen the Sannois alias to escape his investors. After the debut of the *Organ Symphony* in London, Camille had unfortunately committed to craft an opera for the Countess Greffulhe, who was a friend of Liszt and said to be having an affair with the director of the Paris Opéra (whose name was Gailhard). She approached us near the shrimp, where we were often most vulnerable, and began her assault with flattery, silver-tongued and waxen, then put the finishing blows by claiming, in addition to being the great-granddaughter of Napoleon, to being a descendant of Cellini! Camille had been toying with the idea of an opera about the great Mannerist for some time, likely since reading Dumas's *L'Orfèvre du roi*. And we were also short on money. So when the Countess floated the idea (and Gailhard's advance) toward us like a delicate lantern, there was nothing for Camille to do but reach out and crush it to make it his.

But his heart was not in it, and instead we fled, randomly destined, to Cádiz, Luxor, India, wandered the deserts of Hanaibin bathed in light and silence and solitude and the canal and fell into a coma of Issaoua trance music in Morocco, high on hashish, avoiding music entirely, like Odysseus in reverse, trying to escape our final destiny. We booked a cruise to see the Sphinx and the Pyramids and there was a piano in the bar and a doctor from Berlin was coaxed to assault it, directly in front of us, eventually performing the aria from one of Camille's earliest operas. For three weeks we aped about a tea plantation in Ceylon with Gabriel—the white master and his Arab, as incongruous as a beetle in a bag of rice. It was dangerous work, often perched on the edge of nothing, and it paid so little and they fed us so poorly and we had to frequently catch a ride back in to Kandy to buy some hoppers or kothu roti. Some of the other pickers were Tamils, but many were migrants like us, who stayed only for the most productive part of the season and then returned home across the Palk to India. The rest were children, local boys and girls, maybe ten years old, who rose before the sun and walked all the way from the city, at least eight kilometres away. They would work until eleven-thirty, bring their sacks to the weighing station, and then they were permitted to walk back to school, which started at one. They were very good at it, because their tiny hands were less likely to bruise the leaves. But they also did not last long because they were so soft and the tea plants were extraordinarily sharp and their fingers eventually became covered in bloodied lacerations and with the baskets on their hunched backs they looked like feral gnomes with strips of leather for paws, their bloody, bloody strips of leather. Gradually they began to miss their quotas, and we saw them again on Saturday as well. Then they had to stay overnight. And we pulled out our opera glass and showed them the secret stars that had been hidden to them without it, and they looked at us suspiciously after that but every night came back for more. We spent time in Cairo, then off to China, to Tibet, and hired a Sherpa to take us into the mountains to seek a guru, to be one with the moment, to think of nothing but the present moment, to think of no spare moments and spare moments, marvelling at the communal gathering of our cells, our bones, our muscles, at how they crept together. When we made dinner, which we partook in as a group, we were to consider nothing but the onion in our hands, the knife, the hands, the space around the onion, the knife, the hands. One time the oil smoked in the pan. Camille had made it too hot. He panicked, sliced his finger, and the blood fell on the ginger. He removed the pan from the fire and dumped the oil in the snow and began again. And we waited, and thought about waiting, and in those thoughts we were thinking about waiting.

Eventually we found ourselves in the Canaries, where everything was of a single colour—the mules, the goats, the veils of sorrow—everything the veneer of ash except the tourists in their green silk umbrellas and blue goggles and the detestable German from whom we rented the cabin up the volcano who was various shades of red. There was also a superabundance of dogs, so many dogs, living and not so living; someone had placed a whole bronze collection of them in a town square and sometimes Camille worried there might not be quite enough. There was also another piano—it was like they were following us. In the room looking out at the volcano there was also an imported piano, a tragic British upright, to which the ocean voyage had not been kind, nor the trip uphill, strapped to the side of a camel and counterbalanced with monstrous bags of flour and sugar. The tone was gone. The local humidity had ruined its action. Camille opened it up and found a crudely repaired crack in the soundboard, another in the bridge. But still it felt amazing to begin each morning with some Mozart. It didn't seem to matter which piece he started with or which he ended with or if he switched partway through a phrase or played it backward, as he had sometimes done as a child; even if a device could have been constructed to play Mozart's music completely at random, it would still sound as beautiful. Every time he did it he was like Antaeus come back to Earth and he would hammer down the notes as hard as he could, his foot forced to the sustain, and wait for them to die.

It felt right, finally, to begin on the Cellini, and most days my brother believed the new melodies to be among his finest, particularly the solo to the *Airs de Ballet d'Ascanio. I want people to be carried by the current,* he said, *as the boatsman lets himself be carried on the current of the river,* he would say, *without worrying about the chemical components of the waters that carry him.* He completed the first act by the winter, setting it in Cellini's later years when he was living in Paris. Other times, he was haunted by Berlioz, who had debuted his own *Cellini* around the time of our birth. It was easy to reason why the Countess wanted something new: Berlioz's version had been performed only once, then deemed too difficult to attempt again. For Camille, however, this meant he was competing with a legend. He knew Liszt would have a copy, so he sent one of the Arabs to steal it from his estate and it was everything he'd feared. The typical Italian aria was an exercise in repetition: eight bars of melody, packed neat with wadded fluff, nothing new at all, the work entirely manual over mental; in contrast, the melody from Berlioz's opening forced itself immediately against the bar line, unclear whether it was supposed to be in 2/2 or 3/4. Berlioz had even supposedly invented his own instruments, had someone construct an eight-foot double bass with a bow so large it had to be supported with an oarlock. The director at the Opéra had initially refused the expense, claimed the notes he was writing were below the range of the human ear. And Berlioz replied: *I will know*, as if that were a proof. He said: *People will feel it.* He said: *Art is not something you see or hear; it is something you feel!* Camille tore up the last act, sent Gabriel to Paris with the latest drafts, very incomplete, and ordered him to return with my brother's old Secrétan, which offered greater penetration to the richer parts of the Milky Way than the naked eye or even the opera glass, greater access to the splendid star swarms around the Belt of Orion. He dreamed of finding another comet like Donati's or, even better, another planet, a beast of rock to dwarf our own, so close to its sun, like Icarus still aloft, that a year would pass in a matter of days, temperatures so high that all of life was naught but gas. Every time I looked through it, however, I saw the same thing. Our days, we spent birding. Then one day he returned breathless, trying to describe to our German the things he had seen, and she said: *The chaffinch, you mean? They're like pigeons or crows around here.* My brother was incredulous. What could a woman like that possibly know about beauty? So we walked back to Las Palmas and purchased a book on local ornithology and consulted it regularly, for the harrier and petrel, bustard and a kinglet. Camille maintained a detailed log of all the birds he loved, the birds he loved with the most beautiful songs, and all the birds he loved most were common.

Word arrived from Fauré that Gailhard was growing restless. *When are you returning?* our friend asked. *People are saying you have been admitted to an institution.* April came and with it the rains, and instead of our long walks in the wilderness, we scavenged another guidebook and explored the edges of the town. There were fewer birds at this time of year, and it was always overcast. But the architecture was still impressive. In the cathedral we discovered a marvellous jewel setting made by Cellini himself, something humanity had created that did not destroy, and we rushed back to our rooms to complete the third act. Then one day as we were crossing an adjacent square, Camille passed some small girls playing unchaperoned and free, accosting each other with a game we didn't know involving shouting and screaming and sometimes both. Their voices were shrill and untrained and Camille bore his head forward and down. When we had gone only a few paces farther, however, we heard a cry and turned to find one of them wailing in misery. She had fallen, bruised herself and was covered in mud. Whatever had happened, the others had scattered like rodents to the light, and before I knew it, Camille had the little girl in his arms, her whimpers like the first movement of Mozart's Concerto No. 1, but more desperate, especially when he squeezed her leg just beneath the hem of her skirt, where it seemed she had fallen against some kind of sharp object. There was blood, but it was difficult to discern a wound, so perhaps it wasn't hers. Or was something else, like jam. Camille grazed it and brought it to his lips. He scanned the horizon. There was no one. He made hushing noises to console her. She smelled like slightly rancid honey mixed with flour. Camille's hand fell upon her beating chest, which produced, when coupled with the heart's erratic rhythm, one of the most beautiful sounds he had ever heard. Then he saw it. It was not a serious injury, the skin barely broken, peeling back like the lips of a snarling, toothless dog. She was calming down slightly, soothed by his presence perhaps, but he didn't want to lose the sound, this beautiful sound, and periodically he would graze the wound by accident in an attempt to maintain it. *I can't breathe,* she would say, though it was only this scratch. *It hurts so much, I can't breathe,* though it was only a scratch, and there was no one else to hear it, just my brother and the girl and the pain and my brother, and as it began to fade, as she became reassured by his presence, his comfort, she began to play absentmindedly with the curls of his hair behind his neck, tracing the collar of his shirt, and I thought then of our cottage in the woods, which was not far, and the quiet of the cottage, the peace of the cottage, and I thought of the Pleiads and the rain and I thought of the chaffinch, and I thought: *There are so many children in the world, more than we could ever possibly keep up with, more than we could ever know.*

Miraculously, an elderly man appeared at that moment on a bicycle, wheezy and squinting. I expected him to rush immediately to the girl, assuming they were related like everyone else in this town, assuming he could see our thoughts, but as soon as his eyes fell upon my brother, he seemed to lose all awareness that she was even there, that there was something not right about this strange beast carrying off one of the village children. *I saw you perform in Paris when I was a child,* he said. *My father had travelled there on business and taken me against his will, because my mother was likely sick of me.* He laughed. I said to myself: *I want to be just like that boy.* Then replied: *You will never be like that boy.* And of course once we'd been recognized everything was changed. Instead of the peace and quiet my brother had come searching for, he now found himself surrounded by hosts of people anxious to pay him homage, desperate for the opportunity to hear him perform. The owner of our cottage suddenly had more things around the property to mend. The baker's wife left us each morning with fresh croissants upon the sill. Even with the best intentions, the local villagers rendered his life insupportable.

Camille returned to the faulty piano, traced his fingers along the keys in the way he'd first played his songs for Henri, then sent what we had, minus the final act, back to Fauré, asking him to get Guiraud to clean it up for us while we attended to other business. *Can it be more important than your new opera?* Fauré wrote back. *Gailhard says an artist cannot disassociate himself like this from his own work! It is against human nature.*

My brother sent his reply back through our servant: *Fear not, my friend. The opera continues. I am merely in Sardinia for research.* The truth: we were off to find Henri.

Camille spent every day in Biarritz painting the sun as it dipped below the Pyrenees, trying to replicate paintings we had been sent by Henri (the only map we had to his world). The mountains massed black against the sky, wrought straight up and forged of glass and marked by myriad clouds of every sunset colour—flame, purple pink, green, violet and all the tints of gold. I wish we could stay in that place forever, on the beach painting landscapes just out of view. I wish we could forget the things that weren't right in front of us, framed by a mountain and a water and more of both. To imagine a world that doesn't exist—wouldn't that be Heaven? To live there, only in it, and not have to consider all of the everything and what that included, the everything? Life can be a series of disappointments if you let it. Dwell in the good, think of the good, it all of life outweighs. *Isn't it horrible,* said a voice said beside us.

The American journalist had been hired to write a travel piece on Biarritz and was hating every minute of it. *I suppose it's a punishment of some sort,* he said over dinner, his face strung dejectedly over a boiled egg in stewed oil, trying to dredge up enough saliva to swallow. *On my last assignment I was travelling among the Turks. People in America are fascinated by the primitiveness of it all, and they sent me with a photographer to bring back something new to impress people. Even our editor came along and one day outside yet another temple we found a genie in a bottle and he said—because there were three of us—that we could have one wish each. I naturally said I wanted to spend the rest of my life sailing the world, without a worry for money, as far as possible from those two! My photographer, taking my lead, said he wanted to live forever invisible in a sultan's harem. And the genie turned to our editor and asked him for his wish, and he said:* I want them both back before lunch. We have a deadline to meet!

The American was incredibly handsome and my brother was flattered that he would even talk to him and they ate many meals together and he hadn't felt anything like this for so long and one night found himself telling the incredibly handsome young journalist about Henri, saying this was the path, or as close as he could estimate, that our friend (he called him *my friend*, and not by name) had taken through the mountains on his way to Madrid and the Andalusia, to the mighty Alhambra, that confident Moslem rockpile amidst the desperate Gothic cries for attention that plagued the rest of Europe. Spain was where Henri had gone to renew himself before finally settling in Gibraltar, he said, to embrace Granada's glorious Islamic past. Only through contact with these things Henri had touched and seen could he truly make again sense of the world around him. Only then could he finish his *Cellini.*

And the American said: *Have you heard the story of Georg Cantor? He was a genius of mathematics, able to define infinity in a way that no one had previously. Beyond infinity, he said—if one were to add infinity to infinity, say—was an even larger infinity, and beyond that, adding even this larger infinity to itself, was an infinity still larger yet. Not only was there no end, but there was no end to the number of no ends. He devoted his entire life to this study of not ending. He travelled around the world and each time it brought him no closer. When he ate and the waiter asked if he was finished, he said: Hardly! He had a family he never saw. All he could see was his legacy. Then one day while he was delivering a special lecture in Leipzig, his youngest son fell ill and died. The boy had been frail as an infant but had grown into a strong youth and was always growing stronger. In another four days, he would have been thirteen, so loving, so amiable, everyone's favourite. Cantor had hoped, just as his father had hoped about him, that he might become a famous violinist. And he began to doubt all his life choices. He turned to drink, went to the bar, ordered another, and another, intending to drink himself to death. But the bar-*

keep put a hand on his shoulder, showed him the door, and said: Know your limits.

But what does it mean? my brother wanted to know.

All lives are finite, the American said. *Some are just more finite than others.*

Then one night, Camille was distracted by the moon, caught long on the surface of a curve at the room's far side. He questioned the staff and they brought it to their table, which gathered a crowd, and Camille knelt to the horn of it to listen and the journalist laughed and said: *Have you not heard of the phonograph?* The factory owner (whose name was Tudesq) fell on them with an unwanted story of finding one in Africa of all places, in the hut of some ragged chief. A ship of smugglers had run a nearby reef and abandoned an entire shipment of them and his men had brought them to him and the chief had no idea what he was listening to, nothing was identified at the beginning, the label long eaten by the fishes, nor would he have understood the words anyway, nor heard of Beethoven or even seen a violin, a flute, bassoon, the oboe, had no ability to even imagine what was making the noises that emerged from this magic ocean box. *But he knew Beauty,* he said, *and he spent every evening with one of his daughters rotating the crank with measured strokes until he fell asleep.* But Camille was not listening to him, only to the magic ocean box, to Beethoven's Romanze in F, which he thought less adventurous than his romance in G, to be sure, but also with a richer harmonic vocabulary than its successor. He also could not stop looking at the cylinder as it spun and it began to seem as though every note was simultaneous, that all of music was trapped in that thing and he wanted to either smash it or consume it. It was a joke, a novelty. It was a child's toy. And he scoffed: *Music is not a physical object in the world, to be turned and flipped and molested at whim. Music is magic. It exists in your heart, or in your head, but not your hands. It is not to be owned. It owns you.*

Oh, surely you don't mean it, the journalist replied. *The phonograph will surely spread beauty to edges of the Earth, where weak-*

limbed musicians will not venture. Right now music is an event. Music is in the now. When a performance is finished, he said, *either the shards of the music embed themselves in the listener, survive the experience of the end, or they don't. With this invention, there will be no need to remember. Can you imagine being able to find Beethoven's Ninth whenever you need it most?*

Camille, however, worried no one would ever hear it, that it would be filed away somewhere in a library unnoticed, and that it would create more forgetfulness, because people would no longer be working that muscle of retention, and music would cease to be one's sole focus. Because they could listen to these gramophones while doing the laundry or cleaning the house, they could listen with detachment. It would mean less to them. They would understand it less. Because it would disturb the balance of their minds. *Once you take a piece of music and own it, you destroy the magic. Endless repetition will turn it into a dead thing. Like a clock you've pried open to reveal the spinning wheels. And once music dies, we lose everything.*

Everyone was laughing now. And the factory owner said: *That's what the chief said!* And the journalist laughed again. And my brother began to feel uncomfortable around him, old.

Is it really so bad here? my brother asked one day.

Of course it is. But I'm being paid. What's your excuse?

I suppose I needed a change. It's nice to have something...new.

Something new? I would die for something new. That's the problem with most of Europe, really. Everything feels like it's been here forever. Like the world never gets any better. How do you do it?

He looked Camille up and down, as if noticing him for the first time. *Maybe I'll like it when I'm your age, too.*

We began taking long excursions into the mountains with the heiress, with whom Camille felt much less threatened. We planned eventually to scale them as Henri had, but they were also lovely in and of themselves, the lower paths strewn with all manner of vegetation and flying creatures, and my brother would return re-energized and approach the concierge and ask about this bird or plant or butterfly, and the concierge told us about the honeymoon of Napoleon III and Eugénie de Montijo: *The hotel was originally supposed to be the Imperial couple's summer home, a late wedding gift from husband to wife. After they married, he could see she was unhappy, that something was missing from her life after uprooting her from her home in Madrid. So he built this place so she could always be close to her Spanish roots. When it was complete, they renewed their vows, a ceremony nearly as big as the official wedding, and the Emperor, who often referred to Eugénie as his little butterfly, arranged to have butterflies brought in from every region of the globe for her. Every guest was to bring two butterflies. And when her blindfold was removed in front of the main entrance, everyone released their butterflies at once and she was surrounded in clouds of colours flapping.* Camille seemed entirely disinterested in the preamble, that somehow life was a story about people, and the concierge rushed to his point. *Over the years,* he said, *many of the species perished in their strange new surroundings, whether through inbreeding or competition over habitat. But many others were able to breed and flourish,* he said, *and every time the Empress returned for a visit, the descendants of the original butterflies would still coalesce around her, so that now the area has become well-known for them and a major destination for collectors.* He said: *The resort is proud to boast many of the most beautiful specimens in the world.* And my brother replied: *All butterflies are beautiful and ugly at the same time.*

But on another occasion Camille asked him: *Did they ever return?*

Who?

The Emperor and his wife. After the revolutionaries acquired the building and sold it as a hotel.

The concierge shrugged. He'd only been there for three seasons.

And my brother said: *Do you think she might have come under an alias, though? Napoleon has been dead for so long. And their son. You'd think she'd like to see the butterflies again. These butterflies. They're* hers, really. Her butterflies. Can you imagine owning such things? Two thousand kilometres away? What is the point of owning something you can't see? They might have all died and she'd never know. Or her son? Wouldn't she want him to see her butterflies? You'd think so. It's something about his mother he never would have known, could never have known, would never have even thought to ask unless she told him, and then, could he believe her without seeing it for himself? Could you? Wouldn't she have to bring him then?

I don't know.

...

I don't know.

The night the heiress embarrassed my brother at dinner, Camille found the journalist on his own in his gloom and the sand and commented: I suppose you're unlikely to say anything favourable about this place, and the American replied: Oh no, I'm loving it. I've never seen so many identical bits of jutting rock with plaques on them. It really has that going for it. And there's the market, you know, where you can easily exchange your money for something of far lesser value. And surely we must be setting a record for gathering the most people of low-to-average intelligence in one place.

What about the swimming?

No one swims here. The undertow is so fierce to carry away a child.

You're just trying to be funny.

I have stood by and let it happen more than once already!

But the resort is so popular.

Everything is relative. Most Europeans wouldn't know the difference. But when you have been to America and seen Newport, everything is spoiled. The real selling point of Biarritz is the view.

He swept his arm across the turbulent expanse of the Bay of Biscay where, had the sun shone through the cloud cover, we should have seen the coast of Spain, with the peaks of distant Sierras rising behind it.

Of course, the attraction is not always running. But on the moments that it is, it's the only place in France you can witness real beauty.

My brother turned back to the Pyrenees, said again we'd be

setting off shortly to follow Henri. He asked the journalist if he'd ever crossed them and the American said: *On foot? Like one of those pilgrims?!*

Preferably by wagon or mule, I suppose. Have you been?

Yes, of course. I've just come from there.

Could you offer any advice, then?

Yes. Don't go.

...

Or take the train. Better yet, take a steamer to Santander and skip them altogether.

But he took another glance at the small hatches of dots and lines on Camille's paper and asked: *Are you really a diamond merchant?*

Of course, my brother replied. *Why do you ask?*

You write your notes in that secret code. Is it a map to a treasure?

You could say so.

I knew it! The American smiled.

Am I part of your story? Camille asked.

But the American was no longer listening, had turned to stare at the mountains. *Are there diamonds up there? A treasure?*

I suppose so. Of a sort.

Then I'm going with you, he said. *It will be my revenge on France, to write instead about nearly being killed by men who have no idea their civil war is already over.*

Imagine my legacy, he said.

We asked around for a guide. One morning at breakfast we were approached by a dark man about the height of a fence post. Camille showed him some of Henri's sketches and the Spaniard said: *Yes, I know this place. We cannot reach it with a wagon, but we can still take it most of the way.*

What about the others?

He shrugged.

What if it rains?

He shrugged. *The way is hard*, he said.

What do you mean?

The roads are little better than mule paths. And there will be robbers. But Spaniards can also be obnoxious in other ways.

You mean we should fear for our lives? the American asked.

Only if you value that sort of thing.

Our guide did not look impressed that the American was coming along and insisted this would cost more. He looked at the American's trunk and said *that* would cost more, too. He wanted us to travel with no more than the clothes on our backs, and forward the most valuable parts of our luggage in advance by the *arrieros*. They could bypass the most frequented roads that way, he said, and travel faster and safer. He also suggested, however, that we carry a small surplus of hard dollars to satisfy thieves and bandits should we be assailed. Caballeros like them could not afford to scour the roads and risk the gallows for nothing, so it was mostly a courtesy, to show them we knew what they were risking. The American didn't trust him, either, but we agreed and slept our last night of comfort in Biarritz.

On the first day up there was grass, there was a rock, there was a rock and some grass; there was a tree, and another tree; there was a trail and a rock and beside the trail a rock. There was more grass. More trees. Few children were to be seen, and no dogs. Camille began to sweat almost immediately, uncontrollably. He kept leaning over his knees and wheezing. Two hours in, we stopped for our third break. Our guide took another look at the pool collecting under my brother, shook his head and suggested making camp. There was a makeshift camp. There was sleep. The second day was worse. Camille woke to find he could not bend at any joint. It took him nearly twenty minutes to stand. The day was also much hotter, made considerably worse by the fact there was no shade. There was no grass beside the path, and no trees. There was nothing but the sun's relentless assault. But my brother insisted he was fine to do it and less than an hour later he was curled up beside a rock about the size of a French horn so that his face could be in the shade for a moment. We made camp again. And our guide went back to the town to purchase two more mules and was back with them by dinner. On the third day, the American learned how to sleep in his saddle, and took every opportunity he could to do so. The mules were relentless, and we made fair progress. The vegetation changed abruptly every couple of hours, and each time it was like entering an entirely different world. By noon we had already travelled farther than we had the other two days previous. Camille still looked sickly though he said nothing. Our guide found a spring and we stopped to drink and found a hoard of displaced Sardinian toads. Perhaps they were Corsican. Also: a dead vulture. The American woke because we had stopped, stared down at the dead bird and said: *Are we at the first café already? I'm starving!* Our guide examined the corpse and searched for tracks. He sniffed at the ground. He said, *Perhaps a lynx.* And the American said: *Perhaps?!* There were no tracks, however, and no external wounds. And that night we hung our food from a tree and there was no sleep. We were now already above the flight path of the eagles, and on the fourth morning we drank our coffee and watched them soar in the eddies of the sunrise. An hour later we passed through some low clouds, and I could see how glad Camille was for the mist of rain, then less glad when it began to pour, rained fat water, fat water, then began to hail. Still, he seemed a new man, and we kept climbing. The temperature continued to drop. We came to the town and every home bore the coat of arms of some dead and forgotten aristocratic family. Every home seemed a grave, a stone, from the earth and destined for it. We expected to find no one. We expected to discover an entire population dead a century ago and we were simply the first to discover them. But as we tied up our mules, the villagers crept from their shadows to peer at us and they were even darker than the Spaniards in Biarritz—shorter, uglier. Our guide said nothing about the lynx, just hauled out Henri's sketches and said things we couldn't understand and one of the men drew a map in the dirt with a stick and he nodded and we moved on. We didn't even stay for the night. In a bed. The American said he had seen a bed. We just kept on searching, though we had stopped climbing and began moving more horizontally, which was something, following the ridge. The American and our guide grew increasingly irritated with one another, arguing over the most inconsequential things. At each village our guide would leave us on our mules in front of the posada, tied to posts so they wouldn't run away with us, enter with several packages and then come back with several others and the American would say: *He has no idea where he's taking us. He's just a postman earning some extra money for bringing us along!* The air grew excessively cold. And the next day our guide took us over a ridge where we could look down on a group of chamois goats picking their way across the feeble scree and it felt as though we had left the world, climbed to Heaven itself. He brought us to vague picturesque settings including a fantastic standing stone. Henri had painted several locations with these erratic stones, which were thought to have been placed there centuries ago by receding glaciers, and when we first saw one, Camille immediately dropped from his mule, dumped the entire contents of his satchel on the ground, and held one of Henri's photographs against the sky as though he were placing the final puzzle piece of the world. *This is it,* he smiled. *This is it!* This was where our dear Henri had stood almost two decades earlier, in this exact spot, adjusting the legs of this tripod in this exact spot to leave us this clue. We marvelled at it, my brother and I. The Spaniard allowed himself a moment of accomplishment. He had earned his pay. But then the American moved behind us to get a better look and said: *That could be any rock!* And of course he was right. They were everywhere. From that point, we saw one almost every day. And everywhere they were the same. Our guide had a story for each of them. Our guide would say: *This is where they gathered the people of Sara after they abandoned their village rather than fight the French Revolutionary Army and burned them alive.* And: *This was the cliff where they threw the bodies of the Basque witches in the Inquisition.* At last the American fell on his back and said: *Oh, clearly he's making it up!* And when our guide assured us, the American said: *But why would you ever fight over land so wet and so cold? It's like fighting over a soddened rug!* And every day we seemed to find another dead vulture. I was amazed that so many things could die on their own like that, without any help at all. One day we were standing around a free-standing rock the size of an omnibus, and our guide was saying: *One day, long ago, a luminous cloud appeared in the East.* And he said something that sounded like *Gentiles,* though it was admittedly difficult to tell, and the American said: *The non-Jews, you mean? How long ago could it have been?* But our guide ignored him and continued: *The Gentiles were frightened of the cloud and asked an old Basque man what it meant. He said:* Christ has come. It is the end of our era. Throw me down a precipice. *Which they did. But it did nothing to calm them. They were, by nature, worriers, always fretting about everything. The cloud continued to follow them. They stopped seeing the sun. Their crops refused to grow. And they became so frightened by this coming of this thing called Christ, whoever he might be, that they gathered the strength to rip this stone from the mountains, then hid themselves beneath it. And they hid beneath it so long they became so weak from hunger they couldn't get out and they died.* It became increasingly clear that our plan to match Henri's sketches and photographs to physical landmarks—a repetition of the same images of rock, wood, and water—was an impossible task. When placed against everything Henri had rendered so grand and vast and sublime on paper, could it ever exist? It had been much simpler to match them to the world of our own imagining. Our guide tried to reassure us. He said the other side of the mountains was like a different world. There, perhaps there, we would find more verifiable trace of our friend. But it only became colder. Everything seemed to slow. We seemed to exist outside of time, stuck in an incessant now. One day I was sure that, so long as we remained there, the sun would never set or rise again, and I saw no indication otherwise. We stopped again. Our guide said: *This is where the Basques routed the forces of Charlemagne, massacring Roland and every other member of the French rearguard.* And it was so cold and it had been raining all day and there was an open-air church with an outcropping that could shelter us for the night, used by Santiago di Compostela pilgrims, according to our guide, and the American moaned: *Oh God, oh sweet, sweet Jesus God, can we please stay here tonight?* Our guide felt this was not respectful. *The next town is not far from here,* he said. But the American insisted, said he couldn't spend another night soaking wet with his ass peeling wet and he began to unroll his pack and our guide reiterated the sanctity of the site but the American was already strewing his wet things across the altar to dry and Camille was also so wet, so wet, could we, maybe? Could we? Maybe? In the end, our guide slept outside in the rain. And for once Camille and the American were alone again, though so tired they didn't even speak, like they used to, only stripped down and huddled together for warmth and grew drowsy and poor and stretched long and tense and let their breath fall and let arms fall and my brother rolled over and stretched long again and took the American's cock in his mouth and stroked him briskly and the American rose up and spread himself on the altar and waited and the next day our guide spoke very little, the next morning our guide was already waiting for us at the mules, as though he had stood there all night, and he spoke very little. The American was overly friendly. And our guide was not, spoke very little, until we reached the next village and we were amazed at how close the village actually was and our guide said: *Wait here.* And he left us and entered a small inn. He was gone for so long. And occasionally some other man would exit the inn and stare at us from the steps and say nothing, and then another man would exit and there was a whole lot of saying nothing, and exiting, and the American began to grow impatient and eventually walked up to the inn and began to shout. I've never seen so many men, so many men exiting a building so small, all to come and stare and say nothing, and I wished we hadn't sent Gabriel back to Paris and finally our guide was back and I wondered what he had been saying in there this whole time and the other man gathered behind him like a long flowing robe and then we were leaving. Just like any other town. At the next village it was the American who disappeared. And after an hour of waiting, our guide suggested we leave without him. He began to pack everything up and was clearly swearing though we didn't know the words, and he began to untie the mules and suddenly the American appeared, his jacket wrapped tightly around his left arm, his right hand pressed to his thigh and holding a knife that was rusted and awkward. *It may look unimpressive,* the American said. *But once you've held one in your hands... The Mexicans back home carry knives for show, knives huge and curved and clearly designed to intimidate instead of injure. These people carry only what's needed. There is no show, no fear. Only the pain.* It made a loud snick as it opened, and he nearly dropped it, waving his fingers in the air in pain. *It doesn't need to look pretty to work,* he said. *To cut. To disembowel.* He crossed his arms in front of him, up near his chin, the knife in his left hand with the blade threatening down and away. Our guide made to snatch it from him, but the American seemed to anticipate it and brought the arm with the jacket up to block him. *Never strike,* he said to the guide, *until you are sure of your blow.* He released the guide and began to shuffle like a boxer. *Also, you must look here when you strike there. Hah! And spring when you have cut. Ho!* Our guide turned his back and began checking the ropes on the mules: *Are you hoping to get yourself killed? Maybe,* said the American. *Put it away,* said our guide. But the American swung it through the air several more times before closing it with the same snick. *Aim for the breast.* He jabbed. *Or the groin.* Jab, jab. *The key is deception. The mislead. It's how you know these people aren't trustworthy, by how they fight. In America we pack our rifles with as much debris as we can and point toward our adversary and there is no doubting our intent.* That day we saw two more dead vultures. There were still no wounds. *Perhaps,* the American said, *the lynx is just so big it scares them to death.* And the next day, instead of letting our guide ask the next farmer about Henri's drawings again, the American immediately jumped in and said: *Have you seen a cat the size of a house?* The farmer's eyes narrowed, and the American repeated what he had said, only slower, then threw up his arms and turned to our guide and said: *What's Spanish for* lynx? *El catto? El catto!* But it was the farmer himself who said: *Lince. That is the word. But not the problem.* They had had a lynx problem, once upon a time, maybe twenty years ago. But now the lynx problem was under control. Besides, the lynx did not eat vultures. If anything, it was the opposite. The vultures were killed, he claimed, by the Tartalo. *What's a Tartalo?* the American asked. *It sounds like an Italian dessert.* And the

239

farmer told us about the caves. We'd seen one or two higher up but never thought twice about them. *Once, they provided refuge to humans. During the Time of Ice. Now they are being used by the Tartalo as a base while he hunts our livestock.* The American laughed softly, but seemed more excited than we had yet seen him. *A monster?* he said. *A real monster?* Apparently. The Tartalo was a giant, and had only one eye. One day two brothers were travelling the mountains and ran adrift a storm. They hid in a cave to wait it out and this was the cave of the Tartalo and when the Tartalo returned he found the two brothers and he ate the elder because he was starving but when he saw how sad the younger boy was, he tried to console him and gave him his ring. *I am so sorry,* he said. *I was starving. It has been such a difficult winter. I wasn't thinking.* And the surviving brother found pity in the beast and stayed with him for a time and cooked his meals and tended his house and his goats and then began to realize he was not a guest but a prisoner and he waited for the monster to let down his guard and he stabbed the monster through the eye and ran and, blinded, the monster followed. It was impossible to outrun him. He was a giant. So the boy hid behind a tree and the Tartalo ran past him and he thought: *I've done it! I've really managed to live through something I never thought possible. I never imagined seeing my family again. I never imagined swimming in the ocean again. I never imagined being able to make my own choices. But now I can.* But of course he couldn't. And suddenly the ring on the boy's finger began to shout: *Here I am! Here I am!* And the Tartalo followed the sound of the ring. The boy couldn't get it off. And the Tartalo was catching up. So the young boy found a rock and struck at his hand, over and over, until the finger with the ring became dislodged. And he took his finger and tossed it with the ring from the cliff, and the Tartalo appeared around the bend and went right past him over the edge, following the sound of the ring below.

You seem skeptical, the farmer finished.

No... the American said, *it's just...why didn't the ring warn him?*

240

Perhaps it also wanted to be free.
But two minutes before, it was calling for him.
To be the slave of one man is the same as being the slave of another.
That's not true.
Perhaps it just wanted to make sure they would always be together.
Our guide scoffed, but the farmer insisted. He had seen the Tartalo himself. Had we noticed there were no wounds on the birds? Could a lynx kill them without wounds? Without eating them? Did we think any creature killed purely for fun? No, the birds had no wounds because the Tartalo did not eat their bodies, just their souls. The Tartalo fed on death, fed on those who fed on the death. The vultures were useful as tools because they allowed the Tartalo to rise to the air and scan his domain. He used them as his eyes and ears, entered their bodies with his spirit, and then, when he was done with them, they would just fall down dead from the shock. It was how he avoided their guns and devoured their stock. Our guide said it was nothing but superstition, a story to frighten children. The American insisted we go see. The American said to my brother: *Did you know they say Basque was the language spoken in the Garden of Eden? Just think of all the monsters Christianity has created. How can it not be true?* Our guide insisted we move on, and the American waved his arm at him and said: *This idiot has no idea where he's even going! At the very least we'd have a proper destination!* And the tension between the American and our guide continued to grow, and the American made a big show of sharpening his knife every morning while our guide prepared breakfast. The more we looked at Henri's sketches, the more it seemed as though there were figures hiding within the images that we could not see, either the grotesque shapes of bandits, ready to start upon the traveller such as ourselves, or a friar rolled up in his garments, like a supernatural messenger of evil. I began to worry about the Tartalo. I began to imagine that giant, one-eyed monster behind every bend, that he was following me and had perhaps always followed me, was just getting closer now.

And one evening we camped by a small river and the American spotted a family of otters entering a hole in a stump. This, he felt, was his big chance. *You shall see,* he said. And he wound his knife to a stick and poised himself astride the hole and had my brother beat a rhythm against the hollowness and the terrified creatures made to their escape and the American threw his entire weight into it to pin one against the bottom. He had done such a poor job fashioning his homemade spear that the blade swung sideways, and the end was too blunt to puncture the otter's fur. The otter surged out of the water and stood for a moment upright. Time stood still. The American swatted at it with the flat edge twice, three times in that period, the creature staring at us like a patient Christ, and he thrust once more, the blade breaking completely from its bond this time, lost down the river, but the American's weight was still enough to keep the creature fast against the riverbed, and it squirmed and doubled frantically near five minutes until it finally drowned. The American retrieved his pole cautiously, victory growing. But the otter remained on the bottom, its lungs now full of water, and he had to strip out of his shirt and trousers to fish it out. In the water he had estimated its weight at thirty pounds but now saw it was closer to seventy. Our guide would have none of it. So the American used the same pole as a spit and built a fire to cook his kill, hanging his clothes around it to dry, until the pole burned clear through and the American howled as his catch and covers lurched into the pit and up in flames. That night it began to snow. And it snowed. And we were stuck there for three more days because the next pass was deemed unsafe for the mules in such weather. Because the American's clothes had burned in the fire and because my brother was considerably larger in build, he was forced to borrow from our guide. He complained about the feel, the smell. He said to us, softly: *What will we do now that I've lost my knife?* Camille and I climbed alone to see what we could, if there was any end to the storm, but the clouds had descended around us and it was impossible to see terribly far. We kept looking for shelter and we found one of the caves that the farmer had told us about. Camille shouted into it, to see how far it went, but the echo came back garbled, out of order, like motifs on what he had said, in a different register and in a different language. And for three days we stood there at the mouth of the cave with our bodies pressed against one another because that's where the fire was so we wouldn't suffocate and watched the snow fall and the night. And eventually we all fell asleep and I dreamed that the Tartalo called me away from the others, deeper into the cave, to an underground river that tasted so sweet and yet stank of oil and urine. He had no desire to hurt me, he said. *We are not different,* he said. Could I bring him the others, though? Could I convince the others to come this way, so we could share them, perhaps? And he gave me a ring, as a show of friendship. And when I woke the next day there were no dead vultures but a dead lynx. And the snow had turned to rain again. And the snow melted away. And our guide had disappeared. And he had taken the mules.

The sky cleared and we headed back down, our sunk boots deep in the damp damp and everything smelling like rotten and we never saw another snowflake nor a tree nor blade of grass. The goats had grazed the bluff to ground, hungered hard against the mountains, chewed the soil to gristle, nuzzled their teeth to the bare until there was nothing left of seed nor sapling, the soil carried away by the melting banks, a desert of mud. We no longer had our mules, no longer had any food, no way to procure more and no idea where we were going but assumed, so long as we continued downhill, we would eventually reach a town or village, a road, somewhere; and eventually there was grass again and then small trees and a forest of pine and box and ilex and the view as we crested the next ridge was magnificent. The heavy clouds that hid the mountaintops cleared away. The whole line of the Pyrenees stretched thin behind us, while to the south lay a rugged ocean of sierras and forests and here and there a glimpse of Aragon and the fertile valleys of Navarre. It was an illumined abyss, and there were chimneys that smoked, and we took a short rest and off our shirts and bathed in the river and pressed our bare feet to moss and laughed because we were not dead.

It seemed everywhere there was a palace; not just build-ings, but every man, a palace; every stone, a palace. Palaces of the soul. Of antiquity. Palaces of the now. It was wonder-ful. And as we descended on Pamplona, followed the har-vests downhill and entered Aragon, the road became wide and smooth enough for wagons. We convinced one of them to take us as far as Huesca, and our driver was easily the best shouter of them all; we crossed the river by ferry and for the entire trip he carried on conversations with men on both sides with ease.

Huesca was built on the crest of a hill surrounded by a fortress that had once boasted ninety-nine towers but now only two. Imagine a fabulous paper cut-out, designed to capture the silhouette of a fantastic city of legends; then imagine pulling it out of a bag after carrying it around with you for several months and you should have the idea. Everywhere was the Aragon coat of arms, with four red lines to represent the bloody streaks left in battle upon the shield of a wounded king. The people were gorgeous and happy. And when they saw we were hungry they offered us work and when they saw we were tired they offered us a spot in a barn or a tent or sometimes in their homes and never asked questions. We spent a good three weeks there harvesting peaches then cherries then almonds then grapes and we ate communally and Camille's back ached for the first week or so, but it felt so good to work with his hands again, to earn his blisters, and he grew used to it. It certainly did wonders for his insomnia. It also felt good to be part of a group, and to feel close to Henri again, to imagine that he had experienced similar, in search of his own authentic truth. After a day in the fields, we would retire to our tents and listen to them sing their traditional songs, an oral tradition of passing down their collective histories, and we were so glad we couldn't understand a word of it. The most interesting of their instruments was the alboka, which was similar to a pair of joined clarinets, with a hollowed animal horn surrounding the single reed that allowed for the most spectacular circular breathing. We loved to listen to them improvise around the fires at night, the melodies and rhythms full of savagery, and Camille was overjoyed when one of them tried to teach him how to work it. It was like a hive of bees in his mouth, shook his teeth near loose of his jaw, and they all laughed at his attempts to maintain the continuous drone. Even the youngest child seemed able to do it. Camille laughed, too, and reached for the tiny imps and they scattered laughing all the more. We helped to tend the goats, and the pigs, and during the next descending moon they tried to teach my brother to help with the slaughter. The way the organs spilled out was too beautiful for Camille, the colours so vibrant. Humans are much darker inside, most already starting to die by adulthood, while livestock are just beginning as they're killed, so young. Their organs practically bloom out, while a person merely spills. As the pig was bleeding out, the woman drew a cross on its shoulder and rubbed its flesh with garlic and Camille swore he would never eat another piece of meat again.

If only the American could have been as happy. One day during our communal meal an older gentleman with the stubble of a white beard spoke to us in broken French and told us he had also once lived in Holland, when they had needed more men to work the harvests. He had travelled there with his new wife, who had also found work cleaning homes.

How was it?

What do you say?

How did you enjoy your time in Holland?

I was happy in that place, he said. *But eventually they told me my wife could not stay, that she was a distraction to the Dutch men, and so we returned.*

A distraction? the American laughed, finally interested.

It was thought our women might steal a Dutch man and marry him instead and stay forever. Of course, my wife was worried about the opposite, that I might be lured away by a blond beauty, else I might have stayed for some time without her and sent my wages back.

The American asked if the old man had ever seen a lynx. Or a Tartufo. The old man blinked silently.

Another day we were seated opposite a younger man clothed in dusty brown linen with a demoralized-looking knapsack and a gun of a similar composure. On his breast was a worsted heart, emblem of the sacred heart of Jesus, and on his head he wore the white cap of the country, a symbol we could only imagine represented the snow atop the mountains. On the hat was

246

embroidered, in gold lettering: *God, King, and Country.* He said
nothing, did nothing, simply stared off to the horizon as though
he expected us to be overrun at any moment. I wondered if
he might be one of the separatist rebels we'd heard of. A Na-
tionalist. The American offered him some of our cognac, and
he refused it, perhaps assuming we were Spanish, or at least
sympathetic. Eventually we were brought omelettes made with
bell peppers and potatoes and sausage and the American wrote
on a napkin, in English, *I'll bet we paid for his.* And my brother
didn't really seem to understand, which made the American
even more upset and we ate the omelettes slowly and watched
the young rebel pick his teeth with his knife and occasionally
the young man would look at the American confusedly, unsure
why he was being stared at, and then he would turn his back to
us. *What is it about the Spanish you don't like?* the American finally
asked him. *They think this land is their land,* the young man said.
*If we do not isolate ourselves from them, it will not be possible to work
toward the Glory of God.*

You think the Spanish are Godless?

Oh, yes. Don't you?

Have you killed many Republicans, then?

And he stopped eating his omelette for a moment, his head
listed to one side and he replied, in perfect English: *I killed four
maketos yesterday.*

I don't believe it, the American said.

And the young soldier looked at Camille and said: *I could show
you, if you'd like to volunteer to be next.*

You're a coward, the American said, insulted. *You are a moral
contagion,* he said. And the young soldier said: *They talk about
peace, the Spanish. They want to bring peace, they say. But it is only
because they think we do not play by their rules, because they are terrified
that old women and children might drive them out with stones. Those
people who love peace!*

When will you stop, though? What is enough?

We will continue until every Basque is free.

Then in Zaragoza we finally attended the Plaza de Toros, the most eagerly watched theatre of boredom I had ever seen. At first it was like they were taking the animal out for exercise, trotting it around the ring for what seemed like an eternity. This was our favourite part. But of course they couldn't just let the poor creature be. They had to torment it and tease it and poke it with sticks and wave coloured cloths. We found ourselves secretly rooting for the beast, though to do what we weren't sure. What could mark victory for the bull in this situation? To find some shade? A space to lie down? The American asked a man behind us when things would start, and the Spaniard spoke slowly to us like we were imbeciles: *It's happening right now, of course! This is the most important part!* We looked back but could see nothing but the bull rooting at the dirt, as if searching for something it had lost earlier. Did they hide food for it beneath the floor of the arena? Was that it? The American cheered it on and received multiple scowls from our neighbours. *I get it now*, the American said. *It's like baseball. Grown men performing the same motions, over and over, with long breaks in between. Everyone stands around for hours, hoping something will happen, but of course it never does.* Our immediate neighbour, who'd spoken earlier, said: *There's a complicated strategy. Once you understand it, the whole world is opened to you. Originally they used to put a man into the ring with the animal and see if he could outlast it, to see who could emerge in a battle of species. It was so pointlessly brutish. All it demonstrated was the combatant's lack of real superiority, that we are dominant not because of our intellect but merely because of our physical strength. The key now is not in killing the bull, but in outsmarting it.* And he laid it all out for us, how in the first stage the matadors merely observed, whether the beast charged like a cat or like a dove, head up or chest out, its favourite locations in the rings, where it felt safest, its tendency to throw its horns and in which direction. They were mapping its reactions, how it responded to repeated stimuli. *With this one*, he said, gesturing at the bull as he wandered aimlessly around the ring, *his movements are easily predictable. They already know to approach from the left, for example. They know the patterns of its steps. They know how to please and how to anger. But there is so much more to learn. Sometimes a bull will keep returning to the same spots, no matter what is happening around him. You see how he lingers near the barrel closest to the gates? This is important.* This continued, however, for what seemed like hours. It felt like it must be over, or not yet begun, either way. And either way, no one seemed to care, and the intensity of their not caring was unflinching. *Now,* our instructor said, *come the picadores. They use what they've learned in the first round to truly master the animal.* And they ran up to it when they knew it was safely distracted and stuck it repeatedly with sharpened poles, these great Spanish heroes, and our bull—for we had begun to think of him as ours now, we knew so much about him—stumbled at them, trying to figure out what was happening to him and our instructor said: *You see? Exactly as planned.* And the American said: *It gets angry, you mean?* And this continued for what seemed like another eternity, while we ordered more of that horrible wine and had it brought to us and the heroes ran their poles again, either to see what the bull would do or prove they knew what it would do and made it to bleed so much that the ground was red with it, and it staggered, and it fell, and I looked around to see if—now—we might leave, but *still* it wasn't over, our instructor practically vibrating at this point, with yet another hero entering the ring, this one on horseback, to perform the last effortless stabs, piercing the bull in the back of the head, so that the blade ran through the back of its neck and presumably severed something important and the pathetic beast crashed to the dust and it was finished.

Thankfully someone made a miscalculation or the whole afternoon would have been lost. Other men were dispatched to clean up the ring, to drag the body from the field of combat, but the bull was not as dead as they thought, had not given itself over to defeat as they thought. And rather than stay down and allow itself to be removed with its remaining dignity, the great thing reared suddenly and scattered the cleaners and went directly after the mounted hero, as though he had spent all that time working out who was the ringleader, who was busy accepting his roses. The crowd gasped, leaned forward. This was apparently what they'd all been waiting for. And the bull ignored the waving arms of the clowns and lesser matadors and the athlete on the horse was thrown and collapsed to the dirt, though his horse definitely got the worst of it, one of the bull's horns penetrating her bowels, lifting her from the ground and carrying her around the ring. There was blood on the bull's face and the ground and in his eyes. He felt victorious, not realizing that most of the blood he saw was his own, went after all the bullfighters, but was already too weak to mount a proper threat. They taunted him from atop the walls where he could not reach them. Then one of them remembered the horse. She had been galloping hopelessly around the ring for several minutes, dragging her bowels. The matador mounted her and kicked her close to the wound and she took off back into the melee, almost excited. The bull turned and was successful again at taking her down. But it seemed one last ruse, the bullfighter leaping to safety while the bull stuck the mare over and over again with his horns and became so distracted from goring her that he didn't notice the men with lances all around him. Eventually, one of them thrust his sword back into the creature's forehead and, the greatest injustice of all, the brave beast was dragged away by mules.

Gathering his things to leave, the American leaned into us and said: *If only they could agree on government as much as they do on violence, this whole civil war thing would have been over a long time ago.* But apparently things were just beginning, as the gates from the pens opened a second time and it started all over again. The second bull seemed unwilling to fight, merely tossed his head and pawed the ground. He believed in peace, clearly, or found the whole process beneath him, these insects trying to get under his skin. The crowd grew irate and began pelting the animal with stones because it would not be angered. It didn't matter. Angry or not, eventually it met the same ending, only this time when the *espada* ran his sword into the poor thing's skull, he somehow managed to miss anything important, at least the brain, and the creature shook it out, spraying blood in all directions. Annoyed, the hero tried again, with similarly tragic results, and a second man was dispatched to slice the bull's hind tendons with a sickle so that it fell helpless to the ground and could be dispatched with a knife. Thus ended the second bull. The third was as game as the first, the fourth as naive as the second, the fifth not unlike the first and third, and by that point it had become too much like one of Auber's operas to remain.

We approached Madrid and spied sudden the Escorial. There was grass, and rocks as before, another set of train tracks, and then a massive box sprung unheralded from the earth, built seemingly for no better reason than incongruity, a parody of humanity. *Can you believe*, the American said, *that this is the nation that once ruled the world? It's like their main talent is knowing where they aren't wanted and embedding themselves wholly.* The architect had apparently studied with Michelangelo in Italy and returned only with the ostentation and none of the beauty. We paid a pittance for a tour, and our guide bragged the great building contained four thousand rooms, nearly three thousand windows, more than a thousand doors, sixteen courtyards, eighty-eight fountains, a near infinite number of hexagonal galleries, and nearly two hundred kilometres of corridor. The body of every important Spaniard was there, he said, like it was some sort of library of death, or a history of the world not with words and metaphor but by physically taking things and putting them in the ground. *No wonder the Spanish are so humourless*, the American said. *Some of them probably aren't even dead, they just got lost in the corridors and still can't find their way out.* And when we'd finally escaped for the rest of the city: *How is it possible these people even managed to find their own coast, let alone the ones to whom America owes its discovery?*

If the Escorial were merely a mistake, however, out of place in the beauty of nature, Madrid was a monstrous evil inflicted on the world on purpose, a city designed to make everyone miserable, where no one wanted to live. As we were entering, everyone else was leaving—for the country, ostensibly, although really this meant heading back to the Escorial to reconnect with their misguided sense of history. We made our way through the welcoming regiment of beggars in their holiday dirt, so helpful, always ready to help you, to do things that didn't need doing, to hold the horses we'd already abandoned, to open doors that did not need to be opened. A woman with a holiday baby told us she was praying for all the beautiful people, and that she wanted us to know we were in her thoughts. Everyone was dressed in black, every last one of them, entirely joyless, as though Goya had just been painting negatives for real life. Even their newspapers were full of nothing but child abductions and bullfights. Luckily there was some sort of carnival going on, and everyone wore a mask because even when they danced it seemed of duty, even when they laughed. As we walked down the main street to our hotel, we were confronted by the sound of a bell, the last sacrament of some dying man, I suppose, and immediately everyone went to one knee in their camel heads, monkey faces, devil tails. I imagined them making love in tangles of purpose, striving for procreation. We parked ourselves at a café and had a coffee and a wine, although it was difficult to tell which was which. *Even the water is watered down,* said the American. And yet it was our first real breakfast in ages, so even his disdain was weaker. Then we paid a visit to the Museo del Prado and felt mostly bad for Velázquez because, as a result of his incomparable talents, he had been punished with a lifetime of painting the ugliest men and women Spain had to offer.

The American left us and we continued by rail to Toledo, which was surrounded for some reason by two walls, though perhaps the second was to also keep anyone from leaving— then, on to Cordova, which was a little out of our way but it didn't matter anymore, we were now just tourists in the dreams of an ex-lover. Everything was charred and ruined, as though time stood still while civilization elsewhere was busy advancing. It was hard to believe Cordova had once been the largest city in the Western world, that this was just one more lie we had been told, a fable, like the idea that there were even forty thousand people here now, unless they were ghosts. We saw barely five, and they were less impressive than Italians. The only thing it had over Toledo was that we heard less guitar, and we left in the night.

As we approached the walls of Granada the day was hot, without a cloud, so we stepped into the shade of an olive grove and were lulled to sleep by the humming of the bees and ring dove broods and rolling otters. We woke full of hope, however, and pressed through the aloe hedges, the Indian figs, more olives, and the houses sprang from the earth and it was as though we had passed into a genuine Arabian story, another chamber and another dream, hall opening out of hall, dome after dome, stair beyond stair, with slender pillars and heart-shaped arches and panels of lace work wrought in stucco and niches with painted and gilded stalactites; there were invented inscriptions from a magical book like the Koran, in letters borrowing from Cufic characters mingled with flowers and overlaid *azulejos*; there were tall vases in which grew rare flowers and all the fairy marvels of the East; there was a great archway with cedar gates forming complicated symmetries, and a broad stair of white marble, laved by the water of a far-off stream, a gilded galley with quaint prow and poop, striped carpets and draperies dipped in currants, surely brought to the foot of the steps by tributary chiefs, and vassals from the outer colonies dressed in brilliant armour, starred with rubies and turquoises. Everything was draped in velvet, brocade, silks and fine white woollens, coffers inlaid with mother-of-pearl, perfume burners in filigree work, cups spilling with dinars and *tomaums*, silver vases, jasper ewers, dishes of Balearic earthenware, iridescent with all the colours of the rainbow, colours the eye was not yet trained to see, floods of stuffs, embroidered, striated, laminated with gold or silver wire, saddles and harness bossy with gold, quantities of weapons more precious than gems, prisoners and captives of every race undraped, flowers that would make the nightingale unfaithful to the rose, pigeons, their necks wrung in graceful spirals, disembowelled gazelles gazing with wide-eyed amazement, the total compass of the richest civilization and the keenest cruelty coexisting in titanic, frightful splendour. We reached the Oriental gates of the palace itself. *The doors open,* Henri had written to us, *on a gallery whose steps are bathed by a lake on whose edge the palace is built. A palace not surrounded by water is no palace for me.* But of course there was no such water here, no lake, no urn-poured rivers from thick-armed slaves. It was like a stage set, the walls high but fragile, like an egg wrapped in golden foil; no great Moslem horde, just a handful of super-annuated vagrants playing dress-up, dozing on a stone bench, and a fourth lounging in the sunshine and gossiping with a fifth, an ancient sentinel who, when we approached him and asked if he knew the palace said: *Ninguno más; pues, Señor, soy hijo de la Alhambra.* I am a son of the Alhambra. It was ridiculous to think about and still we stayed, knowing none of it was real, spent an entire week just staring at the honeycomb ceiling Henri had used for the background of *Execution Without Hearing.* Another day we happened upon the columned doorway he'd endlessly repeated to create his hall of great stilted arches, fading off to a vanishing point that existed far off the canvas. He had been such a collector of details, our sweet Henri, gathering them into an enormous puzzle mixed with a scavenger hunt that, when—or, more likely, if—complete, would capture life so utterly. Sadly, most of these had been lost with his death, would remain without match in a forgotten alcove of his mind. And only occasionally, between inscriptions from the Quran that our guide would point out, reading *There is no conqueror but God* or *God alone the conqueror,* etc., etc., would we see how two pieces could be combined in a way that took on a greater significance than either would have had on their own, then a third, and a fourth, a rational process combined with an irrational one, thrusting forward in a double harness.

We continued to Bobadilla, another 125 kilometres by wagon, then boarded a train bound from Córdoba to Málaga and met up again with Gabriel, who had travelled by ship with our bags from Marseille, then at last for Gibraltar, crossing the last part on horseback with a pair of men who were scouting the area for the railroad in hopes of extending it as far as Algeciras. They were British, with dress identical, and names of Lewis and Fry. All they could talk about was distance, these men. That was all that mattered to their French employers. That was the measure of their success. The goal was to own the most rail line in the country, and since the first part of the contest was already over, the land already divvied up by government contracts, the key was to wedge in as much track as possible, as though even adding another metre to the line was akin to scaling Everest. They worked tirelessly on a succession of maps, each with a different potential route: along the coast, weaving in and out of the Bermeja Royals, as far north as Ronda. *My real dream*, one of them said (either Lewis or Fry), *is to secure the land in Málaga near the marina, where the ferries arrive from Morocco. If we built the station there instead of near the Plaza de la Misericordia, we could add nearly a kilometre and a half. If we could make it past the Castillo de Gibralfaro, we could add another one point eight. If we could encourage growth in El Palo...* He whistled.

Then you're just helping the Rothschilds add to their coastal line to Barcelona, said the other (either Fry or Lewis), chuckling smugly.

That's never happening and you know it.

They surveyed the land to distraction, for the most spectacular views, unknown towns, places they could start unknown towns. They redrew their maps at different scales and found that, even with the slightest adjustments, adding a fraction of a fraction of a degree to the path, they could add kilometres of distance and no one would ever notice. They could double the curve, introduce one every metre; triple, every centimetre; there was no limit.

One day Camille asked: *Don't people want to get where they're going faster?*

Do they? said Lewis or Fry. They were convinced that the work they were doing was of the utmost importance, that this was not just the introduction of a people to a new destination but an evolution of humanity on the scale of discovering America. They talked about the world like it had once been a piece of paper folded a million times, and each time it was unfolded again we learned about it and ourselves. Knowledge was life. The outer world was just an extension of the inner one. *Imagine,* one of them said, *when this route is finally open, what it will mean for the world. Did you know the Romans referred to Gibraltar as one of the Pillars of Hercules? They thought it was the westernmost limit of the world, the place where Hercules turned around. Some force in their minds prevented them from moving beyond it, from even entertaining the idea that there was anything more in the world. They even marked it with a plaque that said,* Non Plus Ultra. *Nothing beyond here. Imagine a whole strain of people who were just content to stop. Or was it something that protected them until they were ready? Perhaps there really were monsters out there. And we just needed time for them to die off.* If they happened to make a profit off that, wasn't that just progress?

We saw the city of Gibraltar long before we reached the gates, breaching the sands that surrounded it like an island, not like the Escorial or the Alhambra but something that was meant to be there, a giant mountain ridge cut down the middle by a monstrous sword, entirely unpopulated by nature except for a colony of apes in the city's centre. Nothing grew anywhere near it, not an animal, just some half-grown dwarf palms, and

257

I half expected to find the city empty, too, that the entire population had passed or departed, given up; but of course it was the opposite and after the guards were made satisfied with our nationality (Lewis and Fry effectively waved at the men and Camille decided it prudent to drop the Sannois facade and present our official papers), we were greeted by street upon street of British-looking shops with Spanish proprietors, were passed through a commercial building with a narrow library to an open-air market infested with sailors of every nation, a post-nation populated by Spain's swarthy children, male Andalusians with their little, round, velvet hats and embroidered jackets, female Andalusians with their mantillas and brilliant eyes, but also statuesque African witches in their red cloth and black velvet seams, the beautiful barbarian men of Tangier and Fez, in their wide golden garments and turbans, the Bernous drifting in their mists of white, an African Jew who had somewhere somehow managed to secure a Zouave military jacket, and a monotony of other Europeans besides, bargaining over old bedsteads, rickety tables and chairs, dilapidated birdcages, second-hand food. There was an additional market, specifically for fish, but we were told it was closed indefinitely because of a wreck in the harbour, a genuine tragedy, with weeping and storytelling, and they were waiting for the sea life to finish picking over the unrecovered corpses and duly process them before casting more nets, because it felt too much like cannibalism. Of course, the ones who stood out were the British, who were largely soldiers or politicians or both, stout, with their stout soldiers' women, the shrill cries of the other Spanish towns replaced by the guns and drums and fife and tramp, tramp, tramp of the marching soldiers. It was as if they were sharks and might suffocate if they ever stopped moving. For an hour we watched their impressive manoeuvres and athletic exercises, even managed to sit through a particularly ghastly rendition of "God Save the Queen" performed on brass with a lead of four Highland pipes. They were so handsome, young, and it seemed a shame that all this effort was put into such a group of specimens only to have them kill other men of similar beauty. As Camille well knew, war kills the best of us, and afterward we are left only with members of the species that were too weak to take part.

The Main Guard was just a plain building with a view of the yard and a portico filled with moulding furniture on which one or two soldiers would typically sit and smoke while they surveilled the street, hardly the secure military post we'd imagined from Henri's letters but more of a local jail, filled with drunks and belligerents and those lovers and excitement seekers unfortunate enough to be caught out after dark without a permit. This sentry duty seemed largely unnecessary, as their temporary residents were neither high-risk nor likely to be sprung by comrades in arms. There was no reason for an outside attack. And yet, there was rarely a time that we did not observe them there.

Camille had expected, once he'd told them his story, to be greeted by the members of the Guard with open arms, as a brother. Henri's letters had spoken of their immense hospitality and the general camaraderie of the unit, and my brother longed to share in that, to be brought inside and treated, not as any visitor, not even as himself, but as a friend of Henri, to drink and laugh and be reminded of the parts of Henri he'd either forgotten or never knew. He also hoped to see the three paintings Henri had made for the men as gifts, along with various other sketches, which he knew only through words and his imagination. Instead, when the officer on duty shook his head, denied having ever seen him, and then chased my brother off the property, we rented an estate in Costa del Sol, not far from Gibraltar, to finish the Cellini opera, intent on uncovering the truth.

During this time we carried on several correspondences. Firstly, Fauré informed us that Gailhard was now insisting on our return to edit *Ascanio* or he would cut us off. Even without an ending, they could find no contralto capable of singing the part of Scozzone, and he wanted to transpose everthing so they could use Bosman. Camille was furious. Making the character a mezzo destroyed the balance. But in the end he merely replied: *I trust Guiraud implicitly. They debuted* Lohengrin *in Weimar without Wagner, and* Aida *in Cairo without Verdi; they can debut* Ascanio *without me.*

The Cambridge Musical Society had also been in contact, requesting that Camille represent France in a series of performances to honour Europe's greatest musicians, and at first he said yes, dreaming of composing a new concerto, but when he discovered that they were placing him on a bill with Tchaikovsky and the days creeped past unproductive, Camille requested to play two earlier piano works instead. *The second is in a similar key to Tchaikovsky's,* he wrote, *or at least it begins in that key before passing on to many others and finishing in G major.* Four days later, he sent a second telegram: *I've begun to wonder if this similarity in keys might seem unsettling. If you see any problem, you can replace my Second Concerto with the Fourth, which is in C minor, assuming that Tchaikovsky's symphony will come between the two pieces!* Two weeks after that, he cancelled the entire thing altogether.

The third correspondence came from a young journalist in Buenos Aires named Leopoldo Lugones, inviting us to Argentina for a residence and performance. It was our first invitation to come to North America, and Camille was definitely flattered and feared for saying no, but my brother did not relish the idea of a trip across the Atlantic, not after his frequent battles with nausea while crossing the Mediterranean, and the lack of details in that first letter made the whole endeavour seem hastily conceived and conjectured. There weren't even any dates, no talk about compensation, no specifics of any kind, just a lot of information about Lugones himself, claiming that he had recently started his own newspaper and was firmly ensconced in socialist circles in the nation's capital. He knew President Roca. He knew Senator Quintana. He was close with the famous poet Rubén Darío, who had been the consul to Colombia and recently been appointed Head of Postal Services. The National Autonomists, preaching austerity, had pawned off the old Teatro Colón to some bankers in 1887 to help cover its debt. They promised to build another, bigger and better than the original. The funds from the sale were supposed to go directly to this. Four hundred days, the promise went. Twelve years on, there was still nothing. But Roca had vowed to finish it and set Lugones to find the first production. Finally they would have a building to match the stature of their city. *The new Teatro Colón will be the best venue of its kind in the entire world! No—the galaxy!* Lugones had arranged for my brother, who had made such a grand impression on him and his circle, on an entirely new movement in art in their country, to open it. *Surely you have something else in that bag of yours,* he wrote. *Another opera?*

But the letters continued, forwarded to us through Paris in bunches—as though Lugones was always thinking of something else to say immediately on posting the previous. Some of these included more details about the residency: the duration of three months (extendable), the compensation of fifty thousand lire (a grant secured through Senator Manuel Quintana), regular access to the Argentine orchestra (led by the local composer Arturo Berutti), travel costs, a luxurious downtown apartment owned by Lugones's newspaper in which we could live, any other expenses; they were hoping he might wish them to perform *The Organ Symphony*; and so long as he made it to the occasional rehearsal he could spend his time writing something new, as the earlier letters had inferred, or just travel, whatever he wanted. But many of the letters said nothing about the residency at all, sometimes nothing even about Camille, just pages and pages of Lugones's poems, all in the original Spanish, many seemingly about outer space, though it was difficult to tell, truly, if there was any merit to them. In another he described a short story he was working on, about a future society where everyone had learned to get along, were united in peace—even through other differences—by one shared belief. The road there had not been easy. There had been a previous period of peace. But then a leader arose in one of the nations who promised everything. *This is your truth,* he said. *This is your truth, this is your truth.* And a small child raised her hand and asked: *What is? What is our truth?* And he said: *This!* He said: *This!* He said: *This!* He said: *This!* And eventually the child said: *Oh.* And for the next two hundred years every nation waged war on the next and the sky opened and wept bombs and the soil wept and the survivors wept and the everything was not for lack of weeping and they forgot all about the peace until finally in the future—after the weeping had settled—an archaeologist was called to examine a fallen meteor and they found in it a musical score. It was not clear, at first, that this was what it was. There was almost no more art in the world, no more music, so the notation seemed at first nothing more than random fissures, cracks of erosion. But then someone recognized similarities in the symbols, and then a pattern. For decades they tried to pull meaning from it. There were many scientists, many specialists (perhaps more than there were specialties). And one day a travelling musician looked at the notes and began to play them and everyone felt at peace with the universe. It was the song of the universe. And he travelled the world teaching everyone the melody that made sense of everything. *And from that point on,* Lugones wrote, *everything they said, everything they did, could be measured against that rhythm and melody. Whenever they followed it, everything turned out exactly as it should. Whenever they erred, it was immediately apparent and horrible.* As he was writing the story, he said, he had always imagined the snippet to be a part of Camille's symphony. *Do you know what I felt when I first heard it? Your* Organ Symphony? He wrote as if we didn't exist, like he was keeping a journal he'd left open for us, and it was difficult to take him seriously. *The pain of the world! The assimilation of the sun! The complicity of the clouds! I felt past and future wars combined to one and I thought to myself:* There is no need to go somewhere because we are all already there. *Of course, you already understand all this. You wrote it!*

Finally—and Camille left this letter unopened for at least a week—there was a note from Félicité, Franck's wife, to inform us he had passed. This news did not take my brother by surprise—Franck wasn't young anymore, exactly, and we had heard the news of his illness in Egypt—but while the official story of his death was pleurisy, Félicité wanted us to know it was suicide. Because of Camille. He had always counted Camille as a good friend, she wrote, someone he could depend on. But after our fight in Weimar, Franck had grown increasingly depressed. *He had found financial success through that job, yes, but it was your respect that he always craved. When he was appointed Head Organ Instructor, you were the one he wanted to share it with. He continued to dedicate pieces to you, hoping you might appear at a performance. Only, you didn't.* His works became progressively more disturbing and grim, putting him at odds with his fans and the conservatory, and by the time he published *Psyché*, a symphonic poem based on the Greek myth, he was widely accused, depending on the circle of influence, of either plagiarism or blasphemy. He even began an affair with one of his students (whose name was Augusta Holmés (who stood four feet ten in one sock (who was already having an affair with the ugly and mediocre poet Catulle Mendès (who seemed not to care so long as it freed him to write more)))), and for a while he had two families, two lives, located not far from one another in the same arrondissement, which he dreamed that Félicité did not know about. *When he became ill, the doctor warned him about leaving his bed.* I would like to see Camille, *he told me,* one last time. *But your Arab refused to let us in. And we returned to our home to eat but he would not eat. And his own children brought him no pleasure. It was such a shame that the two of you became adversaries, when everything had begun so affectionately.*

Then the letter came to its point, that my brother finally do right by his friend and join the petition for a monument, so that Franck's contribution to French arts not be overshadowed by rumour and gossip so late in life. *It's not fair,* she said, *that history be rewritten like this.*

Meanwhile, we returned to Gibraltar every morning, a trip of several hours by horse, hopeful to encounter a changing of the guard, so we could ask someone else about Henri. There was a bench directly opposite the main house, and after asking the first soldier of the morning, we would sit there quietly until the next, ask again, wait for the final shift, and then head home. Most of the time they were the same few men, always with the same answer. One of them didn't even wait for my brother to speak, just shook his head as we approached, shooed us away like dogs, clearly angered by our persistence, so we stopped asking him and instead just waited on the bench for the next. The square was often full of people, which made the wait more tolerable. One day there was a special drill, and the entire force pretended to be attacked on all sides, a sham battle on a huge scale that included the entire city. As we were seated across from our typical spot, guns were fired from at least a dozen different points, and red coats swarmed like insects over the crags and heights, the whole city resundant with the thunder of artillery. We hadn't heard anything like it since the siege. Camille felt himself ill, with a sense of suffocation and convulsive snatches in his stomach and limbs, and I was happy we would never have to live anything like it again.

One day the guard spotted us and shooed us from the bench, too. Of course it was perfectly fine that we were there. There was no reason we couldn't be. But my brother did not protest, merely moved farther down the square—far enough that he could still see the pillared entrance but could merge much better with the crowd. He found us there, too, began shouting at Camille, chased him completely from the square, accusing him of being a pervert. Why was my brother staring at him every day? It wasn't normal. But the next day my brother was back at the bench again, refusing to accept the truth, and also the day following. And after the soldier had chased us from the square for over a week, he gave up.

Gradually our soldier's expression—because he was clearly

our soldier now, not like the rest—progressed from frustration to confusion to anger, again to sadness, and one day he was not in uniform, not at his post but at the bench, and he called my brother to him and offered a sandwich and asked if we would like to take a walk. *Do you believe the world changes?* he asked us once we had reached the trees. The macaques howled at us and I howled back and laughed, perched atop my brother's shoulders. It felt so good to be high above him. *Think about these trees, that were here long before we were even ideas in someone's mind. Think about these stones, this hill, this mount. Consider the air that rushes through our lungs but remains the air. Consider the whales and sharks. Did you know there are jellyfish out in the sea who never die? After they breed, they revert to an immature state. Their tentacles retract. Their bodies shrink. They become like newborns, sink to the ocean's floor and start it all over again from the beginning.* And my brother said: *At some point there was no path.* And the guard said: *Well, yes, of course, but wasn't man always there to dominate?*

We are new.

Are we? You and I, you mean? Or people, in general?

The paths became less and less populated, and it was easier to believe what the guard said. Then, in the darkness of the Great Siege Tunnels, the guard grabbed my brother quite roughly and awkwardly, pushed him to the wall, and they fumbled at each other for several minutes, lips and tongues and searching fingers. He was rough, and several times the discomfort of his grip brought my brother back from his fantasies. When the guard finally took his mouth off Camille's he said: *I remember your man.* He said: *I'm sorry. He told me never to tell, that his life was a secret. But you so clearly care about him.* Camille traced his finger around the man's ear, brushed back the curls. *I didn't know if I could trust you.* You can trust me. *But how do I know?* You can know. And the guard said: *I found him one morning in the square, directly across from where we stand, on the same bench you sometimes sit. When night fell, I informed him he had to move. As you know, it is illegal to sleep on the streets overnight, especially in the square. He said he had nowhere to go, and I told him that was no issue of mine. He had to move. And if he had nowhere to stay he would have to leave through the gates before we shut them for the night. Nothing changes in Gibraltar overnight. The gates are closed and no one comes in or out. He said he had no money, could not pay for a room, so I took him to the gate and cast him out.*

And that was it?

As you can imagine, the land outside the gates is not meant for man. It is nothing but sand and rock without means of shelter or shade. The track to San Roque (one can barely call it a road) is nothing but stones and ruts. Gigantic houseplants, geraniums and heliotropes left to fester as vines. He went not far, just kept walking until we shouted it was okay for him to stop. Then he just lay down where he was and went to sleep again. I watched him all that night and he did not move. I thought he might be dead. But the next morning he was at the gate when we opened it and every morning thereafter I would meet him at the gate and we would walk back to the square together and he would reclaim his spot on the bench and I would go inside to have breakfast and go to sleep. One morning, I brought him a cup of coffee and he thanked me with a drawing of a small bird he'd made on a discarded newspaper. The next day, I brought him in for a bite to eat. I've never seen anyone eat so quickly.

And so he drew you? This was true!

Sometimes he ate with us, but mostly he just wanted to observe, crouched in the corner like an evil spirit. Perhaps that's why the rest of them no longer remember. They don't want to remember. He would crouch in the corner and observe us, capturing our very thoughts in those little sketches of his. Everything. Even if we didn't realize we were thinking it. Isn't that strange? That you could be thinking things and not know it? But so visible to someone else? They were so small, too, barely larger than a coin most times, and still each one seemed to encapsulate the entire world. They could barely fit an entire person in them, a body part, although sometimes he would manage to cram several of us into one, so entangled were we that it was impossible to tell one man's legs from another's, one man's arms, one man's tongue and breast and thigh and sigh. I've never seen anyone draw so small. He told me once it was because he had to fit everything into everything, and when I asked him what that meant, he said the only way to capture the whole world was to capture the whole world and what he dreamed of doing was drawing everything on itself, in a 1:1 scale, or maybe that wasn't even enough. He etched directly to the wall. Most of the time you'd walk right past them and not notice; even though he'd filled entire walls with them. But sometimes, if you weren't searching for them particularly, you'd see yourself, from a moment of private shame, and swear you would never do anything like that again. It's amazing what you will refuse to do when you feel you're being watched. I think we became better people, more aware of ourselves, more aware that we were not alone inside our heads. Have you ever read a book or closely inspected a painting and wondered, if you weren't there to observe it, if the characters in it might have chosen differently? Do we root for them because they are good and righteous? Or do they merely act that way so we will think they are righteous and good? Then gradually we forgot he was there, and just went about his doing, and this was now who we were.

Once I asked: Why do you always draw us at our lowest points? And he said: What can you learn from happiness? Nothing. It is only through grief and strife that we emerge transformed. It is only through grief and strife that we find life. *After that, we became lovers. And after we fucked, I would fall asleep and he would sketch directly on my body. And when I woke up and found him sleeping, I would search my body for scenes of us fucking, or me naked, doing unspeakable things. What was I hoping for? Was I hoping to discover that we were really doing something else? Was I searching for some kind of secret world? Like these tunnels under the city? But there was nothing. Sometimes I would pretend to sleep and would feel the nib of the pen trace hard across me cross my bicep cross my inner thigh outer thigh cross the back of my neck that I could not see like he was forcing truth into me through my skin and he would fade gradually and I would wait the fade out then tear the sheet from our bodies then search my body then still find nothing. Every night. I don't know if he was still drawing on the walls anymore. There were the hours I spent on guard, when it was impossible for me to know what he was doing. Maybe he was sleeping with all of us, and none of us knew because each of us had the hours we spent on guard.*

267

If you added up all those hours, after all, multiply the number of shifts by the number of us by the number of hours by the number of numbers, what would you have? What could one man do with all those hours? Especially someone like him? A lot. I couldn't trust him. How can you trust someone who sees everything? Someone who has all those hours to see everything? So one day I asked him. I felt him trying to press the pen through my heart and I reached out and grabbed him by the wrist and twisted it behind his back, nearly broke it, and he said he had been drawing me, that on my chest he had drawn my chest, on my arms he had drawn my arms, on the back of my neck that I could not see he had drawn my neck that I could not see.

Love can't be minimized, *Henri said*. It is everything.

Where are the drawings now? Can you show me the walls? If we go back? Can you?

Some of us went searching for the drawings but couldn't find them anymore. And even though the walls seemed clean, one of the other soldiers suggested we replaster, anyway.

Where did he go?

Do you think that you will ever find him again?
    I hope so.

Do you think you knew him?

I did know him.

Perhaps my French is confusing.

It's not confusing.

I mean... I'm not sure what I mean.

It's not confusing.

Do you really think you can see inside the heart of another person?

Does it matter?

I want to know if there was love. For him. Was he in love? Was there love for him.

If you felt love, wasn't there love?

Perhaps my French is confusing.

It's not confusing.

Did you love him?

It is only possible to love one thing.

And was it him?

To be truly good at something, you need to love it above all else, even yourself. You have to cheat yourself, give over yourself, so that your love of that thing is actually a detriment to you, to sacrifice yourself to it, to be willing to sacrifice anything or everything, even yourself, so that others may benefit from it.

...

To love someone else is the same. To be good at loving someone else, it is the same.

And we rushed back to Costa del Sol to write our letter for Franck, frantic in a desperate euphoria that he had never been our adversary, could certainly not be blamed for the fancies of youthful impatience to which he had been only peripherally connected. He was a good man, a good friend, had been good to us. What would my brother have done without him at the Conservatoire? Would he have survived it? But then there was d'Indy, his signature perched atop the petition like a raven; Tailleferre, Milhaud, Durey, Cocteau; there was Canteloube, there was Auric, there was Poulenc; there was Lekeu, who took the worst parts of Bach and Wagner; Satie, whose greatest success came from being ignored; Honegger, and Ganne, whose best works were the parts he stole from *Parsifal*; Franck's students and the students of Franck's students and it pained Camille that people might confuse him as one of them when, if anything, it was *he* who had shaped Franck! He grabbed the pen and there, in fact, was Stravinsky, whose music was like spoiled fruit, a richly coloured orange that, when opened, is found to be hollow inside; and Strauss, so clearly still a novice, with no grand overture to ease you in or gentle melodies to release the tension. His *Salome* was an insatiable pervert's fantasy, the soprano overwrought, the male performers underused, the music surrounding them commonplace. *Play faster!* the audiences cried at him. *Slower! Crescendo! Calando!* There was Debussy, whose latest ballet (titled *Jeux*) was accompanied not by actual dancers but by a miniature tennis match, between Gobert and Decugis, who had recently been chosen to compete for France in the upcoming Davis Cup in Germany. His *Pelléas et Mélisande* was, likewise, like watching Maeterlinck's drama by itself, with no music at all. Debussy?! Was this the future of music? Where everything was art? Without separation between Beethoven and a bear's claw, just another commodity, and all that remains at that point is to find ways to sell it, entertainment, to keep people talking about it? He ran his eyes further down and there was Berlioz (a genius, but a little bit too much of a genius, you know?). There was Silas and Bussine. There was Fauré. This could not simply be about Franck. His music was too weak to even create the feeling of aversion in someone. This was nothing more than another power move, by d'Indy, to rewrite the books of history against us! He had already succeeded his master as the President of the Société Nationale, but for that to mean anything he had to invent the appropriate legacy, and had simultaneously gathered all of Franck's unpublished scores and corrected the mistakes and removed the inappropriate dedications to his students (especially Holmés (who was already ten times the composer Franck had ever been (who was ten times d'Indy (who cared less for art than he did for putting art at the service of political gain, like one parent using a child against the other parent, the outcome on the child the least of his worries)))). What had Félicité said? It was a shame we had become adversaries? *Adversaries?* We needed no single adversary. We were at odds with almost everyone we encountered. We were at odds with existence itself, at odds with the world. And Camille flipped the petition over and scrawled—hastily—on the back: *To whom it may concern at the Société, The influence of César Franck has been...disastrous...to French art! It would be an embarrassment,* he said, *to attach our nation's laurels to such a sinking stone!* And he proposed statues to others first (Rameau, Méhul, Hérold...) and sent our Arab back to Paris once again because it was important this message not be lost and we left for Argentina.

Finale

OUR STEAMER TO BUENOS AIRES WAS AN ARK OF BOORS, a raft of disenfranchised failures, inanimate objects masquerading as people, who had misunderstood the world so perfectly that they had elected to start afresh: an obstinacy of disgruntled Portuguese hoping to find work on the railroad; a regretful sigh of refrigeration technicians from Bristol; a shrewdness of rough-handed Italians for the Southern harvest while Europe languished in its winter; a languishing of shoemakers from Catalan, Basque shepherds and Swiss surveyors, French foremen and engineers, Russian nobles and Spanish maids; a Dane on prescription to cure his dyspepsia; flat-Earthers, entrepreneurs, other criminals; those who were making the mistake for the first time and those who should have known better; the armchair preachers and politicians and first violins, who talked and talked and talked; a monotony of Irish who all fancied themselves tenors; a dull nest of Welsh with shovels for hands; an ennui of Marxists who had emigrated purely to escape the Bakuninists, and an equal number of Bakuninists who had left because they had found Spain so backwards industrially that it would take too many stages of development before they could truly free anyone from it; a *te deum* of Jesuit, Mormon and Muslim missionaries, and a non-denominational agent of the British and Foreign Bible Society. He was Canadian, this religious Uncertainty Principal (so sure of the generalities of his belief but unwilling to commit to the specifics), and owing to our ship's greater fondness for the horizontal than the perpendicular, we made frequent roost the deck beside him, lodged between catastrophic bouts of gastric expulsion and his improbable tales of Patagonian savages and Icelandic Lutherans.

Did you know, said our Equivocal Evangelical, *that every home in Iceland has a Bible? Not as a demonstrative ornament or sentimental marriage gift, either, but for daily use! In Iceland, the Bible is constantly read, and as a consequence there are no prisons or theatres. There is no such office as sheriff. Military drills are like exotic, tribal dances. Dishonesty, theft and other crimes rarely occur.* And he had a story like this for any occasion, an impressive ability to make points without ever directly engaging in the subject, a metaphor for everything. *Once in Venezuela,* he said, *I stopped to take a drink and noticed a remarkable figure walking along the far riverbank. After all my travels I had seen black men and red men and yellow men and white men but this man looked entirely different in his dress from any man I had ever seen before. Eventually I learned he was dressed like a Highland soldier in full kilt, from Great Britain, but at the time he was just a pale giant in a woman's dress. When he came near I said:* What are you doing here? *He said:* Why should I not be here? Don't you know this is British soil? *I corrected him:* This is Venezuela. *And undeterred he said:* Wherever there is an English heart beating loyal to the Queen of Britain, there is England. *That is like the Bible,* he continued. *Wherever you find it, you find God.*

Still, he made my brother laugh with his stories of travelling without break from Manitoba to New York to Liverpool, arriving only one night before our ship had launched from Southampton, meeting us on the Isle of Madeira. And while it seemed incredible to me that the most expeditious route between these distant parts of the New World should be via the Old, he assured us that it was true, he had made the trip several times already.

The only difference this time was that he planned to bypass Buenos Aires entirely, which was already lost to the Catholics, and catch the first train to the north through Bolivia, Perú, Rioja, Tucumán, Salt, Jujuy, each in succession to be supplied with the scriptures he was carrying, in Tulia, Cotagaita, Caysa, Petosi, and finally to the Pacific coast in Arica where he would be met by a ship with more Bibles and would head back up the mountain again. He seemed so small and frail and my brother asked him how he managed to carry such a load over such distances, over and over, without faltering. And he said the first days were always the worst but he was able to continue through his Faith, confident that God would eventually lighten his load, that he would discover some new group of natives and God would take the weight off him through them. *One time*, he said, *I nearly died cresting the mountains to a pristine Patagonian village to discover the Jesuits had already been there before me, had already prejudiced the Indians against me, and I was stuck carrying my undiminished crate of Bibles up the entire Chilean coast.* Camille told him how he had been offered an abridged version of the Bible during the Siege of Paris, a *Soldier's Bible* that was nothing more than a few pamphlets, really, so we could remain more mobile, and it was still nearly impossible to find space in our packs between our pocket versions of Homer, Descartes's *Discourse on Method*, and the collected works of Voltaire. *The Prussians, meanwhile,* he laughed, *carried only a map of France.* And our new friend from the Bible Brigade said: *The Bible is the map to the Kingdom of God! Imagine removing entire sections of a map to make your voyage seem shorter; it would still be the same voyage, just as tired and toilsome, only more difficult!*

And it was good to have someone to talk to like this, to confess to. And Camille told him everything. About Henri's death. And Mother. And giving up. Wanting to start over. He acknowledged a memory of an uncle of a great aunt who—in his sleep—indicated where one would find lost objects; and that, for several years he had experienced the strange faculty of divining the arrival of visitors some moments before the doorbell indicated their presence. But he saw no reason to interpret that as a plan. He said: *Didn't we get rid of God finally with Darwin? Or at least Thomson?* And the other man said: *You talk about reality like it is a concrete thing that is not constantly changing. That's why it takes true courage to believe. True conviction. Letting scientists discover everything for you removes your freedom to live. We don't understand half the things we know.* And he told us the story of God's temptation of Abraham, and how Abraham endured that temptation, kept the faith, killed his son; and on his way back from the killing, on his way back to the servants that he had left with the donkey (*Just stay here, I'll be right back...*), on his lick back to the fork, his long venture back to the donkey, an angel of the Lord stole after him, into his loneliest loneliness, and told him he could go back, had proven his devotion and could travel back in time to change whatever he wished. He could live once more and innumerable times besides, revisit all that he had moored to doubt and to regret, and make the necessary changes until he was happy. Abraham fell to his knees and kissed the feet of the angel and threw back his head and laughed and of course went immediately back to the mountain and the knife and the fire and found his Isaac alive again, stacking his wood again, levelling his altar for sacrifice again. And Abraham wept before his Isaac and took his face in his hands and stared him deep like he was a not true thing but something he had imagined, his son, his beautiful son—that something so beautiful could not possibly exist, it seemed impossible—and he looked deep into those eyes and said: *You are my beloved, you are my beloved, you are my beloved, there is nothing else. I would do anything for you,* and he raised the knife and struck once again down his Isaac, changed nothing. Because how could he? Who was he to question the will of God?

It is crucial for mankind to have beliefs, Lugones said as he dragged us—almost literally, with the help of a mute, a teenager, a sycophant, and a toddler the size of a malnourished pony—to our apartments for the next three months. He had many of them, beliefs: animal magnetism; hypnotism, deep breathing; that cephalopods were aliens from another planet; that entropy is relative; that America did not exist; that the greatest sin is accumulation; that free will resides not in action but in interpretation; that sense determines reference; that the universe does not change, it is just an image of change; everything is knowledge, the world is information; we exist, each of us, as smaller collections of information; and that each human is the entire world folded in on itself at various intensities. He believed in synesthesia and textual surfaces; zoological symbolism; if there were such a thing as Planck time and length, could there also be Planck thought, or Planck caring; that poems do not attempt to describe life but are what life is all about; poetry is a ritual; poetry is the belief in an unreal truth; art should be life fire because *What is the most pure Truth? The fire. It burns only to burn and knows no else!* He wanted to crush the poverty of his circumstantial reality. He believed in the possibilities of crystal cubes suspended between two bar magnets in total darkness; the likelihood that sleepwalkers were, perhaps, simply allergic to the moonlight; that he could synthesize moonlight through alliteration; that they could have kept the Falklands if they hadn't overthrown Rosas; that Argentina had been made the scapegoat to save the Bank of England in the Baring Crisis; the gold standard; and that the only way to form false beliefs was to mistake the world's cardinality. What he did not believe in, apparently, were taxes of any kind but especially from the blue-bloused porters and uniformed men with pistols who, on watching our long and arduous disembarkation, as we entered the mouth of the Rio de la Plata and the vivid blues and greens of the Atlantic made way for an imposing rainbow of browns and greys and river shallows and our trunks were loaded from liner to lighter with precarious sail made hoist and heave and then, when that too became impassable, transferred to smaller *balleneras* designed for something, I'm sure, but not floating, to a third vessel that can only be described as a bad idea and, eventually, when the water had run out entirely with half a kilometre of unnatural sludge still to traverse, to the shoulders of some mute and a teenager and also our trunks and disappearing into the city before they could lay hands on us. *They're really only looking for dynamite, anyway,* he said as we hid behind some garbage cans in an alley. *After everything that happened recently in the London Underground, you know. And last week with that druggist in New York. Like a bomb is ever going to change anyone's mind! Plus, these crooks don't really even care if you have some. They just want to tax you on it at fifty per cent.*

The tram companies were, likewise, extortionists. *This is why bodies have muscles,* he said. And he pulled us by the arm through street after café-lined street, tugging so often at Camille's elbow that it was difficult to not walk into lampposts or keep free of the gutter, and though we were tired and hungry and just wanted to rest, to be still for one moment so we could feel the ground unmoving beneath our feet and every café seemed so identical to us that to describe one would be to describe them all, Lugones would only shake his head and laugh and say: *Those places only serve Argentine wine,* and then ask Camille to hum parts of *Samson,* or even *Étienne Marcel,* and Lugones would close his eyes and nod and say *yes, yes,* and sway a little, *yes, yes,* he liked to be carried away by it all. Once Camille even nearly lost his head to a passing tram and one of the men with our trunks (whose name was Berutti and who insisted repeatedly that he studied in Paris and Milan and Leipzig, saying, *The Germans are in love with you*) said: *You must always be careful of this one, he will lead you into Hell if you don't watch for it.* And the teenager (who smoked incessantly and whose name was Sux) added: *My arm is still sore from the last walk we took. I still walk like a crab from my last congress with a post.* Lugones puffed himself up and said: *I step not aside from the furrowed track, though they loosen their hilts as they come.* A pause. *Do they read José Hernández in France?* It was not a name with which we were familiar, and Camille apologized. *Truly?!* Lugones said. *His book is a classic here already. Like the story of Juan Moreira, everyone knows it. They sell it in the bars and anyone can recite it provided enough drinks.* He spoke at length about its whining preachiness, its romanticized ogling of the frontier, its reinforcement that all Argentine literature should be about survival, in the face of hostile elements and/or the mystical/magical natives: *Survival?! Hernández was born here in the city! And wrote it when he was working for the Banco Nacional, before it became the Banco de la Nación! What could he know about survival? At the same time, the poem's rhythm is based on the eight-syllable tradition of the payadas, like a galloping horse: dada dada dada dada. And it rhymes in patterns of six, like the strings of a guitar.* He mimed the cheap local style of guitar playing with the guitar at his throat. *And I can almost love it if I don't listen too closely.* Lugones quoted from Verlaine. He quoted from *Faust.* He quoted from *Beowulf.* And the child (who was never introduced) would get a block or two ahead of us with Sux and La Muerte (who was not a mute after all, simply spoke no French and almost no English, though he still laughed at nearly everything) and the three of them would begin scaling a wall or lamppost or would leap up to grab a hanging flagpole and do pull-ups or there was a trick where Sux would wrap his arms around a light post and stretch himself perfectly horizontal using nothing but his arms and talents at rigidity. When we would catch up to them, it was clear that the older man was winded from his exertions but unwilling to cede. *At one point in his life*, Lugones said, *La Muerte was the youngest person he knew, you know, when he first gained consciousness. He refuses to believe it can be otherwise.* And La Muerte grinned and ran off once more to catch up to Sux. We were joined at each stop in our ascent of the local culture by more of Lugones's friends, who trailed after us like a snake through the gutters, until I could no longer see the tail around the last corner, like they were a parade, waving their batons and pumping their fists, launching a revolution at every corner, against the establishment, the weather, freedom, the price of wine, freedom. And after what seemed like hours we arrived finally at the Café de los Inmortales, a literal hole in the wall that led to a ruined cathedral, open to the sky, with some of the worst dancers I have ever seen. Berutti shook his head and said: *All they know here is the tango.* And finally a woman in a costume that can only be described as ill-conceived brought us a full carafe of disturbing-looking red liquid and Lugones said: *Ah, here we are!*—and poured us the smallest of portions and said: *A taste of home, M. Saint-Saëns?* Camille was eager for a drink, but as he brought the glass to his lips he was overcome with the reek of bad coffee and vinegar, as though it had been long exposed to the air and perhaps even a burnt cigarette. *A friend works at the Jockey Club on Calle Florida,* Lugones said as he poured everyone the smallest tumbler. He swished it liberally around his mouth, leaned back so he could insufflate around it. *He has to smuggle it out one mouthful at a time,* he finished, *but in the end,* we *are the beneficiaries!*

We returned to Los Inmortales almost every night, and in many ways it was like being back at the Viardots, though more democratic, without Pauline as a curator; and chaotic, because it was mostly in a language we did not understand and felt like they were wild creatures and we were on safari. They would talk about protest, class struggles, how to get published, as well as painters and poets and radicals we'd never heard of, referencing them all so casually it was as if they were old friends: Abùlico, who was working on a series of interconnected poems under various pseudonyms to question authorship and cultural history; Vila, who had rid the world of the need for capital letters—literature without punctuation until the final period, as to be exhaled in a single breath; Dominguez—*He's been trying to paint clouds! Not on canvas but directly on the clouds themselves!* Everything seemed an effort to redefine art, and they were in it together, warriors on the edge of truth. It even seemed like they were all happy.

And why not? Reilly announced. *Argentina is a paradise! We lack in nothing except money!* They had all found it difficult to find paying work, especially with the recent flood of new Europeans. Hundreds of thousands of them arrived every year. Reilly estimated that at least twenty-five per cent of Argentines had arrived within the past ten years, took all the jobs, and the cost of housing had increased in tandem. A few of them, like Lugones and Reilly, were journalists (though Reilly said he had also worked in construction, as a security guard, as a teacher, and even briefly as a *vijilante*). But many others would not insult their talents through misuse, so they took what they could find. Danel said he cleaned houses. La Muerte ran packages. Sux said he typically spent his winters in Brazil harvesting coffee. It was hard, wet work, he said, especially as the season climbed the surrounding peaks. But that was partly why he enjoyed it. They needed to walk four hours to buy groceries from the company store. But he liked being outdoors. And it was good to get out of Buenos Aires. It was also where he had lost his virginity, the first year when he was only thirteen but he was big so he lied and said he was older. Unfortunately the government in São Paulo had started paying immigrants to come from Italy, providing them with lodging because the price for beans had fallen so sharply and they would work the plantations for less, and now he was stuck rolling cigarettes in Gerchunoff's apartment.

Gerchunoff, like Sux, was also in his teens, born in Russia but had followed his father to Argentina to escape the pogroms, raised in the tiny town of Moisés Ville. The town had not existed before them. They created it, along with dozens of other families who, afraid of others, had decided not to integrate but start their own village, as far from the capital (and, indeed, as far from Santa Fe, even) as possible. They wanted nothing to do with anyone else, and having arrived together and living with no one else but themselves, they could still believe they lived in a tiny part of their original home (or perhaps even in Palestine, where they had originally intended to flee), at least until they reached the town limits and looked out on nothing, surrounded by the nothing. *We ignored the nothing,* he said. *Because we didn't feel like we needed anything else. What was the point of things we couldn't see? And I went to yeshiva like all the other children and learned about God and the laws and how to read and write in Hebrew but I never once learned about the nothing, which seemed like such an important part of my life, since I could always see it, any day I chose. We ignored it, even though on the other side of the nothing—not even the vast nothing between us and our original home, or us and Buenos Aires or us and Santa Fe, but a nothing much smaller—we knew there was another town called Monigotes that was inhabited by criminals and bandits. I couldn't sleep at night, thinking of these Monigotans coming down to our world, wondering if they might be friendly or would enslave us. I would sneak from our house and set up strings and bells around as much of the perimeter of our town as I could.* Why would they come here? *my father would assure me. And I slept. But they did. They learned we had gold and they came in the night to take it. From the nothing. And they murdered my father and I learned he had taken down my strings and bells without my knowledge and I decided to learn for myself, to run away to the* city *and to study at the Colegio Nacional and learn more about the nothing.* Now he lived in a *conventillo* in one of the outer barrios because it was all he could afford. And when Sux's mother kicked him out, he had invited Sux to stay with them, assuming based on the extraordinary number of roommates he already had that one more person would not greatly affect anyone else's percentage of floor space. Truthfully, no one really noticed he was there.

Other than Berutti and a painter named Tlön who whistled the entire theme of *The Swan* while sitting beside us, Gerchunoff was the only one who seemed aware of who my brother was—not just that he was from France and somehow important—and he often engaged my brother on several subjects: Spinoza, Heinrich Heine, the great woe. Gerchunoff spoke Yiddish, Spanish, Italian, English, Portuguese, Russian, Latin and near-perfect French and was familiar, because of his own adoration with the poet, with the piece my brother had written for two pianists inspired by Heine's *König Harald Harfagar. His linguistic structure is totally smooth,* he said, *unblemished in any way. It's like he doesn't normally speak in words and is somehow just assembling them by their look. And you*—he could not even look at Camille directly—*your interpretation is the same, each piano part so perfectly textural and virtuosic, it's impossible to tell which set of hands is playing what at any given point.* And his questions were so sincere and earnest and detailed, wondering why my brother had selected it, for example, what it had said to Camille when he had first read it, and wondering what my brother thought of the laziness, *a blip for Heine, of course,* of the metaphor of a woman's laughter,

287

when the nymph kisses him with her laughing mouth, it feels...hollow...
and cheap to me... Camille felt bad to have to say: *I'm sorry, it was*
so long ago, you understand... Though, naturally, Gerchunoff could
not. He probably still remembered everything of his life, had
not yet run out of space to care for it all, in the way my brother
once held Mozart. When you love something, you keep it inside you. The rest of it is wiped out like it never happened. He
also asked my brother about *Samson*, citing the importance of
Jewish characters. And Camille told him about Halévy, who'd
been dead for, what, almost fifty years now? Gerchunoff had
never heard of him. Was it possible? That someone could exist
and then just not? Gerchunoff, seeing that my brother was disappointed, smiled and said: *Have you heard the story of when Ovid*
sold the Metamorphoses *to his publisher? He celebrated by taking his*
advance to the nearest bar and spending it all on a martinus. Confused,
the bartender replied: Don't you mean a martini? *And Ovid said:* If
I could afford a double, I wouldn't be writer.

Gerchunoff claimed to work part-time at a bakery, part-time
as a mechanic, part-time rolling cigarettes with Sux (all the other anarchists mocked Gerchunoff because he didn't come to
their readings, but he and Sux were quite close), and part-time
in a textile factory making, of all things, Argentine flags. He also
rarely made it to his classes and spent most of his free time just
roaming the library and crashing political conferences. That's
how he had met Lugones, and Ugarte, who was the envy of
most of them, because he'd been appointed to a government
position overseeing water safety in the city. I could not help
but think of our father as he said this, asleep at his desk, writing
meaningless numbers into ledgers. He had never contributed
anything to the world. Had there possibly been a moment in the
day when he'd thought of something else but rolling the stone?
But Ugarte said the pay was very handsome, and allowed him to
complete several manuscripts over the past few years.

Don't you have to be at work? Camille asked. *At an office or some*
such?

The office? Ugarte laughed. *I haven't been to work in almost two years!*

So who tests the water?

It's water! What are they hoping to find?

Besides, Sux added, *you can never be successful and important. Let the last generation write from their inheritances. Men like Uriarte and Laretta, flaunting their wealth by writing so much about their travels in Europe; even Mármol, who spent so much of his life abroad, have you read his* Amalia? *No? With its mongrels, mulatto and mestizo? Monsters! This is what we've had to put up with for generations, writers who want to copy Europe, writing not a country of reality but a pale facsimile, applied overtop of the people who had previously walked the land without permission from them first. If you are too comfortable, you cannot feel the injustices and write about them justly.*

Another carafe of wine had materialized and my brother turned over his glass. To lighten the mood, La Muerte performed a short pantomime. And while Sux continued to sulk in the corner, Reilly joked: *Of course, failure is no guarantee of success, either!* Then Lugones called for silence so he could recite one of his poems. Since we spoke no Spanish, it washed over us leaving little more than the articles and the pronouns, some proper names. I thought I heard Samothrace, for example, assuming it to refer to the famous statue of Nike, as well as Belgrano, Castelli, Cipeda, Pelayo, which we could only assume were Argentinian of some sort. Other poets, perhaps? They might equally have been place names, titles for famous works of art, sites of other military victories? Chubut? Something about roses? And was that Barrès he mentioned in the fourth pass? Bourget? Sixte? Meanwhile La Muerte would raise his hand in the back whenever Lugones paused for dramatic effect and Lugones looked mildly perturbed but continued as though he hadn't heard him, wherein La Muerte began to moan, softly. As soon as our host spoke his last word, La Muerte leaped to his feet and requested, as far as we could tell, that Lugones translate one of *his* chapbooks for us, either from the first called *Diez Días de Dios* or the

289

other titled *Las Perras Calientes*. *Haw-t beetch-es,* he drawled in English.

Lugones refused, claiming we would understand none of it.

Why is that? my brother asked.

He thinks poetry has to use every word in the dictionary.

La Muerte laughed and said: *Apuntó en su matiz crisoberilo?*

But Lugones brushed him off.

What did he say? Camille asked.

Nothing. Oh, nothing. He is an idiot.

Instead, Reilly told us of his friend Güiraldes, whose last book had sold so poorly that he'd stolen the remaining copies one night from his publisher and thrown them in the harbour. They'd all gathered to watch him, apparently, all the poets of Argentina, lining the construction of the new port, kilometre upon kilometre of cement quays and dilettantes, as he launched them, one by one, into the water. But he had mistimed it horribly, the tide at its lowest, so they just struck the mud like wounded birds and lay there, slowly soaking up the sewage. *Can you imagine anything less poetic,* he said, *than a harbour soaked with books?*

Let them flaunt their inheritances, Sux scowled. *We will flaunt our poverty.*

Even the city itself was so perfect, like a little Paris but without all the destruction from the siege, everything gleaming and new. Camille began each morning in our new apartments by brewing his coffee, poured the water through it three times, as always, and then, as always, after he had his cup, poured it through again, not to drink, but to set aside as his water for the first pouring the next day. He sat in his chair. He addressed the piano on his way by, then threw open the windows and listened to the bird sounds: the rufous-bellied thrush that rushed to the morning before it was even there; the chalk-browed mockingbird; the starling, so similar to the ones back home that I almost felt ill. He began by sketching a little piece called *La nuit*, nothing terribly serious, just something to get him going, modelled after the nightingale he heard calling from the eucalypti stride the street. It was simple, so simple it made him giggle, an *amuse-bouche* of music, with notes that never fell too far astray, a song to be sung wherever you might find a light soprano, a flute, a choir, any ordinary place with ordinary talent. Sometimes, to challenge himself more, he would work on a cantata about the blessings of electricity, inspired by things he was reading by the Croatian, Nikola Tesla, particularly about the great tower he was building in America to shoot messages around the world (like Zeus!) on bolts of lightning. The first half he wished declaimed by ritornellos and the second by a soprano and choir and a repetition of a single line: *This flame to the vault of Heaven is flown;* a feeble spark, a flickering flame, a mighty blaze increasing in speed and power with huge mounting arpeggios climbing rapidly in fifths to approximate the feel of the lightning flash. He also imagined the entire audience strung with wire beneath

291

the seats, with a violent shock at each strike of the tam-tam, then wondered if it were too advanced, too *fin de vingtième siècle*. Then we would walk. *Be honest,* Lugones said on our first outing. *When you think about Argentina, what do you see? A few flippant paragraphs in an encyclopedia or magazine article? Aztec temples? Is it something real or something defined more by what it is not? Are we the not-Spain? The not-Italy? The not-Mexico or Uruguay? I think people consider us, if they consider us at all, in the same way an investor considers stocks. They put their money into us and don't really think of us again until they are roused by default in the payment of half-yearly interest. We might as well be Mars,* he said. *A planet worth nothing but resources, free land and a new beginning.* Desperate to prove to us how cosmopolitan they were, Lugones took us to the city's downtown parks, the canals, to show us the arch of an entrance hall, the grillework on a gate. We took walks to admire the City Hall, the Stock Exchange, the San Martin. We walked to the old Teatro Colón and the French Embassy; to the Plaza 25 de Mayo and the Cathedral that was said to be the largest in South America. Ugarte even took us on a tour of the magnificent palace on Riobamba, which was not a palace at all but his legendary water treatment plant. But the biggest surprise to me were the streets, as though we had stepped right into one of Haussmann's dreams. A city's streets are like its signature, its grand statement, and those of Buenos Aires were infinite and straight, endless: streets that led places, of course, but mostly streets with grand vista points, and streets that were shows of importance. Even the diagonals were perfect, as though everything were a shortcut and, through a tiny shift of direction, you might skip entire parts of the city and end up on the outskirts of the opposite side.

We walked to the Plaza de la Victoria, with its spectacular Pyramid of Liberty, and the Retiro, once the location of an enormous bullfighting ring until they made the practice illegal in 1822 and tore it down and let the bulls escape into the plains. The Library in Calle Perú had once been known for its theological collection but had fallen into neglect and been over-taken by an Americanist. Every wall of the grand reading hall was covered to the ceiling in books, protected by glass doors and iron galleries placed at different heights, and upstairs they kept the real collections and when they learned who my brother was of course they gave him the key and we wandered that great hall alone, marvelling at the knowledge being pro-tected from the greater population. The post office walls were covered with names, the right side of the building devoted to telegraphs and the left to the delivery of letters, but these lists were for recipients of mail that was undeliverable. Some ad-dresses did not exist. Some were illegible. Some recipients had simply disappeared. But the best of all was the Museo Público, which contained many curiosities of natural history and was an invaluable resource for acquainting ourselves with the fauna of this country. First were the fossils, unique to the area: the *Megatherium, Scelidotherium, Glyptodon, Mylodontes, Mastodontes, Toxydontes, Orthodontes*; so many random bones forced into all sorts of fantastic creatures. But there was also an impressive assortment of real, living creatures: the pink fairy armadillo; the massive carpincho; the Patagonian mara, a rabbit the size of a small deer; miniature opossum and rats; birds, so many birds, the black-and-white hawk eagle, orange-eyed ground doves, yellow-legged Andean flamingo; cryptids and ceti eels; snakes and four-eyed frogs.

Meanwhile, Reilly took us on the commuter trains, rocket-ing along the earth at thirty kilometres per hour, a mere twen-ty minutes to cover the eight and a half kilometres from his neighbourhood in Flores to the Plaza de Mayo. This was his daily ritual, and we spent an entire week with him just riding back and forth and then from La Plata to Rosario and back, which was considerably farther, and then from the Central Station to Ensenada, to Altamarino, from the Plaza Once de Septiembre to Bragado, not as destinations but rests, drinking brandy and calvados and dust and talking about Sarmiento.

Have you read Sarmiento's Viajes? Reilly cooed. *He travelled as an ambassador to Europe and said he found nothing but gaps, empty spaces of such completeness that he was convinced reality was unravelling around him, as though you had decided to wipe out your worst memories but had nothing else to replace them with, so you just hid them, these empty spaces, behind mountains or cathedrals or marvels of architecture and called it Europe, as though moths had gnawed through your blankets of morality. And he returned here to create something new. Something real.*

Camille earned great respect for the Argentine railway through Reilly, their efficiency, so solidly upholstered, and also that Reilly dreamed to likewise someday create a book that would break barriers and change their nation, the book Argentines needed now. It was why he worked as a journalist, he said. *It's no longer a profession or a craft but an art. An art of goldsmiths, of poets, of philosophers. Art has heroes and victims; the true artist is both.* He told us about an exposé he was writing about drug abuse, and another on men who dressed as high-class women in order to rob men downtown. *These thieves are men who love music, flowers, sewing and poetry!* he said. *They play the piano! They just also live off stolen property.* And science could explain it all. It was a pathology that went back to the Bible, to the Greeks. He praised science. *The Irishman, Kelvin, has already affirmed that there is only enough oxygen in the world to last mankind another three centuries. But that is the date of complete exhaustion. We are already dying of suffocation. Do you know the expression* free as the air we breathe? *Soon the air will no longer be free. It will be manufactured and sold like any other commodity. The artificial air will be stored up in enormous reservoirs, and to these receptacles applicants will come for their daily supply of oxygen. This will then be carried home and doled out to the family as part of the day's means to support life. The manufactured oxygen will be breathed in as a diver inhales the air supplied him when he sinks beneath the waves. Those who will not work for their daily air supply will perish. We are on the edge of a new age, poised to break down the walls of the impossible. Time and space died yesterday, and we already live in the absolute because we have created eternal, omnipresent speed.*

A devoted Americanist, Reilly claimed the entire rail system—not to mention the new dock and the dredging that was being done to increase the capacity of the harbour—was being funded by companies from Boston and New York to access the extensive groves and orchards that engorged the land until the Pampas. *We have been fucked by the world for so long, finally the Americans are making a legitimate city of us. Last year I took a vacation to New York and Boston and do you know what I saw? They don't care about beauty anymore. They care only about the thunder of mechanism. The clang and a holler. It's so liberating. Buildings fifty storeys tall. You should see them digging the subways under New York City. I looked down into those holes to Hell and thought to myself: If da Vinci had lived today, would he have painted his Last Supper? Or would he have designed this great tunnel, this great bridge, these massive ships that would have seemed like monsters to the people of his time? Plate by plate, rivet by rivet, beam by beam, the birth of a million, the shapes of half a hundred. With this much power he would have torn the top from the mountain just to see what lay beneath and then, his curiosity sated, would just toss it in the ocean and never consider it again. He would have engineered the entire gold rush of Tierra del Fuego and never have thought twice about displaced Indians. All the Americans want from us is fruit and we have more than we need. It just falls on the ground and rots. Thank you, United Fruit Company!*

Berutti would take us around the city's cultural landmarks—the Opera, the Alegría, the Victorian, the Politeama—typically accompanied by one of the dancers we'd seen at Los Inmortales, the one they all called the Little Russian though it was clear she was not Russian at all and her real name was Lelia but we didn't learn that until much later. Camille made the mistake of mentioning Turin and Berutti went off about the squares and the covered sidewalks. *It was the first time I saw a painting by Titian! The finest work I still believe I have ever seen. His* Venus *is practically a study in painting hair, the auburns and yellows so perfectly rendered, as though the description had leaped from Homer's words to the canvas.* The Little Russian, on the other hand, asked many questions but always seemed disinterested in the answers, rarely waiting for my brother before moving on to something else. One time she placed her head on my brother's shoulder and asked him if he believed in electrons. Had he seen a dirigible? *Have you ever tried heroin?* she asked. *I wonder what it is like to have an abortion,* she would say. *Would you get me pregnant,* she joked, *so I can find out?* At one point Camille found himself trying to console her over her supposition, likely correct, that Berutti did not love her. Of course she wasn't really in love with Berutti, either, was living with another popular musician named Ángel Villoldo. *Have you heard of him?* We had not, and she found this extraordinary and gradually she wandered off.

Does it pain you as it does me, Berutti said as he watched her walk away, *to see what's happening with popular music? It makes you question democracy when you see such things.* Of course, he felt the same way about anything that was not directly within the purview of his own experience, including any and all opera written before the late 1800s. He talked as though nothing had existed before Mascagni, before the *Cavalleria rusticana. Do you know he wrote it in only two months?* Berutti said. *Of course, when art comes directly from your own experience like that, there's no stopping it.*

I thought it was from a book, my brother replied. *And the libretto was written by someone else.*

But Berutti just said: *Yes, yes, a book, and his friend sent him the libretto on postcards, one line at a time. But one day the wind swept all the postcards from the table and scattered them around the room, and what did Mascagni do? He just picked them up and used them in the order they came to him, and when he heard the final piece, his friend admitted it was even better. He was a genius. It's like the opera I'm working on about the* Revolución del Parque. *I was in Italy when it happened, but it's a part of all of us.*

It was very important to Berutti—to be of the time, and to be as real as possible. His first opera he'd based on a story about immigrants by Balzac, followed by *Evangelina*, which he'd taken from Longellow's beautiful poem about the genocide of the Acadians, and the third came from a story by Gogol, though admittedly he had nearly gone for Dostoevsky instead, because he'd been born twelve and a half years later and had such an affinity for Edgar Allan Poe, whom Berutti had also grown up reading to learn English. *Dostoevsky actually translated three of Poe's stories for a journal run by Gogol. There were, in fact, four stories, but if you read them closely, you can see that one is an imitation—a stylistic plagiary—written by Dostoevsky himself. It is full of Dostoevsky's trademark rush and roughness, convulsive thrusts of passion, general provincial clumsiness and ridiculous polyphonic narration. He's more concerned with voices than anything else. It's why his novels are my favourite books that I hate reading.* When he returned to Argentina, Berutti told us, he knew he wanted to write about the great gaucho outlaw and murderer Juan Moreira, and of course about the Revolución: *Because fifteen hundred dead and wounded! What could be more true than that!*

Maybe he was right. Maybe that was what Camille needed to

do next. He wanted to write about Henri, about all of the emotions he had felt during the war, and the loss at losing him, but he kept avoiding it, making up other stories, and he told Berutti about the opera he had recently started called *Les barbares*, about a vestal virgin in the first century BC who gives herself up to save Gaul when it is overrun by cultureless German hordes and Berutti winced as though he'd been struck and said: *It sounds like you've never been in love before! An opera about a gaucho so adept at the knife the whole world wanted to fight him! That is love!*

Oh, Aníbal, he said suddenly, *come here! I have someone you need to meet!* And he introduced us to the orchestra's first violin, Aníbal Varela, whose resemblance to Henri was so striking that I felt the whole thing must be a cruel trick. He was smiling, always smiling, tossing his hair, smiling, and it wasn't so much that he walked but that the ground shifted beneath him to meet his feet and, miraculously, like the night we first met Henri, we found ourselves alone with him, watching his mouth move until Sarasate's name brought us out of our reverie to a clearer focus. Was that right? Was he really saying that one of the first pieces he'd learned was Camille's *Introduction and Rondo Capriccioso*? It was impossible. I was sure he was lying. My brother had composed it for Sarasate when he was only nineteen, half a lifetime ago, and it was more than difficult; for anyone but Sarasate, it was impossible. But our gorgeous young friend persisted, saying: *It took me months to begin to comprehend it. So many of the melodies in the piece are Spanish, as you know, which of course comes more natural to me, it's in my blood. We are surrounded by it. But my master was never satisfied and had me focus on my bow control and, most importantly, my shifting. Do you play the violin, M. Saint-Saëns? The problem,* he said, *was that I was moving my hand, and of course I was a child and so I responded*: How can I get to another position without moving my hand? *I thought he was crazy and ignored him. And every day he would scowl and tell me to stop moving my hand, would yell at me, and I would try to keep it as rigid as possible as I slid up the string but could never do it to satisfy him. I locked every bone in my hand and*

298

forearm until they were one. I performed it perfectly. And he walked out. He said: I can feel the movement. Why are you wasting my time? There should be no movement. Stop thinking about your hand or your fingers and think about the position. The original position must cease to exist and the new position appear. There must never be any sense of you going from one to another. You must just be there. *I replied, once again, as a child, and he said*: You should always be asking yourself three questions: Where is my first finger? Why is it there? And: Would it be better if it were somewhere else?

Of course, by the time I was near to finally figuring it out, my master inserted Paganini's Sauret Cadenza *directly before the coda, with its impossible double-stopping harmonics, and it nearly broke me. But here I am. I still play it and am never bored playing or listening to it.*

They talked about music for the rest of the night, eventually coming back to the *Organ Symphony*, and Varela said: *What you did with the* Dies Irae, *it's like gazing upon the profile of Christ himself. In bas-relief. On snowy marble. Such hope. Have you heard Strauss's* Tod und Verklärung? *I can still recall watching the lead violinist as she launched into her solo, the moment of divine light through the physical and spiritual torment, thinking, how does such a pretty girl play so ugly? And Mahler's* Resurrection Symphony, *with its gut-wrenching shriek of despair! The trumpets attacking from the wings! All of the metaphysical questions raised by Beethoven's Ninth answered! If it hadn't been for you, unafraid to make so many mistakes, we would never have had either.*

They were obsessed about the gaucho. Berutti was writing his opera about Moreira. Lugones wanted to write an entire book in the gaucho language. Reilly was working on a book about the Conquest of the Desert. *The gaucho,* Lugones said, *is what unites us. The central symbol of Argentina.* Supervivencia. *Torn, caged, colonized, despairing, undone, he is the outlaw fighting against the law. Europeans like to talk about lineage,* Lugones said, *though in Argentina it's not the name of their father or grandfather or great-grandfather but the name of the ship they arrived on. The gaucho, however, are descended from mountains, from the plains, descended from the horse, descended from the rock and forest. The gaucho are the heirs of Hercules. The gaucho is intangible as the wind, whose name can be spoken only in whispers. He has no fixed point, is always moving. He is the only map of the land because he is the land. The old school tries to fix us with their tales of morality, men committing suicide after visiting a prostitute, women perishing from infidelity, at risk of venereal diseases, crime, alcoholism, homosexuality, women working outside the home. Language bends around the gaucho, as gravity bends time. Spanish only has to get close to them and it bends, is transformed.*

Gerchunoff accused the others of being *acriollirt,* a Yiddish term meant to capture people who took on the gauchesque lifestyle but were not. *They want you to believe that they are the true Argentines, that there is some sort of litmus test, that if you cut them they would bleed sand and grass. But they have not lived among the gaucho, as I have.* Lugones, however, called Gerchunoff a lover of the city. *This city is a monster,* he said, *made from scraps and rare body parts. It's a waste dump for Europe, filled with all the bits the other countries are through with. The people who are born in Buenos Aires want us to believe they're the same as the rest of us. But they were only* born from women. I was born from poverty. From the desert. My parents planted a seed in the arid soil of Córdoba and I stretched my arms to the sun and emerged whole. When you are born from the desert, you must have deep roots. You know where you are there at all times, because how could you be anywhere else? And once this started, it was difficult to settle them down. Berutti said he was born from the mountains; Reilly, from the river. Reilly climbed atop one of the tables and began to orate. The Spanish don't worry about the future because they have the past. They let language evolve of its own accord, confident in their numbers and centuries of natural selection, and have always hated this whirlwind of energy and creativity that menaces their traditions (whatever they may be) and shames them for their inability to keep pace. The Spanish are richer and fatter than us. Lazier than us. They eat more than us, sleep more than us. But that is fine. It means only that we will work harder. We will write harder. Our poems will force their poems from the shelves. We will tear down the old order every day, both within our society and abroad. Time is not a line to follow, but a fortress to infiltrate and break down. We must destroy them to advance our historic mission. We will write ourselves into existence. Like the Americans.

Sux, meanwhile, began to clap slowly and loudly until everyone stopped to look at him. Oh, please, Reilly, he said, turning to my brother like he was shielding us from the others. He goes on like this all the time; false poverty, alienation, a genetic heart defect, he needs the story to give his art validity. Next thing you know, he'll be telling you both his parents worked in meat-salting plants.

They did both work in meat-salting plants!

You see? Sometimes he says he was born in Concordia, and other days he says Uruguay, his mother setting him adrift on the river because she thought he was Moses. Meanwhile he has an apartment above a shop in the north end with the Jews in Flores! He'll even tell you he's a journalist but he makes his living writing propaganda for the large companies, creating stories for us to live inside, writing whatever they tell him to, about the hospital they built recently, for example, their happy employees, all that bullshit.

Sux likes to think he's an anarchist.

And Reilly's only real dream is to be excommunicated. Like Vila.

I have suffered as much as anyone! I worked with Lugones at La Protesta!

And Lugones told us the story of the Gaucho and the Wealthy Spaniard.

Once upon a time a wealthy Spaniard came to Argentina with a sizable inheritance, looking for a ranch, and settled ultimately on the largest parcel bordered by the Río Areco. Before signing the papers, however, he wanted to walk the fine print of it, traverse all 180,000 acres, long the lush arroyo that split it near symmetric. He trekked long the tallsome grass and thrust his hand to loam and lime and mid the quivering wools and thew and grist he was surprised to discover a *pulpería* that had not been included on the maps from his Scotch seller. Inside he discovered three gauchos playing cards and sat down with them but they would not speak to him so he went to the bar and ordered a shot of *aguardiente* and told the bartender to leave the bottle: *They do not trust you. You are a stranger.*

If they want to work for me, they will need to trust me.

Who says they want to work for you?

This is my land.

This will never be your land.

The Spaniard laughed. He had been hunting with his father since he could walk and was an avid naturalist, knew there were at least a dozen plants and animals he could live on and identify by sight or smell or even touch and could distinguish subtle differences within the same species so that, even in impenetrable darkness, he could pull the herbs and smell their roots and chew their leaves and confirm the proximity of a lake or underground stream, establishing it as salt or fresh water. Did they really think he couldn't make it to the farthest edge of the plain, in La Rioja, and return? Without even returning to his home, he purchased the hat and poncho from one of the men and a magnificent-looking horse and cart and a proper knife and, without so much as another word and only these clothes and horse and knife and what he'd already had in his small shoulder bag (including a strip of dried beef, a water pump, a change of socks, three oat cakes and his copy of Darwin's *Naturalist's Voyage*), he chose a point on the horizon and began to ride. But of course the Pampas were larger than the entirety of Spain, and the rain from the previous night had made the earth heavy and the horse stubborn and the cart the gauchos had sold him snapped its rear axle and he had to get out in front of the beast on more than one occasion to pull, and eventually he abandoned it and took everything he could from the cart and tied it to the sides of the horse and still thought it was nothing, even when he spotted his first rabbit with ears and teeth and cuteness budging, tumbling and teasing the grasses beside him, and took it as a sign from home, a sign from God, and then discovered they weren't rabbits but *biscacha*, widely known as great scavengers and thieves, woke on the third night to the sound of their gnawing at the tent peg he'd driven into the earth to pin his horrible horse, carrying off his compass, water flask, boots, the useless tube pump and was lucky enough to keep the horse from bolting.

By the fifth day it didn't matter which way he turned, it all looked the same. To the left it was desert; to the right, desert; to the sky, desert. There was nothing but sand and grass and sky unmoving. And somewhere, farther off, the sky continued beneath his feet. He was sure he was going to die. He could no longer find water and he prayed for rain and received it, the clouds grouped to gather, and he walked in the rain with the horse in the rain and drank from his hat and danced in the rain but the rain did not stop and soon the ground was run with rivers so he made for some nearby hills and camped on the highest ground he could find and the rain continued and made its way easily into his shelter and a lightning storm the likes of which he had never seen, with hailstones the size of pigeon eggs and so little fallen wood suitable for burning and so he read as fast as he could and tore the pages from his Darwin as he finished to feed the fire and huddled beneath the horse and howling and eventually it collapsed and he was too exhausted to even move it so he wrapped himself around the beast's remaining warmth and fell asleep and when he woke at least the ground was scattered with dozens of dead biscacha and he cooked one using the *Beagle*'s threading of the Strait of Magellan all the way to Valparaiso.

He began to think like the animals. He observed a pampas fox seize the burrow of an armadillo and after that night smoked out some more biscacha and every morning his body was covered in dirt and scratches and at last he reached what he assumed was the Salado River and stalked an ostrich but could not get close enough to snap its neck and he killed an iguana with a rock and it was over a metre long and stringy. In the distance he saw a grouping of Indian *toldos* and headed toward them, hoping he might avail of them some hospitality but they were all empty except for an old woman and a child, maybe eight years old, left to watch over the oxen, he supposed, while the rest were out hunting partridge. They understood nothing. The old woman was blind and he wondered if the child might be brain-damaged. The wealthy Spaniard tried to tell the child how hungry he was, pointing at his mouth and his stomach and doubling over as though in pain. The child stared. He said the word *food* in Spanish and the child stared. Perhaps he was mute. Or feeble-minded. A simpleton. Perhaps that's why they left him when they went to hunt. He dug to the bottom of his bag and found an old candy and a piece of glass and offered both to the child and showed him how the sun played in the piece of glass and he thought about his own son back in Spain and how he must be playing back at the *estancia* and wondering where his father had disappeared to and he showed the child how to balance the piece of glass upon its edge, so that there was no space between it and the rock, and they laughed together when he couldn't do it, over and over and over and so he said: *Then you try!* even though the boy could clearly not understand

him and still the boy took the glass from him and began to try
and try and try again and the Spaniard stood and looked at the
empty horizon and looked at the old woman and he stepped
back softly and coaxed one of the steer to follow him away. He
had his own son to worry about, his own son to return to and
he was so very hungry and of course once he had created a safe
distance he had no idea what to do with it and all he had was
his tiny *verijero*, which was very sharp but barely long enough to
peel a potato let alone slash the bull's throat, which was wide
enough that he couldn't wrap his arms around it and yet he
had gone through so much effort already and with the dagger
dealt him a deadly stroke—or so he thought—to the back of
the neck, thinking to cut its head right off. The Spaniard had
never before used a knife as a weapon, however, and the bull
was likewise unfamiliar with the idea of dying, or even of a man
creeping up on it, and wheeled sudden round and fell the blow
instead to the left shoulder and cleaved the bone but otherwise
came nowhere near the intended target. Up sprang the animal
and dazed by sore pain it threw the Spaniard aside and began
to run, careening off the single tree and sprawling to the grass,
scratching like a started mutt. The Spaniard followed hungry
after, and raised the dagger above the beast's bent head one
more time, struck it bluntly on the nape, once, twice, until finally he lucked into a hit, so satisfying, sunk it so satisfyingly
deep, blood spraying everywhere, and then he found he could
not draw it out, the entire blade lodged in its sternum, its blood
foam and welter, and still it did not go down, turned and stared
the Spaniard down. He would not give. He was a man. Perhaps
they both had some free will at the outset but now the bull's
was clearly diminished and the Spaniard threw his entire body
into it and had to use all his strength just to wrest the creature
over so he could plant his hands back on the handle, trying, to,
work, it, back, and, forth, his left foot planted across the bridge
of the bull's nose and levering, levering, back and forth. And
he was too weak. It had been so long since he'd properly eaten,

he was so weak. And the bull struggled to its feet again and the Spaniard who could not give up, could never, wrapped his arms around its neck and hung there and thankfully the bull was also weak, from the loss of blood and possibly what it saw as betrayal, and it slipped again to one knee, wobbled, too disoriented to find escape, and just crawled in circles, dragging the Spaniard for over a kilometre without getting anywhere and then, finally, it fell, came crashing to the ground on top of the Spaniard's right arm, dislodging the *verijero* but also pulverizing the Spaniard's arm with every pant and wheeze. The rich Spaniard was covered with the beast's hot blood and the flies and swarm and, ultimately unsure of how to properly butcher it, he left the rest of the carcass where it had fallen, he was in so much pain, his arm was useless, and he fashioned a sling from one of his trouser legs and continued toward the distant mountains. He learned to avoid people. He went still when he saw a puff of dust in the distance, or a swarm of condor or crows, or was startled by the movement of the ostrich and deer and guanacos and yet, when more biscacha made off with his last pair of socks, he set fire to the grasses around their burrows and walked slowly away and didn't wait to see when it stopped. Occasionally large tracts of country appeared purple, or spotted with pink and yellow, and others again brilliant with crimson, and amongst the verbenae over a metre high he found some lovely mushrooms and carried them off to relish for dinner. And he lived off armadillo and brightly coloured tinamou eggs and deer, leaving a trail of blood and ashes behind him until the land finally succumbed to him, and bore the freshness to him, with vines of grapes and grand oaks and ferns as large as a man and the humus was nearly a foot deep, this layer between death and life without the cellular cake that confines the rest of us, and felt like he was walking on cushions and he removed his boots and left them there and walked deeper to the thicket and when he was tired now he just dropped where he was and closed his eyes and woke refreshed and one night he woke to find himself swarmed by lightning bugs and imagined each a distant galaxy he would never reach, already dead, perhaps, and he was drifting, drifting. Another day he rounded a copse of black and Aleppo pine aggressing a Portuguese oak and came face to face with another wild bull— in the middle of the forest—as though it were his earlier life— his nightmare—manifest. He rubbed his eyes and it was large and twice as large and he put his hands out to the animal and it snorted, tossing its horns, so he lay down to the humus and tried to press himself into it, to loose his structure, and he and the bull and he were one.

Finally, in the distance, he spied a monastery, surrounded by bushes of spikes and they tore. And he saw a circle of gauchos and they were first people he'd seen in months so they looked like him, to him, they were now the same, and he neared them in friendship but when they saw the face beneath the hat began to dispute his passage and were not disinclined to take the only things he had remaining, which amounted to the shirt and pants and hat, of course, the one pistol, no bullets, *his shoes!* they laughed, *where are his shoes!,* his crown of ruscus, red-berried and cross, and they took everything from him, everything he had left, but could not bring themselves to kill a one-armed man and they let him go.

The bartender was amazed when he walked back into the *pulpería*, freshly washed and wearing the most spectacular northern *campero*. He poured him a drink on the house but the Spaniard said nothing, addressed no one, he was truly a gaucho now, pulled a cigarette from his pack and, just as it settled on his lips, realized he had no matches. He approached one of the original card players with a long scar down his left cheek, who had little more than a quarter inch remaining in his own. The Spaniard gestured to the man to see if he could use it to light his own, and to show his gratitude, rather than return the stub, he tossed it to the ground and offered him a new one in thanks—untouched, pristine and machine-rolled, the latest thing in America. The gaucho stared at it in wonder. He'd probably never seen such a thing, such perfection and uniformity. The wealthy Spaniard wondered if the man would even know what a machine was. They probably didn't even have electricity! And he turned to the bartender to translate for him, saying: *Tell him they have robots now*, he said, *that can roll two hundred in a single minute. Someday they will replace all of us! It's*— But before he could finish, the gaucho had buried his knife in his side, insulted that the wealthy Spaniard thought he'd been smoking the cigarette to the end because he was too poor.

This is what it means to be the gaucho, Lugones said. *No true Argentine wants to feel indebted to the world!*

Alone, however, Lugones was not as vocal in his opposition, had so many questions about Europe, confided that he dreamed one day to visit, to walk the catacombs, to see the paintings of the Louvre, to stand at the birthplaces of Hugo and Verlaine. I was shocked. Was Verlaine so famous now? All the way across the Atlantic? The hotel where he had drunk himself to death—imbibing a not-so-careful blend of whisky and cyanide—was a short walk from our childhood home. *They say he was so ugly, the ugliest man in France. And his poems are...perverse...and indecent. My dream is to ascend that garret and look out over all of Paris, to see the landscape of Verlaine's soul and then understand the world the way he did—a European, like yourself, who saw the cancer of Europe.* I tried to imagine it. Would he, I wondered, see our childhood home from there? Had Verlaine? And what would our home have looked like from there? Like the birthplace of a genius? Or just another rooftop like any other? It was not terribly far. Lugones said he would never leave. He would just write until he died. Even if it came quick, it would be worth it. *All you have to do is write one true sentence. The truest sentence you know.*

And what would that sentence say? my brother asked.

Perhaps that was it.

I thought you devout, Camille said. *Are you not distressed by his rejection of faith?*

Lugones shook his head. *Sin isn't a rejection of faith. It is a moment in the parable the faithful tell about themselves. There is no redemption without it.*

He also confided he longed to take in the magnificent achievement of the new Eiffel Tower, such a building to God, had we seen it? *Of course, it is impossible to miss.* What were our impressions of it? He had heard of the protests leading up to it, the petition that had been signed by so many French architects and artists: Dumas, Maupassant, Huysmans, our dear Gounod, as well as so many names Lugones didn't even recognize. Who were these people? he asked. Did people know of them even in Paris? What was the value of their opinion? And Camille answered that many of them were quite prominent figures back home, so, yes, people did know them. *Does anyone listen to them?* Lugones asked. *Yes,* Camille said, *of course.*

But why?

Because they understand beauty.

Do they, though? They claimed it was not an attack on Eiffel as a person but on the process of choosing, that there should have been more artists involved, not just engineers. It should have been more open. And really, did the president want to be responsible for imposing on the Parisian cityscape a tragic street lamp, a belfry skeleton, a deformed gymnasium apparatus, a factory pipe carcass, a hole-riddled suppository? *What was it that Eiffel replied?* Lugones grinned. He said: *Are we to believe that because one is an engineer, one is not also preoccupied by beauty?* He also pointed out the potential scientific uses, for transmitting radio signals, studying meteorology and astronomy. Of course, it would open up the world, such a thing, would allow man to greater understand the universe, as all great creations of the imagination should. Not through the science experiments people were planning, but by breaking through layers of possibility. *They suffered from a great failure of imagination, those men. Afraid of losing their dominance on something they cannot own. It is its monumental uselessness that makes it so necessary; like a tunnel beneath the ocean; or launching hundreds of mirrors into space to create a giant ring, to manipulate the light from the stars, to reshape them into anything we want. Sometimes I think the Eiffel Tower doesn't even exist, that it was just an idea in someone's head, and so forceful an idea that now everyone sees it. Someday I want to see it, but I worry it won't live up to my imagination and yet I still want to see it, all the same. It is the problem* with most art, making ideas into art, concepts into things, it's entirely inhuman. Making ideas into realistic-seeming characters, into people, but they can never be more than things. Our things. Art is the residue of thought. It's what remains when we try to understand the world. Characters are constantly being victimized by their creators, forced to do things they might not otherwise, had they the agency. The world is set out for them in such concrete ways. And yet there is still the illusion of this agency. Is it likely that the characters would feel bad—if we let them? I'm not sure. Signs must be allowed to signify. Like the Eiffel Tower, we should only create impossible things. The greatest highs and the greatest lows, packed together. Only then can we finally just put it aside and start the real work: deciphering truth. Art is belief in the unreal Truth, after all. It doesn't matter if you understand it; it won't wait for you to understand it; it's already on to the next idea.

Short fiction, Lugones claimed, was the future of Argentine literature. Stories about impossible things. He had written one about the world before the Great Flood. Another was based on a gardener training flowers to defend themselves. Another about a scientist trying to liquefy thought. Another about trying to project sound through time. Just recently he had begun a story about a giant monster, part ape and part whale, that is awakened by all the mining near the capital, attacking Buenos Aires and crushing every existing monument to Spain. (*It is a story of hope,* he said. *It is only through violence,* he said, *that one is able to rebuild.*) And yet another was about monkeys who refused to speak so they wouldn't have to work. *In the story,* he said, *a doctor by the name of Amo buys a monkey from a bankrupt circus and tries to entice it to words—with a variety of unhealthy foods, alcohol, you follow? He employs a cook to make the most fantastic meals. Anything he can use to bribe the beast into making one manly sound, certain he can use this to spark their evolution. He makes the monkey watch films, makes him read Shakespeare. He employs a series of levers and pulleys to contort the monkey's face into the proper formations for the composite sounds. But it does not speak, only becomes more contemplative and sad, weeping in despair when confronted. The monkey suffers,* Lugones says, *from intelligence, and finds its sole consolation in more drink. But of course he still won't ask for it, is too proud and/or committed. One day, frustrated by his lack of progress, Amo beats him within an inch of his life, forcing him to the ground and kicking him repeatedly in the ribs. Once. Twice. Three times. Four times. Forces. Twigs be. Hind his. Lips and. Levers. Them a. Gainst his. Teeth. To form the appropriate shapes. But then he just feels guilty and breaks down and apologized to the monkey and agrees to bring him whatever he wants.* How can I make it up to

313

you? *he asks.* What can I do to make it right? *And he means it. In that moment, he will bring the monkey anything. He will do anything. If he'll just ask for it. Once.*

But of course the monkey still won't. And the story ends with Amo opening the window so the monkey can have its freedom. And he leaves him there and goes to the kitchen and complains to the cook that he has given up, to finally admit failure, that the animals aren't their equals as he had supposed. And the cook, more saddened by this news than Amo would have predicted, says: I will miss him, too. I will miss our long conversations. *And Amo says:* Conversations? What do you mean, conversations? *And the cook tells him of the weekly philosophy club they started, and how they would regularly discuss politics, though it was clear to him that the chimp did not believe he could understand any of the real complexities of governance and would dumb it down for him.* He used to say that, when he is one day elected president, he will make it a felony to drink small beer. *Small beer is for women,* he says. *He would also often make special requests for foods he read about in his books.* Do you know what it is? *the cook inquires of Amo.* A funeral baked meat? Or a posset? And Amo rushes back to the room to find Yzur still sitting in front of the open window, contemplating something on the end of his finger. *Presented with his freedom, Yzur chooses not to take it. Why? Because it is easier to be taken care of than to be free. Freedom is not easy. It takes great responsibility. Imagine,* he said, *the freedom to sit down at the piano and not follow the score.*

Why would you do that? my brother responded.

To be free.

But it would be worse.

It might be. But it might also be better.

The little boy from the first night, as it turned out, was Lugones's son, Little Polo, who began to arrive with him at our apartments most mornings. Instead of arriving after our morning of work, however, we would now wake to find Lugones sleeping on our couch or reading through my brother's notes or drinking the cold dregs of yesterday's coffee or, on more than one occasion, accompanied by one of the secretaries from his newspaper, talking close in the kitchen, Little Polo colouring at the table. It was unclear how they got in. Lugones had his own set of keys, I suppose, since the apartment was owned by the paper, but he never mentioned them, never spoke as though this arrangement was anything other than ordinary. He would simply act surprised that *we* were there, say, *There you are! The great Saint-Saëns himself!* and the secretary would quietly ask, *Who is he, again?* and Lugones would ignore her and offer my brother a drink and for the next ten minutes we would sit in the kitchen, all four of us, drinking at eight in the morning while pretending the secretary wasn't there. Even she was a participant in this last part; quite possibly she was even better at pretending she wasn't there than Lugones. More often, Camille and Little Polo and I would stare out the window while listening to them fuck awkwardly in the next room and then Lugones would emerge again, tucking in his shirt, and his face would light up and he'd say: *Are you all finished, then? The well has run dry for the day? Me, too!*

Lugones took us to the Recoleta, with its magnificent monastery and cemetery, like a miniature version of the city. The cemetery itself, Lugones said, was nearly three hundred years old, with many unmarked graves, but only recently had it become the final resting place for the capital's wealthiest, a contest of vanity, with thousands of grandiose mausoleums and mini-palaces, Greek temples, Roman cenotaphs, Egyptian obelisks, Gothic, Classical, Classical Revival, many supposedly designed by Paris's greatest architects but each lathered with such anachronistic adornment, a grotesque pastiche of mourning, and Little Polo ran ahead of us to laugh and scream and chase some stray cats and we often lost sight of him as he passed between the silent ballet of obese cherubs, forlorn virgins, Rubenesque angels blowing trumpets, weeping mistresses and mothers of stone. He took us to the tomb of General Guido, and of Juan Manuel de Rosas. *The private social clubs I told you about the other night?* he said. *Argentina is run by these clubs so the wealthy elites can avoid the rest of us: the Jockey Club, the Club de Progreso, or the Yacht Club Argentino, which cost over two million pesos to build. Two million! More than the deficit for the entire nation last year! On a club. For men. To wave straw hats at each other! But it's the Círculo de Armas that is mostly made of the families who were involved in the overthrow of Rosas. They want to force their help on the poor and the provinces but all we need is more people like Darío. He is a true Christian,* Lugones said, *and he understands—as I do—that this lack of faith is the greatest problem of the lower class.* We saw the garish tombs of several presidents, each larger than the previous; others crammed with the full membership of the Topographical Society, the Spanish Aid Union, the Assembly of Loyal Gatherers; another built for an Italian gravedigger who saved his entire life for a plot and a statue, then killed himself on the day it was finished; and another that belonged to the illegitimate grandchild of Napoleon Bonaparte, at the foot of a large blasted tree, split in half and filled with dead leaves, and it was amazing how two numbers, just six digits apart, could mean so much. There was the great Facundo Quiroga, el Tigre de los Llanos, who was buried standing so that, should he be required again, he'd be ready. Sarmiento was also buried there—the man who had betrayed Quiroga as an example of provincialism—with its soaring obelisk perched by a sickly condor. *Sarmiento would have loved the whole world to be city,* Lugones said. *It made things simpler. Have you read Sarmiento's* Viajes? *He travelled as an ambassador to Europe and said he found nothing but gaps, empty spaces of such completeness that he was convinced reality was unravelling around him, as though you had decided to wipe out your worst memories but had nothing else to replace them with, so you just hid them, these empty spaces, behind mountains or cathedrals or marvels of architecture and called it Europe, as though moths had gnawed through your blankets of morality. Then, on his way back, he discovered America, as every person new to America seems to do, and decided the only way forward was to destroy what we were.* Once the graveyard had filled, Lugones said, they had even paid to evict some of the older tenants to make more space. *It used to cost more to die in Buenos Aires than it did to be alive,* Lugones joked. *But now it is wholly and truly full. It's been decades since anyone has been able to get in, and now it is less of a spiritual gate than a historical landmark. When we bury someone's body,* he said, *we are making a tangible connection to the afterlife, to the spiritual world. And the longer we go without doing that, the more pointless it all becomes. Anyone—a local or a tourist—can read the names upon the stones. But they do not create emotions, and emotions are only real in exchange. Perhaps that is the problem with Buenos Aires, that the graveyards are filled with people no one knows.*

We spent June and July of that year in Argentina, so we missed all the renewed rioting back home over the Dreyfus Affair and had to be satisfied with the local strikes and police crackdowns over plans to build another gigantic boulevard like they had in Paris and Berlin. This was opposed not only by the landlords and residents of most of the existing buildings, but also by the workers, who saw the plan as a direct threat to their ability to mobilize in protest. The construction workers could not afford to walk off the job. Many had already lost their jobs to these new European immigrants, or been replaced with Chinese at half the price. *One day,* Sux told us, *two thousand European workers marched on the waterfront and prevented a hundred new Chinese from disembarking, then bashed their Chinese heads and tore down their Chinese shops and Chinese laundries, yanking their Chinese braids and kicking them down the Chinese street. After that, the government had to bring in the army to patrol the downtown.*

Under our noses, the city began to change—like the creatures of Tussaud's wax museum in London, who seemed almost human until the deep peer into those lifeless sweaty eyes. It was like a little Paris, yes, but Paris in an opera by Puccini. The rains came at the same times every day, as opposed to the random sorrows of home. It was like Paris as told to a child to an imaginary friend to a stuffed toy. Even when we looked back, the only thing notable about the Opera was the cocktails; for the Politeama, its ventilation. Everything was too clean, too perfect—lacking in context. They knew nothing, these people, except pomp and display, the appearance of art rather than the art itself, the dissonance of the city's Neoclassical palaces and coffee shops set against tangles of Italian Classical with French Academic as though the custodians of history had quickly swept everything into a box before the guests arrived and the city planners and architects had pulled pieces out at random.

If you want to know more about the real Buenos Aires, Sux said to us, *you need to come where I live in Barracas. Has Gerchunoff told you about our conventillo? They are wonders of science, designed not for space but for the opposite of space, packing groups of unfamiliar men to a room, a family to a room, a family to a closet, a family to a stretch of wall, hung on hooks. This is how we have evolved in South America,* he said. *From creatures of the plains to creatures of tiny boxes. We are breeding to survive the apocalypse, like cockroaches. One day, the whole world will be like this, with Argentines occupying every square inch of the planet, teetering on the brink of the oceans. We are weeds. Homo south-americanus.*

Sux took us to all the *other* neighbourhoods, the ones we hadn't seen with the others, the ones that were all the same: an infinite straggling high street, misshapen masses of brick and stucco they called houses, a bleak plaza with a hideous pile of masonry called a church, and mobs of *vijilantes* (underdeveloped young men with thin moustaches and cigarettes and skins whom the police force had raised from the poor to surveil their own but who instead spent their time playing billiards or harassing women and were passable at one and excelled at the other. Each church also had a bell to signal nothing, apparently, but the end of daydreaming, with a loudness inversely proportional to its musicality.

Has Lugones told you about his plans for a national literature? Sux said. *A national* culture? *Can you imagine that? Culture is as imperceptible to him as water is to fish, only in his case he's as likely to drown as swim. Lugones believes in the principle that immediate survival is more important than long-term survival. He equates the two, in fact, is convinced that the former will lead to the latter, as though winning a battle is enough to win the war.*

His main problem is that he trusts in the idea of government. He wants to set up rules. If the goal is to tear down the establishment, Lu-

319

gones should do so and replace it with the ideal machine, one designed to destroy itself, over and over, until there is no more memory, just the consistency of the now. The now of destruction!

He took us to see the conventillo where he lived with Gerchunoff, and with each step he seemed to take us further from Lugones's imagined Paris and we stopped to rub our eyes and each earlier exhibit of opulence transformed to a museum of poverty, a shop window of vagrancy, a sidewalk of illness. Sux said: *Everyone who lives in my building calls it the Cuatro Diques. Do you know why? Because it leaks like it was made from spare sheaves of wheat. When it rains the rooms that still have paint get sick and grow boils, huge bubbles of water and paint that hang as much as six inches from the ceiling. Occasionally they burst, but more typically they are just slowly sweating wounds that recede when it gets drier. When we complain, the landlord arrives in the night and wakes us up and kicks us out into the street for the night while some people he calls his cousins make the repairs.* Do you know how expensive it is to keep these buildings in working order? *he said to us the last time we waited outside in the cold.* It's a full-time job, *he said. But he only fixed four rooms, the rooms of the people who complained the most. He did nothing for the people who were too scared to complain, and that's why they call it Cuatro Diques. The four dams. All the conventillos have names. There's another they call La Cueva Negra—the dark cave—because the landlord is too cheap to replace the lights. I don't ever need a key to my building, but I do have to subject myself to beatings before anything will be opened to me. It's one of the rules. They know me. They're really quite remarkable, their memories,* he said. *There must be twenty thousand people in my building and they know us all. Not by name, of course, but by the particular stench we must give off, detectable only to them. They have nothing on us, of course. Elsewise, they would charge us. And put us in jail. And perhaps kill us. But since they have nothing, beating is the only option.*

One day I was eating with some friends in the park and one of them snuck up behind me and I was grabbed by the throat, suddenly and without warning, and then tossed onto my friends. I saw a group of police storm the crowd of people relaxing on the lawn, causing panic. I saw more police than I could count, beating people on the grounds with their batons. Is that the right word? Their nightsticks, I mean. Their clubs. And as I turned to look behind me I saw, out of the corner of my eye, a short officer with a goatee come toward me with his baton raised. He hit me on my right hip, causing a red-and-purple welt.

Another time one of the officers broke his nightstick across my back, left to fetch another one, then kept beating me. They took me back to the station and he commanded me to spread a cream, used to scour toilet seats, over the head of another nightstick, which they inserted into me and I fell down and they beat me. I had to defecate. I ran to the toilet to defecate. And they said: You are not going to defecate in the toilet, you are going to defecate on the ground so you can eat it. And what choice did I have? I defecated on the ground and they made me eat it. And then they beat me. And as I was cleaning the floor that was filthy with feces and blood, they were beating me.

Another day we were in the Plaza de Mayo for lunch and a line of police moved toward us and told us we had to move and my friend had broken his leg at work and we were sitting on the bench on the east side—do you know it? the one on the grate protecting the foundation stone?—and so he refused. The Plaza used to be surrounded by a double line of paraiso trees but they all died rather than remain Argentines, so there wasn't even an idea of shade, which meant it was not an especially pleasant location in which to linger, anyway, but since they were forcing us to move, he decided to sit. And when the police approached us, my friend said: This is a public space. We are only having lunch. And the officer said: You are too close to the police station. My friend laughed. Is there a law about lingering too close to the police station? And the officer said: Yes, there is a law about lingering too close to the police station. And my friend laughed again, because it was clearly total bullshit and, emboldened by the ridiculousness of it all, how unbelievable it was, I said: Since when? Since when is that a law? And he said: It is brand new. And I said: How new? And he said: Just now. Just this second. And my friend put a hand on my arm, as if to caution me, concerned now, but he had already emboldened

321

me, *already set me off, and I said the first thing that came into my mind because I was already set off and in no mood for thinking and I said, without thinking:* Do you know who I am? *not entirely sure what I would say next, but saying it sounded presently wonderful.* Do you know who I am?! *I repeated and tried to stand taller. I tried to will my body to be taller—can you imagine that? Through nothing more than confidence I would bend reality and rise up over him and through nothing more than being on the side of the right I would make him see reason, tattooed on the side of my fist, and I would thrash him and his friends and rid the world of people like them, rid the world of hate and pain and intimidation and, when it gradually dawned on me that this was not going to happen, I closed my eyes and waited for his baton to descend, waited to be surrounded by his workmates and kicked and beaten and spat on and someone pushed me down and suddenly instead of the beating there were gunshots going off all around us and it took me a moment of spinning madly in place to realize it was them, the police, not firing at us or at anyone in particular, really, just firing into the air, so that most of the young people went scattering to the side streets, past the cathedral and the mansion of the archbishop, down Calle Defensa, Calle Victoria, Calle Bolivar, Calle Balcarce, past the Cabildo that was already being demolished, the statue of Manuel Belgrano, through the Italianate archway of the pink Casa Rosada, the Avenue Rivadavia, the Avenue Hipólito Yrigoyen and the government offices and the Ministerio de Energía y Minería, de Educación, de Defensa in the distance, most of my own friends were gone, and in the confusion our officers swung through us and the one I'd been arguing with was in the middle of it, pointing, screaming:* These ones! These are the ones! Take these ones! *And there was someone grabbing my arm and forcing me to the ground, my face to the ground, with what felt like an unsheathed knife at my back. I looked up for a moment and saw them pushing my friend into a line and they had taken his crutches and he was walking and he was looking at what his legs were doing and he seemed surprised by them, at their miraculous betrayal, and then I lost him. And they pulled me to my feet and threw me into a group of other prisoners and they made us kneel in a line with our hands on our heads, facing the wall. I heard them talking behind me and learned that a group of men numbering somewhere between fifty and a hundred had attacked the jail in the next neighbourhood, which was only defended by twelve guards. They released many of their friends but more importantly gained the possession of two hundred and fifty Remingtons, ten thousand rounds of ammunition, and two cannons, which they were presently using to attack other jails and police stations, so they could gain even more ammunition, and more friends and soldiers and police had been ordered to protect public buildings but not to interfere with either side, and still there were errant bullets that somehow found their way into the hearts and minds of both sides and it was impossible to know, at any given moment, which side any given soldier was not intervening with more. Whoever was supposed to be watching over us told us not to move or we would be shot. And then he left us for nearly an hour while we tried to imagine the scene behind us. It's surprisingly difficult to keep your hands on your head like this. Even with something to rest on, they quickly start to ache and crick. Many times I thought about lowering them, because the pain was too great, but always at that precise moment I would feel one of them stop behind me, would feel him lean in and breathe, like he was smelling me, like a wolf, so I would resist, and think about something else, mostly—and this is strange—of the first time I tasted ice cream, not a complete vision but like a box of sounds and aromas that I unpacked one on one and one on one until my tongue was cold and alive and the sun felt like my mother's hand on the back of my neck and my mother was laughing at something my father had said, maybe about Pirandello? He was always talking about Pirandello in those days, quoting Pirandello and talking about absurdity, about Pirandello, I'm not sure, maybe it was Jarry, or the weather, and then I could hear it quite clearly, my father's voice saying:* Elephant shoe, *which was a private joke we had in our family, this phrase, but it was never actually spoken, so it was curious to remember it in this way, never spoken, always signed, like he was pulling on his nose and then knocking his fists together, the sign for elephant, and shoe, which was meaningless, especially in Spanish, only really made sense in English, and only spoken, because if you couldn't hear the sounds you could still see the lips moving and it would seem like he was saying* I love you, *but my father had been an assistant, for a while, to a professor at the university and my mother had cleaned rooms for a diplomat from Belfast and they had picked up a word or two of English here and there and my father, who was quite funny, who was always cracking jokes, began to sign the two words instead*—elephant and shoe—*because it removed all sense from it, made it absurd, like Pirandello—he loved Pirandello—and so we signed it, these two words, to mean* I love you, *which was touching and funny at the same time, and that was the kind of people my parents were. We could never really afford frivolities, of course, but my parents liked to treat us, to spoil us, my sisters and I, and one day he blindfolded us and took us to the port and bought some ice cream from a street vendor and spooned it into our mouths with strawberries and milk and I thought the world had been upended, that something could taste this good and this cold and this happy and I began to drool—in the present, I began to drool, just thinking about this—and I was self-conscious about how this might look to the woman beside me, her hands above her head as well. I was embarrassed and it tore me from the memory, shook me through nearly a decade of fondness until there alone was that rotten breath again, and when I finally dared to turn my head, of course, there was no one there. The six of us were all alone and God knows how long we'd been like that. I was so full of tension that I started the punch the wall. Over and over and over and over and over and over and over and over...*

Camille began to wonder if he'd made a mistake, coming here. Rehearsals began for the *Organ Symphony*, and though Berutti had already been practising with the musicians for weeks, the piece was nowhere near ready, the entire production mired in incompetence. The scores had been transcribed by French copyists in the European fashion (for one) rather than the American (which they were accustomed to), so the tuba players had to read one note but actually think and play another. But it was more than that. Varela was, as expected, an overinflated fraud, barely able to play a part that was not even the lead. The flautists were the worst I'd ever heard, could not seem to follow simple notes on a page, and Camille was forced to interrupt Berutti over and over and sing their parts to them from memory. Sometimes, he even had to segregate an offending section and make them play it over and over by themselves until he could determine the exact fault and remedy it. Then, once those issues were fixed, Camille began to rethink the piece itself, especially the organ. And the soloist was forced to forget the interpretation he had mastered the day before and incorporate all of Camille's new notations, each scrawled atop the last.

We also attended a rehearsal for one of Berutti's new pieces, the gaucho or the revolution one, I couldn't tell, and for all his posturing about authenticity it screamed of Italy, especially when we heard the harmony, so simple and obvious, so trapped in its tunefulness, its duets, quartets, its *scenas*, we could see it all coming before it happened, the opening overture climaxing in a series of *ostinatos* with a tonic-dominant seesaw and its awkward, painful crescendo and a deafening *tutti* with the bass instruments scooping up the melodic ball; its high notes, fast and high, and its triple it, triple it, triple it, triple it; its *cabalettas.* Berutti's Argentina was like Lugones's Buenos Aires, all *baciami, baciami, se quel bel labor baciar potrò,* and would not take no for an answer, these melodies without end, on and on, *il solo sperare d'aver a gioire, il solo,* forcing itself on you, forcing it, selfish you and then STOP! *Cabaletta.* So many cabelettas, like he was Bellini, or Donizetti, or Verdi trying to be Bellini or Donizetti, trotting couplets over a contrasting *boompa boompa trala trala.* At least Donizetti had been original, in his own way. Verdi was like an additional blister on the Donizetti callus. And this? I wanted to reach out and slap him. How was it possible for someone who had grown so here to sound so away?

As careful as possible, we slipped into the lobby and found the Little Russian reading Longfellow's "O, Ship of State." Camille was uncertain what to say to her and she did not look up from her book as we approached, nor did she initiate anything, so he told her, maliciously, what the others had said, that this place was like a little Paris, and she said: *Why do you always talk about such boring things? You're like the rest of them, with their theatre of unhappiness. You act as though the world doesn't change as soon as you write it down! Yes, yes, it's like Paris, it's not like Paris—can't both be true? There is no real Buenos Aires, anyway. It's like an imaginary city, or like several imaginary cities, each layered on top of the next. A city of Spanish but also a city of Italians, a city of Russians, a city of Jews, a city of Syrians, all in this place and all different and all more or less real. No one even speaks the same language anymore and we probably have more newspapers per capita than any city in the world but no person can read more than one and you can drift from one dream to another and imagine you're in a new place. Sux likes to say the whole city is made of mud—layers and layers of mud excreted from the Pampas—piled high into skyscrapers and cathedrals and palaces of mud. Lugones describes it as floating in the clouds. He's always looking for the edge, where he can peer down under it and find a way to drop it on the heads of his enemies. Buenos Aires, like the mind, is an iceberg. Buenos Aires is a city of dreams. They dream of success. They dream of revolution. Given a choice*, she said, *I would rather live in the world of dreamers.*

Do you know, she said, *the first half of my life*, she said, *was like I had been born into a Victorian novel, not a question of* What will she do? *which is the luxury that men have in this world, nor even* Who will she be? *but* To whom will she marry? *Because of my father's political affiliations, I had a range of potential spouses, probably of more promising nature than most. The men outnumber us nearly five to one. And yet, probably because of my mother, I asked to have some say, to choose my own, and remarkably, probably because of my mother, they acquiesced. Can you imagine? It was arranged that I should have a series of supervised meetings, conversations, and after that, for whatever reason I wanted, I could choose. And so I devised a set of questions I felt would most quickly allow me to get to know them.*

Like what? my brother asked.

What do you mean?

What kind of questions?

All sorts, really. What does it matter? It's not the point of the story. They were things that were very important to me and likely never to anyone else. Perhaps that's the most backwards way to go about it, and what I should have done was ask them things that were important to them and see how they dealt with it. In the end, however, I chose poorly. My husband knew my brother and was twenty years my senior. I had no recollection of ever meeting him but then he was asking my brother what my parents might think, what I might think, about my becoming his wife. I think that's the way he phrased it: become my wife. *And I recoiled, naturally. But in the end I still said yes. There was something about him. It's impossible to truly see into another person's mind, but I think he loved me. He took me to Europe for our honeymoon simply because I asked. We went to Paris. We went to the Louvre and saw the* Mona Lisa. *In bed he was passionate and caring. I decided I wanted a baby. More than anything. He seemed less sure but went along with it. There was a thing living inside of me, M. Saint-Saëns. Can you imagine what that feels like? To having something with you at all times that is not you and still dependent on you? I simultaneously wished it would* never come out and that it would disappear forever. *Whenever anyone asked, I said it was the best thing to ever happen to me. I was already loving him. Then, when he actually emerged, I was unsure. I had always imagined I would love him from the first moment, and when the midwife gathered him and brought him to lie on my chest I said:* My baby, my baby, my baby, *I just kept repeating it, hoping he would stop crying, I was so tired, and he stopped crying and the bright sunlit room grown even brighter and in my head I was already thinking perhaps I didn't want to be a mother, that this creature did not appeal to me at all, not immediately. It was frail and dependent, clearly it could not survive without me, I had to be forever vigilant, which I was not wont to do. And I tried to fall asleep and I dreamed of happy things and when I woke there he was. He was the one who made me wake. But still I began to love him and long for the waking, long for the tears, long for the hard stretch of loving dreary. I would look at him sleeping in my arms so beautiful and sudden would come over me a chill and I would consider the cold and think about the weather and the coming winter and how there were women with babies who were not as fortunate as I and that they might not have a shawl, as I did, or a blanket against the cold, and perhaps they were even homeless and unwanted themselves, did not have the supports I had from my husband, or my parents, and they had to worry about where they might get their next meal, and where they might get their next meal for their baby and they had nothing and had to live with that constant fear of failing their child and I realized they were sad and in pain like me.*

My brother was silent. *Is it true?* he said, finally.

She shrugged. *Sometimes I like to imagine the worst thing that could ever happen to me. In the end it makes me feel better for not being true.*

But you've already made yourself imagine it, Camille said, *already lived through it, in its own way.*

Isn't that the importance of life? she replied.

Afterwards, Berutti and the Little Russian took us to meet Alberto Williams, founder of the Buenos Aires Conservatory of Music, and Zenón Rolón, who invited us to his club to watch the other black musicians play jazz. The band was led by a man who barely seemed to move except for his fingers and cheeks and eyes, his back, back bent, neck all crook, and everything flaring, flaring, flaring. He dropped boot to the floor, swung a long eye over the crowd. Sometimes they fell into familiar patterns and melodies from other pieces, like a short sample from Mozart, another from Chopin. I could even hear Camille's own extended chords, and the way they blurred the edge between major and minor triads. But just as often he was just giving himself up to chance, flopping from mistake to mistake until it all felt natural, with no respect whatsoever for the transference of sounds, laughing and shouting at one another, stepping off the stage to smoke in the middle of a song. As the music spun and spun and lurched and spun, I tried to imagine what Halévy would have thought of them, giving themselves up so wholly to instinct, lacking in the precision and purpose he prized. It was like they lived in an imaginary world, without rules—a brutal landscape where rocks were living and struck themselves and pronounced it beauty. It was like the worst of Gottschalk, like listening to a series of repeated mistakes, as though they had to test it over and over to find that it was—as anyone with any sense should have suspected—all wrong, like an argument with a communist, aimed to convince, to convince, to convince, saying: *This is music, this is music, no, really, this is music,* until we accepted it as correct.

They upset you. Berutti leaned into Camille as they played. And my brother said: *No.*

They are some of the finest musicians we have here.

And my brother said: *Chaos is simple. The universe tends toward it. True art fights against life.*

Perhaps you have never lived within chaos, true chaos, as we breathe it here. Most of what passes as art today is a machine. What we listened to back there is more natural. Animalistic. Since the Industrial Revolution, humans have created such a world of automation that we no longer understand it.

Lugones left us one morning and we discovered he'd left Little Polo behind. For the first hour, Camille tried to ignore him, sat down at the piano and tried to work. But Little Polo sat beneath the piano and attempted to tie his shoelaces together. He asked for a drink of water. He wanted to show us how he could ascend the mantel. So my brother helped him put on his sweater and tie his laces and we left the apartment and rode the trams together, farther than we'd yet been with Lugones, to scenic Belgrano, wealthy Flores, aspiring Adrogué, pulled by two insufficient nags who probably should have been enjoying their retirement on a ranch eating grass but had instead been pressed into service like this for their country. We trammed to Tigré and the river had overflown the banks and we had to wade through the brown water without stockings or shoes, our pants rolled up past our knees, Little Polo on Camille's shoulders laughing madly. At the Puerto de Frutos the entire river was hidden by fallen peaches and oranges, bobbing rosy and yellow as though they had done it on purpose, to copy Seurat's paintings of the Seine, only in this case the painter had become confused about where the water ended and the grass of the *jatte* began. We were overcome by the water and the stench, emanating from a barge anchored in the river's centre, filled with enough fruit to supply the entire Marché des Innocents. We laughed and stopped for lunch at a *confiteria*. Another day we ventured to Palermo, just to see the old summerhouse of Juan Manuel de Rosas, the terrorist dictator of Buenos Aires province and briefly the entire country. The main building was nothing now, a school for military cadets, and it was hard to believe, as ugly as it was, that it had once housed one of the country's most powerful and

330

horrible men and out back were the sheds where he'd stabled his escorts and past that were the gardens where the flowers had all the colour of flowers but none of the smell and we came upon an artificial military band upon an artificial hill and they played something that was almost music. And on our return, just as we were descending from the footboard, an older gentleman tumbled from the fore (or was pushed) and the wheels of the car trundled over his right knee and left him amputated and bleeding out in the street. Camille stepped forward to help him. He had learned so much about the body, how the blood pumped and flowed and how it could be managed. Quickly he removed his belt and prepared to apply it as a tourniquet. He began to whisper to the man, saying: *Everything will be fine, you will be fine, everything will be fine...* But out of nowhere came one of those vijilantes and he drew his machete and blew his whistle for reinforcements and stood guard over the dying man, waving his weapon at Camille, until the divisional police surgeon could be found to officially diagnose the man and write his accident report and by that time, of course, the victim had already perished of inhumanity and most of his corpse was conveyed back to the *comisaria* to be claimed by his friends or relatives, minus the contents of his pockets.

The Little Russian arrived looking for Lugones and when she learned he'd just left, she decided to wait. *He's left the kid, after all*, she said. Rather than sit around all day, however, the four of us took the train as far as it could go, like a happy little family, beyond the buildings, beyond the vijilantes, left the city, then the province, then entered the adjacent province of La Pampa and swept the singéd grass and the solitary *ombú* and there were fires in the farmers' fields that brought to silhouette the solitary trees and grasses and occasionally a *tropilla* of wild horses standing beside a fence that fenced nothing. There was a young fiddler in our car that we paid to stop, and a man selling impolite literature, and once we'd reached the pastures we assumed we'd go even faster, but the driver slackened speed and blew, its hideous whistle wakening the heads of every passenger on every side swung wide and out window, like a grotesque beast with a hundred heads instead of legs, just to see what the slowing and the sounding meant. And there they were, one of those mobs of wild horses, spread directly across the track. They had ample room to escape, nothing for kilometres in any direction besides the train, and themselves, and us. They merely had to take a handful of steps in any direction. But they were such an awkward mass of stupidity, and when the train made slow and sound, rather than bolt to safety they turned and came directly for us, and oh! the shrieks and screams; the crushing and mangling of bones; the scattering right and left of quivering limbs! Little Polo hung out the window and whooped and kept score.

Once we had run out of tracks, we found a huge open pitch of mud and found two men digging trenches and approached them to see what they were doing. It was as though they were trying to dig a moat around the city, or were perhaps slowly digging under it so they could get rid of the whole thing altogether, the trench was so deep and long. And Little Polo, of course, ran straight for it, leaping down without a second look and disappearing immediately from view, but we approached the two men directly and learned that one of them was the caretaker and the other was his assistant and they were digging graves, getting ready. About a quarter century ago, some immigrants had arrived by ship and brought with them yellow fever and so they created this burial ground and within three months it was full, twenty-five thousand corpses stacked like pallets beneath their feet, with barely a dusting of earth between them, they came so fast there was no time to do otherwise. *So now we're getting ready*, the caretaker said. *People are dying all the time. Before they even know it. This time we'll be ready.* The Little Russian was bored and went looking for Polo and, at that moment, a third young man struggled by, dragging the corpse of an older man on a tray, collapsing repeatedly in alternating grief and exhaustion—left, right, left, right, wailing and pounding at the earth.

The caretaker put down his shovel and stared and said nothing and Camille walked over to the young man with the corpse and took the other end of the tray and together they made it to the edge of the trench and the trench was even bigger than we'd first thought, about two metres across, with enough depth to bury maybe five or six at a time. The young man, who was suddenly resolute, said the body belonged to his father and that the cemeteries in the city were asking too much but he did have some money and the caretaker looked at it and at Camille and rolled his eyes as though he would never have done this if we had not been there and took his money and counted it and called to his assistant and Camille helped them lower the body into the giant trench and, without warning, no one had been expecting it, the son leaped in with his father and addressed the lifeless corpse with a lot of chest-beating and *why did I this* and *what have I that* and rearranged his father to look more peaceful, more prepared, and the gravediggers, who had their own lives to live, who had so much more to dig today and were hungry, urged him to get it over with, to hurry up, that people didn't stop dying, it happened every day. Shamed, the young man wiped his tears and began to climb, but the earth was loose and he made no progress. The assistant swore and shovelled some dirt on him but the caretaker put his hand on his shoulder (was the assistant also his own son?) and instead looked at Camille as though this was all his fault and leaned down to help pull the young man out and Camille did the same, but in ascending the young man partially dislodged a woman in the stack behind him with his foot and for a moment it seemed like the whole prior wall might come down. Ignoring this, the two gravediggers with their spades threw a few shovelfuls of dirt on both of them, then jumped down with heavy wooden rammers, directly on top of the man's father, and rammed both corpses unrelentingly until they were sure there was room for three more. The son wandered off and we went searching for Little Polo, tracing the edge of the trench without luck and a final man

333

approached, with a mule and a tiny hearse, no larger than an apple cart, and this time the caretaker tried to wave him off, it was not that kind of cemetery, he said, but when he saw that the dead infant was only six months old, he accepted what the man had and once the wagon was gone he carried the tiny corpse by one of its arms deeper into the grounds, away from the trench toward the open plain. We followed him, watched him find a spot about twenty metres from the trench and, without putting his foot upon a spade or even lifting up the ground at all, dragged his heel through the dirt to make a small furrow and dropped the baby there. He paused, staring at it for a moment, perhaps reconsidering the amount of space it might take up in the trench, but then simply pushed its arms to its side with the edge of his shovel, then walked away and left it. Camille could not move, staring at this poor thing on the ground, its body broken and still. He walked forward and took the spade, intent on burying the baby himself. It looked like it was sleeping. *Whose child were you?* he said. *Who has forgotten you?* he said. And then: *No one will ever forget you.* But then we heard the caretaker and the Little Russian and Little Polo all screaming at one another, and we ran immediately back.

Gerchunoff and Sux did not join us for several nights, had not been seen for several nights, and we had begun to miss their playful attacks on Reilly. Camille asked about them and everyone went silent. Finally Sux was found and said Gerchunoff had been cycling back to the Cuatro Diques from a rally when he noticed a small child huddled by the shrubs they'd planted to make the neighbourhood feel more like a community. The child was no more than eight, and she was clutching her stomach and crying and Gerchunoff worried that she'd been stabbed or worse and he dropped his bike in the middle of the road and ran to the girl's side, she was moaning loudly, and Gerchunoff bent over her to see if she was bleeding. *Have you been hurt?* he said. *Has anyone hurt you?* And he was trying to turn her body, trying to protect her from every side but also trying to see if she had been stabbed or worse and trying to make sure there wasn't any blood, trying to make sure there wasn't any hurt, but also trying not to be obvious about it, not to worry her. And he was turning her body, whispering such tender things to her, whispering: *It's okay, you're okay, everything's okay*, and he was turning her body and looking for the blood. And the child exhaled so forcefully that he thought she was just giving up, expelling her life from her body. And the child turned her face into his neck and he couldn't feel her breathing, could only feel her not breathing, holding her breath, and then, suddenly, she kissed him, and he felt so warm and loved and protective, every part of her tiny, fragile body melting so perfectly into his. He thought: *There is no greater thing than the innocence of children, no greater failure than if we don't make the world better for them, if they have to live like us.* And before he knew it, the child had deftly

335

slipped a pistol into his hands and it was so warm, warmer than any gun he'd ever held before, and she was pushing away, her face in her neck was pushing away, and the child was running, suddenly, the child was running, and she escaped quickly over a wall and into the Diques and seconds later some military officers appeared from behind some bushes, like, *how do you do, what have we here*, and they approached Gerchunoff to ask what he was doing, what he was doing out after curfew, and they searched him, found the pistol, and kicked and beat him for nearly twenty minutes. He was sure he was going to die, but a light went on in the Diques and he thought, for a moment, that God was looking down on him, and the light was a sign. And someone had seen what was happening and would save him. And the beating stopped. And the soldiers helped him to his feet. And they brushed the dirt from his legs and his back. And they placed him carefully in their car and took him to a nearby scrap heap where they questioned him some more. And then they forced him to kneel facing a wall. And they shot him three times in the back and walked away.

He showed us the scar beneath his rib and the scar beneath his eye and the scar below that. And he said: *You can always be rewritten.*

* * * * *

Except for the pain, Gerchunoff would have thought he was surely dead. He heard more footsteps and thought, for the second time, he had experienced this before, that God had come for him. The air was so cold and the dew had begun to settle on his trash and on his hands and on the wounds in his back, where three bullets had entered, and the ones in the front, where two had made exit. But it was just the same officers returning because one of them had dropped his packet of cigarettes and did not want to lose them, and when they saw that Gerchunoff was still living, they shot him two more times and went home to bed.

In the morning, two of the soldiers returned to drag his body to a nearby trash yard and they left the body to be devoured by the rats and worms and God knows what else.

* * * * *

I was jumped by a number of kids, Sux said, and though it was practically nothing I was still distraught enough—so disparaged by my faith in the future—that I sought out the nearest church and, when no one answered my pounding on the door, I broke a window and just went in. It was quiet and dark, not what I had imagined. There was a peace. And also row upon row of emptiness, an absence of faith. I thought: What is a building like this without the people inside it?

Someone must have reported me. Because as I was finally falling asleep, I heard footsteps in the antechamber and I ran. Out the back doors that were not chained and all the way to my brother's home and the soldiers chased me all the way to my brother's home. And when they caught me outside my brother's home they beat me savagely, until the ground outside my brother's home was soaked with blood in a metre-square area. And I suppose because I wasn't dead they brought me to the police station to finish the job, but I wouldn't stop screaming so eventually they assumed I was some sort of drug addict having fits or that I was crazy and they brought me to a room and left me in a corner and I realized they were more afraid of me than I was of them, because I wasn't quite a human anymore, I was a beast, and they came back to beat me some more but I kept raging and they stopped beating me so I kept raging and they sat back to watch and I kept raging and eventually they let me go and I kept raging, until this day, and I keep raging. I keep raging.

I was brought to a jail, Sux said. They brought me to a room and put me with my hands over a table, curved around the edge, like this, here and here, and they cut me. Here. And here. They made me stand against a wall and then threw a knife to see if they could make it stand. Here and here. Between these fingers. Here and here. They put me with another prisoner named Emilio who also beat me, not because we were on opposite sides but because he needed someone to beat, someone to pass on what had been inflicted on him. I don't blame him. Otherwise it would have sat inside him forever. They kept on giving me showers, then beating me, then putting me back in my cell, where Emilio would beat me, and then it would start all over again. There was never a time when I wasn't doing one of those things, or rather having it done to me. And one day they began to question me about the day in the Plaza de Mayo. They asked me about my friends and they asked me about people I didn't know and they asked about people I did know and pretended not to know and one of them threw alcohol on me and set me afire, and when I tried to put it out he screamed: Stop it, you son of a bitch!

* * * * *

Around noon, another group of soldiers happened upon Gerchunoff's body and realized he was still breathing. And not knowing who he was or what had happened the night before, they rushed him to a doctor. Not knowing who he was or what had happened the night before, the doctor fixed him. Not knowing who he was or what had happened the night before, the doctor removed the two bullets that had not passed all the way through him and sewed the four holes shut and, not knowing who he was or what had happened the night before, the doctor hooked him to a machine that pumped new blood through him, someone else's blood, and he was filled with other people's memories, and he gasped at the weight of the world, at the grief of the world, and died under the weight of the world.

There was a laugh from the corner. *He's just looking for another story,* Reilly scoffed. *He's unable to imagine anything beyond the simplicity of his own self-obsession.*

Am I forbidden to write about myself when Ibáñez can make an entire film about the cost of his new automobile?

And now you think you're Ibáñez?!

338

Not infrequently, my brother was invited to attend chamber concerts at the homes of random dignitaries—anyone with a house, really—joined by whatever local string players could be mustered and soloists as forgettable as pie crusts, dull knives on which to impale beauty. More often than not they were at the home of Ruben Darío, who still lived among the true Argentines, on the outskirts of the city, in Maldonade, close to Arroyo, where he was teaching the workmen of the area to read Spanish and French, and was supporting several poor families he had taken into his home and who acted as servants though he treated them as his extended family, splitting with them everything he earned as the director of postal services and from the publication of his verses. There were so many families in situations like this, having lost their jobs in the recession brought on by the Europeans, the politicians in their private clubs. I recall the neighbourhood chiefly for the number of houses without glass in the windows, and when we arrived, for all their talk of him being such a man of the people, we were astonished to find his home surrounded by a great wall crusted with broken glass so it could not be scaled and the grass swayed so long and the mango trees that shat all over the everything all the every time. Inside, it put the opulence of our London parties to shame, with great feasts that must have been difficult to source outside of Europe. Darío was never there. And Camille would ask: *Who pays for it all?* And Lugones would just laugh and grab another leg of chicken or slab of cheese and say: *The people, in the end, pay for everything.*

At the last of these before the opening of the Colón, the Little Russian told my brother that La Muerte was planning a séance. *An inter-dimensional gate,* the Little Russian translated for us. *The ability to link across time.* But he would also say things like: *Artists are but mediums to another plane able to reinterpret both the past and the future, and therefore our present.* And: *We don't move through time; time moves through us.* La Muerte wanted to collaborate with de Sade. With Edgar Allan Poe. De Quincey. Machen. *Machen,* he said, *is a...Titan* (the Little Russian took some time to settle on the right word there). *Perhaps the world's greatest living author.* He wanted to collaborate with the destroyers. The killers. With Cayetano Godino, aka the Macrotous Runt. With Jack the Ripper. With Henry Howard Holmes. *No pude evitar el hecho de que yo era un asesino,* he said, *no más de lo que el poeta puede ayudar a la inspiración a cantar.* My brother looked to the Little Russian and Lugones, who had been eavesdropping from across the room, said: *Why not God?* We had not seen him since the jazz club and he looked horrible, had not shaved in weeks and reeked of cigarettes and anger. I followed him over the course of the night and realized that he never sat with the Little Russian but was also never too far from her that he could not overhear. And the Little Russian would ignore him but would also allow her hand to linger on the back of his chair as she passed behind him. And La Muerte would say something and Lugones would storm from the room and after a suitable pause the Little Russian would translate. One time she said: *It is better for man to fail at the utterly contemptible than to succeed at mimicking beauty.* And Camille replied: *Really, he said this?* But then she looked angry, leaned back and pressed her pelvis to the sky like it was a beacon and said: *Something like that. What do you want from me?*

Lugones's wife, Juana, had tossed him because—apparently—he had been sleeping with the Little Russian. No one had suspected. Lugones and the Little Russian rarely spoke or were even near one another. And yet, he had gone to Juana to end it, had gone to tell her what had happened and that he was in love, *they* were in love, had packed his things and told her she would get over it, that she would find someone else someday, someone who was much better suited to her than he was, someone who needed her, that she was still a desirable woman and he would always love her as the mother of his child, this was just how love worked, it was either to grow or to die. Unfortunately for him, by the time he'd made it back to the Little Russian she was already deep in rethought. Did she want to be tied down to a man with a son and ex-wife to support? So now Little Polo was his for good, it seemed, and spent most of his time sneaking drinks and eating food from the floor and screaming, screaming, screaming. He was not a camel or a lion but a tiny child, his throat full of might, a champion, this boy, this beast of childhood grown fierce. This boy. Lugones cornered us once again to talk about the hours of his vice, the hours of his misery, his hours of hunger, his hours of humiliation, his writing. His poetry book had stalled and he blamed it on the Little Russian. He blamed it on a lack of sleep. He blamed it on Juana. He blamed it on Little Polo. *He refuses to learn to piss when a man should piss,* he said. *You take the opportunity when it is presented to you, not when it is necessary!* He had been begging, he said, and in two days had not eaten, had not collected one five-cent piece. There had been another beggar on the same street, he claimed, who had done famously, had perhaps even gone off and purchased a house with all his earnings, or tossed his hat in the ring as the next president. *People were dropping their wallets on him. Several women made love to him on his cardboard sheet. But me?* Lugones wondered if he were not real enough, was not convincing enough as a beggar. Perhaps people could see through his desperation, or only saw a metaphor, saw right through him. *Poets aren't real people. We have so much empathy we just blend into the world.*

He saw us looking at the Little Russian and said: *You know she is not a Russian at all? Or whatever else she told you. She is closer to a god,* he said. *A descendant of Itúrbide. Related to Olózaga. And Lanteros. A descendant of ancestry. Glorious chiefs.* He was convinced she was sleeping with La Muerte, and the fact that she might have been doing so was, to him, a travesty of the gravest propor-

341

tions. That he might be entering her, vaginally and anally and orally and mentally, morally, the son of a provincial attorney, it was repellent to the idea of greatness. *You know, I once drank with the Little Russian until the late hours, and nuzzled her neck and felt her breast in my hand and wondered if she were too much for me, this seed of Itúrbide, the Augustine of the Americas. If this is what the world is to be, let the buildings crumble,* he said. *Let the institutions dissolve to the ground. There were no buildings when we arrived and what we have built is crass and unshapely. We are People of the Earth. People of the Mountains! People of the Tiger!*

La Muerte said he was ready to begin, and Little Polo took the Little Russian's hand and Lugones followed behind and behind and La Muerte, who was delighted to finally be in control, made a big show of drawing circles on the floor, pentagrams, various shapes that were meant to look arcane and, through the Little Russian, said: *You who wish to embark on such a journey must be resolute and steady of temper!* And my brother assured him, yes, he had the fortitude *and* resolution that he believed was required and La Muerte did not look entirely convinced but continued to draw, seemingly inventing, off the top of his head, the most impressive ceremonies imaginable. He pulled asafetida from out of nowhere, several precious perfumes and other unidentifiable compositions that nonetheless diffused multiple noisome odours. He built a fire. And when it was burning hotly, he made an opening in one of his circles and took us by the hand while instructing Lugones to cast the perfumes into the flames—the order didn't seem to matter, he did not specify—and began to incant the names of several demons who were the leaders of several legions, in the name of the eternal uncreated God, who lives forever, hallowed be His name. It went on forever and I was, to tell the truth, entranced by the burning of one of the powders and the stench of garlic and fennel when he turned quickly on my brother and asked him (imploringly, through the Little Russian, of course) to ask a question of the spirits that had apparently swarmed about us. It was so ridiculous I began to laugh and yet my brother choked out: *Henri. Are you there?* And La Muerte, who had no idea what we were talking about and seemed totally unprepared for this response, shook his head and said the spirits were confused or angry or something, it was lost in translation, and said they required a repetition of the question. In his haste, he kicked over a candle and the room was sudden filled with such smoke that they had to vacate prematurely.

When we reconvened, the Little Russian had brought Little Polo and La Muerte redrew his artwork, albeit more solemnly, and incanted half-heartedly the names of two or three demons, the leaders of a legion or two, in the name of the eternal uncreated God, who lives forever, hallowed be His name, while Lugones sucked loudly at the legs of his lobster and said: *Poetry is a luxury commodity*, he said. *As is music, I suppose. Do people need us? Of course they do. But art is still not a right. We must fight for it. Like privacy—some might argue that privacy is a basic human right. The right to be left alone, no? But think about the future. The population of the world is growing so fast. In the future, privacy will be something we recall only in dreams, inaccessible to most, disproportionately costly to the average individual's ability to acquire and retain it. To be alone in an overcrowded world will one day connote social status and advantage in the way that displays of social connection do today. Poetry and the future of privacy are the same. Art is the same. It does not come cheaply. Not to the creator of the weapon nor to the soul it strikes. To experience true art is to pay a price and be changed forever.* And *shush* said La Muerte, La Muerte said *shush* and repeated his question to my brother, with whom would he like to converse, was there no one else? And Camille again requested to be reunited with Henri and La Muerte was clearly perturbed and said brisk that the demons had replied that we would see Henri again within the space of a month and who else? He also ordered Camille to come nearer and embrace him, because the demons were greater in number than he had anticipated and as my brother stepped forward he loosened the robe and sash and Little Polo began to scream, claiming there were enormous four-armed giants trying to break the circle, and a million other tiny warriors besides, which were somehow the worse, a tiny boy, like him but not like him, who was lost, *There is a boy here,* he said, *a boy, a boy, a boy, a boy,* and La Muerte, trembling now, began to try to dismiss them (or at least this was what the Little Russian said he was doing), screaming at Lugones to put out the fire, *put out the goddamn fire, why were you not burning the proper perfumes!* And I don't know why I was afraid, but I actually began to cry, not from fear exactly, because it was nothing I understood, Little Polo pointing at me and screaming, how could I be afraid of it, but out of confusion. And Little Polo crouched to the ground and put his head between his knees and began to whimper: *In this posture I shall surely die, for we shall all surely perish.* And I couldn't bear to see him like this so I knelt beside him and put my arm around him and said: *These things are not real. We are in another place, another time. None of this is real.* And finally we all exited the circle together, keeping as close to each other as possible, especially Little Polo, who kept to the middle and held to La Muerte by his coat and me, astoundingly, by my cloak and Lugones complaining that we had gone through all of that and not even managed to negotiate any riches or fame or anything out of them. Later, however, when everyone else had gone home, Lugones said: *I think I am done with Buenos Aires. It is no place for me. I think I might return to Córdoba, where it is still okay to be true to one's self. But the horrible tentacles of this city have me. No one will publish me if I'm not here.* Though he had told almost no one else yet, he had also quit his job at the paper, and was living on liens from his publisher against future sales, on his last book of poetry but also on future books. *I am surviving on books that are not real,* he said, *that do not exist. They are buying my future and I cannot afford my present. If I decide not to write them, will the money also disappear? I have already spent it all on alcohol, to drown the suffering. Sadly, suffering is a cockroach that will not drown.*

And we followed him out to Darío's gardens and were surrounded by the rarest of shenzhen nongke, kinabalu, saffron crocus, gifts to him from foreign diplomats, the walls hung with redweed and inkvine and so many butterflies and he crushed the bud of an imported kadupul between his fingers and said: *The other day I went to the country on my bicycle and the world slowed and was just that moment, and then that moment, and then that moment, and in the moment there was no regret nor anxious creep, only peace, and my lungs and legs burned in perpetuity, a beacon, a cross, a body pushed to its limits always and when I could go no further I found a stone wall and made stop, a wall some farmer had set with his own stone hands, likely, and sat back to smoke and look at what he had done and marvel.* Perhaps I am not the God of this entire world, *he probably thought (can you imagine?),* but I am at least the God of this parcel. *This* I can control. And the wind will be held back and so the rising waters and so the steer and so the ram I've raised here and what else can a person do, after all? *And I left my bicycle and book to one side and straddled long the stony wall and stared back at the city and a vaporous mist shift off the land, great rose clouds of dust and red western glow, grown deep. I saw the murky cast from the trains and chemical works upon the Rio de la Plata and Salado, the electrical plant of burn and coal and factory of wool and cotton, imitation cashmere, factories of dreams, the dust kicked up from carriage and cart, and tram, and the great dump piles from the hydraulic gold and silver mines. And I saw a small shift and shape upon the adjacent hill and saw it was a child and knowing it was a child clad in their wisp green cloak and gashed red hood I was more drawn. It was a Sunday afternoon in late autumn. The air smelled of sick and sulphur and burn and such a jewel of quiet colour crept upon the landscape that changed everything.*

Maybe I'll go to America.

Notes

This book contains quotations and allusions, many of them altered to various degrees, from works by or about Camille Saint-Saëns, Henri Regnault, César Franck, Eugène Fromentin, Fromental Halévy, François Benoist, Daniel Auber, Adolphe Adam, Adolphe Botte, Vincent d'Indy, Gustave Courbet, Théophile Gautier, Henry James, Fredric Jameson, Herman Melville, Russell Hoban, Robert Lopshire, Oscar Wilde, Washington Irving, Stephen King, Bram Stoker, Lord Byron, Mary Shelley, P. B. Shelley, J. K. Huysmans, T. S. Eliot, H. D. Thoreau, C. S. Lewis, J. R. R. Tolkien, F. Scott Fitzgerald, Robert Louis Stevenson, Samuel Taylor Coleridge, Edgar Allan Poe, Arthur Conan Doyle, Joel Chandler Harris, Charles Dickens, Ann Radcliffe, Victor Hugo, Georges Perec, Ernest Hemingway, Gertrude Stein, Dorothy Kunhardt, Michael Bernhardt, William McFee, Leopoldo Lugones, Rubén Darío, Alejandro Sux, Arnaldo Danel, Jorge Luis Borges, Bret Easton Ellis, Bill Kennedy, Michael Ondaatje, René Descartes, Søren Kierkegaard, Friedrich Nietzsche, Frederich Engels, Arthur Schopenhauer, Walter Benjamin, Theodor Adorno, Wikipedia, Marcel Proust, Fyodor Dostoevsky, Sofiya Feodorovna Rostopchina, Franz Kafka, Henry Wadsworth Longfellow, Benvenuto Cellini, William Shakespeare, Giovanni Boccaccio, François Rabelais, James Joyce, Jesus Christ, Saint-Saëns's biographers (including Stephen Studd, Brian Rees, Rollin Smith, Timothy Flynn), and various travel writers from the 1800s (including Arthur Morrison, Margaret Harkness, Mrs. H. Lloyd Evans, Ernest Feydeau, K. F., Charles Augustus Stoddard), as well as from Jack the Ripper autopsy reports.

CHRIS EATON is the author of three previous novels, including *Chris Eaton, a Biography* (2013), selected as one of the Books of the Year by *Quill and Quire* and the *Toronto Star*. He spent many years making music in the band Rock Plaza Central. He currently lives in Sackville, New Brunswick, with his partner and two children.

Colophon

Manufactured as the first edition of
Symphony No. 3
in the fall of 2019 by Book*hug Press.

Edited for the press by Malcolm Sutton
Copy edited by Stuart Ross
Type + design by Malcolm Sutton

bookhugpress.ca

Book*hug Press